DAUGHTER OF AFRICA

SHADOWS OVER AFRICA

T.M. CLARK

DAUGHTER OF AFRICA

Published by Wilde Press, P.O. Box 275, Bribie Island, Queensland, Australia, 4507

Edited by Creating Ink

Cataloguing-in-Publication details are available from the National Library of Australia www.librariesaustralia.nla.gov.au

ebook © Published 2026 ISBN 978-1-923129-32-0

Paperback © Published 2026 ISBN 978-1-923129-31-3

Hardback © Published 2026 ISBN 978-1-923129-33-7

ABOUT THE AUTHOR

Zimbabwean-born T.M. Clark weaves her fascination with diverse cultures, wildlife, and storytelling into her literature. Her books cater to a wide readership, from children to adults.

T.M. Clark is the author of the critically acclaimed My Brother-But-One, nominated for the Queensland Literary People's Choice Award in 2014, and Song of the Starlings, winner of the 2022 Killer Nashville Claymore Award for Best Action Adventure. Her picture books, Slowly! Slowly! (a 2018 CBCA Notable Book) and Quickly! Quickly! are beloved by young readers and are companion pieces to Child of Africa.

When she's not writing thrilling adventure stories, T.M. Clark is dedicated to helping other writers. As the coordinator of the CYA Conference (www.cyaconference.com), she provides professional development for both new and established writers and illustrators. She also co-presents at Writers at Sea (www.WritersAtSea.com.au), guiding writers on their creative journeys.

Tina Marie loves mentoring emerging writers and collecting books for creating libraries in Papua New Guinea.

Visit T.M. Clark at tmclark.com.au and follow her on social media.

- facebook.com/tmclarkauthor
- instagram.com/tmclark_author
- amazon.com/stores/author/B018N3D2QY
- bookbub.com/authors/t-m-clark
- goodreads.com/tmclark
- linkedin.com/in/t-m-clark
- mastodon.au/@tmclark
- pinterest.com/TMClark_Author
- tiktok.com/@tmclark_author
- threads.com/@tmclark_author
- bsky.app/profile/tmclarkauthor.bsky.social

ALSO BY T.M. CLARK

ADULT BOOKS

Shadows Over Africa series

- Child of Africa
- Cry of the Firebird
- My Brother-But-One
- Nature of the Lion
- Shooting Butterflies
- Song of the Starlings
- Tears of the Cheetah
- The Avoidable Orphan

PICTURE BOOKS

- Slowly! Slowly!
- Quickly! Quickly!

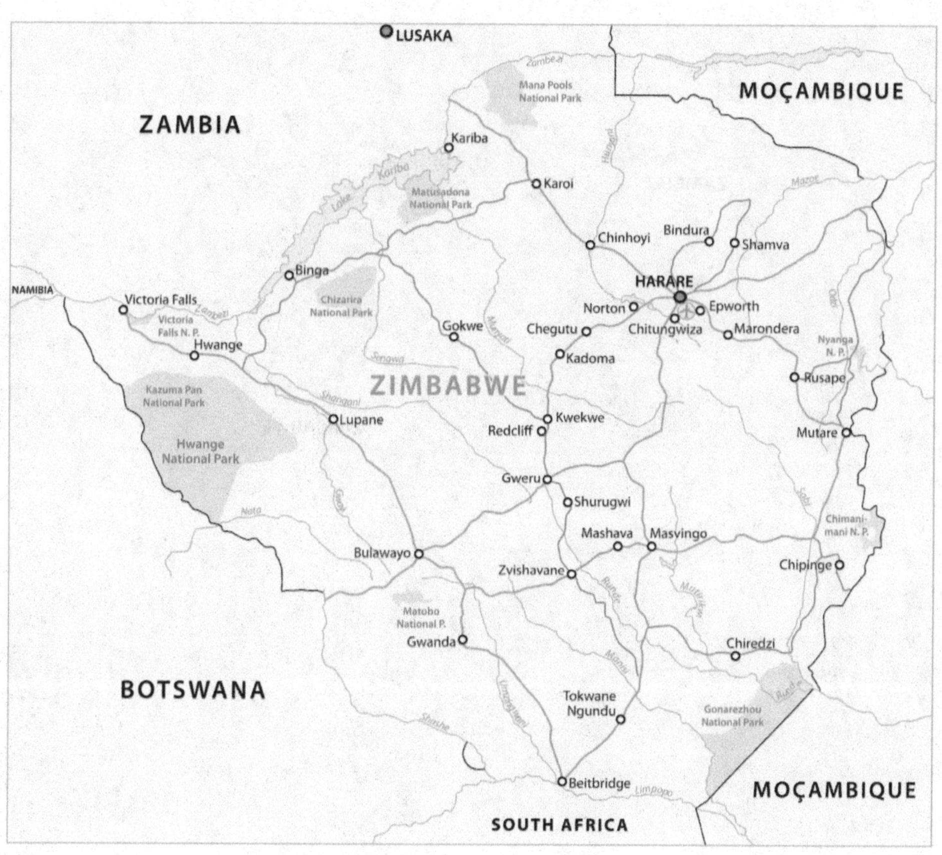
LUSAKA
ZAMBIA
MOÇAMBIQUE
Mana Pools
National Park
Kariba
Matusadona
National Park
Karoi
Chinhoyi
Bindura
Shamva
Binga
NAMIBIA
Victoria Falls
Victoria
Falls N. P.
Chizarira
National Park
HARARE
Norton
Epworth
Chegutu
Chitungwiza
Marondera
Gokwe
Kadoma
Hwange
Nyanga
N. P.
Rusape
ZIMBABWE
Kazuma Pan
National Park
Kwekwe
Lupane
Redcliff
Mutare
Hwange
National Park
Gweru
Shurugwi
Chimani-
mani N. P.
Mashava
Masvingo
Bulawayo
Zvishavane
Chipinge
Matobo
National P.
Gwanda
Chiredzi
BOTSWANA
Tokwane
Ngundu
Gonarezhou
National Park
Beitbridge
Limpopo
MOÇAMBIQUE
SOUTH AFRICA

MAP

ZAMBIA
ZIMBABWE
Lake Kariba
Chisekesi
Pemba
Gwembe
Salamuka
Sialumba
Sianambwe
Munyumbwe
Siavonga
Kariba
Batoka
Choma
Madonda
Bumi Hills
Dandawa
Magunje
Matusadona National Park
Siakobvu
Sinazongwe
Maamba
Chete Safari Area
Siabuwa
Nenyunka
Sijarira State Forest
Chireya
Binga
Manjolo
Chizarira National Park
Nembudziya
Mlibizi
Saba
Sanyati

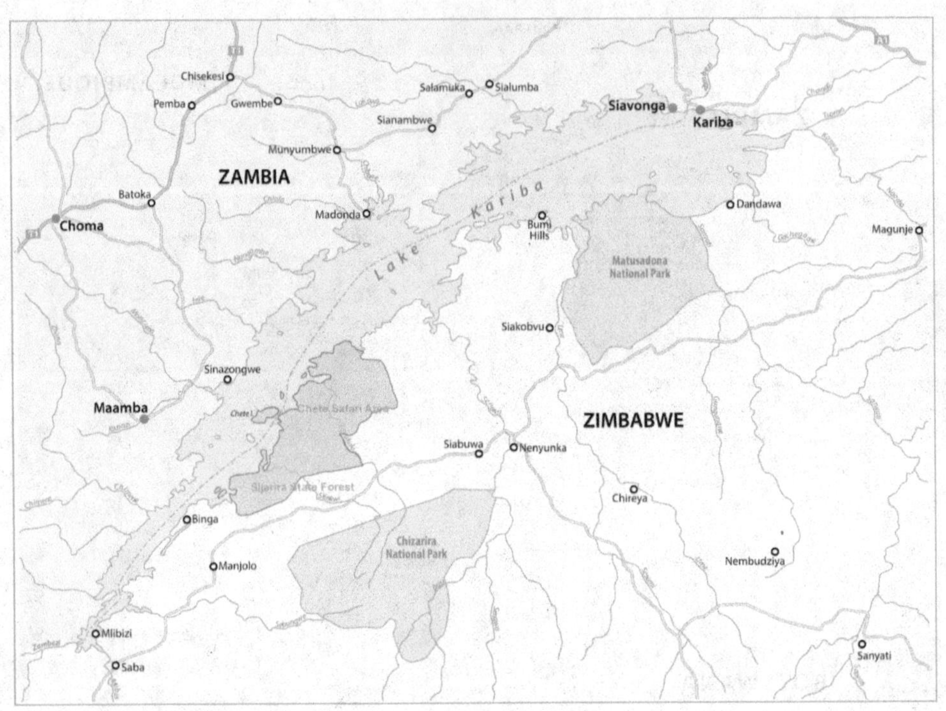

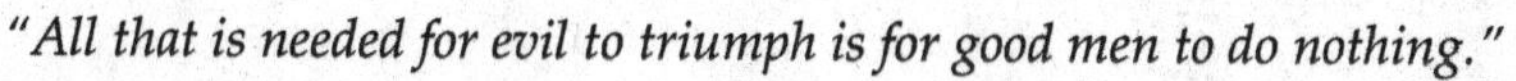

"All that is needed for evil to triumph is for good men to do nothing."

~ Modern paraphrase of Edmund Burk's (1729–1797) quotation.

DEDICATION

To Shaun who always believes in me.

For my mother, Carole Vivienne Wilde, 1943 – 2020. maNdhlovu, to those who were with her in the last few years of her life. You are loved and missed.

CHAPTER 1
AN ELEPHANT'S LIFE DIVERGES

HWANGE NATIONAL PARK, ZIMBABWE

October 1983

The thunder sounds from the humans had finally stopped. The steel birds in the sky, still circling, like vultures, forced us to group tightly together.

From beside my mother's carcass, I lifted my head to see Aunt Nomusa, the matriarch of her own herd, rush away under a big grove of trees, followed by what remained of her family. Escaping.

I trumpeted.

Again and again.

I pleaded for Aunt Nomusa not to leave me behind with the humans and their destruction.

My mother and everyone else in our small herd were dead, from my newest brother, born only a few moons ago, to the large bull Mandlenkosi who had joined us recently to mate once again with my aunt.

I had watched, one by one, as they fell to the earth and didn't get up.

The human bird machine in the sky circled once more.

There was more thunder.

Aunt Nomusa continued to break a new trail as she led the others away through the bush.

She wasn't coming back for me while the humans and their thunder were near.

She was hidden by the thick bush.

I stopped calling.

There were no answering trumpets. No rumbles for me—only the scent of primal panic as she urged what was left of her herd to move faster. Run. Flee. Stay under the trees.

I understood now. I was beyond any herd's help and protection.

At the mercy of humans.

The sun beat down. I stood lost, surrounded by carnage.

I shook my head. The stench of blood and death coated the inside of my trunk and refused to clear away, a new sensation. I was no longer able to smell the mopane forests.

Flapping my ears, I listened. From the pounding of feet growing softer, I knew Aunt Nomusa was leading her herd north. Away from these lands. Towards safety deep in the mountain country, where forested gorges would hide what was left of our family, and the water in the lake was plentiful. Where humans did not visit often and animals lived in peace.

I'd seen enough death to last many lifetimes today. If I was going to be allowed to live, I would always remember.

Even if it broke my heart each day, I would never forget.

Men with guns had destroyed my family, leaving only me alive.

I longed to run away with my aunt, but my family were all here. I had not been allowed to share in the silence of death.

This was genocide.

How was I to go on living when they were all murdered? Why was it, only I was spared?

A man walked towards me, waving a big stick.

He herded me away from my family's carcasses.

That was when I saw that there were many other youngsters around my age, from smaller herds scattered around the clearing. We had been enjoying a large gathering of the families. It had been peaceful in the abundance of the rainy season, where food and water were plentiful.

But it had become a slaughter ground. Bloodlines were decimated.

The only ones of us left were those who were no longer milk-dependent, but not fully mature.

We were forced up a ramp into a space with a hard, cold floor. Thunder sounded when I walked on it. The sides were made of dead tree trunks, spaced close together. We could see through them. They were so strong that even our matriarchs could not have broken through, had they still been here to protect us.

No one trumpeted anymore.

We huddled together. Our collective fear was too real to break the unnatural silence.

There was a rumbling underneath us, and the ground began to move. I could still see my family behind us through the gaps between the log sides. Men began removing their skins.

I blinked, trying to dislodge the scene in front of me.

But it wouldn't dissipate.

CHAPTER 2
COUNTERTERRORISM OR COUNTERPRODUCTIVE

USA MARINES COVERT TRAINING MISSIONS, SOMALIA

March 2002

Chad Whitney wiped the sweat from his face with the sleeve of his desert fatigues. Unrelenting heat radiated from the building they patrolled, his body perspiring in the Kevlar vest against his chest and the pack on his back, amplifying the heat.

Beside him walked one of the militias that the USA was training in the counter-terrorism fight. The scarification on Jamiel Omer's face identified him as being from Sudan, not Somalia, where they were currently stationed. Still, it was no surprise, given who was at the *Qalcad* they protected. Hiding inside was Farid Al-Qadhafi, a politician and activist from Sudan, and his family.

Chad turned the corner, checking northwards. The area beyond their hill-side fortress oasis was desolate and flat with only the odd bush battling for survival in the inhospitable environment. Nothing moved out there but sand. His eyes looked at the horizon, searching for any telltale signs of reflections that would give someone away. A few clouds gathered across a dull blue sky, proof that the winds that blew across the desert were absent today. He shifted his attention to the ground closer to them, using his elevated position to its full advantage; burnt-out armored trucks tangled with civilian vehicles. Monuments of death from previous attempts on Al-Qadhafi. As were the large shell holes before the foundations of the solid rock wall.

Somalia was no stranger to war. The land bore the scars as deeply as the people did.

He imagined the Sudan was similar. Same shit. Different country.

Warlords and militia. Everyone was armed with a rifle and fighting.

Greed, politics and religion had been tearing Africa apart since ancient times.

All clear.

They walked the next wall.

Jamiel was two steps behind him.

On his second six-month Special Operations Deployment, Chad was considered a local, by the militia. There were two reasons for that:

One: he had been there so long.

Two: while hiding behind the USA flag, he now behaved more like the militia than an American soldier.

It had never been his intention to be part of the militia when he was stationed in Mogadishu, but when Jamiel found him coming out from his unsanctioned sniper's nest he had been invited to join their operations.

The local Somali he had chosen to execute, had the unfortunate honor of being around the same age as Chad's Uncle, Walter Whitney.

Walter, the man responsible for making his childhood a misery.

The man who could have saved him and his mother from poverty, but hadn't bothered.

The man who had given him the ultimatum of join the army or go to prison.

Instead of punishment and judgment, Jamiel had pointed out so many ways they could do more together, instead of him alone, and make money while killing.

Killing was easy.

He had trained for it.

He was good at it.

And making a little extra money from it never hurt, him.

He didn't know or care about the fundamentals of any militia group, but he did know that much of their money came from 'protecting' local businesses and people. Money he was happy to hoard until the opportunity arose to annihilate the Whitney blood line forever.

The only other thing he cared about, and was thankful for, was that the militia helped him remain off the military police's radar.

Chad was finally counting the days until his deployment was over, and he could fly back to the USA. It was time to put his skills to work on a task he longed to carry out.

He would deal with Walter first. The old bastard did not have personal security with him on the ranch. He was an easy target. Then he would deal with his cousin Marissa. She would be twenty-one now and at college. She could disappear after a frat party. Another college statistic—a student committing suicide due to the pressure. Her bloody elephant would be last…

Revenge would be sweet.

He would inherit everything.

A flicker in his peripheral vision drew his attention.

He stopped.

"See something?" Jamiel asked.

"Movement. Eleven o'clock."

Chad focused on the area. Al-Qadhafi's son, Ismail, was sneaking along the path, towards some bushes that would give him better cover. On his back was a pack that was too yellow to blend into the desert sand. The kid was only twelve years old but already had an attitude worse than any teenager Chad had ever met.

"Fuck, not again!" Chad exclaimed. "Come on. Let's go grab him before he gets into more trouble. What's with this kid and running away?" Then, into his radio comms, he said, "Falcon, team three retrieving Fledgling, again. Will be off rotation approximately thirty minutes."

"Roger that," Comms came back.

"Can't say I blame him," Jamiel said, slinging his rifle onto his shoulder and beginning the climb down to the next level of the wall. "It's tough for a kid to move from a bustling city like Juba to an isolated fortress like this one."

"Give me a USA city the same size so I know what you're talking about," Chad said.

"You Americans and your lack of geographical knowledge," Jamiel said.

"Fuck you," Chad said, making the last jump down the terrace. "I haven't been to Juba, but if you'd said Khartoum, I'd know what you were talking about. One or two million like Dallas or Houston—not nearly ten million like New York."

"About three hundred thousand people in Juba."

They had reached the bottom. They hadn't exactly been stealthy. The boy glanced back over his shoulder and broke into a surprisingly fast run over the uneven ground. Chad and Jamiel increased their speed and caught up with him in moments.

"Ismail, come on. You have to go back inside. We can't protect you out here," Chad said, wiping sweat from his forehead onto his sleeve.

The boy cringed and pulled away.

"Move it. Inside," Jamiel said. "Now." From the sternness in his tone, it was evident he was taking no crap from the youth.

The boy opened his mouth to say something, then closed it again, his shoulders slumping in defeat.

"I admire your tenacity to keep doing this, but I have no idea where you think you can run to. Look out there. Nothing but sand, heat and death," Chad said, gesturing to the barren landscape beyond.

"I'll take my chances. Better than inside," Ismail mumbled.

"Not today, and not on our watch," Chad said as they escorted him back inside the *Qalcad*.

Chad tagged the replacement guards going out the door and breathed a sigh of relief as they escorted Ismail inside. Chad's eyes adjusting to the dimness as they moved deeper, the closely packed stone of the outer walls keeping the light out, and the inside cool.

"Come on, kid. Let's get you back to your room," Chad said as they walked through the building toward the family quarters.

Al-Qadhafi crossed the entrance area so quickly that his jalabiya billowed as if in the wind. He grabbed his son by the arms and slapped him hard across the face, speaking in Sudanese so fast that Chad couldn't follow.

Images of Walter chastising him flashed in Chad's head.

The humiliation.

Only now, he was older. He didn't have to accept men like this anymore.

Anger bubbled up at Al-Qadhafi. And at Walter.

He physically separated the man from the child, pushing Al-Qadhafi roughly, forcing distance between them, and keeping Ismail behind him. Protected. "Enough. There was no harm done," Chad said. "He didn't get far."

Al-Qadhafi's eyes widened, and he looked down to where Chad's hand was firmly placed on his chest. Chad straightened Al-Qadhafi's *jalabiya*.

"This time. He didn't get far this time," Al-Qadhafi said. "What will happen when he gets out and is used as live bait to get me to come out of hiding?"

"You wouldn't pay the ransom, so what do you care?" Ismail said, hurt causing his voice to break. "You could afford to pay millions, but you wouldn't because you hide here in Somalia instead of being in Sudan."

Chad looked at Ismail. The kid was younger than what Chad had been when went to live with Walter, yet he showed far more spine–standing up for himself and speak his mind. This kid would be okay.

Al-Qadhafi took a deep breath, and let it out, slowly. He looked directly at them. "You have done your jobs–"

"Even the servants say you're a coward. That once you were a revolutionist, and now you're soft," Ismail said. "You do nothing but hide."

It seemed that when Ismail got started, he had a lot to say to his father, with the hired protectors standing between them.

"Everyone's waiting for you to bring peace, and yet here you are, hiding. No one even knows where we are," Ismail said.

"How did you get this information?" Al-Qadhafi demanded, his voice rising before he clenched his teeth together.

Chad knew that look. It was the same one he'd seen on Walter's face when he'd discovered the useless racoons Chad had killed and discarded in the old mineshaft.

Chad took in a deep breath and released it, trying to control his rising anger at Al-Qadhafi.

Ismail looked at his father defiantly. "I have eyes and ears."

"You stupid child. You are listening to some militant army made up of renegades and misfits. And the American soldiers who know nothing of the liberty and freedom they claim to fight for. They do not know how quickly it can all be taken away. None of them respect our traditional ways or care what the people of Sudan want."

"At least they are doing something. Not hiding like you," Ismail said, his jaw jutting forwards.

Chad cleared his throat to remind Al-Qadhafi that he was still standing there with Jamiel. Listening to him spout his bullshit to the child. The last place he wanted to be was anywhere near the dress-wearing idiot.

This man was testing his temper today.

Chad needed to get it under control.

A new wave of heat rose in his chest at the insult to both the American soldiers who were being expected to give their lives to protect him, and the militia who were being paid to do the same.

"Out," Al-Qadhafi said to Chad and Jamiel. "This is a personal matter between my son and I. I will need to deal with him."

The words enraged Chad further. Images of Walter merged with the present movements of Al-Qadhafi. He clinched his fists.

"Keep it together. This is not our business," Jamiel warned him. "Come on. Let's go."

With heavy feet, Chad turned to leave. The kid seemed to have really stepped in it this time.

He admired that. He had never had the balls to stand up to Walter. He had protected the kid as much as he could, without being in trouble with his superiors. He didn't need to be there for more of Al-Qadhafi indoctrination of his ways on his son. Chad turned to leave.

"Why can't you be more like Fatima? You don't see her trying to run away. You don't see her sniveling like a dog because we came here," Al-Qadhafi said to his son, still in English.

Fatima became Marissa.

Chad took a breath. Blowing it out through his lips.

An unrecognizable squeak came from Ismail.

Chad turned and Al-Qadhafi face was right close against Ismail's. He knew that action too well.

Al-Qadhafi became Walter.

Chad had never been physically abused by Walter, but the loud shouting, constant put downs, and comparisons to his darling Marissa, those he knew well.

He was a constant disappointment to Walter.

Chad roared and ran at Al-Qadhafi', knocking off his *taqiyah*, as they both fell to the floor. "Leave him alone. Why can't you treat us fairly? Stop playing favorites and pitting us against each other, you manipulative piece of shit!" His punches landed where he most wanted to hurt Walter.

Walter, who had enough money to run a foundation to help strangers have a better life, yet ignored the needs of his own brother's son.

Walter, who refused to give him and his mother a cent to live on. Forcing his mother to hide in a drug-and-alcohol-shamed stupor. Forcing him to steal food so they did not go hungry.

Jamiel tried to grab at Chad's pack and drag him off Al-Qadhafi, but Chad was landing military-trained blows on Al-Qadhafi's head, fueled by years of pent-up rage at Walter.

Al-Qadhafi was no fighter.

Chad pummeled Walter's face, making him pay for every moment his uncle had humiliated him.

Cast him aside.

Chosen his precious daughter over him.

"No, no, please," Ismail said, putting his hands into the fray to try and pull him off.

Chad drew his arm back for another blow to Walter's face. His elbow connected with something soft. The kid went backward and fell hard, yelping.

The cry of pain cut through Chad's rage, and the image of Walter faded.

He stopped.

He stared at the man lying on the floor under him, his nose pushed back into his brain, his cheek and jaw bones broken.

It was not Walter.

A small sob echoed in the quiet room as Ismail reached for his father.

Chad looked at his own hands, where the knuckles were split and bleeding. He couldn't tell where his blood ended and where Al-Qadhafi's began.

Al-Qadhafi would never be able to torment Ismail again.

CHAPTER 3
PRESERVATION

LAKE KARIBA, ZIMBABWE

January 2014

Former Australian Special Forces operator Mitchell Laski's friendship with Zimbabwean and ex-British Marine Joss Brennan was as tightly woven together as the liana vines of the Victoria Falls. Which was how Mitch had come to be in charge of the anti-poaching unit at Yingwe River Lodge, Animal Rescue And Rehabilitation Center. Or AP, as they referred to it.

A lone go-away bird called loudly, warning of the poachers' approach, letting everyone in the area know that their territory was being disturbed.

Mitch held his breath as he lay against a fallen log and waited for the poachers to pass along the forest track. Reeds stuck out from his cap, and camouflage cream covered his face, helping blend his six-foot-two, muscular frame into the African bushveld.

The AP team was based inside Chief Bongani's lands. He'd walked the boundaries often enough to know where the borders ended. And right now, they were heading towards the very edge, nearly in the Sijarira State Forest.

The poachers had come in under the light of the almost full 'hunters' moon, despite the unusually cool night temperatures. They had attempted to hide their boat in the taller reeds. His anti-poaching team had already seized that along with the illegal fishing nets on the lake's bank.

The informant had told Mitch that the poachers had already killed at least one animal, so he'd decided that the AP should wait for the poachers to return to their boat.

The sun was climbing in the clear blue sky. The day was going to be a merciless scorcher. The African continent in its flaming fury.

He would never understand how the poachers could put their lives at risk by trusting their homemade boats, constructed of old tin roof sheets held together with bitumen. When it was cool, the bitumen held well, but could become brittle, and pieces would break off, causing leaks. When the relentless sun softened the bitumen, it would begin to ooze, and the boats began to leak then too. The locals were constantly bailing their boats. A lot of people had died in the lake when their boats fell apart.

Now, hours later, the temperature was climbing rapidly towards its expected daytime high of thirty-five degrees Celsius. A potential mistake by the poachers.

Luckily, Mitch and his team would save them from that end.

The heat today would be oppressive.

Ordinarily, poachers came in the night, did their hunting and left by sun-up, to be back across the border line in Kariba before anyone was awake. The hunt had taken longer than they had allowed for, this time.

A win for the anti-poaching team, who had time to maneuver and get into position.

Mitch waited.

The first poacher walked past him, the heavy tread of his bare feet crushing the reeds next to the log where Mitch lay. Two other men close on his heals.

The sharp metallic smell of fresh bush meat and unwashed human bodies hung heavily in the air as the poachers labored under the weight of the bush meat. Sweat pumped from every pore, their mahogany skin glistening in the hot sun. The blood from the waterbuck's dismembered carcass dripped on the sandy path, and flies landed where the thick red liquid splashed.

Mitch stared at the putzi fly's golden body with its dark abdomen and suppressed a shudder. Just last week he'd helped pick maggots out of one of his young guard's stomach area. The flies were active year-round, but worse in the wet season; it always paid to be vigilant in Africa.

"*Gijima*, the *Askari* will catch us. We must hurry," the lead poacher said, adjusting the head of the waterbuck he carried by the horns, slung over his shoulder.

"We should have brought the *inja*," the second poacher said, his clothes stained red from the blood of the severed leg he carried. He spat into the reeds.

"Dogs would bark and bring the protectors," the lead poacher said. "*Shesha*!"

The man increased his stride and started to move faster as instructed.

A third man passed Mitch. Slower than the first two, his load too heavy for his weary body.

Mitch remained hidden.

A guinea fowl called *rippe pee peep*—one of Mitch's team signaling that the poachers were all past him, and he could cut off their retreat. Rising from where he lay in ambush, Mitch stepped up onto the log in the reeds and jumped off the other side, giving it a wide berth just in case a puff adder had slithered there while he waited. The bastards were known to strike from hiding places just like that. His desert combat boots covered his ankles for such attacks, but he still took the precaution.

The poachers had only gone a few steps, with Mitch and his two guardsmen close behind when Luckson, his lead team member, appeared ahead to block their path.

Faced with an armed guard, the men turned as one to run, only to find Mitch and the others behind. They dropped the butchered animal pieces, lightening their burden, and ran into the thick reeds. Mitch was always impressed by how these men could dodge like a rugby player and then run like professional athletes. They had inhuman speed when under direct threat.

But escape was not on the cards for them.

The thick bush was the very reason Mitch had laid their trap here. They had been too late to save the waterbuck, but he'd be damned if he was letting the poachers get away. After a short chase and lots of swearing, the men surrendered.

With their wrists bound behind their backs with thick cable ties, they walked to the edge of the water where the anti-poaching boat was moored.

"Why do they always come in from another area, thinking this is an easy place to kill animals?" retired Lt. Jason Carpenter asked, standing close to the water, but still out of striking distance should a crocodile happen to think they might be a nice snack. "You'd think that word had got around that we protect Bongani's lands."

Mitch shook his head. It was a common question from the volunteers. Despite all the community training they put the locals through and how much the tourist dollars in the area were shared, there were always others who thought the region was wild and unprotected. Ripe for just taking whatever they wanted.

On the wall of their operations office at Bishu, was a map from a publication that showed that over fifty percent of the elephant population in their area had been poached or disappeared between 2001 and 2011, an astonishing statistic for a ten-year period in this day and age.

And that data didn't include the less iconic animals that were suffering steep declines because of urban encroachment and the bush meat trade. There were areas where the game had been hunted out around them and it was even barren of birds.

It worried Joss, Bongani and Mitch, as the game within the boundaries didn't recognize where the safe borders were.

Like the elephant who used the area as a corridor to migrate north and south, up from Botswana, through Hwange and Victoria Falls, and up to Kariba, past Mana Pools—and then they'd return. Ancient trails that many researchers were only now mapping thanks to elephants who still remembered, or had the knowledge passed down from their matriarchs.

The land and its animals were in trouble, and while so many scientists, activists, and ordinary people on the ground, like him and his team, tried to help, Mitch feared that many of the species would never be seen again. Small hedgehogs, the humble duiker, the dik-dik and even klipspringers and dassies that clung to the rocky koppies were becoming less frequent. Not to mention the pangolins—the most trafficked animal in the world, according to the latest statistics.

Zimbabwe was in a crisis, and people were starving.

"They don't carry enough meat," commented one of the local AP team members, Kat, as she walked over and inspected the parts of the carcass the poachers had dropped. "The waterbuck would need at least six people to carry it all. They would try not to leave even the intestines behind. They only carry two legs and the head. Where's the rest?"

Mitch shook his head. "Take Greg and Jason with you and see what you can find. They probably have a biltong tree somewhere. Easier to spot when it's still red."

"Biltong tree?" Greg, the newest of the Marine volunteers, asked.

"They hang the meat to dry in the tree. When it's dehydrated, they come back and take it. It's lighter to transport dried. And in these winter months, not so many flies, and the weather is kinder to them. To an untrained eye, it looks like seed pods on a tree, but to those who recognize it, it's a sad sight. They keep it high enough that hyenas don't get to it, but often, leopards will raid the cache. If they catch the leopard doing what comes naturally, scavenging on older kills, it'll become another statistic."

"Right," Greg said.

"Kat can spot one of those trees from far away, and you're not going to need many tracking skills anyway. Just follow the blood trail. Take pictures before you gather the supplies."

Kat took off down the path with the other volunteers behind her.

Mitch turned to where the three poachers were restrained and under close guard.

"Come on; get them on their feet. Let's get to our boat. We can return for Kat's team later. Time to get these three to the police and start the process of getting them convicted. If they even come back to Binga for their court date," Mitch said bitterly. "They aren't known to us, so chances are they'll get bail and quickly disappear back across Kariba into Zambia. The best we can really hope for is that we never see them again. Such a waste of a magnificent animal."

"Holy shit," Luckson exclaimed. "Look at the size of that flatdog."

A huge crocodile, attracted by the smell of the meat, was lumbering out of the water. Quickly, the men pulled the poachers off their knees by the riverbank and away from the danger as the crocodile burst into a sprint, its mouth open to reveal spectacular teeth. Mitch dropped the hindquarters he had been dragging up the bank and ran.

"At least we have photographs, and the meat won't be wasted," Mitch said as looked into the crocodile's cold eyes and saw the determined will to survive.

The crocodile dragged the leg into the water. Two more crocs had gathered in the shallows, and when the bigger one began swimming, they attacked the meat, all wanting a share.

The water boiled as they gripped the hindquarter and tossed their bodies, spinning three hundred and sixty degrees, breaking off chunks.

Mitch turned to the poachers. Their widened eyes, still focused on the crocodiles devouring the food they had risked so much to gather. The superstition and the natural fear of such an apex predator, clear.

"What gives you the right to live when the waterbuck can't? Give us one good reason not to throw you in there too?" Mitch said in perfect Ndebele.

One of the poachers had wet himself, the patch growing on his tatty shorts, the smell acidic.

Mitch shook his head. Despite being a soldier and taking lives in a kill or be killed situation, he wasn't about to commit murder, but the poachers were clearly terrified of what might happen.

"Come on team." Mitch said. "Once we're away from those crocs, make sure to rinse him down. No one deserves to be coated in their own fluids. Good thing it'll be an easy ride back to base from here. At least we can be certain that we don't need to bail out our boats."

CHAPTER 4
A FREE MAN

NAVAL CONSOLIDATED BRIG, CHARLESTON, SOUTH CAROLINA, USA

3 January 2014

Chad Whitney strode out of the high-security prison.

The gates clanked shut behind him. He drew in a deep, ragged breath. Turning slowly, he took in his surroundings, letting his newfound freedom settle over him.

His six-foot-one body was more honed for battle than it had been before he was incarcerated. He wore civilian clothes: jeans, a T-shirt, a hoodie and some nondescript boots. A duffel bag was slung over his shoulder.

He knew it was the same air as in the prison, but somehow it smelt different.

Freedom carried a distinctive aroma.

Liberty.

He'd taken a plea deal for second-degree murder of Al-Qadhafi and served twelve of the fifteen-year sentence. The remaining three years were to be served under martial supervision. Chad had been paroled early for good and remorseful behavior.

What a load of fucking bullshit! Remorse. Repentance. Regret.

He would do it all again in a heartbeat.

He had killed Farid Al-Qadhafi, but it had not been a pre-planned assassination.

He'd acted on raw emotion. It was not a calculated decision. Anyone who treated their son like Al-Qadhafi did, deserved to die.

War had taught Chad a few valuable life lessons, such as patience. Good things were worth working and waiting for.

He'd also learned that life was even cheaper than he'd been led to believe.

A taxi cruised along the asphalt and came to a stop in front of him. He climbed in, ready for the trip to the halfway house.

Half an hour later he walked into what would be his room for the next six months—the first private space he'd had in years. He put his bag down and locked the door. Blue curtains covered a window. The only furniture was a bed, a lockable closet, a desk and a chair. The door to the right led to his own bathroom.

He stripped for his first shower as a free man, leaving his clothes next to the bed. He lingered under the spray, taking his time to wash every inch of prison off his body with steaming-hot water and the soap dispensed from the wall-mounted container. After scrubbing his body dry with the towel from the rail, he brushed his teeth with the new toothbrush that had been supplied. *What he would give for mouthwash…*

He walked back into the bedroom, then lay naked on top of the thin bedspread and closed his eyes.

He slept the sleep of a dead man.

He had spent so long sleeping with one eye open while in prison.

Here, in his own space, he could finally relax.

Chad woke sweating, despite the winter cold. He leapt up, fists already in a defensive position, his feet slightly apart. Strong.

He looked around his drab room. It smelled of the cigarette smoke coming from the men outside as they destroyed their lungs with poison. It was a filthy habit he had never taken up. Someone cursed crudely, and he heard glass smash.

"That's enough. Whoever did that, get it cleaned up. You know the rules. Obey them or you know what happens," a raised voice of authority threatened.

He felt the chill run down his spine. It kept him from opening his door to tell them to shut the fuck up.

They fell silent, and soon a vacuum could be heard.

He remembered where he was. Halfway house. The drill master's word meant the difference between freedom and jail here.

He took a breath and relaxed his shoulders.

After grabbing yesterday's T-shirt, he wiped his face, rubbed his eyes, and laid back down on the bed. Using a relaxation technique he'd learned in prison, he took himself to a time when he was in a happier place.

The Balkans. Where the northerly Siberian wind carved death threats into his skin, reminding him that he was alive, and he was finally totally out of reach of Walter's money and influence.

He was using his memory to self-regulate his breathing. *Calm. Safe.*

He saw himself adjusting his scope.

Breathe in.

He was AWOL again. Roaming the streets for a kill.

A man, Walter's age, walked along the road. He'd seen him in the market earlier in the day, wrapped heavily in scarves and a thick jacket against the bitter cold of winter in Kosovo.

The man blew into his hands. At a guess, Chad would say his gloves probably had a hole in them, letting in the frigid air.

Breathe in.

Hold.

Breathe out.

Walter never had gloves with holes. Everything was always perfect, the best of the best, when you had money.

Chad remembered the chilling coldness and wearing gloves with holes in them. And poverty, when he didn't know where their next meal was going to come from, unless he raided a dumpster and took the end-of-day cast-offs from the fast-food bin home to feed him and his mother.

Chad had been fifteen when his mother had overdosed, and his Uncle Walter, with all his money, had let his own nephew suffer all that time. Walter had finally sauntered into the picture. And even that was only after social services had contacted him. Walter had begrudgingly taken Chad from the foster system to his ranch.

All those years of moving from place to place. Of having nothing. There had been a blood relative with the means to fight his mother for custody, if he'd cared enough—a relative who had done nothing to save Chad from the things he'd had to do for his drunk and drug-addicted mother.

Anger rose, pulling him further away from his calming memory.

His breathing was ragged.

He started again.

Taking a deep breath, he forced his mind back. The cold in the room helped put him back in time.

He was seeing the snow falling. Faster. Thicker. A whiteout was coming.

He'd been a younger man when he'd served there, barely twenty-one. Naive, thinking he had a plan for the future. Yet he was still developing his skills and gaining experience, and it would take time.

Walter had thrown him off the Lucky 7 Ranch in Nevada before his eighteenth birthday. Other than securing Chad's admission to the United States Military Academy, West Point, Walter had never done anything for him.

It was as if, to Walter, Chad had never existed.

Almost three years of living on that ranch, and he wished he'd never met his Uncle Walter. The constant comparison between him, the orphaned boy with a screwed-up mother, and the precious heiress had a deep psychological impact. Even if he tried hard to cover it up.

While he was at West Point, he had received a letter notifying him that a truck had moved his possessions from the Lucky 7 Ranch into a storage locker in Pinehurst, North Carolina—close enough to his college on the military base to be useful. It had been paid up front for eight years.

There had also been a letter from Walter's lawyer, Jeffery Myers, of Trout Creek Law Firm, P.C. On the thick paper were instructions that Chad was never to return to the Lucky 7 Ranch. It also stipulated that Chad would receive his inheritance from his biological father, Norman Whitney, at twenty-five, and that it would remain in trust until then.

Thankfully, his mother had been unable to access it and hadn't spent it on booze and drugs.

A bank account statement was attached, showing the balance. Chad had whistled when he read it. Walter had not added to it, but the interest over the years had helped.

Substantially.

He breathed heavily.

He opened his eyes and looked at the ceiling of his room in the halfway house.

Just thinking about it today still brought him anger beyond what he'd learned to control with his training.

He clenched his fists, then straightened his fingers.

Voices outside his door reminded him he was not alone, but he was at last free.

Free to follow the plan he'd spent so many years planning.

Bosnia now totally forgotten, he allowed himself time to think about his favorite subjects instead.

Back then, if the intention was to keep him penniless, both Walter and his lawyer had failed. He didn't squander the money he'd earned in the army or from the militia and had built up substantial cash reserves to add to that inheritance. He had hired a stockbroker who was good with his money. A brother of one of his inmates who was jailed for a drunk driving fatality, the man was a genius.

Having a nephew had made no difference to his uncle.

Walter had already told him on the night that he had the ranch manager drive him to West Point, that he would never get anything from the Whitney estate.

Nothing, despite being family.

That money had called to Chad all these years. How could one branch of the family have so much of it, and yet not share it with the rest? They were part of the same darn tree, and things like wealth should be shared.

When Walter died, everything would go to his precious Marissa.

And how she'd grown over the years. Matured. She was thirty-three now to his forty, and despite trying hard not to, he still remembered her birthday every year.

It was easy to stay up-to-date with the news about his family. They were always in the paper. His uncle lived for being in the news and took his precious daughter to all the McDermitt New Frontier Foundation events, now that she'd grown into the perfect trust fund princess.

Always smiling.

She'd attended university and apparently had an internship within the United Nations in their international relations division. Chad guessed she'd been already sorted with a cushy job lined up for when she completed her final year. He was sure her daddy had paid handsomely for that position for her.

Of course he had.

She'd been born with everything given to her—the wanted child.

But then she had disappeared from the papers. Not attending as many events as previously.

He took a deep breath.

He admitted that when he was younger, he'd made a mistake.

This time when he tried to kill her, he knew he would succeed. It would be meticulously planned and executed, just like a military exercise.

Forgiving his younger self, he admitted he had needed time to understand his anger, and his purpose in life.

Time to learn how to kill a person with no remorse.

Time to access his inheritance and make his own money to finance his revenge.

Time for Marissa to make her own delicious mistakes and fail in life.

He breathed out. Perhaps she'd made that mistake, which was why she had disappeared from public view. He knew from his sources in jail that she was a bit of a hermit now, spending a lot of time with her elephant on the ranch. Unmarried, with no children, she dedicated herself to the ridiculous foundation, according to his information network.

The bitch and her expert avoidance skills, she was still doing it. Not once had she reached out to him when he went to the army, or even in jail. Not one letter. Not one call.

Marissa had never antagonized or reminded him that he was just a nephew; she had simply been polite, as if pretending he was just a visitor at the ranch.

She was spoiled. Her father, besotted with her.

What type of present was an elephant for her fifth birthday?

If he remembered his fifth birthday, he was probably stuck in a dark cupboard, waiting for his mother to finish with her latest client's dick and get a few dollars. He doubted he even received a present that year, or any following that until he had moved to the Lucky 7 Ranch.

He didn't believe it was a cool, calculated move on his cousin's part to ignore him; she didn't know how to share, and she certainly didn't appreciate the privileged position she was in.

Not at all.

And that was eventually what made him try to kill Marissa.

Her coldness and a lack of awareness of his existence. As if she was the mistress over the whole ranch, and he was a gnat to ignore.

Of all the places on earth the army could have sent him, Bosnia had never been on his radar. Yet, ironically, it was there that he tasted freedom for the first time. He'd been learning the skills to enable him to remove Walter and his precious Marissa from his life and leave no trace.

Chad opened his eyes. Looked at his watch and knew the day was about to intrude on his thoughts.

He needed to remember the endgame. That was the important part: to kill and not be caught.

When he was finished here, he could cash out some of his funds and use that to be ready for the strike. Take down those bastard-spawn, Walter and Marisa, who should have had his back as a kid, but instead were living a life of opulence, while he was in slum conditions.

Then he would shoot that elephant and have its head stuffed and put it in the ranch's men's communal restroom for them to piss on when they got drunk.

The drill master in the halfway house banged on his door

"Get your lazy ass out of bed. You have breakfast duty."

Chad stood, grabbed his shower bag, and walked to the bathroom.

Before being imprisoned, he used to think well in the shower. That was not a luxury you had behind bars. It appeared that it wouldn't be a luxury in the halfway house either.

CHAPTER 5
FOUNDATIONS ARE CREATED TO HELP

ELLINGTON AIRPORT, HOUSTON, TEXAS, USA

5 January 2014

"Thank you for waiting for us. I didn't expect to be this late," Marissa Whitney said as she and her father climbed into the limousine and shut out the biting cold.

"Think nothing of it Ms. Whitney," the driver said.

Marissa took a bottle of water from the fridge and offered it to her dad.

He nodded and she popped it in his hand and grabbed another.

"Thanks," Walter Whitney said. "Wish it were something hotter. It's freezing here."

"Would you like me to stop for a coffee? There is a shop just off the main road," the driver offered.

"No, that's alright. We'll grab something at the hospital," Marissa said, taking a sip. "Water's better for you, Dad. Remember what the cardiologist said? Healthier choices."

"Healthier choices my ass. He knows there's nothing wrong with me. He's being a scaremonger."

"Do you have the same degree he has in health?" She raised her eyebrows.

Walter grumbled. "Still think we should've flown back to Nevada and done this meeting another time. Would've been a whole lot simpler." He stared down at the newspaper he'd reopened, despite reading it several times on the plane on the way from Washington, D.C. to Houston. His glasses were perched on his nose like always, and he was wearing a crisp white shirt, his tie loosened but not undone. Even now, at sixty-two, her father was not a man many wanted to tangle with. She angled her head to peek at the newspaper article, but he shifted it away.

She wondered what was so interesting. Something was bothering him, and he was finding it difficult to share with her.

She knew when he was ready, he would tell her.

Marissa shook her head. "You know I wanted to be here. Being late is one thing; not turning up would have been something else altogether," she said, settling back into the seat, looking at the city's skyline as it drew closer.

She'd given her word. The latest recipient of their McDermitt New Frontier Foundation patronage, Sophia Brennan, was scheduled for surgery in the morning. Even one more day might make the difference between having both legs amputated or just one.

"And you are still sure you want to meet her?" her father asked. "Make it so personal? Her parents knew what they were getting into when they brought her to the States. And the risks involved."

"I know, but there've been complications," Marissa said as she looked out the window. "Did you read that they were reluctant to even accept the Foundation's help? They seem so proud and hesitant to receive handouts. The story behind the child is so unusual; she was abandoned because she was disabled. Adopted by a bachelor who's a war hero and a double amputee. It intrigued me."

She knew his view of the military. She wasn't sure if it was because his brother Norman had been killed helping evacuate people in Operation Frequent Wind at the end of the fall of Saigon. Or because that was where Chad, her psychopathic cousin, had landed up.

"I read it," Walter said. "It's not that unusual in humanitarian work. I just don't think you should get so personally involved. You might get hurt if it doesn't work out."

"Dad, you know that I'm also here to meet the father, Joss. You do recall he owns an animal sanctuary on the edge of Lake Kariba, in Zimbabwe?"

"I haven't forgotten where you elephant comes from," Walter said.

"Good, see the water is working, good hydration in the brain and body." She laughed. "I like meeting the people we help. Adding the 'personal touch'. I enjoy the progress we're making with the foundation work; it means a lot to me to see this kid get a second chance at life."

"The foundation," Walter said, then reached for her hand and patted it. "When your mother was alive, I loved to see the recipients' reaction to her. She would light up the room when she walked in, and somehow it just made their world seem like a brighter, happier place. You take after her. She'd love that you're taking a personal interest in this couple's daughter from Zimbabwe."

She squeezed his hand. "I wish I'd had more time with her, Dad."

"Me too," Walter said, letting her hand slowly slip out of his as they drove. "Me too. You do understand my girl, I tend to focus more on the patients than the families' backgrounds. I'm just looking out for you."

Marissa reached over to her father's hand again and squeezed it. Holding tight. "Dad, I'm thirty-three years old. You could have stopped 'looking out for me' years ago."

"I didn't get that memo," he said. "I think the fact that you chose to follow your mother's footsteps into the foundation work makes it even harder." He flicked the newspaper closed, tapped it on his knee, and sighed. "That's true. Sophia's a worthy recipient. Joss is a bonus. It's not often we get a recipient of the foundation's help where we can look to expand the aid we can offer."

"What's really got you on edge?" Marissa asked, unable to keep waiting for her father to open-up to her.

Her father hesitated, tapping the newspaper again. "As you said, you're an adult, and you can make your own decisions. The army called me yesterday to let me know that Chad has been released from prison."

She took a deep breath. "So much for not keeping things from me."

"I know, but it's Chad. He's always known how to push my buttons."

She watched her father. He looked ready to strangle the newspaper.

"I'm not a teenager anymore. Besides, I kicked his ass last time he came at me. Dawn taught me well. So, what does that matter to us?"

He threaded his fingers through his grey hair. "I remember only too well. Including how Amalee was the one to alert us that you needed help. You might not have held him off much longer. Things could have been so much worse."

"Let it go, Dad. He's not worth getting an ulcer for. He chose his path, despite being welcomed into our house after Alice died," Marissa said. "Your PI searched for them for years. Chased them all over America. Alice hid him well. It's not your fault your brother married an addict who spent all the money you once gave her on drugs, and then kept your nephew hidden all those years. All because she refused to go into a drug rehabilitation and chose drugs over her son's welfare."

Walter frowned. "If I had tried to take custody of him as a baby when she first came to me, he would have been so much better off. He might have been stable. Normal–not the animal who tried to kill you."

"Dad, don't go there." Marissa said reaching out to and running her hand down his arm.

"If I could do it all differently–"

"I'm a stronger person for it. More compassionate and definitely more aware of my strengths and weaknesses. Besides, what difference will it really make if he's out?"

"None. If we're lucky," Walter said. "We don't know if he changed in prison, and I certainly hope he at least found some peace within himself. That he's more settled and has matured."

"Me too. It's a sad story—"

"Norman must be turning in his grave knowing he has a murderer for a son. After Alice got pregnant, they married by proxy; he didn't even get to meet his child before he was killed. Then, she decides to disappear on us and drags Chad all over America, causing him God knows how much pain and suffering, just because the little bit of money Norman had was locked up tight for Chad. She kept him away from his family. We had to find out from a social worker that she was dead, and what she'd been putting him through…"

Deep frown lines showed on her father's face. He swallowed hard and she watched his Adam's apple bob as an emotional lump formed in his throat, "If–" He cleared his throat. "If it wasn't for her selfishness, Chad would have been so different. He could have been the brother you never had–"

Marissa put her hand over his and gave it a reassuring squeeze. "We can't change any of that, Dad. You gave Chad a home when we knew he needed one. He messed it all up for himself. Did they tell you anything else?"

"He'll be in a halfway house program for six months, and still under their supervision for three years. In a different state, so the chances of him dropping in on us are slim."

"Did they say where?"

"No, just that they would closely monitor him."

"See? He's still the army's problem—not ours," Marissa said. "And maybe he has changed. Twelve years in a prison is a long time to think about your life choices."

"Five minutes to your destination," the driver's voice came through the intercom.

"Right," Marissa said, taking a deep breath. "Time to put our lives aside and find the Foundation's game face. There is one scared girl who's going through hell, and we have the ability to make it all easier."

The Texas Children's Hospital in Houston was a collection of modern buildings, standing stark against the stormy sky. The largest children's hospital in America, it was known for its international patients who came to be treated there. The enormous facility, with over nine hundred beds, was a hive of activity. Doctors, nurses, patients, and visitors all swarmed like ants around a grain of sugar, and yet everyone seemed to know where to go and what to do.

A warm blast of air swept over Marissa and Walt as they walked inside. A volunteer with a huge name badge that read 'Sally' approached them. "Are you the Whitneys?"

Marissa nodded. "Please call me Marissa, and my dad, Walter."

"Doctor Maine asked me to watch out for you both. The orthopedic wards are this way, in the West Tower. Please follow me." She crossed the large foyer and headed toward a bank of elevators.

Marissa straightened her blouse and her jacket, checking her reflection in the lift mirror.

"You look fine, love," Walter said.

The bell pinged as they arrived at the eleventh floor—the orthopedic surgery inpatient unit.

Sally stepped out of the lift and walked to the reception area. "Please can you let Doctor Maine know that the Whitneys are here?"

The nurse looked at her chart. "Doctor Maine was called away and wasn't sure when she would return, but she gave permission to please introduce them to Sophia in room 1116. You're welcome to do that since you're here."

Sally nodded and then walked them to the appointed door and knocked quietly.

"Come in," a male voice said.

Sally pushed the door open, and Marissa followed her. Like all pediatric rooms, it was decorated in soothing tones of green and blue. It had a large, brightly colored mural of a dog superhero on the wall.

"Mitch, got to go. Our visitors just arrived. Chat later," the man said, and hung up the phone.

A smile slid across Sally's face. "Joss, good to see you. I have Walter and Marissa Whitney for your appointment this afternoon."

"Thanks," Joss said as he stood from the chair next to Sophia's bed. "You made it." He shook her father's hand, then hers. "Nice to meet both of you. This is my daughter, Sophia."

Marissa turned to the little girl in the bed, but not before she swept her eyes lower over Joss's legs. He wore long chino pants that hid his prosthetics. Defying her circumstances and medication, a bright button of a four-year-old sat there, her hair half-braided in traditional pink beads. Drips and drains decorated her body, and Marissa noticed a small pouch of strong pain drugs keeping her comfortable. Buried beneath a white sheet were her legs that had caused so many problems for such a young girl. Balanced on her legs was a bowl, and inside that were more beads, but she smiled broadly.

"Hi Sophia," Walter said. "This is my daughter, Marissa."

"You're the people who are like the Make a Wish Foundation, only you get people healed when we are not dying," Sophia said.

Marissa laughed. Kids always had their own unique way of saying things. Straight to the point—no beating around the bush. "I guess that's us, sure."

"Y'all set here then. If ya need anything else that the nurses on this floor can't help you with, please ask them to fetch me," Sally said before she turned and opened the door.

"Thanks," Marissa said to her departing back.

"We're taking the beads out, getting ready for tomorrow's operation,"

Sophia said. "It's more comfy without them when I have to lie down for a long time."

"I can believe that," Marissa said. "Not that I ever had such wonderful beading in my hair, but I did threaten to have dreadlocks when I was in university. You should have seen my father's reaction. Nothing like yours."

She snuck a look at her dad, who had the courtesy to blush.

"I don't think that Sophia's lovely braids and your rebellious teenager's dreadlocks are a very good comparison," Walt said.

"Is this your real dad?" Sophia asked.

Marissa smiled and patted her dad on the arm. "Every last grey hair on his head. I don't even have to share him with a sister or a brother. Do you have a brother or sister?"

Sophia shook her head. "Just me, but there are lots of other children around the lodge that I get to play with. So that's okay."

Marissa smiled and looked at a photograph next to Sophia's bed. Joss held Sophia in his arms, and a woman with smokey eyes and pretty girl next door looks, complete with freckles across her nose, had her hand on his shoulder. Beside them was a mother elephant and a baby. The baby had its trunk kissing Sophia's face. "Is that you?"

Sophia laughed. "*Yebo.* And that is Ndhlovy," Sophia said, pointing to the bigger elephant. "She was rescued by my dada when he was younger, and that's her baby, Khwazi. Ndhlovy has returned to the wild, but she brings Mamma all the elephant that need help, hey, Dada?"

Joss reached over and took the bowl off her legs, her hair now bead-free. "That she does." He walked around the bed and placed the bowl next to the photo.

"They are wild, but you let your daughter near enough for a photograph?" Marissa asked.

Joss smiled. "They're special. It's a long story but Sophia is never in any danger when she's near that herd."

"There are more than those two?" Walter asked.

"Of course," Sophia said, as if Walter was silly for not knowing. "Elephant are always in a herd, except if they are a bull. The bulls need to be alone. Ndhlovy is the matriarch of her herd. There are her and her baby, and her sisters, and her cousins. When we got our first orphaned baby, Isibane, Ndhlovy was like an auntie and came in to look after her all the time."

Marissa looked at Joss. "You own a single elephant or a herd? Sorry, I'm lost."

Joss chuckled. "Ndhlovy is not owned by anyone; she's wild and free. The herd too."

"And they are classified as wild?" Walter asked.

Joss nodded. "They were never tamed. The chief of our land and my friend, Bongani, we rescued Ndhlovy when I was a kid. Her family came and found her and took her back into the wild once she was healthy. I didn't see her for many years, but after I returned home from Afghanistan, Ndhlovy and I found each other. Make no mistake—she's wild. She just has the greatest compassion for people who need a little bit more love and attention, doesn't she, Sophia?"

"And Khwazi too," Sophia added. "I miss them."

Joss put a bright pink headscarf on her head and tied a big bow. When he was done, he dropped his hand, turned to his daughter, and smiled. "Perfect." He reached out and tapped her nose.

Marissa looked where Joss held his daughter's hand now and absentmindedly rubbed his thumb on her little wrist in a comforting way. Her heart fluttered at the obvious love between them. She was away from the ranch in Nevada and Amalee often due to her frequent travel, so she knew what it was like to miss an elephant. "I can only imagine how hard it is to be so far away from them and not know when you'll see them again."

"Mamma tells us when she sees them, and what other animals are visiting," Sophia said. "She got a new tortoise and a bat-eared fox yesterday that need help."

"She looks after all the animals—not just the elephants?" Marissa asked.

Sophia giggled. "You talk so funny. It's not elephantsssss," she emphasized the 's'. "It's just elephant."

"Sophia!" Joss said.

Marissa looked at Joss.

He shrugged.

"Really?" Marissa said. "Goodness, all these years, I always have put that 's' on the end, but you know what, I think it might be one of those American-versus-the-world words."

Sophia smiled. "Do you know that Mitch always says Mamma looks after all God's creatures. Mamma says it's just Bongani's ones. She's silly because we get people outside the chief's lands bringing in animals. Remember that lady who came from Binga with the little hedgehog, Dada?"

"I do," Joss added.

"How much time do you get to spend with your elephant?" Marrisa asked with a little exaggeration on the 't' at the end.

Joss smiled. "Depends on the day, and what's happening, Ndhlovy comes and goes. When she needs it, we make the time for them."

Marissa reached out and touched Sophia's arm. "Once you're given the 'all clear' to get out of the hospital and are in rehab, would you like to come to my ranch and meet my elephant, Amalee?"

"You have an elephant too? But you live in America," Sophia said.

"Here," Marissa said, digging her phone out of her briefcase purse. "This is my Amalee. I've had her since I was five years old. She isn't wild, so my best friend Dawn looks after her full time for us, and Brandon too," Marissa said as she showed Sophia the photos.

"She's an African elephant," Sophia said.

Marissa nodded. "Yes, she is, but she's as gentle as any horse—maybe even more so."

"And this is her stable? It is fancy," Sophia said with a giggle. "Even our new rescue center is not smart like that."

Marissa smiled and turned the phone to Joss, who took it and studied the pictures.

"How did you come to have an elephant?" he asked.

"Dad and I rescued her from a circus that was mistreating her. Before that, she was one of the JumboLair Elephants rescued in 1984," Marissa said.

"Your Amalee is what us Zimbabweans refer to as one of 'the stolen elephant.' A sad time for our country and for all sixty-four of the elephant taken," Joss said.

Marissa nodded, well aware of the controversy behind the supposed 'rescue' because of a drought—elephant that later made the man who sold them all off even richer. "She had a questionable start to her time in America but know that she's had nothing but the best care and love since she's been in our family."

"She's one of the lucky ones. Many weren't so fortunate," Joss said.

"She's rather special to us. I can only imagine the horror others have experienced," Walter said.

Joss nodded.

"My dream was once to rewild her," Marissa said. "But here we are, two old ladies still together after almost thirty years. My life would be so empty without her." She ended on a weak note as she moved to another photo on her phone, of Amalee, where Dawn was feeding her apples.

"She's spoiled rotten. And I admit to worrying that Amalee would think something bad had happened to Marissa if we rewilded her—that it would be yet another abandonment in her life," Walter said, putting his hands on his daughter's shoulders.

"She would adapt," Joss said. "She must be lonely without her own kind 'round her."

"I don't doubt it," Marissa admitted, "but Dawn and I do everything we can to enrich her time. I just can't imagine moving her to another rescue center in the States."

"I would like to meet Amalee, if you're serious about us visiting," Joss said. "It'd probably make a huge difference to Sophia to spend some time with an elephant while she's recovering. She really has a special bond with Khwazi."

"I meant it. I'd love for you to visit. I've never met another four-year-old who is just like me and sort of has her own elephant," Marissa said.

Sophia was grinning.

"But first, you have to have your surgery. And work hard in rehab to get strong enough to travel," Marissa said, turning her attention back to the patient.

Sophia nodded. "One day, when I have my new legs, I'll be able to twirl with Khwazi, hey, Dada? Artificial legs are just part of someone special," she said with a look that hinted at something shared between her and her father.

Marissa smiled. "Twirl? Now that I look forward to seeing. It brings up memories of when I used to dance with Amalee when I was younger."

"You did?" Sophia asked, excitement edging into her voice.

"I did, and when I began Taekwondo lessons once I was older, she would patiently stand by while I practiced," Marissa said. "I doubt she ever understood why I would spend hours kicking the hay bales."

"Here," Walter said, showing his phone to Sophia. "This is a picture of Marissa doing ballet with Amalee. She loved to wear that pink tutu everywhere when she started dancing."

Sophia laughed; the tinkling sound touched Marissa's heart. "Is this really you?"

"It is," Marissa said. Then she looked at her dad. "I guess we all grow up."

"It's an old picture, but one of my favorites," Walter admitted, handing the phone to Joss.

Sophia looked at her dad. "I miss home. And our elephant." It came out almost a sob.

Joss was by her side in an instant. "I know, my girl. Once they sort your legs out, we can go home again."

Sophia was frowning. "If we get to visit your elephant, can Mamma come too?"

Walter frowned. "Where is she?"

"In Zimbabwe," Sophia said.

"Peta had to stay home and watch over the sanctuary," Joss said quickly.

Save on the expenses, thought Marissa.

Definitely a worthy family.

"Every princess should have her Mamma with them, especially during rehab. We'll sort something out and bring her to you, Sophia," Marissa said as tears glistened in her eyes.

CHAPTER 6
THE NEXT REAPING

HARARE, ZIMBABWE

7 July 2014

Shumba Chitepo sat at his mukwa hardwood desk. Behind him, certificates from Oxford University declared him qualified, with honors, and others certified him to practice law in Zimbabwe. He was proud of the effort he'd put into obtaining those on his boxing scholarship. It proved he was really clever.

Cleverer than the idiot head ranger of Hwange National Parks Service, Frank Hadebe, who sat in the visitors' chair and threw the paper down on his desk.

"This is a death sentence to my career and to me," Frank complained.

"It was not a problem for you three years ago," Shumba said.

"That was only eight elephant babies; this is one hundred and forty," Frank said. "This is too many; this will decimate herds and take them many years to recover."

"Focus on the now—not the whole amount. The first shipment, thirty elephant. That's all. Can you handle that, you *gutless wonder?*" Shumba said.

Frank flinched at the insult, but he dared not show weakness. "We can do that. Know it will take time, but what is the use if they just die in transit like last time? What we did in 2012 did not work," Frank said. "Why do you think it will work this time? What is the difference now?"

"That was regrettable," Shumba said. "The Chinese have changed their policies to allow more jumbo to be together, to stay in groups. They are also allowing a single handler per plane to go with the elephant through the journey and to spend twelve months in China. That is why we are going to supply more." He looked at the pathetic man in front of him. Despite being in his late fifties, the man's body was still scrawny, like a teenager's. He was short, probably about five foot eight, if that, in his boots.

Frank shook his head. "This won't work. No one can expect this many babies to be taken from the wild."

"Ah, please, spare me the sob story," Shumba said. He was beginning to tire of the whiny man, but he needed him to get the job done. "Your rangers lost over fifty adult elephant alone a few weeks back to poaching. And there are always more elephant coming here from Botswana. Too many elephant eating everything. You cannot stop the poaching here anymore than you can stop these elephant babies being exported. Your job is to capture them and get them ready to send overseas. I don't care if they die in China. In fact, that is good; then they come and buy more."

Frank looked at the papers again, shaking his head.

"It is not a choice for you. It is an instruction," Shumba said. "What do we need to do to make this happen?"

Frank massaged his neck.

Good—he was uncomfortable. It always helped when you were getting a man to step over a moral line that he was aware of his own mortality.

"So?" Shumba pressed.

Frank frowned, appearing deep in thought. "Older babies. Ones that are no longer milk-dependent. Allowing for two months of quarantine in their pens for their two rabies injections and all their inoculations to ensure that there are no infections or diseases carried on them before they ship out. You should move the month they are flying out; between October and February, it is the hottest time of the year to move any wildlife. There would be the most casualties from dehydration during those months–"

"The timeline is not negotiable, but I can see what the Chinese delegates say about the age of the elephant. I know that they need to be under two meters to get in and out of the plane," Shumba said. "But older is probably a better idea. Then they are not so dependent on their keepers."

"Do not use individual crates. If they load like cattle, all together, it will be easier for them. Less stress," Frank said. "Less tranquilizers and manhandling."

"I will let them know."

"The receiving station in China needs to not be in snowy conditions. These are African elephant. They don't do well in extreme cold," Frank said.

Shumba nodded. "I will endeavor to press that home to them. I do not have a destination for where they plan to quarantine them because they were adamant, they wanted them to go on display first thing in the springtime."

"Thirty, even in one year, is a lot of babies to take from one park," Frank said.

"Do not take from the Presidential Herd. The President only wants you to take them from elephant groups that are not under public scrutiny, to keep people's eyes and energy away from it all."

"What about the CITIES mandate on elephant? How can our President do this?" Frank asked.

"It is not your place to ask such questions," Shumba picked up the papers from the desk and handed them to Frank. "This is a copy of the signed letter from your President. You do what it says. I will be coming to Hwange periodically to check on your progress."

"This is going to cost a lot of money. Where do you expect us to get the funds to build these bomas? To arrange the capture of these elephant? The feeding of elephant babies is a specialized business if they are going to be in good condition."

"Everyone just wants the greenbacks." Shumba got up and opened a drawer in a steel cabinet, took the bag, put it on the desk in front of Frank, and opened it.

Inside were slabs of American one-hundred-dollar bills. "This is enough money to do everything. There is a letter at the bottom with who you are to contact to bring in helicopters and shooters. Make sure the bomas are better than the ones used in 2012, as there will be additional game capture too. Your part is to capture the elephant and get them ready. Everything else is already arranged. You will select the herds to take the babies from. No excuses. Your President has asked for a job to be done."

Frank shook his head. "Our President has overstepped–"

Shumba pulled his arm back, bunched his fist, and let fly, smack into Frank's face.

Blood from his nose splashed over his shirt and his suit, and splatters were on the desk.

"Disrespect the President again and you'll be just another Matabele to disappear," Shumba said as he shook his hand.

Obviously, he was out of practice with his boxing. He had felt the fat jiggle all the way up his arm, and Frank should have been knocked out.

Frank held his nose, trying to stop the bleeding.

"Of course, how much of that money from the bag is used to restore that boma, or pay your wages, is up to you. Come December, have things ready or you'll regret it."

CHAPTER 7
DANGER! DANGER!

LUCKY 7 RANCH, NEVADA, USA

4 July 2014

Marissa stood beside Amalee in the enrichment area. July was one of her favorite months to be out, playing with her elephant. Being the 4th of July holiday, the ranch was down to a skeleton crew; the rest had gone into McDermitt to enjoy the parade and celebrations.

The weather was beautiful, with lower humidity and hot days that went on endlessly, and even now, just before the sun sunk behind the mountains and the cooler drop of nighttime, it was magical.

Dawn and Brandon had put fresh hay, acacia branches, and elephant cubes in the enrichment area outside earlier. Attached to the elephant barn, it was about three times the size of a football field, surrounded by an elephant proof fence. Amalee could see through most sections, except the one at the end that protected her from the bitter winter wind. At the outer edge was the outdoor mud bath and wallow area, for her to bathe and cool down in summer. She loved to play in the different depth pools, plunging deep into one while laying on her side in the shallows of the other.

Long poles and thick tree stumps were used for scratching and rubbing against. A new barrel with foraging holes in it, had been moved into the dusting area, and various morsels she loved; apples, thick slices of watermelons and pineapples were hidden inside.

They had swapped out the big tire that Amalee used as a giant stress ball, and there were three new aspen logs that Thomas, the ranch manager, had some of the younger cowboys bring in. Thomas was her Dad's best friend and always called a duck a duck. *"That elephant of yours can strip the bark off, piece by piece. Like I saw on a wildlife documentary."*

Amalee loved logs, tossing them around and rearranging them again and again. And she had already begun stripping the new logs. Eating the rough bark, rich in salicin, and often used in medication much like aspirin. She lifted her trunk, sniffing the air, and took a step closer to the outer edge of the fence, her trunk still raised, she rumbled a warning.

Marissa could feel it in the ground and through her bones, she stilled and looked closely at Amalee. While she was giving a warning, the danger wasn't immediate, her ears were not pinned back. She was not mock charging.

Dawn came out of the elephant barn, a frown on her face, her worry mirrored Marissa's own.

Something or someone was around that the elephant was not happy about.

"It's been many years since Amalee has given any such warning," Dawn said, walking towards them. The elephant turned her head and looked at Dawn, then went back to smelling the air. Dawn approached closer now that Amalee was aware of her presence. Sneaking up on a five-ton elephant would never end well for anyone.

"I know." Marissa nodded. "But what can she smell?"

Amalee was standing at the far side of her enclosure, looking out, beyond the ranch buildings, towards the grazing lands and the mountains in the distance. Amalee swayed from side to side, a clear sign that she was agitated. Her ears tilted forward, her trunk reaching out, tasting the air, her left foot closing over her right repeatedly, kicking up dust with her huge toenail.

The danger wasn't immediate, or she would have trumpeted, but something out there was making her uneasy. And she was letting her humans know.

"It's okay, girl; it can't get to us in here. We're safe," Marissa said as she stepped closer. "Amalee, it's okay."

Marissa put her hand on Amalee's shoulder and looked back out through the thick bars. The ranch stretched all the way to the mountains and beyond. Cattle roamed there, eating the summer grasses.

"What do you smell, girl?" Dawn asked as she stood gazing out with her. "Is he back?"

Amalee rumbled even louder, and Marissa put her hand on the elephant's cheek.

Her mind had immediately gone to Chad, now she knew he was out of jail. It was a logical explanation given that he was the only person her elephant had ever had that reaction to, other than her elephant trainer whom she attacked when they had rescued her. God knew she had enough reasons for hating both men.

"It's okay, girl," Dawn said. "Thomas and the men will be ready for him if he comes to the Lucky 7. We've been tightening security for six months now so he can't get to you, me, or Marissa. Just in case he hasn't given up on his obsessions." Dawn patted the elephant.

More rumbles came from Amalee.

Marissa frowned. "She's sharper than any watchdog. She's trying to warn us that something's out there." She couldn't help looking too, straining her eyes to see any movement outside the fence. "We'll be fine. Many years have passed since last time. He might have changed; all this additional security might be for nothing."

Dawn smiled as Amalee looked all over her for a treat. She pickpocketed the apple like a pro.

"And pigs might fly," Dawn said. "I do worry, though." Patting Amalee, who crunched her favorite fruit. "I taught you well, but I'm not sure how you'll hold up next to a Special Forces nutcase."

"Let's hope I don't need to use those Taekwondo skills out," Marissa said.

"You and me both. We're getting on in years, Amalee and me. We might not be as agile as we once were," Dawn said then laughed at her own joke.

Marissa smiled. "Oh please, you'll always be more remarkable than anyone else in their sixties. You're still as fit as anything, and you don't age. And Amalee is an elephant, in her prime."

They stood together looking outwards. Saying nothing

"The peace was wonderful while he was behind bars, wasn't it?" Dawn said, shattering the uncomfortable silence.

"That it was," Marissa said. She scratched Amalee's ear. The big elephant dropped her trunk and wrapped it around her.

Marissa smiled.

Amalee was affectionate to both her and Dawn. While Dawn fed the pachyderm and looked after her everyday needs, Marissa was the five-year-old girl who'd asked her father to rescue Amalee from abuse at the circus, and the two of them had a deep bond.

Whatever had alarmed Amalee, it was clearly Marissa she thought she needed to protect. As if she were Amalee's own kin.

Amalee swayed, turned and grabbed a trunkful of hay from the basket.

Whatever was out there, Amalee was no longer worried about it.

Or perhaps the threat had retreated...waiting for the right opportunity to strike.

CHAPTER 8
BUSH NEWS

BINGA AREA, ZIMBABWE

25 July 2014

Mitch stood in the middle of the road beside his anti-poaching bakkie, as an old man cycle towards him. After the frosty morning, the day was heating up with the bright winter sunshine. The road was wide here, where two cars could pass easily on the tarmac, and thick bush lined both sides. A large mopani tree was on the side opposite him; a warthog slept in its shade.

Esulu Dazis came to a stop next to Mitch and climbed off the bicycle. His green overalls showed that he was part of the game rangers from the national park. The uniform wasn't new, but it was clean and ironed. Clearly, he took pride in his job. A bag was strapped to the saddle rack on the back, and a long fishing rod was sticking out over the front handlebars.

Mitch stepped forward and clasped his strong hand. "Good to see you again."

Esulu nodded. "I only have two days of leave, then they will expect me back. I cannot be here with you for long, *baas*. I took the bus from Hwange town and then a taxi to the turnoff. I have cycled since then." He looked around, full of nervous energy, his motions jittery, despite the isolated location of the meeting place. "I do not want anyone to see us talking." He looked down the road again.

Mitch smiled. "You just look like a man on a bicycle, off to catch some fish, to me."

"Do not tell anyone that the fishing rod is broken," Esulu said with a wry smile.

"I promise," Mitch said with a smile. "Come sit in the shade of the ute-*bakkie*. I have cold water with me." Mitch took two bottles from the Coleman and passed one to Esulu, who placed his bike on the side of the road and sat in the shade.

Esulu looked around again. He shifted his weight, as if he couldn't relax, and might be ready to bolt if anyone came along.

Mitch asked, "What's happened that you wanted to meet out here and not at the office?"

"I am dead if they find out I talked to anyone. Dead-dead, I tell you!" Esulu exclaimed.

Mitch nodded. "Who're you so scared of?"

"The government." Esulu took a long drink of water and removed his hat. He mopped at his sweating face with it like a towel. "It is like in the 1980s when the Fifth Brigade was after us Matabele."

Mitch knew it had been a terror regime when the government had systematically killed about 20,000 Ndebele people in a genocide that later became known as the Gukurahundi—a dark time in history for the people in Zimbabwe under oppression.

"You're describing every day in Zimbabwe. People still hide from Mugabe's spies. We're all looking over our shoulders. I've learned that well enough since I moved here," Mitch said, taking a swig from his water bottle. "Who's threatening you?"

"No one yet. But they will kill me if they find out I am telling you this. You said when you did our training that if anything ever feels wrong, to come and tell you," Esulu said, checking the road again. "*Eish,* this is like that. It must be done, but it is wrong. It is like 2012. Once again, they are stealing the elephant from the Hwange National Park."

"Who?" Mitch asked.

"They are not relocating them to another reserve like we used to do. They plan to fly them to China. It is as if our very ZimParks rangers are poachers," Esulu said.

"You certain?" Mitch asked.

"I have been a ranger my whole life. First in Matusadona, and then in Hwange, before you came to Chief Bongani's lands. I have seen many things. This–this has happened before. Management, they told us the animals were for relocation. But they did not capture groups of animals like you would when you are relocating. Or just bulls." Esulu stopped and looked around again.

Dread grew in Mitch's stomach. It couldn't be true. "What did they capture?"

"Babies. All weaned so that they do not have to be bottle-fed, and all under two meters high. This is to be able to fit on the plane from Victoria Falls. The last time they sent elephant like this to China, it was the same. Only smaller ones."

Mitch shook his head. "How?"

"Before, it was all hush-hush… then. Then, I did not know what they were doing. I believed it was a relocation, something new the research scientists wanted to try. Not now. *Aikona*. Not now I have done training with you to protect the animals. Now I know that I must come and ask for help. We have been instructed to capture thirty."

"Thirty baby elephant?" Mitch asked. "That's a lot of elephant babies being ripped from their families."

Esulu nodded. "We are holding them in the Elephant Graveyard boma. We are also building a bigger boma at Umtshibi. It is north of the park. Closer to the Victoria Falls Airport. Away from the nosey eyes of the ranger station and out of the eyes of the tourists."

"Hidden well?" Mitch asked as he stripped the plastic label off his water bottle.

Esulu nodded. "No access except by the service roads. I was there to pick the site, but I was sneaky. You can see it from up on one hill if you know what to look for. Doing my job, and I made it almost as hidden as a poacher camp. Lots of big trees covering it. Shade and space to fit the elephant babies, and all the other game that is to be relocated to China. Sable and impala now. Lion captures closer to the date." He hung his head in shame. "Frank, he told me the last time only one baby survived in the end to be on show. It made my heart sore."

"I wonder why he told you that?" Mitch frowned.

"Because he knows he can do nothing," Esulu said, traced a bead of perspiration as it dribbled down the side of the water bottle. He held it on his finger before it fell to the ground, before taking another sip. "They have him by the family jewels. He took their money. Not me. I did not touch that cash. I am old now. I have nothing to lose. My sons, they died of the thinning disease, and my wife has passed on too. I am alone."

"I'm sorry. HIV has touched a lot of people here, it's a cruel indiscriminate disease." Mitch said.

Esulu nodded. "They will pension me off soon. I might or might not get money from the government scheme, but it is okay; I can come home to our homeland. Frank is not so lucky. He does not belong to a homeland. He is not for Chief Bongani to look after."

Mitch frowned and drank some water. "Well that's a lot to take in. Do you trust Frank not to tell anyone it was you who came and told your chief?"

"*Aikona.* No. He does not know I came here," Esulu said, shaking his head slowly. "*Udakiwe,* drinking too many Zambezi beers. Trying to forget he has taken a bribe to poach the animals he swore to protect, when he told me, and I swore to keep his secret. I am not a good friend to a man who needs a friend now. I do not know if there is anyone else to tell who might be able to help. This is the land where the elephant sanctuary is. It is the land where people learn how to protect the wildlife for everyone. If I must betray my *baas* and a friend, then this is the right place to do it."

Mitch looked at the old man and nodded. "We'll see what we can do. We cannot exactly rush in there and take the elephant from ZimParks; that's not how it works. You know that?"

Esulu looked skyward and then back down. "I understand. If we do nothing this time, then next year there will be another quota. This is worse than trophy hunting. And the world wants to know about that. So why not now, when the live trade is happening behind their backs?"

"We'll see what we can do to bring eyes to it. You keep away from here, and you keep your nose clean at work. Don't let anyone know that you told someone about the babies. Especially not Frank," Mitch said.

Esulu nodded and stood up, getting ready to go. He offered the water bottle back.

"You keep that. Hang on," Mitch said as he opened the door, then the cooler box in the bakkie. He took out a tinfoil-wrapped package in a material flour bag. "Here. If you are going back already, take this fish with you. I caught and smoked it last night, so you can eat it on your way home. That way, anyone who smells you will think you came to catch tiger fish in Kariba." He also piled another six half-frozen water bottles into the old man's basket for his journey. "You be safe cycling back to the bus stop. You know you're welcome to come to Bishu if you want to. You can always tell anyone that you came for a copy of your training certificate."

Esulu smiled and nodded. He clasped Mitch's hand in both of his, in a gesture of respect. "Thank you. I will take the fish and go home. Even though I can only do my job, it is good that you know what is happening. You cannot trust ZimParks. The orphans in the nursery here—I fear they might come and take them if they are needed for the quota because they are already tame."

"Lucky at the moment, the babies here are all too young, and the older ones are already rewilding with Ndhlovy. Still, I'll get some additional guards to monitor the orphanage."

The old man bowed his head. Then he turned his bicycle around, stood on the one pedal as he pushed, then took his other leg around the back and hopped onto his saddle. He began a slow pedal back south.

Mitch watched him till he disappeared over a hill. The bus stop on the main Victoria Falls Road was more than ten kilometers away, through wild predator territory. Still, Mitch knew that Esulu would glide there on his bicycle easily now that he'd unburdened himself.

Mitch opened his door of his bakkie, climbed in, and slammed it. Hard.

Damn it! Just when he'd thought things were going so smoothly in the neighborhood, with only the occasional poacher coming through.

He started his *bakkie* and then slapped the steering wheel in frustration.

The old man told the truth; Bongani and Mitch would have to tell Joss and Peta, and they had so much on their plate already. Peta had flown out to the USA to join Joss and little Sophia after her last round of surgery, when she had lost one of her legs. They had volunteer vets, Zola and Danie from South Africa, covering the sanctuary now, while Joss's family regrouped with the help of the McDermitt New Frontier Foundation that was helping to make sure that Sophia would have everything she needed, with her new prosthetics.

He had to ensure that when they came home, there were still baby elephant to come home to.

If he knew anything about Peta and her passion for the elephant of the wild in Zimbabwe, she wouldn't just kick the hornet's nest when she found out about the planned capture and export of the babies; she would go at it with a blow torch.

CHAPTER 9
SHARING AMALEE

LUCKY 7 RANCH, NEVADA, USA

29 August 2014

Marissa looked out the kitchen window at the clear blue sky above the ranch and right across the mountains. The National Weather Service had forecast a dust storm later in the day. Not the most ideal weather for entertaining her houseguests. This was the first time she had invited any of the foundation's recipients into her home for a few nights and into her personal space.

Things were so different with the Brennan family. She felt connected to them because of their understanding of elephant. Comfortable.

Some people thought owning a cat or a horse was a lot of work. They'd never had an elephant. Amalee had the ability to help Marissa through anything. She wouldn't have changed her four-legged companion for all the gold in the world.

Amalee might be an inch too big to tuck into bed with Marissa at night, but that didn't mean that there was any less affection between Marissa and her elephant than between her and a child, if she'd chosen to have one.

And when she spoke with Dawn, Dawn said all elephant handlers would say the same thing: *Bonded elephant in captivity do better than those whose handlers constantly change; they are calmer and more stable.*

But despite all this, there was a restlessness in Marissa. A broken promise long made to Amalee that she hadn't kept: freedom.

Peta walked into the kitchen. "I wanted to catch a few moments alone with you, before Joss brings in an over excited Sophia, and we can't get a word in."

Marissa nodded, smiling. "Coffee?"

"No thanks. I had more than enough on the flight. Flying on your private plane was a first for us. It was quite the experience, and it made it so easy for Sophia. Thank you for everything." She touched over her heart with her hands. "Being able to come and be with my family, it means the world to me to be here too. It's been a real journey. And not the one we imagined we were taking Sophia on," Peta said.

Marissa smiled. "I'm glad we were able to help."

"And I can't thank you enough for employing Zola and Danie to fill in for me. They were unexpected, and relieved my biggest worry, besides how Sophia was doing," Peta said. "I almost feel embarrassed to admit that for the first time in my life, since varsity days, my callused hands, from working the land, are softening." There was a genuine warmth in her - voice.

Marissa smiled again. She realized that she seemed to do that a lot around the Brennan's. "My pleasure. It was Dad's suggestion to ask you if you knew anyone. After all, you're in a far better position than me to select the right people to stand in for you. Once we met with Sophia, I wanted to help more, but it was you who pointed us towards those siblings; we were just glad they had all the skills you needed."

"They have done great work. Thanks," Peta said.

"Seeing Sophia doing so well after everything she's been through, that's all the thanks Dad and I need. What is the use of having a foundation like ours if we can't help make a difference to those that matter in the world?"

"Please let it be time to meet your Amalee? I'm dying to see her," Sophia said as Joss wheeled her into the kitchen.

Peta started to speak, but Marissa cut her off.

"She's right," Marissa said. "I forget how excited I would have been at your age to see my elephant. Of course, waiting is so boring, isn't it, Sophia? Come on. Let's go say hello to Amalee."

Marissa's eyes brimmed with tears. Amalee had taken to Sophia as if she were a miniature version of herself. Her elephant wrapped her trunk around both father and daughter as Joss held Sophia in his arms.

Dawn also stood nearby, but neither of them had expected the instant love that Amalee was pouring out towards her visitors.

The Brennan family was so comfortable around elephant, and it showed. Amalee must have felt their lack of fear and capitalized on it, looking for more scratches and treats, as if she had always known them.

Peta had her phone out, taking photos.

"Go stand with them. Let me take some for you all," Marissa said.

Peta went to her family, and with the big grey backdrop that was Amalee, Marissa took several pictures.

"Can I stay here all the time while we're staying with Marissa, Dada?" Sophia asked, as she snuggled her little face against the hairy trunk of Amalee and smiled. "Mamma, she feels just like our elephant."

"I bet she smells just like them, too," Dawn said, laughing. "We try hard to feed her close to what she would eat if she were in the African bush."

Peta nodded, one hand stroking behind Amalee's ear, while she talked animatedly with Dawn spoke about elephant diets.

Marissa zoned out their conversation and really looked at her elephant. Amalee was thirty-three years old now. Same as her. Certainly, time was marching on. While Amalee looked ageless, the same since she'd arrived at the Lucky 7 Ranch, time was taking its toll on Marissa.

The stress of the last few months as they waited for Chad to show his face. The burden of the foundation; a family they were working with had lost their little child when things had not worked out during a transplant the week before, which had added to Marissa's drained feeling. The project to restore part of the prairies for American buffalo was slowing as it became more difficult to find willing landowners to buy from.

But it was more than just those pressures. She needed a break. Time away from everything where she could be Marissa, herself, not the face of everything that the Whitney / McDermitt bloodline stood for.

"Amalee and Ndhlovy could be friends if she came to live wild with us," Sophia said.

Marissa's eyes widened. "What?" she asked, then realized she probably sounded a little abrupt.

"Ah, I wondered if you were listening to the conversation or lost in your head somewhere," Dawn said, walking towards her. "We were talking about you when you were Sophia's age and how you wanted to take Amalee back to Africa."

"I did," Marissa admitted, "But then life…" She still wanted Amalee to go back to Africa. She just hadn't done anything about it...

"You're welcome to come and see our sanctuary. Perhaps it's an option," Peta said.

The words were swirling around in Marissa's head. *Amalee. Gone. Sanctuary.*

From all the studies that she had read about captive elephant, if Amalee was ever going to go back to Africa, now was probably the time, because if she stayed longer, she would be too old to handle the move and would end up dying in captivity.

"I'm not sure. Thanks for the invitation. But it's–"

"This would be a huge decision, and not one that you can make on the spot," Joss said, saving her. "Don't let my ladies' excitement railroad you into doing something that you're not ready for. Just think about it. You could come stay with us, enjoy our Zimbabwean hospitality and meet our wild elephant and the orphans. Give rewilding Amalee more thought."

Marissa nodded slowly. "A visit with you all would be a welcome break. Thanks, I'll do that. Once, I did want her to go home to Africa, but I wanted her to be wild. To rewild. I don't want her in a sanctuary where she's still fenced in."

"There're no fences once she's wild with us," Joss said. "One of my ex-service buddies, Mitch, and his anti-poaching guards do an incredible job keeping the area safe. I have to admit that the word is out that he's working that space, and now we have a lot less problems than we used to. He's even taken to teaching other communities how to do it for themselves."

Marissa raised her eyebrows.

"I'd trust Mitch with my life," Peta said. "Ndhlovy's fate is often in his hands when she's out and away from us. He has trained many of the guards in the national parks."

Joss said. "He's a good *oke*, you'll see. If you bring Amalee, she'll most likely join Ndhlovy's herd, and they come and go all the time. If she doesn't, she will soon find her own family, perhaps adopting orphans of her own. Who knows? Africa might be her playground once again."

"I will think about it," Marissa said.

Sophia kissed the elephant on her trunk. "Amalee's lucky to have had you all this time. Just like Dada and Ndhlovy."

The sky was already darkening with the predicted storm was approaching, and particles of dust had begun to blow in on a threatening breeze. Amalee made a loud sound, not quite a trumpet but an excited noise, and started walking towards Marissa, pushing the big ball that she'd been playing with alongside Dawn and Joss. Sophia sat with Peta and watched from just outside the enrichment area.

Marissa couldn't help smiling.

When Amalee got to just inside of sixteen feet, she whacked the ball directly at Marissa with her trunk.

Marissa caught it and walked to her elephant.

"You're welcome to take over playing for a while," Joss said.

"Only for a bit, then we'll all be hiding from the dust storm," Marissa said as Joss joined his family sat on bales of hay. There was something so special about them all. Despite everything little Sophia had faced, she stayed so bubbly.

And Amalee had recognized it.

"Dawn, do you still think about her going home to Africa?" Marissa asked quietly as she patted Amalee's trunk.

"All the time," Dawn admitted. "I think you should be giving Joss and Peta's invitation to view their sanctuary some serious thought. They seemed keen for you to take her home."

Marissa nodded. "It's easy to listen to them and think it's the perfect place for Amalee to go back to Africa."

"The question here is, are you ready to let her go?" Dawn asked.

"To see her free, back in the wild? Where she doesn't have snow and has to stay inside? I used to dream of that all the time. I guess I gave up. Having the

Brennan family here has re-awakened the idea. I wanted to know what you thought of it though?"

Dawn smiled. "You know that I was always for it, and she's getting long in the tooth now. Time's moving on all of us."

Marissa nodded. "I'm not so sure I can afford the personal detachment. Can she survive in the wild, or will this be yet another rich American's dream gone wrong? She landed with us after her last 'home' became a nightmare."

"That she did, but then she got you and me," Dawn said. "And I don't think she had it so bad after that."

Marissa smiled. "What if she does rewild easily? Then how do I make sure that poachers don't get her?"

"You're overthinking things. It's one thing to talk about a dream; what happens once you achieve your dream is another matter entirely. What's best for Amalee is the question. Remember, you'll still live here, and you're going to come home to this empty barn reminding you every day that she's not with us anymore," Dawn said. "And if you do send her, she'll probably have a tracker on so you can follow her progress for a while."

"Is that really letting her rewild then?" Marissa asked. "I know she'll pass at some point anyway. I guess it's working out how we say goodbye." She put her head against Amalee's forehead. The hardness of the elephant's wrinkled skin, covered in hair, was as natural to Marissa as the fur of a cat or a dog might be to someone else. Marissa moved back slightly so she could look into Amalee's amber eyes, with their long eyelashes that held such wisdom and so much kindness.

"How long will you be able stay with her in Zimbabwe? You'll need to spend time during the rewilding. She's bonded with you; giving her another family doesn't mean that you can disappear without her having time to get used to it." Dawn said, a deep frown on her forehead.

Marissa nodded. "It's a lot to think about."

"My advice is go and visit the sanctuary. You don't have to decide now. It's a big one for you— and for Amalee."

"It is," Marissa said as she scratched Amalee's ear. "It's not like I can't run the foundation from there for a little while if I need to. Dad will be fine looking after things that have to be done from here."

"What's holding you back then?" Dawn said.

Marissa nodded. "Everything. Nothing. An unexpected opportunity." She took a breath, as hope bubbled up from deep inside her, almost like butterflies being set free. She smiled. "I'm going to tell Peta and Joss that I'll take them up on their invite."

"And while you're there, just think about it. You might be taking her back to her roots," Dawn said with a smile.

Marissa frowned. "Will you come with us if we go ahead with taking Amalee over?"

"You just try and leave me behind," Dawn said. "I've never been outside of the USA, but my ancestors crossed the sea in worse conditions than I will, so this old bird will go with you."

"You sure?" Marissa looked at Dawn, frowning. It was one thing for her to make a decision like this, but Dawn was still a paid employee. Even if she had been with the family and Amalee all these years. It would be a huge adjustment for Dawn too.

"To see my life's work go back into the wild? Go free like she was meant to be? Any zookeeper who says no to that doesn't care about animals." Dawn said, with a wide grin spreading over her face.

Marissa smiled. "Guess that's settled then. I'm going to scope out a sanctuary in Zimbabwe."

CHAPTER 10
WHERE THE HABOOB BLOWS

NEVADA, USA

29 August 2014

An alert went off on Chad's cell phone. A chorus of similar noises sounded from other diners' phones in the café. He looked at the screen: a message from the National Weather Service.

Emergency Alerts – Severe Alert: Dust Storm Warning in this area till 23:00 PDT. Avoid travel. Check Local Media. - NWS.

August 29, 2014, 14:37.

The weather would give him the perfect opportunity.

Who knew? Maybe the dust storm would transform into a haboob. The huge, intense dust storms were common in the area, but they hadn't had one in quite a while.

He knew that his uncle's private plane was supposed to land at twelve o'clock today. That would mean all three of them would be at the farm. Walter, Marissa, and Dawn.

A three-base hit.

Chad had been waiting for just such an opportunity since coming back to

Nevada and hiding out in the great city of Winnemucca, just under seventy-four miles from the living ghost town of McDermitt.

Here, he could blend in and keep a low profile.

After six months of weekly parole check-ins in Charleston, South Carolina, they'd been changed to a monthly schedule, and he'd been transferred to the veterans' affairs program.

That was when he was allowed to travel interstate. No babysitters.

His next parole was still a week away, and he hadn't bothered booking the flights back.

He had suspected he would miss that meeting, and probably every one after that too, if things went well; it was a waiting game. The weather report was forecasting winds.

Contingency plans had already been made.

That was the last thing the military had taught him. Have contingency plans upon contingency plans.

Now was the time to act.

Emergency services would be consumed with other calls. A ranch on fire would be the last place they would come to help. Chad knew the land like his own body; he could find his way in a dust storm.

Others wouldn't be so lucky.

He could hear the other patrons' chairs scrape the floor as they said their farewells and wished each other good luck for weathering the storm before quickly scurrying off to secure their homes and make sure loved ones were not driving in the approaching storm.

He finished his last mouthful of Key lime pie, casually drained his coffee, wiped his mouth, and threw the money on the table for it, leaving a decent tip. After all, the waitress hadn't done anything wrong to him.

Unlike others, she didn't deserve his revenge and wrath.

16H40

It took him two hours to hide his pickup and walk to the cave on the Lucky 7 Ranch, which he'd found shortly after arriving at the ranch as a lanky, lost fifteen-year-old. He uncovered the camo net that hid his quad bike, stashed there a few weeks back when he'd begun traveling interstate, for just such an opportunity.

Patience. He'd learned it well; now he was using it.

The wind was picking up.

The weather bureau had predicted perfect weather this morning. Anyone looking at the rapidly darkening sky now would think the bureau was on drugs. But only if they hadn't received the dust storm alert, or if they didn't know to look to the horizon for the massively approaching dust that towered hundreds of feet into the sky, that could happen at this time of the year.

As a local, he knew better.

Within half an hour of him leaving the cave and coming towards the Lucky 7 Ranch home base, huge clouds could be seen in the distance. Dark grey masses rode higher in the sky; below that, what looked like giant, puffy cotton wool rampaged over the mountains and swept into the valley from the south. Several hundred miles high, the monster dust storm clouds were whiter, despite being polluted with desert sand.

Dense.

Good. The smoke from the ranch fire would be disguised for longer.

Even through the mask over his nose and mouth, Chad could taste the grit. His goggles kept most of the dirt out of his eyes, yet they felt abused anyway. Used to storms like this, and worse, while serving in Somalia, he tightened his *shemagh* scarf, ensuring it was snug, protecting his face and keeping the sand out of his clothing.

The wind was increasing; he knew from experience that if this turned into a haboob, it could bring winds up to sixty miles per hour. This one sure felt like it was whipping up a frenzy. He could hear the *ting* as small particles hit the front of his goggles.

He parked his quad bike and ran along the line of trees planted so long ago as a windbreaker for events like this, to protect the buildings and stock pens when the wind came from the south as it was doing.

The elephant barn was in front of him to the west.

The wind hadn't let him down. He knew the storms and what direction they came and went, and he'd made sure that his escape route wouldn't be engulfed in a fireball.

He glanced at his watch.

Almost five o'clock.

The storm still had a few hours to intensify before it would blow itself out, and the dust would settle on Nevada once again.

The cowboys would have received the same text he had and readied the ranch. The cattle would look after themselves, turning their backs to the oncoming wind if they couldn't find shelter. They would weather the dust storm, as would the wild animals out there.

The fucking elephant. She would be inside in air-conditioned comfort, along with that bitch Dawn, and hopefully, Marissa. He had noticed the private jet being tied down on the runway earlier, the crew at the small airport looking after their plane with care. He wondered if, now she was older, Marissa still slept in the room in the barn near her elephant…

It must be nice to be a daddy's girl and never have to leave the comforts of a rich home.

They'd never suspect what was coming.

According to Walter's electronic diary, which Chad had hacked using another handy skill he'd learned in prison thanks to Uncle Sam, Walter would already be in the house, as would the guests who had arrived on the flight from Houston, to visit with him and Marissa. They would burn too.

The ranch itself hadn't changed much in the twenty-odd years he'd been away. The elephant barn that had been built before he'd first arrived as a teenager still towered over the other buildings, despite being designed to blend in. It was weathered a little more now than it had been when he was seventeen.

The wind's immense wail covered his approach. He came up to the first of the outside barns, and Chad slipped inside.

He lifted a backpack flame-torch kit from the storage rack on his left. The firebreak equipment was still in the same place where it had been stored years ago when he was younger. Evidence that Thomas, the ranch manager, didn't like change.

Had Chad just been a change they didn't like?

No, he was the change they detested.

He was the proof that the family wasn't as perfect as everyone thought.

The dirt that needed to be cleaned away.

He shook his head. He didn't have time to think about 'what if' or 'how it was' now.

A container of deworming medicine on the next shelf for the horses on the ranch that were used to round up the cattle. The stables were situated a little southeast; in this wind, they would be spared. He'd loved to ride the horses and spent hours in the saddle as a boy exploring the ranch.

After quietly putting the flame-torch kit on the floor, he walked to the window. Here, he had a clear view outside into the main bunkhouse kitchen. A couple of quad bikes were parked up on one side, but he didn't know or care whether they belonged to the cowboys or the ranch. It was a radical change for both Thomas and Walter if they used the quads to round up the cattle.

Another quad came in. The tall cowboy pulled up and walked into the kitchen, stomping his boots on the mat before opening the door.

As expected, the cowboys had gathered, waiting out the storm.

Chad walked back to the flame-torch. After opening the storage box fully, he picked up the fuel canister and shook it. Full. He smiled as he slipped it onto his back. He put the empty storage box back and reached for a drip-torch. This one dribbled fuel and flames, a more controlled and accurate tool for starting a fire than the first flame-throwing-style-torch. It was heavy, which meant it was also full. Having both fire-starters would be useful. Thomas was always so organized; it was pathetic how easy it was to rely on his skill to create maximum havoc.

Chad stepped out of the barn again into the raging dust storm. He left the door open. It wouldn't matter if it banged in the wind; the cowboys wouldn't hear the little noise of a door slamming, besides it would give readily available oxygen to the building, which would help with his fire. Facing into the wind, Chad bowed his head and made towards the first of the feed barns.

From there, the fire would spread quickly through the equipment barns, where tractors, harvesters, and other stored farm fuels would feed the flames. With the wind like it was, the fire would have a direct path to the elephant barn.

The rage inside him twisted into something darker, colder, and more calculated. Marissa and Dawn wouldn't last the night. He'd see to that. The fire would spread fast, racing toward the old farmhouse, and when it did, Walter Whitney would finally choke on regret.

He'd understand too late that Chad wasn't the one to discard. He was blood. His brother's son.

Dawn would learn he wasn't some kid to push around; he mattered.

Marissa would pay for every time Walter had chosen her over him.

Every time she'd played the helpless baby girl back then.

And Amalee? He'd savor that one. She'd die because she deserved it. Without her meddling, Marissa could've been gone years ago, first back when she was nine, the first time that Chad had tried to take her out, and then again when she was twelve. The fucking elephant had robbed him of that satisfaction.

He would inherit it all.

Claim the insurance money and sell the land to a ski resort developer.

Only then could Chad finally be happy and find peace within his restless soul.

CHAPTER 11
AN ELEPHANT'S PERSPECTIVE

LUCKY 7 RANCH, NEVADA, USA

29 August 2014

I loved having visitors. New humans like Joss and Peta, and the young girl Sophia. They were not at all scared of me—just like Marissa when she was a child. Fearless.

The child reminded me of another place where I'd been able to reach out and pluck green shoots from growing trees with my trunk. Glimpses of memory were filtering through my mind—memories of trees that tasted different. Looked different. Felt different.

Lifting my trunk, I could smell the dust as the wind whipped it up.

I could taste the ferocity of unleashed power.

I'd experienced storms like these before. This was a big one. I could sense the majestic nature of the ground as it rumbled beneath my feet.

The herd I had joined in this strange land didn't have the same abilities as me, but they seemed to be aware that a storm was coming.

They'd tied down things that could fly away, and despite us being out here, they had shut the rest of the big cave up tight.

They were all sitting on the hay bales with the little girl Sophia, so much like my Marissa was at that age. Only her legs were different from Marissa's, and most of the time, she moved around in the chair with wheels.

Sophia's body was different, much like Joss's.

I could feel the approaching storm. The winds had gotten stronger. The dust had changed the light; the sky was starting to take on a browner hue.

The temperature had dropped.

This was a sign that the ferocious wind would arrive shortly.

Time to get inside, where my herd would be safe.

I trumpeted.

Dawn walked around the outside of the poles to where I stood. I smelt the air again.

I flapped my ears in annoyance, trumpeting, warning her about the approaching storm.

She frowned. I turned towards the cave, shaking my head.

Come on, follow me.

Peta stood. "Your elephant is agitated. Her behavior has changed."

I wanted to hug that woman with my trunk. She knew elephants, as if she had our blood in her.

I wanted my herd to follow me. I wanted all the humans inside the cave, where it was safe. Where the sun didn't shine, and there was coolness or heat when needed.

I walked towards my cave.

Come. Follow me to safety.

My baby girl Marissa seemed slower. Distracted. I trumpeted and swayed, sending out signals to them all. I needed everyone inside the cave, away from this storm.

Marissa reached her hand out and patted my trunk. "I know, time to go inside." The gesture was soothing even after all our years together. But not what I needed. I needed her to be safe.

I wrapped my trunk around her and brought her close.

I let her go and pushed her gently towards the gate in the cave with my forehead.

Go inside.

"That was a rather clear, she wants us inside," Dawn said.

Peta nodded, moving Sophia into her chair with Joss.

Marrisa rubbed the back of her neck with her hand. "We know the storm is coming, girl. Right, everyone move into the stable. She must feel the storm is getting too close for us to be outside."

"They predicted it, and here it is," Dawn said as she walked in front of Marissa towards the cave. The little family moved in the same direction.

I encouraged them all to walk faster with my own rumbling, louder than the approaching storm for now.

Faster, move faster.

As the matriarch of this herd, I always made sure my humans were safe before the storms unleashed their might over my cave. There was an electrical charge in the air.

Dawn walked inside with the new ones close behind. Joss wheeled Sophia, with Peta at his shoulder.

Marissa opened the door with the push of a button.

I moved my body to face the outside and smelt the air.

Danger.

I trumpeted. Again and again.

Go inside quickly. There is more out there than the storm.

I turned and walked briskly into the cave.

The fine particles flew around despite Marissa closing the larger outside doors that keep the weather out of the cave. The sound of the storm was muffled, but it was still out there beyond my cave.

As was the danger.

The humans were talking as they got settled to spend time with me.

They thought we were safe from the storm.

Little Sophia was just outside the bars of my stable. I liked her.

I remembered when Marissa was that same height; she would sleep there too. I could touch her.

Sophia giggled as I checked on her with my trunk.

The cave had been safe in storms with more lightning and thunder than this, and with higher winds too. But could it keep out the other danger?

I tested the air again.

It could not be–

I smelt deeply.

I listened for sounds.

A scent I hadn't detected for at least a full moon cycle was present.

How could I tell them that this storm was hiding something else, an eerie haunting?

He was there.

The one who'd tried to hurt Marissa, the one who'd wanted to kill me.

His scent was the same.

The wild boy.

I trumpeted another warning, shaking my head. I ran at the scent. He was out there.

Danger. He is here.

I smelt it then. Smoke.

Acidic—not the natural wood smoke of an outdoor fire that I had experienced before.

I trumpeted again.

Can you smell it? Can you smell him? There is another danger.

Marissa came to me at once. "What is it, girl? We've been through worse storms than this. Why are you so unsettled this time?"

I trumpeted again.

"She senses something else," Joss said. "Surely if she's used to storms, she wouldn't be so agitated?" He lifted Sophia from her chair, up into his arms. "She's warning you of something else."

The smoke was getting worse. The smell coated my trunk, almost choking me.

Why couldn't the humans smell it?

I knew their sense of smell was bad, but I never realized it was this useless.

They couldn't smell him, and they didn't know he was there either.

"I agree," Marissa said. "This isn't normal for her. We need find out why she's so stressed."

"Definitely not the behavior of a happy elephant," Peta said. "It's more than the storm."

I moved to the door, but it was closed, keeping us in the cave.

It wasn't safe anymore; we had to get out.

I smacked the door with my trunk. *Come on, we need to get out of here. There is fire.*

"Wait. Can you smell that?" Marissa asked. "Smoke?"

A loud, piercing siren began.

"Fire," Marissa shouted. "That's the fire alarm. Come on, outside. Get Amalee and everyone outside."

"What do you need us to do?" Joss asked, holding Sophia tighter.

"Keep close to Dawn and me. We're getting out of the barn," Marissa shouted above the noise, and the big door began its slow opening just as the cave went dark.

Silence. The siren stopped.

I could hear my heart pumping blood. It rushed through my body abnormally fast.

"We'll need to open the door manually," Marissa said. "Dawn, please stay close to Amalee."

"The emergency power will click on in a moment," Dawn said reassuringly. "We just need to wait for it."

The room was illuminated in a natural soft orange glow. Joss held Sophia in his arms. She was safe with him.

"I'm scared, Dada," Sophia said.

I sent her soothing sounds. My humans would get us out of the cave and away from the fire.

"It'll be okay. Marissa knows her barn like we know ours. She'll lead us outside. I got you," Joss said.

"But my chair is still here," Sophia said.

"It can stay here. I'm not letting you go. I'm better having you in my arms than in your chair." Joss said, giving her a kiss on her cheek.

The electronic screaming started again. Lights flicked on.

Marissa opened the door. We rushed together down a long passage.

Good, we are getting out of the cave. I don't want a fire roof to fall in on us. We don't want to go to sleep with the smoke. Wait, there is heat here… We can't go there. That way is death.

I stopped and trumpeted.

"The fire's right outside," Marissa shouted. "I can feel heat coming through the wall. Get out through the other side of the building."

There was more fire behind us. I could smell the smoke.

Marissa ran towards me. "Come on, Amalee, turn around. Not safe. Not safe."

I trumpeted at her.

Not safe; we have to get out of here. The other side is worse.

There was fire in front of me. I could feel the heat, but it was less intense than what was coming through from the enrichment area.

"It's okay, girl. Come on, trust me. Calm down. Help me get you out of here," Marissa was saying.

The screaming continued. The noise hurt my ears.

"Hang on," Joss said. "Before you turn her, let me check back there." He gave the girl to the mother to carry and ran back down the corridor on his strange metal legs.

Marissa seemed unusually calm. I could hear her heartbeat in her chest and smell the tang of fear in her sweat. She understood the danger, and she wanted to get me to safety.

But she was in control.

I put my trust in Marissa; she wasn't the oldest human in my herd, but she was not a child either.

Those two humans had saved me before from the trainer in the circus. They'd saved me from the machete of the wild boy. My herd had never let anything bad happen to me in all the years we had been together.

Joss came towards us, his arms waving in the air as he shouted, "Go out this way; the flames back there are huge. Quick."

Marissa ran in front of me to open the door to the outside.

There was heat there. But it didn't extend up my whole body; it was concentrated at the height of my knees.

I trumpeted, giving my encouragement.

The smoke was getting worse. The incessant shrill sound continued. At least the heat had not increased.

Marissa slapped the yellow button on the wall.

Nothing happened.

"Damn it. The emergency electricity hasn't kicked in properly. We're going to have to manually open it." She began moving levers, and then she pushed the wall.

Joss came past me and helped her.

They pushed it together, but it didn't move.

"Shit," Marissa said as she rechecked the levers.

"Try again," he said.

She moved one up and then down again. The door rattled.

Marissa and Joss pushed on it, and it glided open. A rush of wind, sand,

and smoke entered the barn. Fire licked inside. But the wind was not blowing it towards us.

They let the door go, and it began to close.

"I'll hold it," Joss said. "Everyone, get out. The flames are not that big yet. Run!" He used his whole body to keep the door from closing again.

While the gap was small, we could fit through it to the other side.

I trumpeted. *Come on, everyone. Run.*

Dawn had her hand on my shoulder, guiding me. I took a step forward.

Marissa turned towards me and shouted, "Peta, run."

She went to push past my bulk, back to help Peta, who carried Sophia.

Fire had broken through behind us in the cave. A wall of orange and red flames was coming down the passage, which had turned into an air turbine, the open door sucking the fire in our direction. A hollow sound vibrated overhead.

Before Marissa could go any farther, I turned, blocking her way to Peta.

"No, Amalee! No!" Marissa called. "Please, forward. You need to come forward."

Peta pulled herself and Sophia against the wall, giving me space if I needed more.

The fire licked at my tail; a deep burn began. I blocked some of the flames with my bulk. I backed up past them. As Peta shifted Sophia on her hip, I wrapped my trunk around the girl and lifted her from her mother. I told Peta what I was doing with deep rumbles.

"Keep her safe," Peta said, letting her hands drop from Sophia.

Trust.

Marissa now understood. "Peta. Run."

And she and Peta sprinted towards the open door.

I thundered behind them, holding Sophia higher, through the flames, to the cleaner air outside.

The fire was hot on my feet and legs, but it was only for a moment, then I was through it. I turned to the side to get out of the way of the funneled fire as it came busting out of the tunnel in a river of orange.

Once there were no flames around us, I stopped running and put Sophia back in her mother's arms. The wind was powerful. The grit, abrasive to my skin and in my eyes, so I could only imagine how much it must have hurt the humans. The smoke was thick, and flying embers that looked like fireflies were everywhere.

Joss was the last to come out of the building. His pants were on fire. He dropped and rolled over and over.

"Joss!" Peta screamed as she passed Sophia to Marissa, and she ran toward him.

I stroked Sophia with my trunk, reassuring her that I was there. I would protect her.

Once Peta was sure that Joss's pants were no longer burning and that he was safe, she gave him a fierce hug. He was lucky that his legs were metal and did not burn.

Joss stood up, as if to test his legs would work, and then they were walking fast towards me.

I trumpeted. We were not safe yet. We needed to get away from the burning building. *Move away from the fire. It's coming closer again.*

"Head for the lawn in front of the house, near the stream. Rather the sandstorm than the fire," Dawn called.

"Come on, Amalee. Come on. Stay close," Marissa said, lifting Sophia up into her arms as if it were the most natural instinct in the world. The child clung to her like a bush baby. "When we get to the stream, I can check you for any injuries. Come on, Amalee. We're not out of danger yet."

I put my trunk in Marissa's hand, like we had done since she was a young girl. As a herd, we walked at pace, away from the cave and the fire and into the monster of a sandstorm.

CHAPTER 12
EAGLES VIEW

NEAR SINAMATELLA CAMP, HWANGE NATIONAL PARK, ZIMBABWE

1 September 2014

Mitch, Bongani, and the two of the AP unit members, Kat and Greg, leopard-crawled on their stomachs to the top of the *koppie*. From their vantage point, they would soon look towards the spot where Esulu said the new holding pens would be.

The sun was just rising above the horizon, and the coolness of the night was already fading. It had been a long hike from where they had driven their *bakkie* through the concession. They'd stashed it under a camo net and then gone on foot into the reserve, making sure no one would know they were there.

Finally, they were hunkered down for the recon.

Mitch made a mental note that after the elephant problem was over, he would approach the Friends of Hwange group about doing more to combat poachers getting in so easily from the hunting concessions.

"Happy Spring Day, Chief," Mitch said, nudging him playfully with his shoulder. "Always wanted to trespass in a national park to celebrate the arrival of the growing season."

Bongani's body shook as he stifled a chortle. "Shut up."

Mitch smiled.

Kat whispered, "As long as Chief laughs and doesn't have a heart attack. I never knew him to do so much physical activity."

"You have him all wrong. He's a legend," Mitch said. "When they stole the kids from his village a few years back, he went all Rambo on us. You need to get to know your Chief better. He's quite the bad arse when needed."

Mitch looked at Bongani, who smiled and kept quiet. Bongani's hand went up to bring them to a stop, and he pointed forward.

Mitch strained to see through the grass in front of him, then, moving it aside, he scowled. "Thanks, Es, you beauty. Right where you said it would be."

He shifted to a more comfortable position before he pulled his camera from his backpack.

He looked over 'the new graveyard' as Esulu had called it.

Mostly made of thick wood, the bomas were not built for full-grown elephant, but to hold babies, and compared to the orphanage, they were pushing it when it came to housing the two-meter-high three-year-olds. The first holding pen was made of steel. It had been painted forest green to give it a little camouflage, but the paint on the inside of the fence had been rubbed off by the elephant. The rest of the pens were made from unpainted wood. A group of juvenile elephant stood inside the main holding pen, their trunks hanging downwards, limp. Unhappy.

Toddlers, whose spirits had been broken.

As Esulu had described, this wasn't like in 1984 when they were saving the babies from the culling.

This was the destruction of family groups. The purposeful removal of a generation.

These people had learned nothing in thirty years.

Inside the bomas, the elephant, sable, and impala stood impatiently, stomping their feet, getting rid of the incessant flies that plagued them. Some had shade over their heads in the form of tarpaulins, and some huddled under large camel thorn trees.

"Why do the sable have pipes over their horns?" Greg asked from where he had settled on the other side of Mitch.

"It's a common practice in wild game husbandry," Mitch said. "Protection, so the horns don't break in transit, and sable are also territorial, so in a small space, those horns can kill."

"Several empty pens. I wonder what they plan to fill those with?" Bongani asked.

Off to the right, some distance away, Mitch could see huge, fully enclosed cages with smaller partitions, which were double-fenced. "Looks like they are also going after predators."

"Most likely lions," Bongani said. "If it is hyena, they had best fortify the pens."

"Interesting," Mitch said. "Both our informant and those papers we received were right."

Esulu had chosen the spot well and had taken the weather into account for the animals. He was an asset to ZimParks, and it was a shame they would soon cast him aside because of his age. Still, he would be a great benefit to Bongani's lands when he came home. Mitch could see the potential in his skills.

Bongani and Kat both had binoculars out, but Greg had a laser rangefinder pressed to his eye.

"Breaks my heart to see those babies in that state," Bongani said. "To think, they still have to face a flight, packed like sardines in a tin. And there is nothing we can do about it except document and wait."

"Wait, my arse," Mitch said. "I see no security there to stop us from freeing them now and destroying the boma and cages."

"And take them where?" Bongani asked. "Trucks moving the animals will be followed. You cannot let those youngsters out into the wild; they have no herds. No matriarch would be as good as a death sentence for them."

Mitch sighed. "Just because you're right doesn't make it any easier. That's Frank Hadebe in the uniform, sitting on the fence. He's the head game ranger of Hwange National Parks Service and as crooked as they come. Apparently, even he's not happy about taking this many babies, but he was quick to take the bribe money." Adjusting the camera's lens, Mitch took a photo for evidence.

"Do you know the fat guy in civilian clothes?" Greg asked.

Mitch focused on the man perched uncomfortably next to Frank. He wore formal black shoes covered in dust, and his suit was as out of place as his footwear. It was tight across his shoulders and didn't close over his belly. He took a handkerchief from his pocket and wiped his brow, sweating even before the sun rose. His multiple chins wobbled like the neck of a ground hornbill each time he moved. The man looked like he may have once had huge muscles, but now, his belly spilled over his belt like an apron of fat.

"That's Shumba Chitepo, the bastard behind the deal with the Chinese. He's got no moral compass. Between him and the businessman Wang Wu, you are about to witness the creation of brand-new wildlife parks all across China, each stocked with Zimbabwean animals. I bet you that the resurrection of the railway system for transporting coking coal from Hwange to Mozambique for shipping to China will come back to life soon. One hundred and thirty-two elephant in three years—that's the down payment, to secure the deal. Delivery first, then the investment will happen."

"And it's legal?" whispered Kat.

Mitch nodded. "A presidential mandate. Signed by Zimbabwe's Minister of Environment, the director general of Zimbabwe Parks and Wildlife Management Authority (ZimParks), and a CITIES certificate."

"*Eish, aikona.* No," Kat said.

Mitch nodded. "Our copy arrived disguised as anti-poaching reports from a reliable source. We knew about this place because an informant pointed it out to us. It's well hidden and not easily accessible to anyone other than reserve workers. They were trying hard to keep this on the down-low and off the public's radar."

Kat clicked her tongue. "Slimy lawyer. I bet he's making a private fortune out of the deal, too."

Greg grunted. "That aside. Bloody CITIES is involved? The world organization that was supposed to look out for endangered species is selling the Zimbabwean elephant? What a surprise—not. This is Africa. Money changed hands, I bet."

Bongani dipped his voice low. "There is a rot starting here that needs to be stamped out before it spreads to the other parks."

Mitch nodded. "My source said thirty juveniles are to be flown out of the reserve between October 2014 and February 2015."

"Not long to go," Bongani said, rubbing his chin.

"Will they be shipped all together or split into multiples?" Greg asked, his voice still kept low.

"We don't know yet," Mitch said.

"No baby in any reserve is safe," Bongani said.

"Apparently," Mitch said, "the only stipulation is that none are to be taken from the Presidential Herd."

Kat said, "*Sis* on them. All eyes will turn to ZimParks, and they will ultimately be the ones responsible for exporting the elephant. And the people will lose trust in the very organization that still cares for and tries to protect the animals in their custody—except for a few rotten eggs. And the President can still claim the elephant he said he would protect, are all accounted for."

Mitch looked beyond the men to the bomas that held the juvenile elephant. His heart sank again. They were so young, just weaned from their mothers and finding their own ways within their herds. Now they were scared, traumatized, and had lost their souls to the cruelty of man.

"I can now understand you not talking about all this till we were here, so no one could overhear. What do you want me to do now?" Kat asked.

Mitch smiled. "You're the best we have at moving through the bush without leaving a trace. You get in and out of places the rest of us wouldn't even try, same way a lioness ghosts through the grass. We need you to slip in and set up a few cameras where they'll never be spotted. The more evidence we bring back, the better positioned we're in for the next step."

"Truly? Aww thanks, *baas*," Kat said sarcastically.

Bongani nodded. "Cool as a Kat."

Kat snorted.

"Those babies will not last long overseas," Bongani said.

"Perhaps. But you know how this plays out. Beijing won't just walk away. They'll come back; they'll keep pushing. There's a level of appetite there that leaves the wildlife dead last on the priority list," Mitch said. "Unless we've got hard proof of what went on here, no one's going to take us seriously when we put the story to the news."

"This is well-thought-out. By putting other game with the elephant, it just looks like ZimParks are moving animals from one of their parks to another. This will be no different until the end," Bongani said. "Anyone who stumbles across it would never have known this site is for exportation across the world."

"It's sad, and exactly what I came here to volunteer my time for—to help the animals. What's my job?" Greg asked.

"You get to protect Kat while she does her thing," Mitch said. "As the best 'ghost' we have at the moment, we need you to ensure she isn't caught, but you also need to ensure they don't know we were here, so no deaths. The workers are not our enemy."

Greg nodded.

The sound of a helicopter broke into the morning.

"'Make sure your poacher's net is covering you," Bongani said. "We still have at least twenty-four hours here. We do not want to get discovered."

The helicopter circled above the bomas, the pilot with his shooter clearly visible before they turned and flew north.

There was a flurry of activity in the boma area, and a small truck drove out of the bushes in the direction of one of the camps, followed by another, twice as large. They stopped near Frank. He climbed inside, but the man in the suit remained seated.

The truck cut a large circle and drove back into the bushveld.

The helicopter left the vehicles behind as it navigated the sandy road. Off in the distance, it banked right and started circling.

Today's capture was not far from the holding areas.

"Do we take a chance and go look?" Bongani asked.

"I don't see anyone in the boma area other than that 'muscle,'" Mitch said. "Kat, and Greg, see if you can get closer and mount the cameras. Bongani and I will keep track of that capture. Perhaps we'll get some photographs faster than we'd hoped." He held out a backpack to Kat.

Kat snatched the bag, "Time to play."

Greg nodded, already moving to be Kat's shadow.

"Good luck. Make us proud," Mitch said. It might not be much yet—but perhaps this would be the start of them exposing this operation.

Whatever it took to save the juvenile elephant.

CHAPTER 13
ANCIENT AFRICA

VICTORIA FALLS AIRPORT, ZIMBABWE

28 September 2014

Marissa stretched from her nap. The plane droned on. Houston, USA, to Victoria Falls, Zimbabwe, was a heck of a long flight, including refueling on the way. She'd was finally getting to visit Africa, but this was not the leisurely safari trip of her dreams. There was business to take care of before she could enjoy any adventure.

Her elephant's future depended on her.

The barn had been burnt to the ground, and the next day they had finally stood with Amalee under the pink morning sky, after the haboob had died down and the fires had been extinguished from the Lucky 7 Ranch.

"Now is the time to come look if you want to rewild her with us, before you think of rebuilding." Joss's voice still rang in her head.

She shifted on her couch. The arson investigators had found a quad bike with Chad's prints on it near the cave, and the new security cameras had caught a picture of him entering the sheds, loaded with the fire-starting equipment, preserved on their off-site digital storage, which hadn't been destroyed by the blaze.

Marissa hadn't stopped shaking for over an hour after the fire. That was the final incentive to get Amalee away from the USA and into the wilds of Africa.

Sadly, Chad hadn't changed in the army or prison.

He was still out to destroy himself and everyone in his path. Like a virus, he'd adapted and was trying once again to kill them. Toxic was what he was.

Who in their right mind burned down a ranch deliberately?

Marissa shook her head, getting rid of the gloom.

She opened her eyes and smiled as Sophia sang her own tune, and her little body almost danced in her seat.

A month after that horrendous afternoon, the Brennans were aboard her plane, heading home with her. And despite the distance, it seemed Sophia couldn't have been more excited if it were Christmas.

Time was of the essence; if Marissa wasn't going to rebuild the elephant barn, then she had to decide now. Winter was just around the corner, and Amalee hated the cold. If she were to reconstruct, she might need to take Amalee south to Florida or someplace warmer for the season. Until then, she was doing okay in the horse barn and had taken well to the daily walks in the horses' arena. Dawn said she was fine, but it had been years since she'd slept rough to be with Amalee.

Marissa was the one who didn't like the setup.

A decision had to be made.

"You're awake, hey?" Joss asked.

Marissa nodded. "I am. I was trying hard to keep that sleepy feeling going, but I'm not winning. You need something?"

"No, just to say that we're so glad that we got to fly Sophia home with you. This is pure luxury," Joss said. "She's had such freedom on the trip; it's made a huge difference."

"I'm glad for the company," Marissa said. "It's nice not to come to a unfamiliar place alone, so thanks to you guys too."

"You would have still flown on your private plane without us? Not on a commercial flight?" Joss asked.

"Absolutely, mostly because I think my dad believes I don't do cattle class well. I'll blame it on being brought up a snob by my father." Marissa smiled and pulled her feet up and tucked them under her.

"You are certainly no snob," Joss said.

"Don't let that get out around the charity circles. People might expect me to socialize more, not hide away with my elephant." Marissa laughed.

Joss grinned.

She turned back to the window. Below her were vast tracts of green, with larger brown areas. Small hills were dotted here and there. She knew the summer season in this part of Zimbabwe was between November and March, so she wasn't surprised by the dryness while the bush waited for rain. Having seen Peta's photographs of the lightning over the lake, she wasn't looking forward to the storms if they came early.

"Almost home," Peta said, her voice thick with longing. She reached for Joss's hand, and he lifted hers to his lips and kissed it.

Marissa didn't feel like a third wheel; instead, she felt honored to be in their company. She silently thanked her father for insisting that she take the Foundation's jet; despite the extra fuel-stops along the way, it made sense.

"Please take your seat for landing," the pilot said over the intercom.

"You knew we were close?" Marissa said. "But it all looks so similar."

"Landmarks. I have flown this route many, many times," Peta said with a smile. She moved to one of the chairs near her daughter. "Sophia, your seat belt still on?"

"Yes, Mamma."

Marissa stood from the sofa and took a chair next to the window and fastened her seatbelt.

The plane dipped downwards, and her stomach followed suit. Butterflies fluttered, and she felt lighter than she had in years. Shortly afterwards, they touched down with a bounce on the tarmac before starting a steady taxi towards the building.

She was finally doing it. Considering a sanctuary with a view to rewilding Amalee. Marissa looked out the window again.

Victoria Falls Airport was more modern than she'd expected. It had clearly undergone renovations recently, bringing it up to date, not only in appearance but also in infrastructure, if all the electronic equipment on top of the tower was anything to go by.

Marissa had done her due diligence for the trip. There were questions about how the President would account for the fact that the Chinese government had paid for the upgrade. There was growing concern in the USA about the extent of China's investment in Africa and what it would take in payment when the bills came due.

Zimbabwe was just one more African country that had gotten into bed with China, and the long-term consequences were yet to be seen, as were their effects on the world as a whole.

They taxied to an allocated parking bay, off the main runway, and Marissa could feel the ground staff chock the plane before the jet engines powered down.

Sophia was literally bobbing in her chair, the excitement getting the better of her. "Almost home. Almost home," she chanted.

Marissa wondered how the family had really coped with being away from home for almost a year. Outwardly, they appeared reconciled to the setbacks that had occurred—Sophia losing a leg, then having it cut even shorter because of infection. She'd had almost every bone in her remaining foot broken and reset. Joss and Peta had been living apart for much of Sophia's treatment.

Stress like that took its toll.

The co-pilot walked through from the cockpit and opened the sealed door. Bright sunshine flooded inside, along with an incredible blast of heat. Once the steps were in place the co-pilot said, "You may disembark. We'll be right behind you, we just need to organize the unloading."

Marissa nodded, undid her seatbelt, grabbed her hand luggage, and walked towards the exit.

Standing on the top step, she smelled the Zimbabwean air—aromas of smoke, vegetation, and heat as it hit the asphalt of the runway. Shimmering mirages danced farther along the runway as a dust devil whirled onto the same tarmac. She looked up at the clear blue sky above and felt her shoulders relax. She hadn't even known how much tension she'd carried in her body during the long-haul flight.

"Dada?" Sophia said from behind her. "I can walk."

"I haven't forgotten," Joss said. "Come on. Show us. If you need me, you just have to say so."

Marissa hurried down the stairs, making way. Joss stepped in front of Sophia and walked backwards down the first step to make sure she didn't fall.

Sophia took the first step with her calipered leg before bringing the new artificial one down to the same step.

Marissa let out her breath.

One down—eleven more to go.

Slowly, Sophia made it to the tarmac. When she was off the stairs, she lifted her hand for a high-five from her dad before throwing herself into his hug.

"I did it. I did it all alone," Sophia said, her voice a few octaves higher and louder than usual in her excitement.

"I'm so proud of you," Joss said and lifted her up. He gave her a cuddle, then put her carefully back down on the tarmac.

A man in an official uniform greeted Marissa at the bottom of the stairs. "*Salibonani.* Welcome to Zimbabwe. Do not worry about your luggage, it will be brought to the terminal by our staff. Please follow me."

"Let's go see how many metal detectors you and I can set off, shall we?" Joss said, laughing.

Marissa smiled and turned to make sure that their plane had good, well-placed chocks securing it from moving, a habit she had picked up as a young girl. Their luggage was being carried off the plane and put onto the waiting trolley. Looking at it all, she wondered how Joss and Peta would have managed on a regular commercial flight.

Sophia called over her shoulder, "Come on, Marissa. Don't get left behind."

"Don't worry about that luggage, the airport staff said they will handle it," Joss said as he turned his attention back to his daughter.

Heat radiated off the tarmac, a dry heat with no humidity. Much like Nevada in summer.

Marissa quickened her pace to catch up to Sophia, as did the pilots walking quietly behind them. When they got to the doors of the airport building, Peta asked, "You okay there, Sophia?"

"I'll get her wheelchair," Joss said, turning back toward the plane.

"No, I want to walk," Sophia protested. "I practiced so I could show Mitch and Gani I can walk now."

"What if, while we are going through customs, you sit in your chair, then when we move out into the main area, you can walk again. Would that work?" Peta said.

Sophia nodded.

They walked into the building. A blast of cold hit them. Apparently, the air conditioner was working overtime in the heat.

Joss came back with Sophia's bright, multicolored 4x4 wheelchair, and soon they headed for a counter under a large *customs and immigration* sign.

"Goodness, little one," the official said. "Looks like you got an upgrade on your leg from when you were last here. *Sharp-sharp* girl! Hot stuff! I almost didn't recognize you after all the time you spent away from us. I saw you walking down the stairs of that fancy plane! Come, we can zip around. Show your new friend our moves."

Sophia beamed.

The man started to walk with Sophia toward the doors, away from them. Marissa looked at Peta.

"It's fine," she laughed. "You can stroll along with boring old me, or you can go with Sophia at top speed. The staff here have been fantastic. We've come and gone so many times that they have come to know us and have watched her progress. She's in good hands."

When Marissa finished at the immigration counter, the customs official said, "Madam, walk around the corner and follow the signs to the Makuwa Lounge. Your luggage trolley will meet you there. If you need to wait while your pilots return to get your plane tied down, we hope you will be comfortable."

Turning to the pilots, Marissa asked, "Do you want me to wait for you?"

"I think you have your hands full enough. Take off," the first pilot said. "Have a good time."

"Hope you two enjoy your safari and white-water rafting. I'll see you back here in ten days," Marissa said.

She watched as her pilots followed the uniformed man back outside.

"Right, Miss Sophia. I believe you wanted to walk into the main airport terminal," Joss said. "Time to get your groove on."

Sophia nodded.

"Remember, it's only Mitch and Bongani, and then you're in your chair. You don't want to overdo it and cause problems with your legs. We are under strict instructions as to what you're allowed to do in bringing you home early, so we could travel with Marissa."

Marissa held her breath as Sophia began her slow, deliberate walk around the corner.

"Gani, Gani," Sophia shouted. "I can walk!"

A large, masculine, Black man rushed quickly towards them. He was clearly a man of authority, yet he carried himself with the grace of a dancer. His skin glistened under the lights; his khaki shirt matched the one that Joss wore in the photograph Sophia had carried with her in hospital. Tears showed in his eyes as Gani lifted Sophia, spinning her around. "Look at you. You're really walking! I saw you come down the steps of the plane, and I almost couldn't believe it. I'm so proud of you!"

"Gani, see?" Sophia said. "Told you I would walk to you!"

"I saw that," Bongani said. "I always said that you would; you just had to be determined. You are a daughter of Africa—you are strong. You are Africa herself. You can do anything that you put your mind to. And look at this—you have a new leg. Electric pink with pictures of flamingoes on it. My, my, where did you find something so colorful?"

"In America at the hospital, silly," Sophia said and laughed, the sound loud in the arrivals hall, and a joy to Marissa's ears.

Sophia deserved to laugh. She deserved to be able to walk and twirl.

Bongani stepped forward and shook Joss's hand—a weird shake, slide, shake again combination. "Good to see you home."

"Great to be back. Meet Marissa," Joss said. "This is Chief Bongani."

He shook her hand. "Welcome to Zimbabwe. Thank you for everything you have done for the Brennans."

"Nice to finally meet you," Marissa said.

"Hi Bongani," Peta said as they hugged. "Thanks for fetching us."

"Anytime. You couldn't have kept either me or Mitch away today. Such an exciting time."

"It's monumental. We're all home at last. I admit, it was a much longer trip than expected," Peta said, stepping past Bongani to a man standing behind, to hug him.

That must be Mitch.

Joss had said Mitch would fetch them and show Marissa around the area while he and Peta caught up on things. Mitch was an absolute cliché of a safari guide. Tall and muscular, with sandy brown hair flecked with silver at the temples. He wore khaki shorts, which were possibly a size too small, and a shirt that only just concealed what promised to be more man underneath. Despite the air conditioning, his skin glowed with perspiration, as if he had just run into the terminal. He shifted from one booted foot to the other as if he were a caged animal.

Her heart skipped a beat. She hadn't felt anything like that in a very long time.

His eyes were cornflower blue and—they were staring at her.

Were we both checking each other out?

She purposefully walked towards him to cover her embarrassment, hoping he didn't notice that now her face burned with a blush that had started on her chest and rolled upward, heating her. "Hi, I'm Marissa. I assume you're Mitch."

"In the flesh. Welcome." Mitch's voice was deep and rich as he put his hand out, and she had to let go of her small case to shake his. It was firm and warm, but he quickly let hers go, as if holding it would give him girl cooties.

"Australian?" she asked him.

"Guilty as charged. Hope you won't hold it against me," he said with a mischievous grin. "I'll just instruct the luggage trolley guy where to go. Hey, mate, the people carrier is this way." He tipped his head towards the door.

"Thank you," she said to his retreating form. He certainly was something else. She'd seen her fair share of cowboys and good-looking men, both at the ranch and in the boardrooms, but there was something about the way Mitch moved that said he was unlike any man she'd met before. She was suddenly looking forward to the next ten days for a very different reason than earlier.

"Come on." Peta said, as she fell in step next to Marissa. "We can stroll with Sophia in her chair. The rest of them can go do their He-Man stuff and put all that luggage into the transporter. Bongani said he brought the ten-seater, so there will be plenty of room and air conditioning. Despite sleeping on the plane, I'm exhausted."

Marissa watched Mitch's backside as he strode off. *Yip, he was one fine man.*

CHAPTER 14
UNCHARTERED TERRITORY

VICTORIA FALLS TO BINGA, ZIMBABWE

28 September 2014

They bypassed the traditional singers and performers who stood just outside the entrance to the airport, singing their hearts out and dancing for the tourists to earn a few dollars. Marissa went to get money out of her purse that was hanging from her shoulder.

"Yeah, no," Peta warned. "Put that bag across your body and don't open your purse in public. The people here are more than below the poverty line. You flash cash, and you'll get us followed from the airport. Right now, we probably look enough like tourists without you taking a picture or giving them a tip."

"Surely I can give them something for their performance?" Marissa said.

"You can tip them double on your way back. They'll be here. This is how they earn their living," Peta said, as she checked on Sophia in her chair.

Marissa nodded and adjusted her bag to go across her shoulder and between her breasts. It was the most uncomfortable way to wear a bag that she knew of, and she made a mental note not to wear one next time, but rather to switch to the small theft-proof backpack she carried in her suitcase.

They walked up to a people carrier, and while Bongani and Joss were loading in the luggage, Mitch opened the sliding door on the side.

"Put Marissa in the second row so she can see things better through the front window," Peta said. "Sophia and I will be fine in the back row."

Mitch used the release mechanism to unlock the seat and helped Peta in, then he put in the child seat they had brought from America. Lastly, he carefully lifted Sophia from her chair, as if he were used to doing it, and fastened the restraints. Only once she was secured did he put the seat back in the upright position and held out his hand to help Marissa as she navigated the high step. Luckily, she'd worn linen pants, and the height didn't pose too much of a challenge for her.

Marissa took his hand anyway. The rough feel of working callouses, was overpowered by a radiating warmth. Then she let it go.

Mitch took the wheelchair to the back and stashed it.

Joss climbed in next to Bongani in the front. Mitch sat in the same section as Marissa, with space between them.

"Yingwe River Lodge, here we come," Bongani said as he started the vehicle and began the drive.

Mitch turned in his seat and said, "Joss and Peta told me that you decided to come and look around the sanctuary. That you are hoping you'll bring your elephant here."

"We'll see," Marissa said. "Peta told me that between you all, I'd get to see everything there is to see while I'm here."

Mitch smiled. "Let's just keep it to the good stuff. Why are you moving your elephant now?"

"Amalee is only coming back to Africa if she can rewild," Marissa said.

Bongani nodded, clearly listening while he drove. "Joss said that if you come, you will have one of your elephant handlers come over to help settle her, as well as you?"

Marissa said, "Dawn was the animal keeper at the circus where we rescued Amalee from, and she talked my father into taking her with, mainly because she drove the truck Amalee was housed in at the time, but she also knew how to look after and control an elephant, and my dad's cowboys didn't. If Amalee comes to Africa, Dawn's coming too and will stay with her as long as it takes to settle, even if it's the rest of her life. And those are her words, not mine."

"Must be hard to dedicate your life to an elephant and harder to let her go," Mitch said.

Bongani nodded again.

Marissa smiled. "Blame it on Joss and Peta. They convinced me that if she's going back into the wild, that's different from letting her go. She's coming home. It's taken a long time to make this dream a reality."

Bongani had turned off the main Victoria Falls/Hwange road and there were signs pointing to Binga. She took a moment to look out of the front window.

The road remained sealed, thought it had grown considerably narrower. While the gravel on either side remained unchanged. There was an oncoming vehicle, and it looked like they were going to have a head on.

Just as she put her hand to the seat to grip tightly, both vehicles moved over and shared the road. They put their passenger wheels on the gravel while the driver's side remained on the tarmac.

They passed without incident and were once again the only vehicle on the road, towards Binga.

"You'll get used to the roads," Mitch said. "Wait until it becomes a gravel road, you'll find you miss the tar strip."

"I'm just grateful I'm not the one driving. You're on the wrong side of the road and now sharing it with oncoming traffic."

Mitch laughed. The sound deep and infectious.

Marissa smiled.

"What type of trees are those?" Marissa asked.

Mitch looked up. "Teak."

"Do the elephant eat those?" Marissa asked.

"They do, especially the younger ones. They love to strip the bark to get to the cambium layer," Mitch said.

Marissa grinned. "Amalee does that with the felled aspen logs. She spends hours rearranging them by tossing them all over her enrichment area."

Mitch smiled. "Guess that's one of the things that will change, if you rewild her here. We don't have aspen anywhere. It's far to tropical and hot."

"She hates the cold," Marissa said. "And as the years have passed, I think she hates winter more and more. She spends all her time inside, in her heated stable, so I don't think she will mind the change."

"What about you? How will you be, with her not being around all the time?"

Marissa was silent. She frowned. She was going to have to share her thoughts with someone, and Mitch looked like he was going to be it. "I worry that Dawn will be the one most affected by Amalee leaving us; she's devoted to her. The three of us are bonded, so we will need time for her to accept a new family and not mourn us if we disappear from her life."

"When you've both seen your elephant go free, you'll be different women," Mitch said. "I remember coming to Zim to see Joss after he came home to recuperate, and it was as if being here settled something wild inside of me. I didn't know it was needed until it happened. Now, I'd give my life for those jumbos. I protect them with everything I have. All the veterans that come and serve in our anti-poaching program do."

Marissa stared at him. She'd never heard a man speak so passionately about what he felt for an animal. There was more to him than just some very nice eye candy. He sounded like he had substance too.

"Peta told me you run an anti-poaching company partly staffed by military veterans," Marissa said. "Sounded like an interesting program."

"She outed you," Joss said, ribbing his friend. "But in a nice way. She didn't paint you up to be saving anything large—just like the odd spring hare or tree squirrel."

The men all laughed, and Peta threw something from the back at Joss.

Mitch smiled. "Big and small, they all need protection. The AP unit was something that I started with a group of friends, and it keeps growing. When other combatants heard about it, we began receiving ex-servicemen and women from all over the world who volunteered to help protect the wildlife, join anti-poaching units, and assist with training locals. My unit isn't based at the lodge where you'll stay while you're here. It's out near Bishu, a community in Bongani's land."

"Have you had any luck with eliminating the poaching?" Marissa asked.

Bongani sniggered.

"I tried to explain this already, so good luck," Joss said.

Mitch shook his head. "Poaching will never be completely shut down. That's the reality. What has shifted is the operating environment. The heavy hitters, the offshore syndicates, the ivory and rhino horn players with real money behind them now know this area is a hard target. High risk. High consequence. They understand they will be dealt with. They've moved their efforts elsewhere.

Marissa looked at Mitch. "You seem okay that your problems have moved somewhere else. Perhaps somewhere where they are ill equipped to deal with it. What about their needs?"

Mitch shook his head. "We're working on that, training other AP units to be like us. Change needs time. But what we're left managing on the ground here now is local-level activity, largely tied to bushmeat. That's a very different threat set, and one we can control. Bongani's trust lands have invested heavily in community buy-in, with clear messaging around why wildlife matters, not just morally, but economically. Tourism dollars put food on tables. People understand that."

Marissa nodded. She thought she understood but she still wasn't sure. She looked out the window as they passed a big tree with a troop of baboons under it. The baboons seemed to know to kept away from the road.

"Amalee will be fine here," Mitch said. "She will be protected, given space, and allowed to transition back to the wild on her terms. She'll settle in quickly."

Marissa frowned. "And what if she doesn't? It's going to cost a few million to get her here. What if she stresses being in the company of other elephant? She's been alone with Dawn, me, and a few of the volunteers who come and go for over thirty years. It's just been our little family unit."

Mitch nodded. "This is Peta and Joss's specialty—making people and animals that come from far away feel at home. Making her see the beauty of being wild."

"I'll be able to help," Peta said from the back seat. "But we won't know until she's here; unfortunately, we don't get a test run."

Marissa smiled. They certainly had made her feel special when the chips were down, and her cousin had tried to kill them all; they had risen above that and still pushed for her to consider rewilding Amalee, even when it would have been easier to walk away.

Marissa looked at the back seat. Sophia was asleep. "Poor thing. She's worn out."

"When she wakes up, she'll be like the Duracell Bunny again. Kids this age have energy to spare, and then some," Peta said, yawning. "Me, on the other hand? Can't keep my eyes open lately."

"How do you usually cope with jet lag?" Marissa asked.

"I'll be fine after a few nights in my own bed," Peta said.

Joss turned, frowning, and said, "Try get some sleep, love."

"I will," Peta said, rearranging herself in the chair and closing her eyes.

"Look at that," Bongani said as he came to a quick stop. A herd of buck wandered onto the road.

Marissa looked out the front windscreen. "Those are kudu, right?"

"I'm impressed," Mitch said.

"Guess I watched too many *Nat Geo* programs growing up. I still do. I'm a tragic environmentalist," Marissa said, and she laughed.

"Nothing tragic about caring for animals," Mitch said.

Marissa smiled, and her heart jumped as the huge grey antelope began to cross over the tarmac.

Bongani switched off the engine.

Marissa stared as another one came to the edge of the road and then jumped right over it, as if it were playing 'the floor is lava.' Its horns looked like an elaborate crown on its head.

"Those first two were older bulls," Mitch said. "See how their horns are twisted almost three times? And the grey of their coat is going quite dark. The one who just crossed is a younger bull. His coat is more brown than grey."

"They're beautiful. Bigger than I'd expected," Marissa whispered, worried they might hear her with their big ears. She took her seatbelt off and leaned forward to see better.

Another two younger bulls ran across the road, looking both ways as if checking for traffic.

"I was introduced to Zimbabwe road blocks by a herd of elephant," Mitch said. "It was a few weeks before I got to see a kudu. They took my breath away. I can't believe they walk around in such large groups and through villages and towns. These animals are truly wild. They clear six feet from standing; no fence keeps them in or out."

Marissa looked at him questioningly. "Zimbabwe roadblocks?"

"A saying going back to when we had a lot of police roadblocks—um, blockades here. Now it's the elephant who do that to us more than the police. Unless it's election time—then they are all out in the road, collecting their bribes." Mitch's tone was acidic.

Marissa frowned. "Sounds like you don't like the police force."

"It's not a matter of liking them. We know good guys on the force. Many are willing to do their jobs, but there are always a few bad ones in any organization who make it hard for the good ones to do theirs. You need to remember that here in Zimbabwe, and much of Africa, the police force is for sorting out trouble—a military presence. You don't run to the police for protection in Africa. Often you need protection from them. A lot comes from the bush war when the police were a mobilized military unit too. People have long memories. It's complicated."

"I see your point," Marissa said. "That elephant welcome must have been something to see, though. There's another one."

A kudu walked onto the tarmac, stood in the middle, and flapped its big ears, as if challenging the vehicle, before it whipped around and bounded into the thickets on the side.

The forest here was different from the wilderness at home. Domineering. It had trees, but then there was this mass beneath—smaller trees and bushes tangled together, as if no one could get inside without knowing where the path was. It was filled with black, grey, and green dappled shades—and Marissa was sure it held secrets. She looked back at the kudu that had been on the road, kept her eyes on it until she couldn't see the white fleck at the back of its tail as it blended into the bushes, fully camouflaged.

"There'll be more on either side of the road. Wildlife roadblocks in this area are common," Mitch said.

"Get belted in again. We have a bit of a drive still ahead," Bongani said as he started the engine back up and began driving.

Bongani overtook a bus that crawled along the road, its old diesel engine belching dark fumes into the sky. Its roof was piled high with suitcases and crates, and even a few goats and chickens were visible.

Joss pressed a button and opened his window. "Listen"

The sounds of a traditional song flowed into their vehicle.

"I used to think all transport was like that in Africa," Marissa said. "And then I watched a documentary on how South Africa became a car manufacturing powerhouse, and how they are adapting to early technology with hybrid and electric vehicles. I know it's an environmental nightmare as is, but it's still nice to see some of the old-world romance of a community bus still exists."

"Don't romanticize it," Mitch said, adjusting his bulk in the chair. "It's hot as all hell in there. There's no air conditioning and they are overcrowded, and while people sing together to pass the time and celebrate going home, in reality, they are also scared that they won't get there. If that bus breaks down, many will pull and drag their belongings far down the road because there might not be another bus to pick them up. You really don't want to travel in rural transportation."

"The people here suffer under a dictator who takes the money from his country for himself and his party members, and doesn't put it back into his people, who really need it," Bongani said.

"That's so sad," Marissa said. "I did research before coming over, and read about Zimbabwe switching to the American dollar to try to stabilize again. Must be really hard to run a business in these circumstances."

"It is the way it is," Bongani said. "Many still support Mugabe, and many must appear to support him because he has a spy network, causing one brother to turn on another just for food. We all hope that someone will come in and overthrow him. The big problem is that they'll probably be just like him. Or we might be lucky, he might die soon. One thing is for certain: it will take many generations to recover without aid. We look to places like Rwanda and see how they have recovered with help from around the world, and we live in hope."

"That's not how it's portrayed in the newspapers back home," Marissa said as she shook her head.

"Politics and newspapers go hand in hand these days; the golden years of knowing what is really happening are gone. Everywhere is influenced by someone else," Bongani said.

"Please don't get him started on social media and how it's being controlled; he'll go on for hours," Mitch said.

Bongani and Joss both laughed. Marissa glanced into the back to see Peta was sleeping, despite the talking.

"'Tomorrow will be better than today'—that's our belief for Zimbabwe," Bongani said. "As a Chief, with tribal trust lands, I try to live by that motto."

"Joss also called you Chief. I thought it was a term of endearment," Marissa said.

"I inherited the title and the lands from my father," Bongani said. "I am the custodian of those who live there, and I am responsible for all of them. We do things a little differently here; we run the area like a kibbutz… so everyone who works and puts in effort to make their home a better place gets to share in the profits."

Marissa nodded and looked out the front window, hoping for a sight of something bigger, but all she could see was the road continuing far into the distance, a scar through the landscape. "Do you think we might see an elephant?"

"Maybe, but you'll get to see plenty of them once we get to Yingwe; the herds visit there all the time," Joss said.

"I've compared the photos from Peta and Joss with Amalee, and the wild ones here are huge," Marissa said.

"Is she an Asian elephant?" Mitch asked.

"Do you take me for an idiot? Fly thousands of miles to the wrong continent?" Marissa said.

Bongani broke the awkward silence that followed with a belly laugh. "Oh, I like her, Joss. She can stay."

"Fair enough. I deserved that," Mitch said.

Marissa grinned.

"When it comes to elephant, you need to know most of us out here are dead against pulling calves out of the wild and shipping them off anywhere. They belong here. And it'll be great to have her back where she belongs," Mitch said.

Marissa heard such emotion in his words. What was happening, or had happened, that he was so passionate about the elephant being taken?

"We look through different eyes than we did just thirty years ago at many issues," Marissa said. "Animal capture is one of those things. We can appreciate small progress being made, especially in the first-world countries."

Mitch nodded. "Given you already have experience with elephant, your stay here will be even richer. You're going to love spending time with our elephant families."

"The whole experience will be magical," Marissa said.

"I'm not sure what Joss, Peta, and Sophia told you," Mitch said. "We really do live in the best place in the entire world. The elephant might be big and take center stage, but there is so much other beauty here. I'm sure when you settle in, you'll never want to leave."

Marissa nodded in acknowledgment. She sat back in her seat, content to watch the forests pass by on the way to the sanctuary. The vehicle moved along the road, bumping and groaning, and the sound was hypnotic.

She snuck a glance at her travelling companion. Mitch was right—there was a lot of beauty here.

Heat flushed her cheeks.

But Mitch was also wrong.

Her home was in America; her life was in Nevada. Why would she want to leave?

CHAPTER 15
THROUGH ENRICHED EYES

YINGWE RIVER LODGE, ANIMAL RESCUE AND REHABILITATION CENTER, BINGA, ZIMBABWE

28 September 2014

"Come on, sleepy head. We're almost there," Mitch said as he woke Marissa from her nap, his hand gentle on her arm.

Marissa snapped awake, lifting her head.

She looked at the sign reading Yingwe River Lodge, Animal Rescue And Rehabilitation Center as they drove through the gates. The building's exterior matched the photos Peta and Joss had shown her. With a thatched roof and stone walls, it was rustic, beautiful, and seamlessly integrated into the surrounding landscape, appearing to be a natural part of the environment.

There was history here but also modernization. A sense of belonging radiated from the building.

A group of khaki clad men and a few women in a safari styled uniform stood on the porch, smiling as they approached, waiting on the porch to greet them.

Mitch opened the door and helped her climb out.

She was sure that his hand held hers a little longer than was necessary. But then the moment was over. She folded her fingers into her hand, holding onto the feeling for a few seconds and she wondered if she was suffering from a little jet lag and hallucinations herself. Once she was out, Mitch moved the seat so Joss could reach his dozing Sophia. Mitch then went to the back to grab Marissa's cases.

"We're at the lodge," Joss said, gently rubbing his daughter's cheek. "You want to show everyone you can walk or go to our house first?"

Sophia blinked her eyes a few times, then they stayed wide open. She looked up and smiled. "I want to show them."

Joss unbuckled her and lifted her out before putting her on her feet, and said, "Go for it, my little love."

Sophia stood, steady and strong, and walked towards the staff.

The singing, dancing, and clapping started at once, as more staff poured out from the wide doorway that led inside the lodge, to welcome Sophia home.

A chant went up.

"You're walking. You're walking!"

Sophia beamed, her joy visible as everyone swamped her with hugs. Joss and Peta stood with their arms around each other, next to Marissa who had remained near the people carrier.

"That's our girl," Joss said, smiling.

After a while, Sophia walked back to her parents. "Now, it's time to go home."

Joss lifted her back into the vehicle. Peta waved to the staff, and climbed in, before Joss closed the door.

"See you later, Mitch, Marissa," Joss said. He waved goodbye and climbed into the front passenger seat. Bongani put the vehicle into drive for the last leg of their long journey home.

The people carrier disappeared down the road, and around a corner before Marissa followed Mitch to the lodge entry.

A slender woman, dressed in a similar fashion to Mitch, with her hair held back with an ethnic-patterned headscarf, drew Marissa's attention. She had dark, almost black eyes with small laughter lines on the sides. A face that was used to not taking life too seriously, but someone who had experienced real hardship too.

"So beautiful. Miss Sophia, she's walking." She dabbed at her eye with the back of her sleeve. "Welcome. Welcome. I'm Christine, the lodge's host."

Marissa shook Christina's hand.

"I have you in the Lion rondavel. Can I organize something for you to eat and drink before I take you there?" She glanced at Mitch, who was still standing next to Marissa, and her suitcases on the porch. "If you're still awake after that, I'm sure Mitch can take you to look at the stables and meet our little orphans. I think that Joss and his family are going to be getting reacquainted with their home after all this time away, and Mitch is a good one to tell you all about the set-up. He's been here from the beginning of the rehabilitation center and helped build everything."

"I'd kill for an energy drink," Marissa said.

"Mitch, please take Marissa to the veranda. I'll have drinks and snacks delivered there," Christina said, and walked inside the building.

Mitch guided her around, this time through a massive door, under the arch of bougainvillea. It was not at its best; although it had a mass of red flowers, it still showed lots of green foliage, and Marissa knew it would be a real showstopper when in full bloom. It was one of the plants her father loved, and their gardener had to bring pots of it into climate-controlled greenhouses in winter, as it was just too cold to grow naturally at home. Here, it sprawled over the structure and continued to creep unchecked, decorating the roof.

Inside the lodge was immediately cooler; the floor was made with stone and concrete that gleamed with polish. The roof was pitched high, and the smell of thatch was inviting but tinged with a hint of something acidic. The furniture was large and overstuffed, matching the African theme perfectly. Couches with plump cushions invited guests to sit and share the shade. While there was a safari theme, there were no taxidermized animals all over the place, as she'd seen in other lodge pictures. The decor was subtle and understated in beautiful chocolate, ochre, and black, with splashes of white.

They walked out through the large doors onto the deck. Marissa took a deep breath.

The view was out over Lake Kariba. Far in the distance, she could see where the building clouds touched the water. "The photos don't do this place justice."

"There's potential for a storm coming in. You'll be able to watch the squalls travel across the lake and over us from here, if you want to, but it might fizzle out. Maybe the rains will come early this year," Mitch said as he drew a chair out for her to sit in.

A soft breeze blew her hair around her face. "What a lovely wind," Marissa said.

"Appreciate it while it's here," Mitch said. "The heat gets oppressive when it's absent. It's like a hot, heavy blanket that settles on the land."

A waiter arrived with their drinks.

"Thanks," Marissa and Mitch said at the same time, as the waiter placed the cans next to tall glasses filled with ice, on a table.

They sat at one of the tables under a thatched umbrella. Other guests were scattered across the deck, sipping their own drinks. Avoiding the hot afternoon sun and enjoying the same view, as a noisy troop of monkeys, swinging in the trees below.

The waiter flicked his towel at them. "Shoo."

"We love the monkeys, but they become pests if they start to expect food," Mitch explained. "Aggressive ones need to be taken care of as they bite, and like a lot of wild animals, they can carry rabies. It's easier to keep them away than to have to put them to sleep. Hopefully, this lot will move on soon."

"They're so cute," Marissa said. "Look at those little faces, and the speckled grey hair. Are their tails usually that long?"

"They're Vervet monkeys, so yeah, they have long tails," Mitch said. "They're sweet until they shit on the chairs and tables. The staff have their hands full, ensuring that this area is clean."

"They sound like groundhogs at home—cute but destructive," Marissa said.

They chuckled as one of the baby monkeys used its mother's tail to swing from where it was to another branch, only to leap back when an older male bared its teeth.

"You can see your rondavel from here," Mitch said, looking past her to the left and pointing it out, a small thatched roof nestled into a sea of green bushes. "Make sure you have a guard with you at night when you move from the main building to your quarters. The lodge isn't fenced, and elephants often wander in, but sometimes lions and hyenas also make their way into camp. Most of the jumbo don't bother guests, but we can't take the chance that Torn-Ear hasn't brought in another bull to the clinic. And bulls in musth are trickier to handle than you would imagine."

"Torn-Ear?" Marissa asked.

"An old bull who we helped years ago. He seems to have become like Ndhlovy. He brings any bulls who need our help here. If they're wounded from a fight, spear or bullet, he guides them in," Mitch said as he took another sip of his Coke. "The bulls are different from the cows that Ndhlovy brings home. Hers are usually family groups, and when one needs help, the whole herd comes along for a visit."

"It's hard to believe that these wild animals trust so easily," Marissa said.

Mitch shook his head. "It wasn't easy, believe me. A lot of the sanctuary's success goes to Ndhlovy. It's like that elephant has a sixth sense as to when she needs to come in and settle a new baby down."

"Yet she's still wild; she doesn't go to any other humans like she does with you guys?" Marissa asked.

"Not that we know of. The people around here know her, and they leave her alone. She wears a collar so we can track her. Anyone who sees her, knows that she's part of a monitoring program and will hopefully give her space. Poachers tend to try to avoid animals with trackers on. Having a tracking device go silent is a sure way to bring attention to themselves."

Marissa looked at him. "She never goes far?"

"She travels. There have been months when she's taken a long walk, right up into the Matusadona, a game reserve north of here. As the crow flies, it's only about seventy kilometers, but the elephant meander up there, much like the road, making it about three hundred kilometers."

"So, about one hundred and eighty miles?" Marissa interrupted, making sure she understood.

"If you say so, I have no idea. We use the metric system in Australia and here in Zimbabwe." He grinned. "But if your math is right, that's awesome."

She smiled. She thought it was quite close-ish.

"We think she did her longest walk when Joss first went overseas with Sophia this time. It was like she knew he wasn't here anymore, and she could follow some old elephant trail to some faraway destination. After Peta left to join him in America, Zola and Danie brought in an orphan; it was as if she knew she needed to come home again, that was special. But then she left again…"

Marissa nodded. "Do you think if Amalee comes, that she should have a tracker?"

"She would do well to have one," Mitch said, taking another sip of his Coke. "After she's rewilded, it might be nice for her to have it off eventually, but it also gives her a little bit of protection."

Marissa yawned. "Excuse me. Jet lag."

"You have two options," Mitch said. "Sleep now and take a few days to get into the time zone, or just stay awake and busy, and then later tonight, collapse into bed and beat it. I usually do the latter. It's harsh but quicker in the long run, and you only have ten days here."

"I've often found that last option works best for me; besides, I couldn't sleep now if I tried," Marissa said, and took a sip of her drink.

"Not that I'm a dietician, but consuming lots of energy drinks isn't very healthy," Mitch said.

"Says the guy drinking coke!" Marissa snorted. "I know, but we all have weaknesses. For me, it's sick kids, elephants, and energy drinks."

Mitch nodded, and a hint of smile tugged at the corner of his mouth. "I'll remember to let the waiters know to have more in the fridge." His Australia drawl prominent on the word fridge.

"Perhaps I should try detox from them while I'm here," Marissa said. "Different environment, different pace."

Mitch held her eye contact for a beat longer, and Marissa smiled then looked down at her drink, studying the silver can. There was something about him that she found far too interesting.

Marissa shook her head. Different environment, different place—and a different accent.

CHAPTER 16
LEGAL ADVICE

MCDERMITT, NEVADA, USA

27 September 2014 – 22:50

As far as Chad was concerned, Jeffery, the lawyer was a waste of space.

He'd considered him as insignificant as a flea since the day he'd received the letter from him on behalf of Walter all those years ago, the one telling him he couldn't access his inheritance until he was twenty-five.

There was one thing about people working late in the office: usually it meant they didn't want to go home to their wives or lovers or whatever. But this ambulance chaser generally worked late every night.

He had no family to go home to, so he had married himself to success instead.

When Jeffrey left the office, he didn't take any of his job home with him—not even a briefcase. It was almost overgenerous to spend any oxygen on digging a hole to kill a man with such a small footprint in life.

Jeffery got ready to close up ten minutes earlier than usual tonight, at eight-fifty instead of nine. The fluorescent lighting illuminated the unsuspecting lawyer.

Exactly what does this man do once his clients and the rest of the staff leave?

Satisfied, the lawyer grabbed his coat from the stand in the lobby, then switched the last light off inside. McDermitt was a sleepy town, so either he and his partner were guarding dangerous secrets, or he was a paranoid bastard.

Chad stood from the bench in the pretty park opposite the office. He walked briskly to the door so that as Jeffery unlocked it and turned, ready to set an alarm code, Chad yanked the door open and pushed his 9mm barrel into the lawyer's gut. "Step away from the alarm panel and keep real calm."

Jeffery didn't argue as he stepped away. "If this is a hold-up and robbery, I don't have anything of great value. There is no cash kept on the premises."

Chad flicked the lights back on. "You go back into your office now."

Chad marched next to him and indicated for him to sit at his desk in his own chair. When Jeffrey visibly flinched at being manhandled, Chad smiled.

"You know who I am?" Chad asked the lawyer who had his eyes on his desk.

Jeffrey looked up, making direct eye contact. "I do, regrettably. What's this about?"

"Unfortunately for you, you're Walter Whitney's lawyer," Chad said, leaning against a filing cabinet, his weapon aimed at Jeffrey. "You've been his legal aid for so many years. There must be multitudes of secrets you keep hidden for him. Like the money he paid to get me accepted into the military academy?"

"I don't have to tell you anything; it's called lawyer confidentiality," Jeffery said. "What do you want, Chad Whitney?" The words were spat with contempt.

"Ah, so you have a backbone after all. Fire that piece-of-shit computer up again, get his will, and we'll make an amendment."

"You'll need his signature on any will change. How do you plan on getting that?" Jeffrey asked.

Chad stepped close and right up against the man's ear, said, "You have your secrets; I have mine. Now get it, or I'll put a bullet in your stomach. You'll have a slow, painful death, with no chance at life at all." Chad remained behind him, so he could read what was on the screen.

Jeffery sweated, a sign of fear. Good. He would be compliant, if still a little mouthy.

"If Walter was going to amend his will, it would just be a minor amendment so I wouldn't have to redo the whole will. That would be more than twenty pages long," Jeffery said.

"Do whatever you have to," Chad said. "You're the lawyer; just pull it up and make a change."

"What do you want done?" Jeffery asked.

"Half. He's leaving me half of everything when he dies. I get half as his nephew, the son of his darling, dead brother. After all, blood is blood."

Jeffery hesitated.

"Think carefully and make sure you get it right," Chad said.

Jeffery nodded, and he began typing. "Anything else?"

"No. Just make it so I get my fair share."

Jeffery typed for a while, then stopped. "I need to print this. He always signs in person."

"Then print it."

Chad heard the printer on the counter kick in, and he fetched the paper, all the while keeping his sidearm pointed at Jeffery. "This has a place for your signature as well as Walter's?"

"Correct, and the amendment needs both the lawyer and the client to sign to make it legal," Jeffery said.

"Real slow, open the drawer and get your pen and sign the will," Chad said.

Jeffery signed the single sheet of paper.

Chad glanced at the signed document. *Amendment to will and testament. I, Walter Whitney, born…*

"Make sure you save that document, so people know it's real," Chad said.

"It's legal. The only thing it needs is Walter's signature; just having mine is not enough. This is only another piece of paper until he signs it," Jeffery said.

"It will have his scribble soon enough. Shut down, like you do every night, and walk out. Set the alarm. Act as if I'm just a regular client you were seeing a bit later than normal."

"That's it? Nothing else? You know, you didn't have to hold me at gunpoint. For something like this, you could've come in and discussed it as a former client. Taken a bit of legal advice while you were at it. There was no need to threaten me."

"Would you have done it if I didn't threaten you?"

"Hell, no," Jeffery said.

"Then it would've been a waste of our time anyway. My way, we both achieve an outcome," Chad said.

The lights were turned off, and still with the barrel of the gun in his back, Jeffery went to set the alarm.

"No funny business with codes," Chad said.

Jeffery stepped outside with Chad close behind. He pulled the door closed and Chad looked up and down the street. It was deserted, as any small-town street would be. One street over was a pub and a diner; you would find people there, but not outside the lawyer's office.

"Get in your car, and I'll give you further directions once we get closer to the Lucky 7 Ranch."

"You know Walter won't sign this amendment. He can be a stubborn old man at the best of times," Jeffery said.

"Just drive while you can still breathe," Chad said.

He smiled. It had worked.

His plan was coming together.

CHAPTER 17
THE ELEPHANT ORPHANAGE

YINGWE RIVER LODGE, ANIMAL RESCUE AND REHABILITATION CENTER, BINGA, ZIMBABWE

28 September 2014

As Marissa and Mitch walked toward the elephant stables, Sophia's words came into her head about Amelee's fancy accommodation.

These were not. The buildings we functional, yes, but no one would ever call them beautiful.

The surprise was the roofs. "Why would you thatch the stables? Isn't that a fire hazard?" Marissa asked.

"Thatch is cool in summer and warm in winter here," Mitch said. "It's a natural insulation against the weather. It might be a tad warm here now, but in winter we get down to single digits some nights. It can be really cold being so close to such a large body of water. The thatch helps the animals and humans to regulate temperature. Both cooler and warmer."

"I had no idea," Marissa said as she looked around.

Fancy versus functional. Electricity guzzler from the first world versus using what was readily available from the environment to heat and cool.

If it went down to zero temperatures, and Amalee didn't have her heated barn to retreat into, would she cope?

"I bet it's different from what you have in the States," Mitch said, as if reading her mind.

"Rather," Marissa said. "And Amalee's been in America for thirty-five years. She's going to find this quite an adjustment."

"It's a big decision, but if you decide against it, at least you've seen where her roots are from," Mitch said.

It was as if a weight was lifted from her shoulders. Mitch understood that while she was here on what others had referred to as an LSD trip (Look See Decide), the D part could wait. She had no idea why that mattered to her; he was a stranger she had just met.

Curiosity got the better of her. "What enticed you to move from your home in Australia to here?"

"Joss. We served in Afghanistan, and when things went wrong, we all stuck together. We ended up in England—now, that's a dreary place. When I visited Joss and saw how well he was doing, I figured the magic must be in the water, so I stayed."

"In the water?" Marissa asked, frowning.

"A joke. Something to blame. For me, it was that Joss believed in this place, and its people, were worth returning to fight for. The least I could do was join in the war beside my brother for a cause that was worth it. After I met Ndhlovy, I knew nowhere else in the world would ever be home for me." Mitch looked towards the bush as if he willed her to appear, or he could be out there in the wild with her.

"Come on, this way. The nursery where the other orphans are is over here," Mitch said once again, touching the small of her back, as if his hand belonged there.

A man, in a green coat and overalls walked out of the stables, a small elephant lumbered behind him. The baby wore a purple blanket as if it were a horse and needed coverings. The man and Mitch smiled broadly at each other.

"Watch this." The man turned left, and the baby elephant followed. He turned right, as if they were playing follow-the-leader, and the baby followed again.

"Finally," Mitch said, and then, as if remembering that Marissa was there, he explained. "Despite Ndhlovy paying several visits to this little one, Moloi has been a little slow with the training. She's like Houdini—gets out all the time to try and run away from us. We weren't sure she would make it, but look at her today, following Bryson like he's her mother. The bonding has started. She'll be okay."

Bryson walked to them. Mitch reached out to Moloi, who wrapped her trunk around him, clearly recognizing him as family.

Marissa thought about Amalee, who had made the exact same gesture with her and hugged her the same way before she left on this trip.

Despite the thousands of miles separating them and their age differences, the elephant showed similar behavior. Apparently, genetics couldn't be altered by being an ocean apart.

"Bryson, this is Marissa."

"Madam," Bryson said, taking his hat off and nodding.

"Hi," Marissa said as Moloi moved to her and put her little trunk out, smelling her.

Marissa reached her hand forward and Moloi wrapped her trunk around Marissa and started feeling her front for pockets, no doubt hoping for snacks.

"Ah, they learn so fast about snacks and treats in the pockets," Mitch explained.

Marissa patted the baby elephant. "Amalee does it too. I think I could get used to being hugged by a baby. Amalee was a fair bit older than this when we got her. Moloi is so beautiful. May I take a photo?"

"As many as you like," Mitch said. "I had noticed you hadn't taken any so far."

"I have to be very protective of my privacy, so I usually don't take many photos myself. But this moment is too special not to capture. Dad, Dawn, and Brandon will love this little one," Marissa said as she dug into her bag for her new camera, a gift from her father for her trip, and got ready to take a few pictures.

After a few more minutes with them, Bryson touched Moloi on the head to get her attention. "Excuse us. We need to walk to get her stomach to work. Nice meeting you."

Marissa watched them go towards a large gate at the end of the building, which Bryson opened, and Moloi followed him through.

"There are others out there; they're going to socialize," Mitch said as if once again reading her mind. "Bryson will be showing her off to the other handlers. She's one of the lucky ones."

"How so?" Marissa asked.

Mitch's body language changed; he stiffened and took a moment too long to answer. "We got to her before the predators did, after her mum was killed by poachers. She came from the Matusadona area, north of here."

"Poor thing," Marissa said.

"That she is," Mitch said. "I have a huge soft spot for elephant babies. They are a delight at that age. Actually, at any age."

They were silent for a moment. Marissa didn't find it awkward; just being there together, watching an elephant walk away meant they didn't need words to be spoken.

She stopped. Dumbstruck as to where that 'comfortable silences' thought come from?

Mitch was still a stranger, and yet there was something about him that put her at ease.

If he noticed her hesitation, he never commented on it.

Too soon, both the handler and the baby elephant disappeared into the bush beyond the gate.

"Can I ask something about Ndhlovy?" Marissa asked.

"Of course," Mitch said as they walked towards the stables once again.

"Peta said they don't know when Ndhlovy will arrive; she just does her own thing?"

Mitch nodded. "Has anyone mentioned that Peta's name here is maNdhlovu."

"maNdhlovu?"

"It means *mother of elephant*. Everyone here calls her that. You can guess why with her job and Ndhlovy coming here all the time."

Marissa loved the name; it was deserving and fitting.

"Ndhlovy is an elephant who defies all logic," Mitch said. "She's wild and comes and goes, but she treats this sanctuary like her own petting zoo. We brought a giraffe baby, Mnene, here for treatment. Ndhlovy was all over her, checking she was okay."

"So, it's mostly babies here?"

"A lot of the time," Mitch said. "We generally don't get many fully grown animals, except the elephant. Ndhlovy is inherently inquisitive; she wants to know everything and everyone who comes in. You'll get to meet her soon. We tracked her coming from the Chete Safari area direction yesterday."

"You mentioned she has a tracker. How do you know if she's bringing in a new rescue or dropping in for a motherly visit?" Marissa asked, frowning.

Mitch smiled again. "We don't always know. Honestly, it doesn't matter which; we love her visits either way. However, this time, one of the community rangers in the outer rim of Bongani's trust lands let us know when he saw her, and it was just her and her normal herd. They all recognize her and her family group. They know most of the elephant that come and go through their lands. Different ear tears, different tusks. The locals take a keen interest in the wildlife as it's an important revenue source and helps support the people who live here."

"Is this a community outreach program you run?" Marissa asked.

Mitch looked at her. "I'm not sure how much Joss told you, but the more you have the community on your side, the better off your lodge, animals, and tourists will be. We're lucky. Our lodge is inside Bongani's tribal trust lands: his territory. He and Joss are longtime friends, so little goes on here without both of them knowing, and they include the whole community. It's a long story, but while Joss is slightly younger than Bongani, it's not by that much, and they have gone through hell together. I don't think there are two other men, who are not military brothers, who would do what they would do for each other."

Marissa smiled. The dynamics of the sanctuary were complex. If Amalee were to be rewilded here, she wanted to be sure it would be as easy an experience as possible for her elephant. It wasn't as if she could reload Amalee back on a plane and take her home if it didn't work out.

There was only one shot at this.

She had to be sure, for Amalee, and for her.

Rewilding Amalee would take Marissa away from home for a long time. Was she ready?

Mitch stepped through a doorway to the elephant stables. "Let me show you the kitchen and the stalls. There used to be horse stables here when Joss was a kid. When Peta came to live here, they got torn down, and we built these instead. That way, the sanctuary can treat any animals who come—even the largest of them, the elephant bulls, if needed."

They walked a little down a passage, and Mitch pointed to a room. "Peta's operating theatre."

Marissa nodded as she looked through the door. A modern surgery with stainless-steel tables and counters stared back at her. She knew that Peta and Joss had spent a lot of money on the sanctuary, but this room was superior to what she'd expected to find.

"She tends to do any surgery to the larger animals like the antelope and the elephant outside. They have all their drug cupboards in there; it's kept locked," Mitch said.

"That kind of makes sense," Marissa said.

"The interim vets you arranged love this space. They have been doing a lot of local dog and cat neutering here to keep them busy when they are not hiking all over this area, helping goats and cattle." Mitch had continued down the passage.

"I'm glad to hear that it's worked out for everyone," Marissa said.

"Next are the stables we use for the twenty-four-hour care and quarantine when an animal, especially a baby, comes in. Can't be too careful sometimes with the wild babies. Except for the elephant, whom Ndhlovy controls. If they look sick, Peta might decide to quarantine them."

"Careful of what?" Marissa asked.

"There was a bad rabies outbreak a few years ago, and we can't afford to spread something like anthrax. Just because a baby is rescued doesn't give them the all-clear right away; we have to consider all the other animals' health, too." Mitch said.

There were diseases here that Marissa hadn't given a thought to. *If Amalee was wild, she would be exposed to them.*

Mitch reached out and touched her arm. "Peta and her team don't cut corners; they take every precaution with the elephant. She'll be safe here. And don't let the talk about disease spook you; it's a tiny risk in the bigger scheme of things."

Her arm was warm where he'd touched her, and she rubbed it. She wasn't sure if it was because the gesture had been unexpected, or if she was untrusting of how her body reacted to him.

They entered the stable area where the babies were kept at night. There were several single stalls, and a large gathering room. Most of the structure was made of thick wooden poles, and the spaces were roomy, but there were two stables made of yellow painted steel poles.

Adult elephant-proof.

There was a cot at the back of each stall, built into the wall, no doubt so the human on duty could sleep there if they needed to stay with their charge. Marissa smiled. "Dawn, will love this place."

"How do you think she'll manage letting your elephant go?" Mitch said.

"I don't think that she will. She's prepared to move to Africa with her. Her great great, perhaps another great, grandparents were taken to America as slaves, and she sees it as coming home," Marissa said.

"Is she aware that she'll need a different visa?" Mitch asked.

"She'll have everything that she needs. If she decides to stay here, she'll still receive her salary, and we'll pay Peta for her food and accommodation. Dawn won't be a burden on Joss and Peta. She's more than just an animal keeper to me. She's more like a precious aunt who's been there for me through everything. When my father was away, it was Dawn at home. If this is what she wants, then I can make it happen for her."

"And you?" Mitch asked simply, looking at her.

"Me? I keep telling myself if I see that Amalee is happy, and I know I can visit sometimes, then I think I'll be okay too. But I really don't know. This is an incredible place, but I still haven't made up my mind. There are so many factors both for and against moving her so far—"

He smiled, reached out, and touched her shoulder. "You're clearly passionate about her rewilding and making sure it's the right thing for you all. It's a huge responsibility on you to make that decision. Come on." He dropped his hand and gestured with his head to keep going left. "The last thing to look at is the main outdoor area. There are also three different spaces there that they can gather in."

Marissa immediately missed the feel of his hand. She hadn't been around anyone in a long time who touched other people as much as Mitch did. *Was it just her that he was so hands-on with?*

She couldn't stop her smile.

She could see Amalee settling here; the facility seemed promising, but she wanted some time with the staff to see if they were all like Mitch. And to meet the other elephant. After all, that was who Amalee would be hanging around with—others of her own kind.

Mitch's voice interrupted her thoughts. "The elephant babies have been taken for food; come, we can walk to them. They are not far. Afterwards we can come back and help with the afternoon feed. Unless you want to rest?"

Marissa shook her head. "No rest. I'm with you all the way."

She followed Mitch out of the barn and down a well-travelled road, wide enough to fit a truck, but the bush at the side was also trimmed back, giving it a sidewalk of mowed stubble. They walked for about fifteen minutes, then she could hear people talking. The low baritones of men and, every now and again, a higher-pitched woman's voice came through, making her smile.

She breathed deeply, tempering her excitement to meet more baby elephants. After years of just being with Amalee, she was in awe that a place like Yingwe River Lodge existed, and how it had been so far off all their radars.

"Here you go—the baby herd," Mitch said. "I'll introduce you."

Marissa looked at the elephant that browsed the trees. Real acacias, not ones that she had to fly in from Florida. There were other bushes there—some with thorns, some without, and some with leaves that looked like angel wings. She ran her fingers along one leaf.

"A mopani tree. Elephant love these," Mitch said. "This area is full of them. And those with the big thorns, those are camel thorns. Their pods, when they drop, are velvety with fine hairs and are a favorite in the bush among most grazers and browsers. Inside is the protein package of a black bean. Careful—those thorns can hurt."

She'd never seen anything like these trees, and she knew that Amalee wouldn't recognize most of the plants here either.

An elephant ran up to Mitch, and he reached out and patted it as it lifted its trunk "This beautiful little one is Nkazimulo. It means *glory*," Mitch said as the elephant walked over to Marissa, its ears flared forward, and its trunk down—then it stopped, turned, and ran back to its carer, its tail bobbing up and down.

Marissa smiled. Such a beautiful name for such a beautiful elephant. This one was larger than Moloi but not by much. It swished its trunk around, looking at her, and went behind its carer, as if playing peek-a-boo.

"Madam," the carer said, nodding a greeting as he carried on pulling the tip of the tree towards the baby elephant, picking the softer foliage at the top and giving it to the baby, teaching the elephant what muscles to use on their trunk.

Mitch pointed to their left to a grey rock. "That sleeping little baby is Sifiso. You met Moloi earlier, and the one trying to play with her handler is Isibane. She's the oldest of the milk-dependent orphans at the moment, which means she's also a little larger. She only has milk at night now. And we'll keep her on milk for a while yet." He seemed to say the last bit with steel in his voice, as if there was a reason for keeping her on milk.

Marissa looked around. Four little elephants. Each with a dedicated carer. The people who watched over them seemed so relaxed.

"Is this paddock fenced?" Marissa asked. "What about predators and snakes?"

"No fences; they end by the stables. From here on out, it's open veldt. The babies go into the wild as soon as they can. Besides, fences don't work well with elephant. And as for dangers, they learn the scent of predators naturally. Usually, the human presence is enough to keep the real predators away; if they do come, they radio the anti-poaching guards. Someone is never far. The carer will move the babies away from something like a snake if they see it. Ah, here comes trouble." Mitch looked back towards the orphanage buildings.

A half-grown Zebra trotted down the path they had just walked on, its tail swishing and its neck arched. Its fat little belly bobbed up and down. Next to it, a bi-colored baby goat pranced. Behind that, a tall giraffe baby stopped at a tree for a nibble, and in an animal conga line came a man, a small warthog, an ostrich, then a second worker. They looked like a parade out of the *Dr. Dolittle* book she'd read as a child.

Marissa couldn't stop smiling. The man stepped around the giraffe and carried on walking. The goat turned and ran at him. He grabbed it by the horns and circled it back the way he wanted it to go.

"I see James-Bruce is just as full of beans as normal," Mitch said.

"Yebo and Alexander-Lang too. Too playful," the man said.

"Those two are named after early explorers," Mitch said, nodding to Marissa, who laughed.

"Marissa, meet Senzi, and the lovely lady trailing him over there is Patricia. They're animal handlers. Senzi mainly looks after these guys," he pointed to the zebra and the goat. "Patricia has Mnene, the giraffe, Anele the ostrich, and the new warthog baby, Thunderbolt. We had one veteran in our anti-poaching team—he was an ex-pilot—and apparently there is a plane nicknamed The Warthog, so he thought it would be good to give the warthog the plane's name. It kind of stuck."

The zebra Alexander came and said hello to Marissa while the goat went and bothered the baby elephant handlers. The giraffe stood close to her but didn't want to interact. The baby warthog, with its little vertical hairy mane, came up to her for a big scratch.

"Thunderbolt is delightful," Marissa said. "Who would have thought that a warthog baby could be so adorable?"

"She won't stay that size, unfortunately. Thunderbolt will probably remain close to the lodge now that she's been rescued, attract a mate, and have babies when she's older."

Only then did the giraffe bend its neck and give Marissa a big, sloppy kiss on her face, its rough blue tongue licking both her chin and her cheek, trailing the scent of acacia over her, with a thick green saliva present.

"Mnene likes you," Mitch said as Marissa wiped her face on her T-shirt, laughing. She looked up and Mitch was staring at where her shirt had exposed her stomach.

He quickly looked at his watch. "I need to get back to help get the milk feed ready. You can stay here or come with me. The orphanage is just through those trees."

Marissa dropped her shirt and heat spread from her chest up into her face. This man had made her blush more in one day than any other person she could think of. "I'll stay for a while and come in with them."

Mitch nodded and walked away as Marissa resumed taking photographs, until a loud gong sounded.

The baby elephant turned as one and headed toward the barn, walking quickly and running as they got closer. The handlers jogged to keep up as their wards moved toward the stable.

"Guess it's milk time," Marissa said as she followed the animal race at a brisk pace. She'd never seen Amalee at this stage in her life. She knew Amalee would love this place as much as she did if she was given the chance.

Perhaps this was the place to keep her promise and rewild Amalee.

CHAPTER 18
CONSEQUENCE

LUCKY 7 RANCH, NEVADA, USA

30 September 2014

Chad looked at the Lucky 7 Ranch house through a spotting scope. Thomas had upgraded security across the ranch. Chad had needed time to learn the layout of the new security system and familiarize himself with all the cameras. On analysis, there were blind spots.

He'd found them.

The weather would be his greatest ally today. A hot day of eighty-two degrees. There was a whisper of a wind with passing clouds. No rain forecast, so no footprints would betray where he walked.

There was no movement inside the house, except for his uncle and his security detail.

Dawn had retreated to a temporary cattle barn, along with the annoying elephant; no more air-conditioned comfort for them. All the men were in their rented Airstream homes on wheels, after their bunkhouses had all burned to the ground. Even Pia, the long-time housekeeper, had left the homestead for the day.

He knew that Marissa was out of the country. He hadn't wasted his years in prison being a thug. Instead, he'd used them to build a network of contacts. The promise of a huge payday always helped grease the way. Flight plans were an easy ask.

His uncle moved from his study, through the lounge, and up the stairs, switching off lights as he went and switching on others. Chad never understood why he chose to live in a fishbowl and never bothered with curtains or blinds, claiming he loved the view too much.

Not that Chad would complain about it tonight. This was the third night he'd silently watched Walter, noting his movements.

Chad was aware that Walter spent many days away, in his DC house, surrounded by all the petty Foundation people and bodyguards, but with Marissa and the jet gone, he was housebound on the ranch. He'd ditched most of those overpriced penguins.

At the Lucky 7, he thought he was safe.

The farm dogs knew Chad. He'd made sure of that during the two weeks he'd been hunkered down at the ranch. Hiding here was easy. It had been his home for almost three years of his teenage life, so his memories of the land and layout were good. Not clouded by young childhood drama and unrealistic expectations.

The ranch incorporated several mine shafts, that cut deep into the ancient soil, hiding many secrets, both old and new.

The old man was in his ensuite bathroom. Chad had seen the security detail check inside his room, before allowing Walter in. If the personal protection followed normal protocol, he would be standing outside the bedroom door now.

Chad pulled on his gloves.

He walked to the house, avoiding the cameras, and climbed the same trellis that Marissa had used to get in and out when she was a kid. He opened the window that led directly into her room.

Much had changed since she became a woman.

Now decorated in white with purple touches, the room looked more like it belonged on the cover of a home décor magazine rather than being a place where someone slept.

The biggest transformation was in her work area. It wasn't where it used to be, which was now home to a fancy curved daybed. He knew she worked when she was at home, so she must have renovated and made a study somewhere else in the house.

He itched to find it and see if there was anything of hers there that would point to the kind of woman she really was. He was sure he would discover that soon enough.

But first, he had to deal with the security and get to the old man.

He didn't want to rush the moment. After all, he'd waited years for this.

He had the change of will in his backpack that only needed his uncle's signature before he croaked. Chad's inheritance would change tonight.

All Walter had to do was sign the paper.

In exchange, he would promise not to hurt Marissa.

If Walter was stubborn and wouldn't sign, it would be open season on his cousin. And this time, that interfering elephant, wouldn't be able to protect the grown woman.

From the pictures he'd seen all over the house, it wouldn't be too hard.

She still seemed like a slight little thing. She sure had matured even pretty, too. Her curves were damn near perfect—just the type of body he loved riding, hard.

He couldn't resist taking just one souvenir from her room.

He opened her walk-in wardrobe and went to the underwear drawer. He wished he could take the gloves off and feel for the softest and silkiest panties, but he couldn't leave any DNA behind.

Not tonight. Not when they'd already linked him to the fire, if his contact on the force was be believed.

He had to be like a ghost.

He directed his concentration back to the drawer. Everything was together as sets: matching. Arranged by color.

He sniggered quietly. Who knew his tomboy cousin would have grown into a woman who liked lacy underwear?

He almost wished Walter would say no so he could take his fantasy and turn it into a reality before he killed her. Give him that excuse to cross the line he'd thought he never would…

He looked in the drawer to see if she had any electronic toys. Perhaps he could tease her with one of those. That would humiliate her.

There was nothing there or next to her bed. Chad searched in her bathroom too.

He opened her medicine cupboard. Of course, she would have some nice prescription pills; no one associated with high-profile charity work got through life without the chemicals from the big pharmaceutical companies. He pocketed her sleeping tablets and closed the cupboard.

Maybe she was too prudish to bring herself pleasure, and too busy sleeping like the dead on her pills. Abandoning the search for toys, Chad pocketed a set of what looked like innocent pink lingerie, except when he looked closer, they were more risqué, decorated with rhinestones on the straps across the chest area, and what he swore was candy floss for the thong part, up the backside.

He sniggered. "Fuck me. Marissa might have a kink after all," he whispered.

He would bet his freedom on that before he burnt the barn down, she probably still spent most of her time in the stable rather than in this bedroom.

He took a deep breath in and let it out slowly, settling his mind.

Patience. One target at a time.

He took his 9mm sidearm from its holster and screwed on the silencer before he opened her door a crack.

No one was there.

He left her room and started down the passage. He kept on the left, close to the wall to avoid the panel of wood on the right that creaked.

At the corner, he peered around. As predicted, a man stood outside Walter's door. He lifted his 9mm, took aim and squeezed the trigger. As the man was crumpling, he ran to catch his body so he wouldn't make a thump and alert the other two guards in the house. He pulled the man into the room opposite Walters, and laid him on the carpet, before silently closing the door and stepping across the passage.

Chad entered Walter's room and heard the shower water tinkle as it pattered like rain against the glass.

Chad closed the door behind him. Everything had been updated, with new furniture and coverings, a more modern setting than when he was a boy. Brighter. He went to open the drinks cabinet; so many times, he'd snuck alcohol from here when he was underage.

As an adult, he wondered what type of man Walter really was that he needed a drinks cabinet in his bedroom. Perhaps he wasn't as saintly as the image he projected to the world.

There was a half-empty glass of the expensive Tennessee whisky Walter loved sitting on the silver tray. Chad pulled out a small container from his pocket. He tipped the salts into the whisky, almost a teaspoon and a half of them. Stirring it with a swizzle stick from the bar, he made sure they didn't touch him at all. Once they had dissolved, he threw the stick in the bin and put the glass on the bedside table. After changing his gloves, he pocketed the older pair.

The old mine had its secrets, and stores of cyanide salts were just one of them. He could have used horse tranquilizers, but they were a more modern drug and easily detected by the medics, where cyanide was a dark horse. The antidote was often not readily available. And it would make Walter suffer, rather than just glide into sleep.

He sat on the bed, then dug into his backpack, retrieved the amended will and a pen, and laid them beside him. He drew his handgun from its holster and placed it close by.

Waiting.

Eventually, the shower stopped, and an electric toothbrush hummed.

The light in the walk-through wardrobe turned on automatically as Walter stepped in. He continued to the bedroom, wearing only a towel that he'd tied around his waist.

Chad was relieved he didn't need to witness the shriveled old family jewels that hung under the fabric.

Walter stopped. His eyes widened. His face flushed red with anger. "What the fuck? Chad?"

"Hello, Walter. Long time no see," Chad said casually.

"Get the fuck out. I thought I made my position clear many years ago when you were sent to the army. And even more now that you burned down half the neighborhood. You are not welcome here. Get out." He pointed to the door, but his other hand had to stop his towel from falling off his hips, so the gesture was fast and clumsy. "Out."

Chad sniggered. "I don't think so. You're going to listen to me, and then you are going to sign these papers I have right here."

Walter began walking towards the phone on the dressing table.

Chad cocked his 9mm.

Walter stopped. "What are you going to do? Shoot me? Make a mess and a noise too?"

"If I have to. You missed that this weapon has a silencer; no one will hear a thing. If I do shoot you, it will not be to kill. Not at first. You would be surprised at how much pain the human body can endure."

"Knowing what you've become, I can believe that you have enjoyed inflicting such agony on others. Why are you here?"

"To ensure I get my share of the Whitney inheritance."

Walter's face turned scarlet. The rage was deep. "You had your inheritance from my brother. Every cent. You are not getting a penny from me."

"Ah, that's where you're wrong. You are going to sign this paper here, which your very own legal eye and mastermind, Jeffrey Myers, typed up for you. Because if you don't, no one will ever find where I buried him. It's a shame, really; he only has about twenty-four hours of oxygen, give or take."

"You bastard. How could you do that? Bury a man alive?"

"As easily as you could push me away after giving me a glimpse of what living comfortably looked like. You can save him. Sign the amendment and put me in your will. I only want half; I won't take Marissa's share."

"And then what? You'll kill me anyway?" Walter spat.

"Maybe. Maybe not. It'll depend on how things go. You see, because if you don't, your lawyer and friend, Jeffrey, dies. And it'll be open season on Marissa. I'm stronger now. I have skills from the service that you pushed me into, and don't forget, special contacts from prison. When I next meet Marissa, it'll be face-to-face. I won't mess up. This time I'll finish what I should have done years ago. Your precious biological daughter will be dead."

"Where does this incessant hatred for Marissa come from? She didn't give you any trouble—always tried to be the perfect cousin." Walter shook his head.

"Only she wasn't, was she? Not to me. She's not perfect, only in your eyes. You always treated her better than me. Always."

"You were a difficult teenager after Alice died—"

"Don't even mention her name." Chad stretched his free hand flat onto the bedside table. "In her own way, she loved me. You just tolerated me. Your own brother's child. After she died, and I came here, I was just another possession. You still gave Marissa all your time, all your attention. You were never there for me. You took me on as a responsibility, not as a family member. You were nothing like an uncle should have been. Nothing I did was good enough for you. I was criticized relentlessly."

"It wasn't intentional, but even so, you were a man. You didn't need any mollycoddling," Walter said. "You needed toughening up after soft city life."

"Is that what you call it? I was tough because I'd seen the prostitution. The drugs. The destitution. I know what real hunger feels like. Do you? Life wasn't tough enough for me? I had to learn how to steal, to survive on the streets, before I came to you." He took a deep, calming breath. Then leant towards Walter. "At least I knew I was honorable then. As a nephew, you wanted me to be harder. More manly? I bet you're super proud of what you got in the end. A real fucking *man's man*." Spittle flew from his lips as he punctuated the last sentence. He stood, unfurling the bulk of an ultra-fit six-foot-one frame.

Walter didn't move. A deer in the headlights. "You're a disgrace to the Whitney name."

"Whatever. Nothing you say has any power over me anymore. Once, it did, but not now. Sign the papers. Half. That's what I'm entitled to, and it's what I'll get," Chad said, slapping the paper against Walter's chest.

"Fuck off. I'm not signing. The moment I sign anything, you'll put a bullet through my heart."

The paper crumpled, and Chad took it away. "Or not," Chad said. "Maybe I'll let you live to see Marissa come home from Africa, but if you don't sign, it's you who has to make peace with yourself, knowing that an innocent man is going to die. Because you let Jeffery be starved of oxygen."

"Lawyers are easy to replace. I could get another one," Walter said.

"Harsh, even for you. How will you keep Marissa safe? If you sign, I'll back away, but if you don't, Marissa might not even make it back from Africa before I get to her. Zimbabwe isn't that different to Somalia. All the beautiful things I could do before I got to end her life—"

"Don't you fucking touch her!" Walter raged and stepped towards him, a vein on his forehead showing.

"Or what?" Chad shrugged. He knew he was now taller than Walter, younger and buffed from hours in the prison gym, heavier. In any pissing competition, he was the physically stronger man. "You'll change your will. See, there is only one way this ends tonight. You sign, and I inherit half of everything."

"I'm not having this conversation naked. I'm putting my clothes on," Walter muttered. "If you're going to kill me, at least they'll find me dressed."

"Don't even look for a weapon. I can shoot faster and more accurately than you ever could. I have you to thank for the lovely military training I received to the best standard at Fort Bragg," Chad said as he sat on the bed.

Walter huffed, turned his back on Chad, and walked to the wardrobe. He dug in a drawer. Seeming without a care, he dropped the towel and got dressed: underpants, trousers, deodorant, and finally a T-shirt. Then he walked out back to the bedroom.

"You still here?" he asked Chad.

"Not leaving till you sign."

"Then you'll be here a long, long time. You seem to be under the impression I'm rich. I'm not worth a dime." Walter chuckled. "I could never give you what is already all Marissa's. That is out of my control. Tied up tightly. You were right; she's worth so much more than you. She did something with her life, and she isn't disrespectful to her family. The same cannot be said for you."

"Just fucking sign the new will that Jeffrey wrote," Chad said, thrusting the paper at him again.

Walter shook his head. "You're not listening. My Whitney money is nothing. Her inheritance comes from the McDermitt side. It was her mother's family that had the money, not me. McDermitt money. Don't you understand? You were never going to get that. You'll never be allowed to touch it. Her mother's ancestors tied that trust fund up so tight even I couldn't get my hands on it. That money follows the blood of a McDermitt. And you don't have a drop of that in you." He laughed, a cynical sound, the cackling of a deranged person.

"I could sign that will and save Jeffrey's life—for now. You have always been like a stray mutt to the bone. You would return with another scheme. You have wasted Jeffrey's life and your own time. I'm surprised Jeffrey didn't tell you that any inheritance from me would be worth peanuts." Walter frowned. "He really was a remarkable and crafty lawyer, making you believe this might work. He doesn't know the extent of rot inside you. Not like I do. I have nothing. I live on an allowance with the grace of my daughter and the family trust. I can sign that paper for you, but it's worthless. There's no inheritance from me."

"Fuck!" Chad said. "Why didn't Jeffrey tell me this?"

"Probably because it's none of your business. I'm only telling you so you might think about how useless the effort of killing me is, thinking it will make you rich. Now get out. And stay out. And go dig up Jeffrey. He doesn't deserve to die in some airless chamber because you were stupid and didn't check your facts before telling him to redraft a worthless will."

"I'm not stupid," Chad raged.

"No, probably not," Walter said. "You're merciless and a natural killer with no conscience. That is why you did so well in the army and in Special Forces. But you were sloppy. You got caught killing for no reason at all. When you killed Farid Al-Qadhafi, you didn't even know that that man was being groomed by the international community to be the next president. Essentially, you assassinated a country's new leader.

"All your scheming and planning, and you never bothered to find out the most important detail: who owned the money. Once again, you didn't get all the facts before you acted irrationally."

"I could still kill you. Right here. Right now." Chad threatened, raising his voice.

"You could," Walter said, rocking on his heels. "But what point would you make? There's no money in it for you, and you've probably left DNA all over the house. Given your prison time, they'll match the samples fast enough. You won't get away with it. The FBI already have you on their list for arson. The fire jumpers had to get involved when the sandstorm picked up embers and dumped them on neighboring ranches and into the state national forest. It took them three weeks to contain the blaze. There was a couple of hundred million dollars of damage. A lot of cattle, horses, and other livestock had to be euthanized on more than one ranch in the path of the fire. Probably gives you an erection, knowing the amount of damage you caused. Do you really want to spend even more of your life in prison?"

"Not really." Chad shook his head slowly and ran a hand along his jaw, staring at the point where the ornate molded ceiling and the wall met above Walter's head.

Why, oh why, wasn't anything fucking simple? But there was still one more chance. "This just means that I'll have to also kill Marissa."

"Maybe you are an idiot. It doesn't work like that," Walter said, his arms animated as he threw them as fists that changed to open hands in the air in front of him. His frustration was clear. "You really didn't do the groundwork, did you? If Marissa dies without an heir, everything passes to the state of Nevada. This house will become a museum, and the state will operate The Lucky 7 as a heritage ranch. No one person gets the money if there is no blood left from McDermitt. No one."

Chad perched on the side of the bed.

If he left now, his uncle would most likely down the whisky, thinking he'd dodged the bullet. It wouldn't be as enjoyable as pulling the trigger himself, but it would still get the old goat out of his way. A small portion of the debt Walter owed him would be paid.

He was sure that if he could get to Marissa and threaten her enough, she would share her money with him, and with her father gone, she would be in mourning and an easier target. Pliable. Ultimately, she still needed to die, but it didn't have to be a quick death. He could milk her of the money and become a rich man in the interim before he took her life.

The plan had to remain in place—just evolve a little in light of the news that had come out tonight. Marissa had to live to pass money on to him—for now.

A man like Walter Whitney, he thought everything was about money, and it mostly was. That was why he'd gambled that Chad would leave him alone.

He didn't understand there was one thing money couldn't buy: revenge.

Uncle Walter still had to die.

Chad put on his best game face.

"Well shit," Chad said aloud. "That's an unexpected turn of events." He took the paper and shoved it back in his bag, along with his pen. Standing up, he threw the backpack over his shoulder, one hand at a time so that he still had his 9mm pointed at Walter. "Guess you'll be hearing from me again soon then."

"I fucking hope not. Get out of my house and out of my life. I curse the day you ever landed on my doorstep. My brother would be turning in his grave seeing the opportunities you were given, and you blew through."

"Keep your pants on old man, I'm finished here anyway."

"What about Marissa?" Walter asked.

"As I said, you didn't sign the will, so it'll be open season," Chad said backing out the room.

He ran along the passage, checked the stairs, then ran down. He went to the kitchen door and glanced inside.

No one.

He made his way to the lounge, opened a window, and headed out the front of the homestead. He made sure he closed it again. Jumping over the flowerbed, he made it onto the grass and then sprinted to the small river where there would be no scent for dogs to follow.

Tonight, he had made sure he was the shadow of death itself.

CHAPTER 19
MORE THAN AN ELEPHANT ORPHANAGE

YINGWE RIVER LODGE, ANIMAL RESCUE AND REHABILITATION CENTER, BINGA, ZIMBABWE

29 September 2014 – 14:00

Marissa had spent her morning with Mitch, Zola, and Danie, the contracted large-animal vets from South Africa, who had been out the day before vaccinating community dogs, cats, goats, and cattle against rabies. Zola had a figure that screamed, *I'm fit and strong. Don't mess with me.*

Her brother, Danie, dressed like her in khakis, was the quieter of the two. Just taller than Marissa's five-foot-seven, he was a much slimmer build but didn't lack in the muscle department.

Peta had left for Victoria Falls for the rescue of a young wildebeest calf with a broken leg before Marissa had even risen from her bed. She'd taken a rescue team with her, including Amos, her long-term friend and worker who'd been with her since her Matusadona days, and Joss had accompanied them.

Marissa was now helping in the front of the stables with the lunchtime feed for the orphans.

Zola smiled. "I can't quite believe that Sifiso just took a bottle from you.

They trust you after less than a day here," she said in her thick Afrikaans accent.

"Maybe they like their milk," Marissa said, as the young elephant took the bottle from her hands. "Hey. Not sure you're supposed to do that."

"*Ag* man, this is bliss. Beats the paperwork I need to get done. I will now have a saying that the only job that is worse than mucking out the elephant stables is the heap of paperwork involved in running a rehabilitation center," Danie said.

"Mucking out stables wins over paperwork any day," Marissa said.

"You muck out Amalee's stable?" Mitch asked from where he stood near them.

"Sure, since I was five years old. Dawn said if you own an animal, you need to learn how to look after it and know everything about it. I'll admit, she and now Brandon do it a lot more than I do. When we have an intern there, they get the honors. It's a rite of passage." Marissa laughed. Then she glanced at Mitch. "That's a look of surprise on your face."

Mitch nodded slowly. "I'd assumed that Dawn would do all the husbandry."

Marissa smiled. "I'm very hands-on. While Dawn does most of the work, she made me learn how to look after Amalee. I think in the beginning, it was as much to keep me near her so she could watch over me as it was to teach me skills. My mother had died when I was three, and Dawn came into my life when I was five. After Chad arrived, the stable became my refuge." Marissa looked at the baby elephant and realized she couldn't use feeding it to distract her from the intrusive thoughts that talking about Chad always brought her. She sighed.

Mitch frowned.

Marissa pushed a strand of hair that had come loose back under her hat and picked up the empty bottle that had been dropped on the ground. She avoided Mitch's questioning eyes and effectively shut the conversation down. One day she might share with him what had happened, but now was not the time.

A phone began to ring. "I have to get this. Hello, Zola speaking," Zola said as she put it on speaker so she could continue feeding the elephant.

"Samson Mathobeni ZimParks, Matusadona. How're you keeping?"

"*Great*," Zola said. "And you?

"Fine, except we have trouble. There's a dead elephant mother in the park on the edge of the lake. Her calf looks to be maybe eighteen to twenty-two months. Under two for sure—still milk dependent."

"*Ag shame,* man. What can we do to help?" Zola asked.

"We wanted to know if you could come take it," Samson said. "We have a team with the calf, and the state vet, Milo, is on his way. It will be a late-night rescue, because you are a distance from us, and there is a boat ride involved. Which brings its own challenges."

"We're up for another baby. You have a rubber duck that can fit a 900-kilo elephant and crew?" Zola said.

Danie was dancing on the spot, giving a *me, me* sign pointing at himself.

"No, but one of the private lodges has a pontoon boat they bought recently. It only has a small ten-horsepower motor, so it will be slow going. It's already on its way," Samson said. "We would prefer you to be there for the rescue. Any chance you can come today?"

"If Milo is on his way, you don't need three vets," Zola said, shaking her head. "But Danie will come, along with the rescue team, and they will be there as soon as they can."

There was a moment's silence, as if Samson was letting out a nervous breath. "Awesome. Is Mitch coming by any chance?"

"I'll ask him," Zola said.

"It would be neat if he can. There are lions in the area, so having him along for protection would be good. Tell them to go to Chawara Harbour; a speed-boat will meet them there to bring them across the water. It'll only take about thirty minutes," Samson said, sounding relieved.

"They'll leave soon as," Zola said. "It's still going to take us over seven hours, so we'll get there around"—she counted off on her fingers—"ten tonight if the drive up goes well. Is the baby going to last till then?"

"It better. Milo will certainly be doing everything he can. Thanks. See your team soon then," Samson said.

"*Totsiens,*" Zola said as she hung up.

"*Dankie,*" Danie said.

"*Ja,* see if you're still thanking me later when you've had no sleep. You owe me big time, *boetie*. I'll get things ready here; you go rescue the baby and bring it back alive," Zola said with a wry grin. "Mitch, you hear Samson? Can you accompany the team?"

"Sure. Marissa, do you want to come?" Mitch said. "It's not going to be pretty, but it will be a real experience."

"Of course," Marissa said. She couldn't believe her first full day would see her attending a rescue. It was a huge responsibility.

"It's going to be twenty-four hours of hard physical work, little sleep, and an emotional roller coaster ready to rattle even the most stable person, with no guarantee that the baby elephant will even live," Zola warned.

Marissa glanced at Mitch. The energy radiating from him was almost overwhelming, electric in its raw intensity. He wanted her to go with him.

She had not known that she'd waited her whole life for this opportunity to go and save a wild baby elephant.

Marissa, Mitch, Danie and Isaiah, one of the elephant rescue team workers, stretched their legs as they got out of the elephant rescue truck at the harbor. Marissa stared at the nondescript, one-story buildings, surrounded by boats on trailers and masts from yachts reaching for the stars, punctuated by the constant *ting-ting* of ropes tapping on metal. She frowned. Everywhere around was dark, but the harbor was lit up like it was Christmas.

"They made it easy for us, knowing we're coming," Mitch explained. "They must have a generator to have all these lights on. If you look in the morning, you'll see that many of the buildings in the harbor have solar, a trend forced by circumstances rather than want of environmental awareness."

Marissa nodded. "Like a beacon of hope."

Mitch smiled.

Danie checked cell coverage and called Zola. He put his phone on speaker. "We have arrived. It's already close to 11:30, and we had to navigate some large herds of elephant on the way."

Marissa didn't think she would ever tire of the sight, despite the herd making them later than planned. The wild elephant were amazing.

"Always a lot up that way. Be safe. Let me know when you are homeward bound," Zola said. "I've filled in Peta and Joss, and they said bring the baby home."

Danie smiled and hung up the call. "*Ja*, folks, let's get going then."

Mitch grabbed his backpack out of the truck and Marissa's smaller one, which he had given her from the anti-poaching unit store at the orphanage.

"Mitch," a man shouted and waved from the opposite end of the parking lot.

Mitch lifted his hand in acknowledgment and started walking.

Marissa stood to the side to keep out of the way. On the trip north Mitch had driven, and she'd sat in the front. They had switched with Danie and Isaiah and back again every two hours, each taking their turn in the back without the air-conditioning. She'd had a lot of time to speak with Mitch about what to expect and what was expected of her during the rescue.

She didn't take his directions lightly and was already taking a picture as the team loaded the equipment onto their backs. She'd seen the thick ropes that Isaiah had explained made it easy and safe for the calf during the rescue, along with a collection of sticks, water cans, and an attachable baby elephant blanket. They left a teddy bear in the back of the truck. Danie had said that every elephant they rescued got a toy of their own once they got into the truck, and that it stayed with them in the stables.

She thought that was a heartwarming gesture.

Marissa adjusted the straps on her backpack, making sure her camera was free of obstructions, and followed the others. She understood that Mitch was taking a gamble by allowing her to come on the rescue.

He didn't know her well yet but was trusting her with this experience.

Mitch laughed at something Danie had said, drawing her attention back to him. For an Australian, he seemed very much at home in Africa.

"Hi Mitch. Samson instructed me to give you this radio when you got here," Banele, the national parks employee said, nodding in a gesture of respect. "Come with me."

Banele led them to where a speedboat waited. On the front, it had a large, mounted spotlight.

"A new addition for the rescue? Or for anti-poaching?" Mitch asked.

"Neither," a tall Indian man she hadn't noticed before said from right behind the boat. "Ragan Naidoo, owner of Tiger Fish Lodge, and this belongs to the camp. Our lodge is inside Matusadona. We use it for emergencies. It comes in handy for avoiding hippos at night."

"I'm Mitch. Nice to meet you," he put his hand out. "You think your boat will take a baby elephant too?" Mitch asked

"Not this one. Samson borrowed a barge boat, so you're good there." Rajan flicked up a tarpaulin at the front. "We have a bigger motor to attach to the barge, give it some go when we come back."

Rajan climbed into the boat, motioning for the others to get on board. "Find a place to sit. Mitch, get hold of Samson on the radio while I get one more thing from the marina."

Rajan climbed out of the boat and disappeared up the dock, and Mitch called on the radio, "Samson, come in. Mitch here."

A few seconds later, a voice crackled through the radio. "Good to hear you. Glad you arrived."

"Us too. You got that baby ready yet?" Mitch asked.

"You're not going to believe this, but no," Samson said. "We can talk about it when you get here. Rajan knows where to come."

"See you soon," Mitch said, looking at Danie. "Wonder what the holdup is? By now they should have the elephant baby on the boat."

Marissa frowned. Whatever was happening didn't sound good.

"Probably another elephant interfering," Isaiah said. "They went in on boats so they don't have a *bakkie* to chase it away."

"Probably," Mitch said. "We'll know soon enough. Get a seat; I think we're in for quite a ride," he said as he climbed into the second row of seats and held out his hand to help her in beside him.

"Excuse my weapons. These bench seats are tricky," Mitch said. His gun bag spilled across his lap and onto Marissa's as he tucked their backpacks around them.

"I've been around guns all my life. We have mountain lions back home," Marissa said. "It's not a problem. That's assuming you have the safety catch on."

Isaiah and Danie got into the next bench seat, fitting their gear in where they could, including on top of the new motor.

"Careful on that," Mitch warned. "Don't want to break anything, it costs a bomb."

Isaiah carefully lifted his bag off the motor and put it between him and Danie.

Rajan jogged back down the dock, and Banele, who had been on the dock, climbed in next to him in the front seat behind the spotlight. "Right, let's go. All six of us are on board."

Both engines roared to life. The motors purred in the water, and the sound which should have been alien in the still of the night became a dull throbbing.

The night worker on the dock threw them the rope. They were free.

Rajan turned the boat southwest. Even before they left the harbor, Banele had the light on the water, sweeping slowly back and forth, looking for unseen danger lurking in the deep.

Mitch held one arm on his weapons and the other braced behind Marissa. She was thankful for both the warmth and the support. Despite the water looking calm, the boat tended to skip along, kissing the surface periodically instead of gliding over it, jarring her as it slammed back down.

The sky above Kariba was so clear and filled with stars. The lack of electricity had its perks. It brought into perspective one of the extreme differences between Africa and Nevada—in one place, there was a choice to switch the lights off, and in the other there was not.

Elephant were meant to be safe here, yet out there, in the dark, was a baby elephant in need of rescue.

She turned and put her face into the wind, and she smelled the freshness of the air, trying hard to ease her worry.

She hoped that they were not too late.

The speedboat hit the shore with a thump, and Ragan lifted the engines and cut them. Banele passed the spotlight to Mitch, flicked on his own torch, and jumped to the shore, taking the rope with him. Holding on, he ran up the floodlit bank, while another man came out from the reeds and helped him to put the loop over a big spike that had been sunk into the riverbank.

Marissa looked left and right along with Mitch as he swept the light across the shore. There were other spikes, and she could see multiple places where the reeds were flattened. She suspected this was a frequent stopping place for the Tiger Fish Lodge and their charters.

"From here, we walk," Rajan said as he climbed off the boat, taking with him an open-carry .303 rifle and a large flashlight.

She smiled. Being brought up on a ranch had its advantages. One of her father's hunting rifles looked pretty much the same, gleaming wooden stock with a black barrel. They were dependable weapons and had brought down many elk and deer for the pot.

"So, you're guide and lodge owner?" Mitch commented as he put down the spotlight and switched it off, and Banele shone his powerful torch at the boat, so everyone had light to disembark

"Don't we all start out like that—work our way up because we love it?" Ragan said. "I hate to admit that I don't get to do the guiding as much as I used to. I'm always stuck with the administration side of the lodge."

Marissa nodded. She understood how business time tended to overtake the more enjoyable experiences. Mitch held his hand out to help her off the boat, and she accepted it.

"Thanks," Marissa said, then stood aside and pulled her Maglite from her backpack. The solid dry soil beneath her feet a surprise, it wasn't muddy or like river sand. Mitch had taken one of his rifles from its bag and held it in his other hand. The cased rifle remained over his shoulder on a strap. Following Ragan and Banele, he lit the way, and she fell into step behind him.

"Keep close to me or Danie," he reminded her.

Marissa's nodded in acknowledgement.

Danie and Isaiah came up after them. Each of the rescue party had their own supplies on their backs, just as she carried her own personal rations, a sleeping bag, and a ground sheet.

They detoured past a large herd of buffalo, their powerful torches picking them up easily. Their eyes were clearly visible, with a reddish-brown muted reflection from the spotlights. She wondered why these animals, which everyone warned her were so dangerous, didn't react to their presence; they continued sitting, like big cattle chewing the cud, dark lumps in the grass.

As if reading her mind, Mitch said, "This is a breeding herd, and they have settled for the night. We're not sending any danger signals. They know we're here and they're happy enough to keep an eye on us as we move through. It's the old *dagga boys* you've got to watch. Cantankerous bastards."

Next, they frightened a genet, with a beautiful spotted coat, an extremely long tail, and huge, bright eyes. When Ragan shone his light, its eyes were reflective and bright green.

The most delightful animals were the bush babies, staring back at them from the trees they passed under, with small, bright orange eyes. They seemed to defy gravity as they bounced from one branch to another with such elegance, despite the dark.

Mitch explained, "When we see game at night, you don't keep the light on any of them for long, only to check where they are, as lights mean that lions and other predators can see them clearly."

"Even the bush babies? Surely they are safe in their trees?" Marissa asked.

"Owls, snakes, *leguaans*—they can all get to them," Mitch said.

"*Leguaans*?" Marissa asked.

"Rock monitors," Mitch said. "It's the South African name for them."

"I didn't think of those as predators. Lions, leopards, wild dog, hyena—that's what I think of when you say predators," Marissa admitted.

"Oh, they come in all forms here," Mitch said.

They had walked for about half an hour before they could hear the commotion.

Elephants were trumpeting. The ground rumbling as they communicated with each other and other herds in the area. Dust clouds rose above the artificial lighting that came into view.

"Something's wrong," Mitch said. "Stay really close to me." He reached out and drew her closer behind him with his torch hand.

In the front, Ragan began to sweep his torch quicker, scanning with wider arcs across the ground and into the bush. Banele and Mitch matched the pace.

Marissa's heart beat faster. She kept close to Mitch.

Breaking through the trees, they found the national parks team standing to the side, close to the lights that illuminated the agitated elephant herd in front of them.

A man walked to meet them halfway. "Good to see you, Mitch, Isiah." He nodded to the rest of the team. "Samson, ZimParks."

"Danie, the vet."

"Marissa, the photographer," she said raising her camera.

Mitch smile. "What's the problem?"

Samson pointed to the clearing. "These guys came in just on sunset and haven't moved. The baby's still with its dead mother. The other elephant have been trying hard to get her to stand, as if by pushing her they can wake her up and make her take care of her child."

Marissa looked at the herd illuminated by the lights. Kicking up dust, the elephant were clearly affected by the death of one of their own.

"A mixture of mums, aunties, and babies." Samson said. "No male travelled with them. A family herd."

"*Ag*, shame," Danie said. "They're saying their goodbyes. Come morning, they will go to the water, drink, and leave. If we're lucky, hopefully, they will adopt the baby if it's strong enough. How weak is it? Will it make it till then?"

"The little one is still on its feet," Samson said. "Hasn't gone down like we feared. The mum had been dead for at least a day before we became aware of them. We wondered if this was their herd, and they were scared to come back until the dark tonight."

"I think there's still hope," Danie said. "Did Milo also think that we should wait it out?"

Marissa frowned. She was glad there was still hope, but she worried for the little baby waiting longer for much needed milk.

Samson nodded. "You know him?"

Danie nodded. "We've met a few times now."

"He said to wait. Not to drive the herd off. There've been hyenas circling. The elephant have driven them away a few times already."

Hyenas? Marissa took another step closer to Mitch, her arm touching against his. She knew stories of hyenas sneaking into campsites at night and biting people's faces in attack. She'd watched documentaries when she was younger of them beginning to eat their prey before it was dead.

She shivered.

"I'm not a fan of the hyena," Mitch said, putting his hand on her back in a protective gesture. "But rather them than wild dogs sniffing around. We'll keep watch and give a warning shot if needed. Hopefully, the elephant will keep chasing them till morning, without us having to take action. "

"That too," Danie said.

"Come sunrise, we can go in there and get the baby. I think the chances of this herd taking it with them are slim, given the presence of the elephant there now. No one is nursing him yet," Mitch said.

"True, but they know the baby is weak already, and if he's not of their herd, his chances are even less," Danie said.

Samson nodded.

"Have you checked the bushes on the other side to see if there are other elephant there?" Marissa asked. "Maybe there are more that we can't see that haven't come in yet?"

Samson shook his head. "We tried, but there was a herd of buffalo, and my scouts saw lion tracks. We aborted the idea and decided to just wait, see what happened."

Mitch rolled his head on his shoulders. "It's going to be a long night."

"Too true," Samson said.

"We'll set up a small camp here. Give your guys some space," Mitch said. "Who's on guard duty?"

"We are taking turns, stoking the fire. There are worse places to wait for the night to pass than in the Matusadona," Samson said.

Marissa looked across the faces of her travel party; most were nodding in agreement, and they seemed content to simply wait while she wanted action *now* to save the baby.

She had to be realistic. The herd milling around it, there was no way they could even approach the little thing.

Was it running out of time while they played the waiting game?

Would their waiting cost that baby its life?

The humans in the small camp were settling in for a few hours' sleep. Danie had taken first watch with Isaiah. A small fire burned brightly between where Mitch had put his sleeping bag and across the fire where Rajen and Banele had put theirs.

"You can put yours this side of the fire, next to mine," Mitch said.

"Why?" Marissa asked. "What's wrong with where I'm standing?"

He shook his head. "It's too far away from me. I can't react fast enough should something happen during the night. I can't protect you if I can't reach you."

"I can look after myself. I'm a sixth Dan in Taekwondo," she said, flipping her ground mat open. "No one's getting one over me if I can help it."

"I'd like to see you try using martial arts on the wild animals, especially a hyena," Mitch said.

She stood up straight and looked at him. He wasn't smiling.

"Ah, okay, I'll give you that," she said, moving closer and then settling down, her bag touching his. "I wasn't thinking of those."

"Keep your shoes on, just in case you need to run during the night," he said. "It also stops scorpions getting in them."

"Scorpions? Are you trying to scare me now?"

"Just keep them on," he warned, then turned his back to her.

She still had her own space but was within easy reach of him. She accepted that Mitch didn't want her scared.

When a roar sounded somewhere in the darkness, Mitch whispered, "Lions."

Marissa stilled.

Next, it was hyenas whooping close by. Jackals called to one another, an airy, forlorn wail of sadness that sounded like children crying. There were even the barks of baboons squabbling as they resettled in their roosts high in the mopane trees after a leopard had hunted one from its sleeping place. Marissa inched closer to Mitch.

It had been a restless night for Marissa. The sounds of branches breaking and larger animals moving through the bushveld kept her awake.

"That's a tiny Pearl-spotted owl. Look up in that tree." Mitch proved his point by shining his torch up into the mopane tree above them, and sure enough, there was the little thing.

Marissa moved closer to Mitch each time she woke. His warmth called to her, and somehow, she knew that she was safe.

CHAPTER 20
AN INCOMPARABLE EXPERIENCE

MATUSADONA GAME RESERVE, KARIBA, ZIMBABWE

30 September 2014 – 04:30

Something tapped Marissa lightly on her shoulder.

"Wake up. You need to see this," Mitch's voice cut into the darkness. "Get your camera; the pictures will be worth it. It's almost sunrise."

Marissa opened her eyes. She lay on her side, her back resting against Mitch's torso and leg, as if she belonged there with him.

She jerked away. Now that she was awake, it was a different story. She was grateful for the predawn light so that Mitch couldn't see her blush.

The darkness of night was tinged with the promise of brightness from the coming sunrise. The sand beneath her ground sheet was hard and cool, despite the sleeping bag she had wrapped around herself, and the second one Mitch had tucked around her sometime during the night. Her back was warm where Mitch's body had pressed into hers.

The elephant were no longer trumpeting. Now there was quiet communication between them, rumbles that she felt in the earth.

Sadness.

"Did the baby make it through the night?" Marissa asked.

"Ja," Danie answered. She jumped, hearing his voice so close to where she lay, and then she sat up, turning her head to see him standing behind them.

Mitch cleared his throat. "Did you wake the others?"

"I'm on my way now," Danie said with a hint of laughter in his voice. "Thought I'd give you two a little time to get up before I did that."

Marissa yawned. "Can't believe I fell asleep." She stood up and stretched like a cat. Her sleeping bags dropped to the ground. She turned and held out her hand. Mitch accepted her help to stand, although he didn't need it, nor did he give her any of his weight. He held on a little longer than necessary once he stood tall. He reached down, picked up the sleeping bags, and gave them a good shake to get rid of any insects and other animals that had been on the floor, then put them into his backpack.

Danie smiled. Then he turned and crowed like a rooster as he walked a little way from them to the other side of the small fire they had kept lit, to ensure predators stayed away during the night.

"That's quite a wakeup call," Marissa said as she smiled.

Mitch looked at Marissa. "I'll give you kudos for coming along and being able to sleep out here. Most visitors we get wouldn't handle what we've thrown at you so far, and they definitely wouldn't be smiling when they knew what was coming today, with the rescue."

"I guess I'm not your average tourist," Marissa said. "Thank you for last night. I do appreciate the effort you went to, to keep me safe and for keeping me warm. I wasn't expecting the temperature to plummet so much."

"It's because we're so close to the water," Mitch said. "And I agree, you're definitely not average. You have been nothing but interesting since you arrived, and the fact that you have an elephant of your own should have been a bit of a giveaway."

She snorted as she swallowed a laugh at the look on his face, then couldn't hold it in and let out a small snigger, covering it with her hand to keep it quiet as she turned from him and looked around. Isaiah was boiling water for coffee while Danie loaded his backpack. Ragan and Banele were rising a little slower. There seemed to be no hurry in their camp. She got her camera out and looked through the lens at Mitch, taking a few photos. "Sleep is for those who are not busy living a full life. When do we start the rescue?"

A rumble of a laugh came from Mitch as he bent and grabbed the ground sheets. "Oh god, she's a morning person. Isaiah is the coffee ready?" he asked in a louder voice.

"Patience. Isaiah has a big fire going. I'll get more water. Ladies first," Danie said as he handed Marissa a mug and offered her a container of what looked like baked bread.

"Take a rusk too," Danie said. "Nothing beats this for breakfast. And don't go giving your coffee to Mitch. That's yours; he can wait his turn." Danie turned to Mitch and grinned. "Rough night?"

Mitch threw the folded ground sheet at him, hitting him square in the chest, causing Danie to nearly drop the container, as he laughed.

Marissa took the squat rectangular biscuit that was so hard she had to dunk it in her coffee to soften it enough to bite without breaking a tooth.

It was delicious.

She looked towards the herd as she blew on the hot drink. The sky had begun to lighten, and hues of gold, pink, and lilac brandished across the horizon.

"Once coffee and rusks are done, Banele and I will be at the boat, getting that motor sorted," Ragan said.

"*Ja*, okay," Danie said. "We should be there soon, I'm sure."

The elephant herd were milling around, and an eerie silence had descended. Each adult or juvenile walked past the fallen mother and laid its trunk over her and then touched the baby as if saying goodbye. Slowly, they were moving towards the water. Marissa put her coffee down on the ground, grabbed her camera, and began photographing the heartbreaking scene.

Eventually, the last and biggest of the herd, the matriarch, touched the baby and walked away.

Marissa's arms shook, and she held back the tears.

"That's why we're here," Mitch said quietly, touching her shoulder. "To take that baby from nature and make sure that little one gets a second chance at life. No matter how deeply elephant are connected, this time they don't believe they can save the baby. The next time they pass here, they will wonder where her bones are when they caress the mother's in passing, paying their respects."

The baby didn't follow the herd.

It stayed with its trunk on its mother's body in a sad display of mourning, as if it had accepted its fate alongside hers.

The elephant herd didn't look back. As silent as ghosts, they blended into the ancient forest, their grey color serving as camouflage; they disappeared.

Marissa captured it all on her camera. She wiped a tear from her cheek and sniffed.

They had left the baby.

Its chance of living in the wild was zero.

Mitch passed her the abandoned coffee mug and a tissue. "Drink it all down. It might be a while till we can get breakfast."

"Thank you," she said.

"*Ag*, I think give it ten minutes; then we can dart it," Danie said. "He's been through enough. The sooner we get him home, the better. He looks underweight, closer to the upper 700-kilo range. We'll go see if Milo agrees or not."

"Wait here with Isaiah," Mitch said to her as he and Danie took off, walking quickly towards Samson and his park board's rustic campsite, where, like at theirs, everyone was just waking and getting organized for the capture.

The shouts started before Mitch was even halfway to Samson's team.

Mitch had his hunting rifle up to his shoulder so fast and shot the ground in front of the hyena that had slunk toward the baby. A whip of dust lifted close to the animal. It stopped.

Marissa jumped at the loud sound, unnatural in the environment they were in.

The hyena darted away, its lopsided gait evident in its departure.

From the bushes came a cowardly cackle.

Mitch shook his head.

Samson met him halfway there and lifted a radio to his mouth, probably relaying what had happened to Milo. Mitch knelt in the dust with Danie and took his second gun off his shoulder. He loaded it with something Samson passed him.

Marissa was frowning as she stood still, clutching her camera, but not taking any pictures. Her knuckles whitened.

"They have done this many, many times before," Isaiah explained. "Mitch doesn't miss. Even if the animal is running. That's why Milo lets him shoot the dart when he's with us. Milo is the state vet and should do it, but they know Mitch used to be military, and ZimParks relies on it. Tranquilizer drugs are expensive, and there is not a lot of money around in wildlife rescue."

"Does he always go on rescues with you?" Marissa asked, lifting her camera to look at Mitch through the lens.

"He used to come with us when we first started, but as his anti-poaching business got busier, he had less opportunity to join us. It is either maNdhlovu or Mitch in our team who takes the shot. Danie can shoot, but Zola is more accurate."

Isaiah threw water on the fire and kicked sand on it to put it out. He lined the backpacks up together.

"I can carry mine," Marissa said.

"*Aikona,* you'll be busy taking pictures of the rescue. The ZimParks guys will bring them with us to the boat," Isaiah said, shaking his head.

Marissa nodded her understanding. "What about Milo?"

"He can shoot, but that one, he's like a *dassie* in the sun—lazy. He's a good doctor with the animals," Isaiah said. "But with people, he's like an aardvark. Awkward, and it's hard to determine just what he's about."

Marissa laughed. "Tell me you don't say that to his face."

"Of course not, but I tell you because you're going to be family if you bring your elephant home," Isaiah said.

Marissa nodded. An interesting concept that if she brought Amalee home to Africa, she would become part of a new family.

Ten long minutes later, Marissa watched as Mitch and Samson crept closer to the elephant baby.

Marissa only knew the shot was fired because she could see the bright blue dart that stuck in the baby elephant's rump. She would rather an animal be shot with a tranquilizer than a bullet but didn't think she would be able to do what Mitch had just done.

"What now?" she asked Isaiah, as he stood silently next to her.

"Wait for the signal. Then we help. You can carry one of the water cans but be ready to run. It is dangerous still in case the elephant herd come back," Isaiah warned.

Marissa nodded. She checked the strap on her camera to make sure it was secure and lifted one of the water cans he had placed at her feet.

Danie motioned them over.

They raced towards where Mitch was.

The baby staggered. There was a little chaos as many hands helped lay it down on his side. Then everyone stepped back and let the rescue team work.

Isaiah knelt down and put a stick into its trunk to keep it breathing. "*Yebo,* come on now, baby."

"*Lowo-olwa,* he who fights," one of the ZimParks workers said. "Lowla. We called him that yesterday when a hyena came close, and he chased it away."

"Good name," Danie said as he laid the elephant's ear over its eye, to protect the eye and also to calm it, so even if it was still a little awake, it wouldn't be traumatized.

"You can stay that side of Lowla and pour the water over his ear and body, little at a time, if you want to, Marissa. This poor baby is clearly dehydrated and stressed," Danie explained. "You can see the trauma showing on its sunken forehead."

The ZimParks biologists needed blood samples, which Milo quickly drew from the back of Lowla's ear. She watched closely as he took hairs from its tail.

She put her water down and took pictures.

"You can touch him," Mitch said. "Just stay by the head where Danie is."

She stroked the baby. Like the elephant at the nursery, it was hairier than Amalee, and it had streaks of thick mud in the folds of its skin.

Isaiah put a second twig in the calf's trunk. "Come on, Lowla. Don't give up now."

"Ready to wake him?" Danie asked.

Milo nodded and pushed the antidote into the elephant's small ear.

Within a moment, Danie smiled. "It's working."

The small elephant struggled to rise and was trying to headbutt Milo and Isaiah, who were monitoring his breathing.

"He fights us even now," Milo said.

"He'll need every bit of that spirit in the next few weeks to get him through," Mitch said, attaching the elephant blanket and securing all the straps.

Once the elephant was on his feet, Mitch on the one side and Samson on the other, they guided Lowla back along the path they had made towards the river. Danie was in front, and Marissa was bringing up the rear, with Isaiah behind her.

Walking calmly behind him, the ZimParks team had picked up their back-packs from camp and carried them to the water, just as Isaiah had said they would.

The sun was up now, the heat baking them all. Workers poured water over the elephant blanket. While a lot went into the fabric, a fair bit dripped into the soft sand, disappearing quickly as if it had never been there.

"Keeping him cool is our main concern." Mitch dropped back to explain to Marissa. "If the baby's temperature escalates, he'll collapse from heat stroke."

"There is so much that goes into a rescue," Marissa said. "And it worries me that we are so far away from a road for this one."

"Actually, this is not a bad spot. We've been in worse places. Ask Danie about Sifiso's rescue, and how he was up to his waist in thick mud. We had to pull that vet out with a tractor and ropes after we'd rescued the baby."

"Time for a top-up," Milo said as they got within sight of the riverbank.

A fat hippo looked at them from where it munched on the reeds before running for the safety of the water and plunging in.

"*Eish*, we'll need to watch where that one is when we leave," Samson said.

"Truly," Banele said, nodding.

"Come on, Lowla," Milo said as he injected more tranquilizer.

Lowla flapped his ears at the sting of the injection, but he remained upright, flanked closely by his minders.

Rajan had been busy, and the new motor was in place. The metal barriers that kept people in the boat had been removed. All they had to do was guide the baby elephant up the makeshift walkway of sand that had been shoveled from the shore against the transport.

Marissa eyed the boat. Would it hold the weight of the little elephant and the rescue team? What would happen if it bottomed out? That would be dangerous for the men, having to push it into deeper water.

She knew that just because you couldn't see a crocodile didn't mean one wasn't there.

Perhaps her thousand worries were unfounded. As Mitch had said, they had been saving babies for a while, so maybe they just knew.

Marissa held her breath as Mitch walked next to Lowla, encouraging him up, and into the boat where Rajan had put a thick rubber mat to hide the small gap between the ramp and the pontoon boat. One false move and Lowla could become crocodile breakfast.

The calf walked onto the boat as if he'd done this before. Marissa let out a breath of relief. "Will Lowla be awake or sleeping for the trip back across?"

"Back to sleep and tied down," Danie said. "There's room enough for him to lie flat on this boat. We can't have him bolt off into the water. We wouldn't be able get him back."

Milo gave him more drugs, and the elephant was soon on its side. The team quickly surrounded the baby, as again once it went down. Isaiah blew into its trunk and put the same stick in there.

"Why are you blowing?" Marissa asked as she took another photo.

"I did that to the very first elephant we rescued, as if to give it my breath and help it through. I do it every time now. We haven't lost one yet in transit," Isaiah said.

If she brought Amalee on the plane, would someone take the time to blow in her trunk and make sure she wasn't lost, too?

"And we won't start today," Danie said, oblivious to Marissa's unvoiced worries about her own elephant. "Come on. Get his feet tied loosely and a strap across him so he doesn't slide, then we can get going. The faster we get him home, the better."

Inky skies, twinkling stars, and the night's coolness had been their companions on the way from the harbor; now light, anxiety, and heat accompanied the boat.

A deep feeling of nausea in Marissa's stomach wasn't subsiding—fear for Lowla's life. So many things could go wrong. The baby could wake up or roll off the boat. A hippo could attack their boat. She took a deep breath, trying hard to still her mind.

Mitch tucked her into his body a little more securely and squeezed her shoulder, as if he had felt her anxiety. Knew what she was going through.

She snuggled a little closer to his warmth.

She knew they were just sharing comfort, sharing an experience, but she also knew that this was a man she could care for. No one had ever taken the time to understand that owning an elephant wasn't a full-time job; it was a lifelong obsession. And the big word in there was *life*.

But Mitch seemed to understand what her elephant meant to her when they talked. He was an Australian living in Africa, and she would be an American there, at least for a while. Hope for a new friendship was a dangerous feeling to let free.

She locked it deep inside. She would let it out slowly as they got to know each other more.

If she was to bring Amalee to the lodge and rewild her here, there would be plenty of time to get to know each other; they didn't need to rush it now.

The boat went a little faster than a snail's pace, as promised; with the new motor attached, it was pushing at about fifteen knots.

Rajan was asking for more, but the ripples in the water and the pontoon's design meant that greater speed would make the structure rock. The motor's pitch changed again as he dialed the revs back. Better to make it there alive than capsize because they were pushing it. She added another title to Rajan's name: *Boat Whisperer*.

Marissa silently took more photos. She peered into the distance through her lens, and could see the natural harbor. Around the central working buildings, to the one side, magnificent houseboats were moored safely, and boat works on the opposite side, showed that there was utilization of the beautiful blue lake. There were other craft coming in and going out of the entrance. "Almost there," she said and looked at her watch. "It's already seven o'clock."

They tied up to the jetty that they had left from, and Ragan gave the all clear that they could move as he cut the engine.

The sound of the boat's engine was replaced with the noises of a busy harbor. People called to one another. Ropes still pinged against aluminum masts, and other boats' engines roaring to life. Someone hammered rhythmically on metal, the echo bouncing around the boat yard.

After removing all the strapping, Milo and Danie rechecked Lowla's vitals.

"Mitch, please back the truck up as close as possible. Ragan, can you help Isaiah bring the ramp we use to get animals onto the truck? Lowla needs to be able to walk off the boat, onto the wharf," Danie instructed.

Marissa stood out of the way while the men worked together, knowing that each moment was precious. They were certainly a well-trained crew for a stand-by rescue team.

The wooden ramp was soon bridging the gap between the boat and the land. Milo walked up and down it, and when he was happy it was steady, he administered half an antidote.

The baby was less responsive this time, a testament to its failing strength.

"Come on, Lowla; you can do this," Marissa said quietly from her spot observing, out of the way from where the action was all taking place. "You're more than halfway on your journey home to safety already. One more vehicle change..."

As if the baby elephant could hear her encouragement, he gave a final push and got up. Milo and Danie helped guide him off the boat.

Isaiah and Rajan joined in, and together the men made their way towards the parking lot, walking the elephant to the truck.

Baby Lowla made it up the ramp before collapsing onto his knees. They maneuvered him onto his side, on the flat bed of the rescue truck and secured the straps.

Milo gave him the rest of the antidote, but Lowla didn't try to stand. Just lay on his side, too exhausted to fight anymore.

"Is he okay?" Marissa asked

"He will be. It's safer he stays down for the trip; our team will make sure Lowla is comfortable the whole way," Mitch said.

Samson and his men had brought the ramp back to the truck. After strapping it in, he shook the team's hands, and then, finally, he stood in front of Mitch. "I knew when Peta left us from the Matusadona that she would do special things, and this orphanage, it is a good thing. Please pass on my thanks to both Joss and Peta." He turned his back and motioned for Mitch to walk a little away. Mitch caught Marissa's arm and brought her with him.

"You can trust Marissa; she's hopefully bringing one of the stolen elephant home to the rescue center soon." He left his hand on her elbow.

Samson nodded. "Did you get my last poaching statistics?" he asked quietly.

Mitch nodded.

"Those who are in charge increased the area of capture for the call for elephant calves of around three to be corralled at Hwange for a game capture program. Now it includes us."

Mitch frowned. And rocked on his heels. "That's—unfortunate."

Marissa went to ask a question, and Mitch shook his head quickly. She kept quiet.

"Many of us rangers are not happy with this new situation. Something is fishy, just like when they took babies to China. I had hoped I wouldn't have to act on it at all. I detest the whole idea of moving elephant anywhere," Samson said, his voice was still hushed. "I know I could be fired working with you, but I can't do this. I will not capture a healthy baby and rip it from its family. I'll email you the poaching statistics when I can."

"It's because of men like you that we can do something about it, and it's not blindsiding us," Mitch said. "Anything we can do to save those babies, we will."

Samson put out his hand to Mitch and shook it.

Together, they turned and began walking back to the group. Marissa accompanied them, but her mind was working overtime.

Secrecy. What was going on?

Would her elephant be as safe as they had claimed? Or was this threat only about babies? This sounded like it was bigger than her rewilding Amalee. Bigger than anything Mitch, Peta or Joss had mentioned to her.

"Remind Peta that when she can afford to pay me to let me know. I'd love to join the rescue center," Samson added a little louder, clearly for others to hear.

"What, and leave here? And your unstable government pension fund?" Mitch laughed. It was common knowledge that the government pension scheme had crashed and was worth nothing with the hyperinflation the country was going through. "Come on, Samson, you told me that your father worked here too; why would you want to leave?"

"Peta and her rescue center are making a real difference. Some days, I feel like I don't make that difference for the animals anymore," Samson admitted.

Joss dropped his voice low again. "You being in a position to make these types of calls with the wildlife, calling in Peta instead of sending the elephant to the Hwange round-up? That is making a difference. Don't be so harsh on yourself; running a game reserve is hard. Lesser men than you have crumbled under the pressure."

Marissa looked from Samson to Mitch. Something big was happening, and she hoped that soon Mitch would open up to her about what it was.

Mitch tossed the keys to Isaiah as he walked towards the truck.

"Right, we're out of here. Thanks, Samson. I'll be in touch, and I'll talk to Peta," Mitch said.

"Thank you," Samson said, stepping away.

"It was lovely meeting you all," Marissa said, "even under these sad circumstances."

"You joining Isaiah in the front with the air conditioning or staying in the back with us?" Mitch asked Marissa, who was still standing in the driveway.

"Stupid question. In the back with Lowla. And you," Marissa said as she reached up to grab the hand he offered and scrambled to get onto the back of the truck.

"Samson. Don't forget to let Peta know those details," Mitch called just as Danie pulled the back doors closed.

Danie tapped on the glass window between the cab and the back, letting Isaiah know that he could drive.

A comfortable stable was waiting for the little elephant Lowla, and it was now their responsibility to make sure he survived the long journey.

CHAPTER 21
A REWARDING EXPERIENCE

YINGWE RIVER LODGE, ANIMAL RESCUE AND REHABILITATION CENTER, BINGA, ZIMBABWE

30 September 2014 – 19:00

The sun had set, and the stars shone in the cloudless sky. It was twilight as they finally drove through the gates of the orphanage. Isaiah parked in front of the isolation section. He switched off the engine.

Marissa hadn't noticed how much the truck vibrated until it had stopped. She sighed in relief. The first part of the little elephant's ordeal was almost over.

Lowla had remained calm the whole way back to the lodge, even when they had to stop and add fuel from the extra cans they carried. They ate from their rations in their packs, minimizing stops. While the meals were interesting, they were not something that Marissa wanted to have too often. She made a mental note to do something about the rations the anti-poaching units were receiving, and to include their nutritional needs into her charity foundation work.

The small elephant stayed lying down during the journey; they encouraged him to lift up only once, and then they settled him back down on his other side.

The drip Danie had set up, even before they had driven out of the harbor gates was still in; the baby receiving much-needed fluids. And Danie had changed the bags a few times during the ten hours, always ensuring the flow was strong.

Isaiah was scratching behind the elephant's ear. "We are home."

The baby lay on his side, the teddy bear tucked into his legs.

Mitch opened the back, and Peta climbed in.

"Hey Peta, meet Lowla," Marissa said. "He's kept us company all the way from the Mat- something-or-other game reserve. Don't come too close to any of us; we stink."

Peta laughed. "It's Africa—we pretty much can guarantee body odors." She stroked Lowla's ear. "Time to move into the nice stable."

Despite the late hour, the staff and volunteers were crowding around the truck. All were getting their first glimpse of the new orphan. The ramp was lowered, and Lowla stood up and allowed himself to be guided slowly off the back and into the waiting stable.

Once Lowla was safely inside, the truck was unpacked and most of the volunteers drifted away; their parts in the orphan's life would start in the morning.

Danie, Peta, Zola, and Isaiah were still with Lowla, and Amos had joined them. Marissa stood to the side, keeping her distance as they worked.

Mitch knocked on the fencing of the stable. "It's metal now. Ndhlovy smashed the original wooden setup. The isolation area is meant to keep the new orphan separate from the others, but Ndhlovy's always got other plans."

"She broke it?" Marissa asked, and Mitch sat on a hay bale alongside her.

"To get to a baby," Mitch said, sitting. "Peta was ropeable, but Joss was kind of expecting it. I'll bet you he'll remind her about it when he sees she put this little guy in here."

As if he knew they had been talking about him, Joss came to the edge of the isolation area. "Not sure why you bother putting them in here; you know Ndhlovy will come and settle him anyway."

Peta looked up from where she stood next to Lowla as the elephant stood on the indoor scale. "I'm tired. I had hardly any sleep last night, worrying about this one, and I don't want to hear about your elephant and her bad habits. Right now, all I want to do is settle Lowla in his stable and make him as comfortable as we can. Give him a few more packets of fluid and get some milk into him. And I would like more sleep."

"Yes, dear. You know Ndhlovy will do what she always does. I'll keep out of your way so you can do your magic," Joss said, hiding a smile behind his hand as he leaned against the fence near where Marissa and Mitch sat.

"Only 750 kilos. Not good," Isaiah said.

"He's still dehydrated and in need of both milk and food," Peta said as she wrote the weight on the new page.

"Danie estimated upper 700-kilos on site; he was nearly right," Isaiah said.

"He's been doing this long enough to make a decent guess," Peta said.

Lowla had already taken to following the handlers, going wherever they needed him. His energy was gone. He'd fought a good fight, and they had made it home. Now they had to make sure that he didn't slip into depression by using Peta's skills, and her team's tenacity, and the wiles of a certain elephant who was always there to help when needed.

Amos offered some hay to Lowla, who ate a few more mouthfuls before he began to lean against Isaiah.

"Amos, I'd like you and Isaiah to take shifts with him tonight to settle him in," Peta said.

"You know you will be here too, maNdhlovu; you never leave us alone with the new babies," Isaiah said with a grin.

"Normally I'd say 'guilty as charged' but I'm exhausted," Peta said as she adjusted the flow of the drip. "I can hardly keep awake. We're against the clock, though. We all know that at sunrise, Ndhlovy will arrive, and we'll need to remove the drip and let nature take its course."

"I thought that having Zola and Danie here still would slow her down, after we got home," Joss admitted. Then a mischievous grin appeared. "Seems instead, with your Foundation backing, you, Ms. Marissa have helped create another two monsters in elephant rescue. Look at those *laaities*—they are not leaving this stable tonight either, are they?"

Peta rolled her eyes at Zola and Danie. "Youngsters? Seriously? Way to make me feel ancient." She flipped Joss the bird.

Mitch and Marissa both laughed.

CHAPTER 22
SETTLING IN

YINGWE RIVER LODGE, ANIMAL RESCUE AND REHABILITATION CENTER, BINGA, ZIMBABWE

30 September 2014 – 22:00

Three hours had passed since Marissa and the whole rescue team had returned to Yingwe River Lodge. Gone was the frantic atmosphere that had followed the arrival of the new baby elephant, replaced with a quiet calmness of the every day. Inside the elephant stables, the lighting had been dimmed, and elephant handlers who were with their allocated charges, used head-lamps to minimize disruptions to the others, all settled into their beds for the night.

Marissa now sat inside the isolation stable next to a yawning Peta on a blanket protecting them from any thorns that had been collected in the hay that was used to cover the floor as bedding. While she hadn't been given a head lamp, being included and able to be one of Lowla's close companions for a while brought an unexpected peace to the end the first part of the rescue.

Mitch, Joss and Bongani were inside the enclosure, their backs against the fencing for support. Giving the elephant a little more space to allow it to settle as best it could.

She frowned, then said in a low voice, "I can't imagine what this little one is thinking after what he's been through. He's lucky there are people like you to help him here and not send him away."

"True," Peta said. "In my father's days as a game ranger, they used to believe it kinder to shoot the baby if they found it in the wild or if there was a dead mother. They even had a saying: 'You have to be cruel to be kind.' Thankfully, we have options these days. With elephant on the decline, we need to save as many as we can. Unfortunately, not everyone in this country believes that." Peta paused. She looked at Mitch and he nodded. "I heard that you were in on an important conversation at the rescue."

"If you're talking about a cryptic exchange between Mitch and Samson..." Marissa said.

Peta nodded. "There's a problem in Africa that China has cash to spend, and Africa is being bought. Our elephant too. They will label this export of babies as conservation and genetic gene distribution, but we know it's payment for a working railway to take the new mines coking coal to Mozambique. We didn't manage to stop the exports in 2012, but we'll try once more for these ones they plan to export soon. Bongani, Mitch and a small team snuck into Hwange National Park, to the holding bomas. They have seen some three-year-olds, already caught. Waiting. They've put cameras around the area to record what's going on. Those babies are already in a bad way. We need to get international exposure for them, but the foreign press and Zimbabwean authorities, they don't go well together."

"CITIES prohibits the sale of elephant," Marissa stated.

Peta shook her head. "It has a few exceptions. One is to provide for conservation benefits. China will claim that they are starting biodiverse populations. CITIES are toothless when it comes to enforcing the law here in Africa—as are we here at Yingwe, and anywhere else in our country. It's a slow process with our court system. We don't have the funds to take on the government in a full-frontal attack. Besides, the repercussions for anyone local doing that are severe. But if the information came from overseas, it's a different story–" Peta looked away to where Mitch, Joss and Bongani were clearly listening. She glanced around as if checking who was in the stable with them, as if making sure those who were there were true and trusted.

Marissa frowned. "That's sad. Something was mentioned about *last time.* What happened?"

"The inevitable," Peta said, her face showing stress and sadness. "Too young to move. Bad husbandry—all dead except one."

Marissa lowered her voice even more, knowing what she was asking was sensitive. "And what type of things happen if you oppose your government?"

Peta released a deep breath, blowing it out through pursed lips. "It's not easy living here. We know a safari camp that stood up to the government about the army hunting in their designated area, and their camp was burnt to the ground. No one could say who the arsonist was, but the message for the safari owner to back off was clear. People still disappear in this country," Peta explained, keeping her voice just as low as Marissa had.

"I never knew that," Marissa admitted.

"It's happening less and less as our President ages, and his underlings take more control. It depends if it is an election year or not. We have opinions, but we must be careful with them. Like opposing the elephant captures. Many of us don't want it to happen, but we can't say anything out loud. To do so would be too dangerous."

"Will Amalee be safe if she comes here?" Marissa asked.

"I have to be honest," Peta said, looking at her directly. "Amalee might be leverage we can at last use against them. They will celebrate bringing one of their own home. When they try and sneak the others out the back door while smiling for the camera. You as a foreigner can expose the extent to which they are exploiting the babies." Peta rolled her shoulders. "I won't whitewash it for you and tell you lies. She'll be a pawn in a dangerous game, but here, she'll have the best chance of rewilding that you can give her. I don't know of another place like ours that has an animal like Ndhlovy, except maybe Sheldrick Wildlife Trust in Kenya, and your Amalee's a Zimbabwean elephant. It'll be easier to move her here. If you can create as many international eyes as possible on her moving home, she might be our best chance of stopping the babies from going to China. In saying that, it's never easy in Africa."

"Is it something that we want to do?" Marissa asked, her voice still low. "Give the international press access to Amalee's rewilding? Won't this be giving Zimbabwean conservation a shield to hide behind, and then they can continue to export babies? Perhaps it's not a good time to move her—"

"It will never be a perfect time, and it's going to be dangerous," Peta admitted. "But, if we control the media, we can use Amalee's arrival to show the world what they are doing with the babies, and then maybe this time it will have a different outcome. To be honest, I'm hoping you'll choose to rewild her here with us. Even if you don't help in the fight against the exports."

"Mamma," Sophia said, poking her head into the elephant stable.

Peta looked up and frowned. "Sophia, what's wrong?" She stood up and rushed to the door.

"Nothing. I wanted to see the new baby," Sophia said, "and I walked all the way here without any help." She smiled as her eyes focused on the baby. She looked like any other child, her hair still without its braids, stood up like bed-hair. Her denim jeans paired with a tee- shirt that had the slogan on it about Zimbabwe girls being the best.

Peta hugged her tightly. "Now I'm dreaming. My daughter walked here? What is this magic you speak of?" She laughed, smoothed down Sophia's hair and, picking her up, carried her to the blanket she'd been on.

Sophia giggled as they sat down.

"The new baby's name is Lowla, short for *Lowo-olwa*." Peta said.

"He who fights," Sophia said, reaching out and touching his ear.

"I was letting Marissa know, Miss Smarty-Pants, in case no one explained it to her," Peta said, and she laughed as she put her hand on her daughter's head, and tried again to smooth her hair down.

"He's a beautiful boy," Sophia said, stroking him more.

"Lowla's still dehydrated and traumatized. Soon he'll regain some strength and probably try and run from us, even though we're trying to save him. He won't know any better," Peta said. "I hope that Ndhlovy is here by then."

Lowla curled her trunk around Isaiah's arm as he offered a bottle.

"He's drinking," Isaiah said excitedly.

"At last," Peta said. "One more big obstacle out the way."

Isaiah held the bottle as Lowla sucked the milk from it. "Wild honey. I always tell you, the elephant love it."

Peta shook her head. "And I always tell you no. Unknown bacteria."

Isaiah shrugged. "It's natural from the wild beehives. No bacteria. It was only a little, just so he got the sweet taste. If it didn't work, I would have tried the butterscotch pudding powder like I did with Mbuso."

Peta shook her head. "I give up with you lot. I try and keep it sanitary, but you're always bringing in other things for the elephant."

"Honey, and butterscotch pudding—these things I'll never forget," Danie said.

"And you thought that you knew everything when you two said yes to come work here," Peta said.

Danie smiled. "This one, he's a fighter, though. I hope he pulls through."

Sophia reached for her mum's hand and held it. "You always make sure they live maNdhlovu."

Peta smiled and kissed her daughter's hand.

Sophia said, "You are Mother Elephant. They know that."

Tears pricked in Marissa's eyes. Those two shared such a special bond that transcended the fact that they were not biologically related.

She tried to think back to a time when her own mother was alive.

There was nothing. She had been too young.

Yet, memories of Dawn and Amalee, always being there, were clear as day.

She wasn't too old to have a family of her own. A child. To be loved so completely, as Sophia was by Peta. A real mother-daughter relationship. Could it be something she might do if Amalee was rewilded here in Africa?

Bringing Amalee here would be doing her best for her elephant, but it would mean saying goodbye to her.

Was she ready to do that?

CHAPTER 23
NDHLOVY – THE LEGEND

YINGWE RIVER LODGE, ANIMAL RESCUE AND REHABILITATION CENTER, BINGA, ZIMBABWE

1 October 2014

It was five in the morning, and the predawn light cast a pink glow over the Kariba lake water. Marissa opened the door of her chalet at the rap of knuckles on wood.

"You rang for a guide from your rondavel?" Mitch said.

Marissa smiled. "I didn't mean you had to come and be my personal tour operator, but since you're here—"

"As if I'd let anyone else do the honors. It's my pleasure." He reached for her camera bag and put it on his shoulder. "Batteries all recharged? It's only been four hours since I was on this same path, guiding you to your room."

"Yes." She nodded and pulled the door closed. It felt natural to fall into step next to him.

Mitch shone his powerful flashlight, illuminating the paved pathway. "I'm surprised you're awake so soon."

"Look who's talking. Did you even sleep?" Marissa said looking sideways at him. She couldn't tell if his clothes were the same as he wore uniforms, but she thought she could detect a fresh aroma of lemon and wood, and his hair looked damp.

Mitch let out a soft laugh. "I will, later. There was lots to organize. But I did grab a quick shower, if that makes you feel any better."

Marissa smiled. "Sure. Did she come in yet?"

"Who?" Mitch asked.

"Ndhlovy of course," Marissa said, then laughed when he rolled his eyes.

Mitch smiled. "I could say 'not yet,' and leave it, but I'll put you out of your misery. She's on her way. Peta was tracking her in just past the last village. Knowing Ndhlovy, she'll make her presence known any second now. If you move smartly, you've got time for a quick breakfast before she arrives, since you're up so early too."

She smiled, thinking of how just a few hours before, Mitch had walked her to her door at one o'clock after she had fallen asleep on his shoulder in the stable. She hadn't wanted to leave little Lowla, but he'd made a point that there was nothing she could do to help the little calf, so she'd headed to her bed instead.

She had slept well but woken early.

As soon as they walked onto the deck, Nyala, one of the waitstaff, appeared and seated them. "I'll grab your coffee and bring that through. It was a big night."

Marissa smiled. "Thanks. Can you bring a slice of white toast with that, please?"

"Of course. Mitch?" Nyala asked.

"A bucket of coffee. Maybe a rusk or two. I didn't get any beauty sleep last night."

"You need all the beauty sleep you can get," Nyala said and laughed as she left them, putting her pad into her apron pocket.

Marissa smiled at the teasing between them as she looked out over the deck, across the lake. A few kapenta rigs and house boats were out there, their lights twinkling lightly, then blinking out as the daylight got stronger. A light breeze blew, and she breathed deeply. She had nowhere to be and nothing to do except meet an elephant. Yet she wasn't relaxed.

This wasn't a holiday. She had come to check out if she might rewild Amalee here. Make a decision based on the whole picture. But she couldn't yet. She needed to ask Mitch to show her the anti-poaching outfit. After all, it would be that unit that would protect Amalee once she left the safety of the stables.

The thought of leaving Amalee here worried her. Marissa wasn't sure she could give up seeing her all the time.

Dawn was right. She'd pushed the dream of seeing Amalee free to the back burner because she'd needed her elephant more than her elephant needed her, and she hadn't wanted to admit it.

Amalee had been there when Chad had tried to kill her.

It was Amalee who had held her in her trunk while she sobbed when she came home after her disaster of a time in New York when she'd suffered professional failure. Amalee who'd held her close and let her sob all the grief and relief out with no judgment.

It was Amalee who was always there when she was exhausted by the charity fundraising events.

Her elephant had a basic need that she had to be cared for, no matter what the world or the weather outside was doing, and from a young age, it had been Marissa's responsibility to make sure it happened.

They were like siblings, having grown up together, but also Marissa was an adoptive parent, taking responsibility for Amalee.

Could she let her go?

"Penny for your thoughts? They look deep. Maybe it should be a US dollar?" Mitch said.

Marissa smiled. "They're not worth that; I was just second-guessing myself again if I'm doing the right thing for Amalee. You know, when we found out she originally came from Zimbabwe, we were told she was part of a rescue by this eccentric billionaire, Arthur Jones. He rescued sixty-three baby elephant that were supposed to be culled because of the bad drought. Even after yesterday, and experiencing everything with your rescue, I keep finding myself asking the question: why would I want to return her to a place that didn't want her?" She dropped her voice. "A place that is getting ready to send more young elephants to China?"

"Understandable, and smart to look at all sides of the rewilding. But see the whole sanctuary first, get a proper feel for it, before you make a decision," Mitch said as he put his hands on the table, fingers splayed. "Don't judge the whole country on what's happening with the calves right now. There are a handful of people who reckon they're entitled to whatever they want within these borders, but most folks don't agree with it at all. Change takes time. Even more so in Africa, where respect for ancestors and elders runs deep."

"It's hard to not judge," Marissa said. "But you're right, I haven't exactly been here long enough to have seen much yet."

Mitch smiled. "I'll take you into some of the local game reserves, so you can get a behind-the-scenes look at what's happening. You can see both sides of the argument that conservationists are constantly wrestling with. Can we really sustain tens of thousands of elephant? Are they damaging the environment through sheer numbers? Is it time to cull again? Or do we let elephant reshape the land the way they always have? Once you've been exposed to all of it…" He waved his hand around.

Marisa couldn't help but notice his powerful arms as he did it, where they disappeared into his khaki shirt rolled up to the elbow.

"…properly and safely, you go home, sit with your elephant, and make that call yourself. Rebuild the barn and keep her in the States or bring her back here and let her be free. Besides," he said, picking up a paper serviette and folding it absentmindedly as he spoke, "you still need to spend some time with Ndhlovy."

As if she knew it was her moment to make an entrance, a trumpet sounded, followed by a few others.

"Speak of the devil. I believe Ndhlovy just entered the sanctuary gates. That's her calling to the family to come to the stables." He smiled. "We have a few minutes. If you can eat your toast fast, we can take our coffee with us and make it to the stables when she walks in."

"Just try keep me away," Marissa said.

Nyala came out carrying their breakfast, but it was already packed to go.

"You're an absolute legend, Nyala," Mitch said.

"I heard the call of the mighty one. She's demanding an audience, as always," Nyala said.

"Thanks," Marrisa said.

Taking their bags and cups, they hurried towards the stables.

The elephant that walked into the stable area was huge. The photos didn't do her justice at all. She was much larger than Amalee, and her tusks were longer

—a beautiful specimen of an African elephant in the wild. Strong, with attitude to spare as she tossed her trunk around, rested it on her tusks, then tossed it again. Marissa couldn't take her eyes off her.

Behind, in single file, came the rest of her herd. Dust kicked up from their walking; rumbles from their communications vibrated through Marissa's body.

"What–?" Mitch asked as she leaned heavily on his arm for support, and she slipped her shoes off. With her toes in the dirt, she could feel them even more.

She smiled. "I thought the herd when we rescued Lowla was incredible, but this is—beyond words."

Ndhlovy trumpeted while Peta, Joss, and Sophia walked right up and patted her. Sophia then slowly walked to the elephant behind.

"Khwazi?" Marissa asked, pointing.

"That's him. Sophia's elephant. He's spoilt," Mitch admitted.

Sophia reached out her hand, and Khwazi was all touching her with his trunk. She was laughing as he kissed her face, and she wiped slobber off her cheek.

"He might be spoiled, but that elephant is devoted to Sophia," Marissa said as Khwazi touched the girl's legs carefully, smelling her, no doubt reacquainting himself with everything that was Sophia.

Khwazi wrapped his trunk around Sophia, and she threw her arms around his forehead, raining kisses all over his face.

"Don't move from here, you have a great view," Mitch said. "Ndhlovy will say hello to the family, then she'll go into the stable and check on little Lowla."

Marissa focused back on Joss and Peta. Ndhlovy was touching Peta's stomach. The movement was more focused and intense than just a reconnection. "Is Peta pregnant?"

"What? Not that Joss has said," Mitch said, frowning. "She's older than him. I think she's in her late thirties."

"Ah, she should be put out to pasture in that case. She's been complaining about being super tired..." Marissa said as Ndhlovy kissed Peta's stomach. "I think Ndhlovy knows something we don't."

"It'd be pretty bloody special. Joss is unreal with Sophia. He was solid with her even when she was a toddler—had the knack straight away. Once he knows, he'll step into it without missing a beat. He'll be a cracking dad with two kids."

Ndhlovy wrapped Joss and Peta in her trunk, and then unwrapped them, and began a slow walk towards the stable area. Her trunk lifted upwards as she sniffed the air.

Marissa smiled at Joss and Peta hugging tight. They'd make great parents to another child.

Low rumbles came from Ndhlovy, and the herd became quiet.

Amos was by the gate. He reached up and patted her as she passed into the stable.

"Come on, Sophia. She's going to see Lowla," Peta called.

Sophia gave one last kiss to Khwazi, then she walked to join her parents as they moved quickly through the door and disappeared inside.

"We can pass between her and Khwazi; he won't hurt us," Mitch said. He took her hand in his and pulled her with him, keeping himself between Marissa and Khwazi so that she had the protection of his body between the small bull elephant and herself.

"Best you put your shoes on. There's no telling when you might step in something hot and steamy with the herd around," Mitch said.

Letting go of Mitch's hand, she knelt down to put her boots back on. Together they made their way to the stable where Ndhlovy was talking to Lowla. The low vibrations were amplified by the building's walls. Lowla's rumbles were softer than the older elephant, barely audible, as he responded to Ndhlovy, who was caressing his little body with her trunk, as if she were getting to know him.

She lifted her head and smelled the air again.

More rumbles.

She turned to go, and the little elephant tucked into her side and walked with her.

They marched out of the stable and into the yard. The other elephant in the herd were curious, each taking a turn to smell Lowla and get to know the new baby. "And that's it? She's taking this one?" Marissa asked.

"No, not this time. Lowla's still milk-dependent; she'll take him to the moringa grove for a feed, then bring him back. But Lowla's once again a member of a herd. Won't be long until he's weaned and back in the wild," Mitch said.

Ndhlovy walked to the big gate that led to the grove, where the other elephant babies had strolled earlier in the morning with their handlers.

Mitch was smiling. "She makes life in the sanctuary so much easier for all the elephant we rescue. She'll go check on the other babies now and introduce Lowla to them."

Marissa let out a sigh. "That is one special elephant."

If she were to bring Amalee here, would Ndhlovy give her the same welcome as she had Lowla?

"Now that you've seen that he's safe with Ndhlovy, you ready to go see Bishu and the anti-poaching base?" Mitch asked.

"You bet!" Marissa said. "Lead the way."

CHAPTER 24
A MAN'S DREAM

ANTI-POACHING HEADQUARTERS, BISHU, ZIMBABWE

1 October 2014

Mitch looked at the Bishu Anti-Poaching Headquarters training camp through the windscreen of his Toyota Land Cruiser. Its corrugated iron roof was painted green and black to blend in with the environment. Built with local stone, the walls stood as a testament that the community was ready to look after its wildlife. Many hands from across Chief Bongani's lands had helped mix bag after bag of cement and move stones to build them. "This is the little project I kicked off. There's a real need for good anti-poaching training here."

"A large building to be called *little,*" Marissa said.

Mitch smiled. "You haven't seen anything yet."

Marissa grinned. "You going to show me, or are we just going to look at it from the vehicle?"

"Sass. You certainly have enough," Mitch said as he climbed out, grinning. Before he could open her door, she was out and down too. Butterflies fluttered in his stomach as he realized he was nervous to show her the facility. Then they disappeared as she looked past the building, and her grin matched his.

"Over there, inside this fenced area, as well as a kitchen garden, we have an indigenous nursery," Mitch said as he walked in front of Marissa. "We have the sickle bush, which the giraffes love and graze on, and bushes for shade and soil retention, like the iron woods, and of course, the baobabs."

Marissa walked toward the nursery, a spring in her step, her voice buzzing with excitement. "I'm involved in ecology initiatives around the world, Mitch. This is the kind of program donors are looking for."

"This is all funded by the volunteers. Bongani and Joss gave me the money to get started because it's on Bongani's land, but, just like the lodge, it's community shared. It's important for us to be self-sufficient." Joss said.

Marissa rocked onto her toes. "Even better. It's community-driven, the impact is tangible, and the outcomes speak for themselves. Think on it Mitch, a community nursery attached to anti-poaching training is a strong proposition for funding. It delivers conservation, supports the antipoaching facility, and adds to the local food security in one hit. Supporting the trainers, sustaining your units here, and embedding that support within the community creates a funding story that is easy to get behind. Donors would respond very favorably to this."

"I've seen how Peta battled to get international funding–"

"So, would you be open to funding from my family foundation?" Marissa said

"I'll give it some thought," Mitch said.

Marissa nodded, but her eyes were still focused on the nursery, as if she were visualizing all the ways she could help.

"I can see your mind working overtime," Mitch said. "This way." He strolled around the side of the building. "Practice range over there, and you can see the fitness and training area over here." Mitch indicated all around them as they walked onto the veranda. "We do a fair bit of combat training."

"It's noticeably cooler under the corrugated panels," Marissa said.

Mitch smiled. "You do feel the temperature changes, don't you. There's insulation in the roof, and the building's set up to catch the breeze. We've also got solar panels topping up the power. When we're running first aid, we shift the tables out here and use this space instead of the classrooms. It gives us more room to work."

He held a door open for her and watched her face as she entered. Her expression went from passive, to looking left and right in awe. He couldn't help but stand taller.

"Impressive," Marissa said. "From the outside, it looks like a straightforward square footprint, but once you're inside, the layout really opens up. The central hub, with the classrooms branching off, is a clever design. Five in total, including the computer lab, if I'm tracking correctly. And I guess that's the armory." She pointed to the heavily fortified door.

"Do you want to see inside?" Mitch asked.

"I take it you have the normal rifles and handpieces. Handcuffs, maybe?" Marissa asked, with a sly grin.

This time it was Mitch's turn to blush.

He looked at his watch. "It's lunchtime. Let's go get a meal in the mess house. If we get out of here quick enough, we won't be run down by enthusiastic rangers. After lunch, they have hand-to-hand combat training if you want to watch that."

"I'd love to. Both lunch and training," Marissa said.

He stopped her with his hand on her arm before she took another step. "Actually, talking training. This is a big ask, but what would you think of going up against a few of my recruits? Your skills against theirs?"

"That is the first thing that's come out your mouth that has sounded crazy. Someone could get hurt," Marissa said.

"They'll be fine, as will you; it's more of a lesson to them. You mentioned you're a Dan. You want to help me while we're here?" Mitch said. "We try to expose the recruits to all fighting skills. We haven't had a Taekwondo teacher before. It'll be good for them."

Marissa looked at him with an uncertain expression on her face. "You sure?"

He nodded. "It'll give them something to aspire to beat."

Marissa frowned. "You're so sure I'll come out on top? Whatever the outcome, I'll do it, but only if I get to teach them a few moves afterwards, so they don't think I'm showing off."

Mitch smiled and patted her arm. "That would be great." He turned her to him before removing his hand and added, "And I know you're better than they are, so I'm not worried about you."

Seated across from Mitch, Marissa mopped up the last of her sudza and *nyama* off her enamel plate. Knowing what was coming, she hadn't meant to eat a full meal but hadn't realized how hungry she was until the food was in front of her. She only hoped she had at least an hour to digest it before she was expected to help teach.

Marissa couldn't take her eyes off Mitch as he spoke of his job. She was intrigued by just how passionate he was. Mitch was building a small army of trained guards to protect Zimbabwe's wildlife. With committed warriors like him and his trained guards, the wildlife had hope.

Perhaps the elephant might still be in the wild longer than the next twenty-five years, as had been predicted.

Perhaps the pangolin and the giraffe might not become extinct during her lifetime.

Mitch reached over the table and gave her hand a squeeze. "Come back to Africa. You're far away in your own thoughts again."

Marissa jumped at the contact, and it took a moment to remember what he had just been saying.

Mitch smiled. "Jet lag catching up with you?"

"No, it's just a lot to take in," Marissa admitted. Mitch's passion for his units shone through, but it was more than that which had her mind sparking with ideas, and her heart reaching out to the project.

There was hope.

In a country in such turmoil, people like Mitch, Bongani, Peta, and Joss were making a difference.

And she wanted to be part of it.

"Come on. Time to move to the training area," Mitch said as he put their dishes with the rest of the items for washing by the recruits. "Jason Carpenter's running the unarmed combat training. He's a retired lieutenant and knows his craft. For a lot of the local female recruits, it's the first time they've felt safe, as they know they can defend themselves if it comes to it after their self-defense classes. Same goes for a few of the quieter blokes. You can see it in them straight away, shoulders back, walking a bit taller. Confidence."

"Unarmed combat?" Marissa said.

"It's something we used a fair bit in military training, along with other fighting skills. You'll see bits of it in mixed martial arts, though those MMA fighters are restricted—no eye gouging, no headbutts, no strikes to the spine. Real life is different. When it comes down to it, there are no rules. You do whatever it takes to stay alive."

"I understand holding my own just fine," Marissa said, walking next to him on the wide gavel path, shaded under a huge acacia tree that looked like the construction team had built around, and ensured remained in their plan to build the antipoaching campus. "How do you train people without weapons and without a rulebook, and still make sure nobody gets hurt?"

Mitch smiled. "The idea's to be decisive and aggressive. You hit hard before the other bloke can even settle. There's plenty of footwork and defensive positioning too. It's all about creating openings. They're taught to throw off their opponent and go straight for the vital spots to shut them down fast. The goal is to take away their ability to see, breathe, or think properly so they're neutralized quickly.

"It's been brilliant for the guards. The conditioning alone toughens them up. Makes them more resilient and confident out in the field," Mitch said.

They walked to the outdoor area where a class of twenty or so students sat on the mats, facing a man Marissa presumed was Jason. There were now ten three-quarter training busts on solid plastic bases to the right of the space, and a heap of safety equipment in boxes sat to the side, such as helmets and protection pads.

"And those?" Marissa asked. "They weren't here when we went past here earlier."

"Training safety," Mitch said with a smile as he took his boots off and put them on the shelf that had also been brought in at the back of the space, now filled with everyone's footwear. "It's not full gear, but it's better than nothing."

"Well, that's a relief. I thought we were going in with no protection at all," Marissa said.

Mitch smiled. "And you still said yes? Come on." He patted the mat next to him as he sat alongside the last person in the line, crossing his legs.

Marissa put her trainers and socks on the rack and sat down beside Mitch.

"Think of this class as your dojang," he said.

She nodded. "I'm definitely willing to give it a proper go. I actually love teaching–"

"Moses, thank you for volunteering," Jason said, interrupting their chatter.

A man nearly as tall and well-built as his instructor rose and joined him.

Together, they went through a refresher of the moves from the previous training class. "I know you are sparring with your own brothers and sisters from the unit," Jason said. "But going easy on each other doesn't do anyone any favors. It creates risk. Training must be hard, deliberate, and honest. At the same time, there are non-negotiables. I don't want any broken bones. No permanent damage. We're building capability, not liabilities.

"Out there, in the real world, there are techniques you can use, but you avoid them if you have any other option. If it comes down to your life or theirs, then survival becomes the objective. Manage the threat. End the fight. Walk away alive."

"Right," Jason said. "Next volunteer. Copper, get your protection gear on."

Once they had on gloves, helmets, and stomach, leg, and arm protection, Moses and Copper faced each other. They were roughly the same height, but Copper had a few pounds on Moses.

"Copper, defending. Moses, attacker."

Jason started the tussle with a whistle, and the men were at each other.

Copper rushed forward to engage Moses.

Marissa flinched as smacks landed on Copper's head. Followed closely by the same on Moses's.

"See those hands? Flat. You don't bend anything that can get broken. These two are going to be interesting," Mitch said.

Copper rushed at Moses again, more willing to engage. More aggressive than Moses, despite being told he was the defender. He wasn't just going to stand there. Moses rammed forward and slammed first one hand then the other into Copper.

"Ha! Good hook by Moses; he's still being the attacker, but he's… whoa, what a kick. Copper took great advantage of Moses. And there you go. Copper has Moses down and defeated. Copper, the defender, didn't want to take a beating, and made sure his attacker knew it."

Moses tapped the mat. The whistle blew, and Copper backed away.

"Good round. You may sit," Jason said. "Malania and Mary, you're next."

Mitch also stood, offered Marissa a hand up, and they made their way to the front of the class. "This is Marissa, who's visiting from the States. She's thinking of relocating her elephant to Yingwe River Lodge and their Rescue Center. She has Taekwondo skills. I'll be interested to see if Malania and Mary can bring her down."

Marissa smiled but shook her head. "I don't even get a warm-up?"

The recruits laughed.

"The difference between what we do here," Mitch went on, "and Marissa's training is that hers is a sport. She warms up, trains, cools down, then heads home to a soft bed. Out here, we don't get that luxury. This is bush work; it's life or death, every time. You or the poacher. You or the rapist. You or a group of blokes coming at you because an elephant flattened their crops the night before.

Marissa shivered. Her life was so much easier than all of theirs.

"So if Marissa's going to get a feel for what we deal with, Malania and Mary, I don't want you starting off easy on our visitor. Just remember she's got a plane to catch in a few days. No bruises. We don't need her heading home looking like she came to Zimbabwe and got mugged."

The students gave a nervous laugh, clearly not sure if Mitch was joking or not.

Mitch continued, "I don't want you giving the win to Marissa either. Marissa, I know that you'll treat our recruits the same. Jason and I will adjudicate."

Marissa nodded as she walked to where Malania and Mary were putting on their protective gear.

The other recruits whispered among themselves, with a note of excitement evident.

Malania passed her a helmet and gloves, with a shy smile, and Mary held out a set of stomach, arm, and leg protection gear.

"Thanks," Marissa said. "Nice to meet you both."

Mary smiled, her much more open character evident over Malania's reserved one. Mary was also shorter than Malania, but not lighter; she carried muscle mass.

Malania put out her hand, and Marissa shook it. Mary did the same after she had finished tightening Marissa's armor. All three women checked that their protection gear was in good order before nodding to Jason.

"Guess we're ready then," Marissa said and walked with them to the mat.

"Marissa, the defender, recruits the aggressors," Jason said.

Marissa stood alone on her side of the mat and bowed to Jason and Mitch for serving as referees, then to her attackers.

They just looked at her through their helmets.

"Another difference between a sport and real life. The respect shown for both the adjudicators and your opponent," Jason said with a wry smile.

Marissa stepped back, pulling her center into line and cleared her mind. *Calmness. Quiet. Control. Strong.*

Jason blew the whistle.

Mitch shifted his weight from one foot to the other. Logically, he knew Marissa would trump the girls. Couldn't she? Sixth Dan was dedication to the sport. But a ball of anxiety for the unnecessary pain that might be caused because of him lodged in his throat. Marissa began moving while Jason's whistle still sounded. He held his breath. She shifted around, trying to get the recruits into single file.

The perfect maneuver.

He smiled. This was going to be interesting. He let his breath go. She would be just fine.

At no point did she stand still; she moved the whole time while the recruits hesitated, clearly unsure what they were facing.

Marissa went in hard. Her roundhouse kick took Mary, who had landed in the front, by surprise. Marissa swiveled and dropped into a sweep kick, taking Mary's feet out from under her. The move was targeted and controlled, and she had already regained her balance and was upright. While Mary was still going down, Malania rushed Marissa and received a jumping, spinning roundhouse kick that took her down with the momentum. All the time, Marissa's hands had been ready to throw a punch if needed. She was not taking the chance that the recruits would get close enough to cause her any harm.

Mary was getting up when Malania had fallen, but Malania had been too close, and they collided. Marissa danced on the outer edge of the mats, giving them space and time to regroup, but as Mary came to her knees, Marissa rushed in with a high kick, putting huge pressure on Mary's body.

Mary went down, holding her shoulder with her gloved hand. She tapped out.

Marissa frowned. Compassion for his recruits.

Malania charged Marissa, who sidestepped her. Clearly, Marissa was still paying attention. Malania shot past and barely stopped herself from hitting the wall. Malania turned, raised her arms in a defensive posture and stepped toward Marissa. She attempted a kick of her own, but Marissa caught her foot and quickly twisted her and brought her down with a sweep.

This time, Marissa dropped to her knee on Malania's chest, holding her gloved hand to her throat.

Malania was defiant, attempting to get up and batting at Marissa. Marissa shifted lower and put her arm against Malania's windpipe.

Within seconds, Malania was tapping on the mat, and Jason blew his whistle.

Both women got to their feet.

Marissa stepped back once again, and when both Mary and Malania were up, she bowed to Jason, Mitch and her opponents once again.

Jason and Mitch bowed back.

The recruits both bowed.

Mitch faced the class. "That wasn't meant as a lesson to knock the skills of our AP unit, or to take away from the work you've already put in. It was about understanding what happens when you come up against someone whose skills outmatch yours. In that situation, the right response, once you establish that their skills surpass yours, is to get your arse out of there. People like that, can kill—no two ways about it. Let's be clear: Mary and Malania, you did bloody well. Marissa is a sixth Dan black belt. She was a tough competitor."

There was applause as Marissa walked up to Mary and Malania and nudged both their arms up in a victory position. "You guys did good."

Both the ladies smiled and fist bumped Marissa.

Marissa kept them on as partners to showcase the moves she'd used, and others, patiently adjusting stances, helping as the recruits adapted from what they knew to accepting what she taught. She was a natural teacher.

Mitch watched the interaction with interest. He hoped she would decide to bring her elephant home to Africa so they could spend more than just ten days together. Maybe even keep her there, longer than she needed to be with her rewilding progress.

There was so much more to the rich heiress than she let others see.

The sun was settling in on the horizon when Marissa and Mitch drove back into Yingwe Lodge. Marissa relaxed into her seat, watching his hands as he navigated the road, and then the turn into the stables. Happiness bubbled inside her. Not on a high from the adrenaline rush of earlier, but because she had found a place that she believed her Amalee could integrate into and rewild. She couldn't wait to call her father and tell him about her decision. Perhaps he might come with them when they relocated Amalee and experience for himself the magic of Yingwe River Lodge and the whole community. Then there was the man sitting next to her, adopted into that same community by the people. He seemed to light up each day for her.

Ndhlovy was walking with her herd out of the stable area, off into the wild again.

"Guess she's happy with the progress of our little Lowla and is letting us humans do our thing," Mitch said.

Marissa laughed. "If I hadn't seen her with my own eyes, and someone told me about this elephant, I would call bullshit."

Mitch parked the vehicle, and together they began walking back to the stable to check on Lowla as Nyala came rushing towards them. "Miss Marissa, there is an urgent call for you in the reception area. They said you need to come, no matter what."

Frowning, Marissa asked, "Do you know who's calling?"

Nyala shook her head. "Just that it was very important that I find you and make sure you come to the phone."

An urgent call couldn't be good news. Her stomach churned. Her dad? Amalee? What had happened at home? "Excuse me," Marissa said, and she followed Nyala to the safari lodge to the landline phone.

Picking up the receiver, she took a deep breath to steady herself. "Hello, Marissa speaking."

"Marissa." It was Dawn. "Finally. I tried your cell, but it doesn't appear to be working. Sit down."

She took a deep breath. This was bad news, if Dawn was telling her to sit. Her hands began to shake, and she had to grip the phone tighter to stop it slipping to the floor. "Wha–what happened?"

"It's your dad. I'm so sorry Marissa. He–he's dead," Dawn sobbed. "You need to come home."

CHAPTER 25
A STATE OF FLUX

LUCKY 7 RANCH, NEVADA, USA

20 October 2014

Marissa packed her father's clothes into his wardrobe. Now that the funeral was over and she'd been given access to the crime scene, she wanted everything to look normal again. She sat on the bed.

The room was a mess. Her father would have hated that.

It was so hard to believe her dad was truly gone.

The coroner's report said that he'd died from cyanide poisoning.

The police had opened a murder investigation and were intensifying their search for Chad. They were also still looking for the missing family's attorney.

Her father hadn't died straight away; he'd had time to tell the paramedics, who had helivaced out to the ranch, that Chad had buried Jeffery alive in a forty-four-gallon drum, and there was a bogus will that he hadn't signed, but it had been witnessed by his attorney, before Chad buried him. But Chad hadn't given him a clue as to where to look for Jeffery. He had also warned that Chad was going to try and kill Marissa, even if she was in Africa.

Marissa took a deep breath.

Chad was officially a psychopath.

When had her only cousin become such a monster?

He'd been damaged when he'd arrived in their lives. Although she hadn't seen him do drugs himself, he'd lived with the worst effects of them, courtesy of his alcoholic mother Alice. When Marissa was younger, her father had tried to hide the details of Chad's upbringing from her, saying Chad was just sad.

But he wasn't.

His mind was sick.

There were times as kids when he'd been cruel, but she'd still always believed that he would come good. He went to the army, and even there, he managed to find trouble. Landed himself in jail after his deployment to Somalia.

His prison sentence, she didn't truly blame him for. His defense attorney had told the courtroom that he was protecting the son from his father.

That was heroic in a way.

She'd thought he was changing for good.

But now he'd burned their ranch down. Buried Jeffery alive and murdered her father.

She hated what he'd become.

And now he had her in his sights.

She shivered.

Right now, she could do with another WhatsApp call from Mitch. He always seemed to know the exact moment when she was low, and his number would flash up on her phone. Despite the circumstances in which she'd left, contact with him hadn't been severed. And she was grateful that she'd made a friend while there, someone to share her experiences with. And she was certain that their friendship was growing into something deeper. More meaningful.

"Ms. Whitney?" Her new security detail, Declan, stood in the hallway. "Dawn is at the back door."

"You can always let Dawn through," she said and rose from the bed. She walked in Declan's shadow to the kitchen, just as he had shown her.

The warm soothing scent of chamomile tea drifted out from the kitchen.

When Marissa was younger, Dawn would give her either lavender or chamomile tea when she couldn't settle in the room near Amalee. It seemed some traditions never changed. Dawn stood holding a steaming mug, with one left on the counter for Marissa.

The private security guards watched on from their posts, one near the door. Declan was just a few steps in front of her, reminding her how much her life had changed in a very short time.

Marissa took a deep breath. Then let it out as she walked into the kitchen.

"Hey," Marissa said as she hugged Dawn, holding on tight.

"You doing okay, kid?" Dawn asked.

She started to nod, but then shook her head.

Dawn slid the tea over to Marrisa as they both sat down at the kitchen table.

"Thanks," Marrisa said as she looked to the head of the table, where her father would never sit again.

Tears threatened again, welling up in her eyes, and she dashed them away with the back of her hand.

"Do you want to go sit with Amalee?" Dawn asked.

"I need to get through the reading of the will. You were called to be present too, weren't you?"

Dawn nodded. "Not sure why, but I bet it's something to do with staying with Amalee and not giving you any trouble."

Marissa smiled weakly. "After it's over, I'll change and come see Amalee. Not sure what they are going to do." She flicked her chin at her security.

Dawn nodded. "Plenty of room for them too. Anything to keep you safe from Chad."

Together, they waited.

There was healing in silence.

They'd sat like this many times over the years, in quiet with a tea, but never with such a sad subject hanging over them.

"I met someone while I was in Africa," Marissa said eventually as she put her empty cup down.

"I bet you met a lot of new people in Africa. Tell me you met one you were interested in for a change?" Dawn said with a slight smile.

Marissa shook her head at Dawn's unsubtle dig at her love life. It wasn't her fault that she hadn't found anyone she'd been that interested in before. No one who understood her like Mitch did. "Joss's elephant, Ndhlovy, is remarkable. She's everything they said she was. A nurturer. She takes in all the babies and helps with the rewilding program. I believe that she'll take Amalee into her herd." Marissa sighed and glanced toward the photo on the mantel of her and her father taken at her graduation ceremony. "It's just so hard to keep going with moving Amalee now that Dad's gone."

"He'd want you to follow your dreams. To keep going. Besides, your father was clear when he said that Chad isn't finished with you. He'll come after you and your elephant."

Marissa nodded. "We both know he's too smart to show his face here today. Even if Dad had signed a copy of that stupid will, he didn't have the authority to do anything with the McDermitt money."

"Thank heavens for that," Dawn said. "You're going to need a shitload to move Amalee. The last thing you need to do is worry about money."

Marissa didn't think that Dawn grasped the amount of money she'd had access to since her twenty-fifth birthday.

"Being out of the country for a bit is probably one of the best things you can do. Maybe you'll be safer for a while," Dawn said. "As a wanted man, he won't be able to get on a plane."

Marissa rolled her neck. It made a horrible cracking noise. "I wouldn't put anything past him," Marissa said. "I tried hard, Dawn. I could never reach inside that shell of his; I couldn't be the cousin he wanted, and he was not the friend I needed."

"You know you've skillfully dodged telling me more about someone special in Africa," Dawn said.

Marissa nodded. "There are plenty of armed guards at the lodge. They have this whole anti-poaching unit run by Mitch. They tackle the poachers head-on."

"I take it Mitch is the someone," Dawn said, taking a sip of her tea.

Marissa smiled. "Uh-huh."

"And?" Dawn asked.

"And nothing. I think there's something there, but I flew home before I could find out. I'd like to give it a chance, but priorities..." Marissa said, shifting in her chair. "We did get to spend a little time alone, which is hard when you're in a tourist lodge. There are staff around you all the time. It was hectic there. There's nothing more to tell than that. Other than he calls me, often and I call him too."

Dawn nodded and then smiled. "Sounds like moving Amalee halfway across the world may have some additional benefits."

There was a knock on the back door, interrupting their quiet conversation. Declan said, "Ranch manager Thomas and your house manager, Pia."

"Let them in," Marissa said.

Thomas took his hat off as he came into the house. "I know I'm early, sweetheart, but Pia and I thought you could probably do with some company before the reading."

She smiled weakly. Thomas and Pia were more like an uncle and aunt to her only love and friendship, not blood, made their connection.

"I have to get the coffee on," Pia said, busying herself with the task.

Declan cleared his throat. "Speaking of the reading–"

A knock sounded at the back door, and Declan opened it, admitting Vincent Pencott, Jeffrey's partner. He still wore the suit that he'd been in at the funeral. The only difference in his appearance was that he carried a black briefcase.

"Hi y'all," Vincent said.

Marissa indicated towards a chair across from her. "Have a seat. Have they found Jeffery yet?"

Vincent sat but shook his head.

"The police will find him," Thomas said. "That shit Chad wouldn't have buried him far away. We've been searching all the old haunts he liked to hang out as a kid on the ranch. We've already found the chamber in the mine he got the cyanide from. If Jeffery is in the ground out here, we'll find him, and he'll get a proper burial."

"You sure you want to do this here and not in your father's study?" Vincent asked.

"I'm not ready to go in there yet," Marissa admitted. "Being in that room without him feels wrong."

After a moment, Vincent said, "We're all set then; everyone's here. Ready?"

"As we'll ever be," Marissa said.

Vincent opened his briefcase and took out a folder. He flicked open a document. "This is the last will and testament of Walter Edward Whitney. We're aware that another will was written after this; however, if that will is presented, we'll contest it in court as Walter's legal representative."

There were provisions of land and a neighboring ranch house left to Thomas and Pia, and her father encouraged them to make it official and get married. There was a trust fund account for Dawn, with conditions that she stay with Amalee, either until she was relocated or until Amalee died.

None of the clauses were a surprise to Marissa, as she'd discussed them with Walter on several occasions.

"And lastly, to my beautiful daughter, everything else I have is yours. You'll find that there is not much monetary value from me. You already possess everything as a McDermitt descendant. Know that as a Whitney, you have owned my heart from the moment my Cherri discovered she was pregnant. My last piece of advice for you is to keep living your life on your terms. Know that you were the light in my life. Always. I love you," Vincent said as he closed the file. "This concludes the reading of the will of Walter Whitney."

"Thanks, Vincent," Marissa said, letting her shoulders relax now that it was over. What her father had said in that last part of his will resonated deep inside her: *keep living your life on your terms.*

She wanted to relocate Amalee.

Before his death, she'd wanted her father to share that with her. Even though he was gone, he was still guiding her.

She needed to rewild her elephant. To take her to Zimbabwe and follow her dream.

And she wanted to have time to explore her feelings with Mitch, the first man who had truly made her think about what it might be like to stand beside someone as an equal.

"Marissa, do you have any plans on what you're going to do?" Vincent asked.

"We're taking Amalee to Zimbabwe as soon as we can," Marissa said, and the relief of saying it out aloud made her smile. "That's why I was in Africa—sizing up a rehabilitation center. Amalee will be rewilded there. We just need to get the clearances to move her, and clear all visas required for Dawn and me."

"That's a big job," Vincent said. "Did your father know?"

"We'd discussed it. That's why we hadn't decided to rebuild the elephant barn yet. He was the one who taught me to check out every opportunity, as often it's the most unlikely ones that work out."

Vincent turned to look at Dawn. "Speaking as a legal representative, are you sure you want to go to Africa? The will clearly specifies you get your trust money when Amalee was relocated. That doesn't mean you have to upend your life and remain with her."

"Thank you, but it's not about the money. I don't need that; Walter knew I'd never leave Amalee or Marissa. The decision's been made. I'm going to Africa with Amalee. Who knows where my life will lead me? Who would have thought there would be two Africans going home to their roots?"

Marissa smiled, as did Pia.

Thomas shook his head. "How many years have your ancestors been in America? And you still think of yourself as African?"

"I do, and this would allow me to make my own decision about where I want to live. But it's more about that elephant. Her life is luxurious here, but she needs her kind around her. Our old girl will do so much better there."

"What, with no air conditioning in summer and heating in winter?" Thomas said. "Whatever will she do?"

Dawn grinned. "She'll acclimatize and be fine. Perhaps one day, she'll long for America. Who knows, but she'll be surrounded by her own kind, and I can't wait to see that."

"One hundred dollars on a bet that you miss your air conditioning and winter heating more than she does," Pia said.

"I'm not taking that bet. I'd lose. I've always admitted to being spoilt sleeping in her barn with her," Dawn said.

Marissa sat in her chair and watched them. These were the people who had always been there for her. They'd spent so many nights around the kitchen table in this very house. Her father would come and go whenever his career needed him; her cousin, when he arrived, would often be absent, and was eventually banished from the family; but the people around now? They were solid.

She was going to need that support when moving Amalee to Africa.

But more so if Chad came after her.

She was no idiot. Chad had killed her father. Was it just sick revenge, or was it really all about the money?

According to her father on his death bed, Chad hadn't known that she already had control of the McDermitt inheritance. And while he'd clearly wanted money from her father, Marissa had a feeling it was more than that.

Would he look at any way possible to come between her and her family's foundation?

Her father had warned of Chad coming after her.

If it was so easy for him to murder her father and bury Jeffery, what chance did she have?

She just hoped that Chad hadn't already dug a grave for her. She shuddered and looked at Declan.

He frowned. "You okay?"

She shook her head and rubbed at the goosebumps on her arms. Aloud, she said, "It's nothing. Something just crawled up my spine."

CHAPTER 26
CONSEQUENCES FROM THE AUTHORITARIAN

VICTORIA FALLS TOWNSHIP, VICTORIA FALLS, ZIMBABWE

11 November 2014

The tin shack in the back of the plot at the Victoria Falls shebeen was hot. It had neither shade nor running water, but Shumba didn't seem to care about the inconvenience that would cause his uncooperative visitor.

The customs official's bloodied body lay on the mud floor, in a fetal position, his hands trying miserably to protect his skull.

Shumba kicked him in the kidneys one more time. "Tell me again, whose fault was it that one of the elephant babies died on the tarmac?"

The man physically shook, and he peed himself, the smell acidic in an already humid room. "*Ungaas*. It was not my fault—"

"You do not know?" Shumba said.

The man shook his head. "I did everything I could to get the elephant loaded as quickly as we could, get the papers done, and get the babies on the plane. They didn't want to move. It took so much time to get them off the tarmac–"

"Whose job was it to load them all safely?" Shumba asked as he twirled the *knobkerrie* between his fingers, much like a baton in a parade.

"It is too hot at this time of the year to be loading livestock. We cannot have water on the tarmac for them. We did not know that the elephant would die. The Chinese man, he said that one looked sick, to leave it till last, so I was doing what he told me to do," the man sobbed.

Shumba dug the tip of the *knobkerrie* into the man's throat. "Did he pay you to do that to the elephant? Take out some US dollars and give you money?"

"*Aikona, baas.*"

Shumba removed the pointed end from the man's neck and twirled it again. "Ah, so you remember I'm your *baas,* and you are paid by me. Why did you listen to the man from China? You left an elephant with no water for two hours in forty-degree heat with no shade, and you expected the animal not to die? You expected the newspapers' people not to take any pictures? You expected there to be no punishment for this stupid behavior?"

The man was weeping. Deep breaths wracked his body. "It was not my fault. He wouldn't load when it was his turn; he didn't want to stand up. It was not my fault."

"Then give me a name of someone whose fault it was. I can go speak to them instead. You are the man who signs the papers for the export of livestock at Victoria Falls Airport," Shumba said, tapping the man's head hard with the knob at the end of his weapon.

"*Yebo,* that is me."

"You're the one who is responsible for all the livestock that goes through the airport?" Shumba said.

"*Yebo,* but yesterday I was sick in the head. I got something wrong. It won't happen again."

"Sick in the head. Now there is some truth at last," Shumba said, digging the pointed end into the side of the man's soft belly. "You were paid well to be there to make sure the elephants were all loaded quickly and quietly. No holdups."

"But my brother, he said he would load that last one." The man attempted to bring his hands to protect his ears again.

Shumba chose not to strike him this time. "So, this was your brother's fault? It should be him in here, not you? Is that what you are saying?" Shumba asked, spittle flying from his mouth.

"Oh no, not my brother. I didn't mean him. He is innocent. He wasn't there. It was the Chinese man's fault."

Shumba smacked the custom official's body with the *knobkerrie* repeatedly in different locations. Each time the man flinched and moved from the pain, Shumba struck in a more exposed place.

"Who was the person responsible? Who was the man I paid to get the elephant through without any problems or delays? The man who took my money and did not do his job?" Shumba kicked the man again; this time, blood squirted out of his mouth.

The man stayed silent; he pulled his body closer in on itself.

"This is the part where you say, 'It was me. I take responsibility because I am an official customs inspector, and I was paid to do my job, which I did not do.' Instead, we have a total cock-up."

The man spat the blood out of his mouth. "Please, I did not let the press onto the runway. I did not know they would take photographs. I am not responsible for that."

"How can you not be responsible? Because you were not there when you were supposed to be? Because you did not protect the elephant like you were supposed to? Or because you did not do your job? Now, international newspapers have stuck their noses into Zimbabwe's business. The news got out of Zimbabwe faster than the elephant on the Air China flight. The pictures of the plane taking the elephant and the dead baby are everywhere."

"Someone must have helped them–"

"Someone could not have just been you. Could it?" Shumba asked.

"No. It is not my fault."

Shumba put one foot on the man's head and began placing pressure on his ear. He then jumped in the air and brought both feet down into the man's skull.

His head was crushed inwards.

Shumba walked towards the door. He might not have the body of an elite athlete anymore, but he was almost three hundred pounds of crushing power.

Shumba kicked the dead man again for good measure. "You useless pile of shit. Because of you, now I have to look for something else for the foreign news people to find more interesting than the sale of the elephant."

CHAPTER 27
CHANGING OF THE GUARDS

TETERBORO AIRPORT, NEW YORK, USA

17 November 2014

Marissa waited in the private lounge at Teterboro Airport in New Jersey, for the car to deliver her two VIPs. Declan sat near her, her constant shadow.

Two long months had passed. But finally, it was almost time.

Mitch was almost with her in person, once again. She smiled.

Mitch and Peta's plane trip had started in Victoria Falls, then gone via Cape Town, and London. Now, at last, they were in New York. Soon they would arrive and climb onto the Foundation's plane to fly home to the Lucky 7 Ranch.

Marissa picked at the skin next to her thumbnail, then checked herself from falling into her old stress habit, and put her hands underneath her, Dawn's voice clear in her head. *"No one needs to see your hands in a mess unless you have just won a fight. Then be proud of bloody hands."*

She smiled and looked up at the door as it opened.

He was there.

"That was a difficult flight. I think it's because you've spoilt me forever in your private plane, my friend," Peta said as she rubbed her tummy that was now showing more than a little bump.

Marissa laughed, and they embraced. "Next one is private, but I think it might be even more uncomfortable, to be honest. Nothing like the business class you just had."

"Maybe it's because this belly gets in the way of everything," Peta said.

Marissa smiled and turned to embrace Mitch.

Hours of emails and phone calls had happened between when she last saw him in person and now. The magnetic pull she'd felt towards him when she'd first arrived in Zimbabwe was even stronger.

A friendship had formed. And something solid on which to base a relationship.

Mitch pulled her close and kissed her on the cheek.

He held her firmly, pressing her against him. His hands moved down her back and rested on her hips, as he pulled her closer.

He leaned his head into her neck, as if he were breathing in her scent in their hug.

Okay, maybe their relationship was already past the friendship level.

"Hi," she said softly when she found her voice.

"I've missed you," Mitch said, his voice filled with emotion.

"I've missed you too," Marissa admitted. Before daily calls, her time had been empty, now she looked forward to sharing her day with Mitch, despite him being on the opposite side of the world.

Declan cleared his throat. "If this is the guy taking my place, I advise against it. He's too emotionally involved. That will be a distraction and could lead to a fatal mistake," Declan warned, without even greeting Mitch.

Marissa stepped out of Mitch's embrace and laughed. "I think so too, Dec, but he's who will be by my side in Africa. Unless you want to change your mind and come with me?"

"I know I said no at first, but perhaps I should, just to ensure you actually make it back here alive," Declan said. An edge to his voice that she hadn't heard in the two months he and his team had been her bodyguard.

Mitch laughed. "Good to meet you too. Thanks for taking such good care of Marissa. I think once she gets to Zimbabwe, my anti-poaching guards and I'll have her covered twenty-four/seven, but we could always do with more help if you do change your mind," Mitch said, sticking his hand out. "You're welcome to join us."

Declan shook it, and Marissa felt her shoulders relax.

"Let's see how you go when back on the Lucky 7 Ranch," Declan said.

There was no pissing contest here between these men. Marissa realized two things:

1. Mitch's other hand hugged her hip possessively, and she really liked that.
    1. Both had put their egos aside for the mission's sake to ensure she survived.

CHAPTER 28
COMING HOME

SOMEWHERE OVER ZIMBABWE, NEAR VICTORIA FALLS AIRPORT, ZIMBABWE

22 November 2014

Marissa sat in the staff seat of the chartered Boeing 747-8F. It was hard to believe that only two and a half weeks had passed since Mitch and Peta had arrived in the United States.

Josha Botha, the transportation veterinarian, had arrived three days later after being delayed by storms while delivering lions to Malawi.

And how much had changed in that time.

She smiled just thinking about how much closer her and Mitch were in their relationship. Not that they were rushing into anything serious, but getting to know each other had been so much fun.

Declan had remained in the USA, confident after a few days that Marissa was in good hands with Mitch.

She had taken up the mantel to save the Zimbabwean baby elephants, just as Peta had asked her, before her father had died. Along with all the information for Amalee's relocation and rewilding progress, was the story of the death of a baby elephant on the airport tarmac in Victoria Falls, Zimbabwe, and the planned relocation of others.

The press had reacted well. With features in national newspapers, and social media posts. They even had TV crews following Amalee's story and with it, the baby elephant's plight in Zimbabwe.

One precious elephant being returned home, but over one hundred were due to be 'legally sold' again.

It had been organized chaos. But with her father's words in her head, encouraging her to live life on her own terms, to make a difference in the world, Marissa called for additional donations to the foundation. Funds she could use to help save as many elephant as she could.

Marissa flipped her laptop closed and slipped it into her backpack, leaning closer to Mitch so she could rest her head against his shoulder. "Even thousands of miles above it all, it still feels like the world is watching my every move," she said quietly.

He gave her a reassuring half-smile. "They are. That was the point, wasn't it when you started your press campaign?"

Marissa nodded. "I just hope it's enough to do the right thing. I still can't believe an elephant baby was left in the scorching sun to die from dehydration. The cruelty is despicable, no matter where you are in the world."

"You know we've got your back," Mitch said firmly. "That escorted road trip to Boise Airport was a whole bloody production. I swear every holidaymaker, local, and protester lined those roads, all eager to witness Amalee's journey." He grinned.

For the first time in weeks, Marissa felt a flicker of peace. She had done everything she could. Amalee was safe; her rewilding was underway.

She smiled. Mitch lifted her hand to his mouth and kissed it.

"Crew, get ready for boarding by Zimbabwe customs once they park us," the captain instructed.

Marissa let out a breath as the wide-body freighter plane finally came to a stop on the Victoria Falls Airport tarmac. She'd been on many chartered flights during her life. Still, never one like this, on a cargo plane used to transport animals. However, an elephant did seem to be a new experience for them.

"And we're ready to run the next gauntlet?" Mitch asked, squeezing her hand.

She squeezed back, nodding.

"Give us a moment to check everything is in order, then you can take your seat belts off," the captain said over the intercom.

She looked across to the jump seat.

Dawn was strapped in, and grinned. "It's hard to believe you pulled this together in less than two months."

"Come on, Captain. We need to get back to Amalee," Peta said, her knees bouncing up and down.

"*Ag*, give him a chance. He needs to make sure-sure," Josha said. "A small delay now is normal."

He seemed so young to be a transportation vet, but when Marissa had asked Peta for some recommendations, she'd said that Wild Translocations was the only company she would use. They had history going back to her Matusadona days, and that was with Josha's father, now the son was part of the operation too.

After a long couple of minutes, the voice returned. "We're good to go. You can unbuckle your seat belts."

The five belts clicked simultaneously as they vacated their seats, and all made their way towards the crate where Amalee was being held just a few feet from where they had been.

The plane groaned as the large cargo door opened.

"Hey girl," Marissa said, putting her hand against one of the breathing vents in the side of the crate. "You doing okay?"

Amalee put the tip of her trunk into Marissa's hand.

"A good sign. Must have taken that landing in her stride," Peta said.

Josha nodded. "She's doing a great job. It was not like we're transporting a wild animal here; she's been a pleasure. Such a well-trained elephant. I can't wait to see her settled back into Africa."

"All credit for any training goes to Dawn," Marissa said, smiling at her friend.

Amalee grumbled, the sound loud in the enclosed space.

"I know, girl. Give us a moment and they will get you out. It's almost over; still got some road traveling to do, but in a few hours… you'll be on African soil again." Dawn put her fingers through an access vent and scratched Amalee's side where it was pressed against the small opening.

Marissa heard Amalee huff, as if to say, *'If I must,'* and she smiled.

The door opened slowly, and daylight flooded the cargo area.

Amalee trumpeted.

Mitch stepped in front of Marissa as a Zimbabwean customs official with a clipboard came onboard and made his way towards Josha in the cargo hold. "Morning. The paperwork says cargo is one elephant, accompanied by two Americans, one Australian, one South African and one Zimbabwean passenger. Crew remaining on the plane for refilling, then immediate take-off. No further cargo load."

"Correct. I'm the Saffa Josha, Peta is the Zimbo, these two are the Yanks, and this gentleman here's the Aussie. And you can hear the cargo is an elephant," Josha joked just as Amalee trumpeted again.

"Passports?" the official asked, not smiling at the attempted banter.

Everyone handed over their passports to him.

The official glanced at them all. "Papers for the elephant? Health certificate and proof of rabies vaccination?"

Josha passed it over.

While Peta had said that the injection was not mandatory, Amalee had already been receiving her annual doses recommended for captive elephants, and Josha had confirmed that the airport officials often asked for proof, and it was easier not to argue with them—just comply. Marissa waited while the papers were flipped back and forth a few times.

The official passed all the paperwork to Josha and nodded. "The elephant can be unloaded. I'll let the cargo team know you are ready. Welcome to Zimbabwe."

"Thanks," Josha said as he distributed the passports back to the team.

The customs man disappeared outside and headed to the rear of the plane. Within moments, a lot of shouting began.

"He's telling the cargo guys to get this elephant loaded on the truck quickly," Peta explained. "He says it's too hot to have her stand here; he doesn't want another dead animal."

"Just so you know, we weren't involved in the 'baby elephant to China' saga," Josha said with venom in his voice. "We wanted nothing to do with it. It should never have happened, as far as we are concerned. A lot of the people in the relocation business are crooked politicians and CITIES people. They should all be left out on that tarmac in this heat and see how they fare. *Ag*, no man. Poor thing."

"Is the elephant ready?" one of the cargo men asked.

"*Ja*, she doesn't need anesthetic. She's calm, hey?" Josha stated.

Marissa nodded her agreement.

Josha stood by the cargo door and beckoned the men to raise the high-capacity cargo loader, as they called the customized truck, until it was the same height as the plane.

The specialized crew stepped up and began pulling the extra chains, and the brakes off the bottom of the crate. Only then did an operator activate the specially designed floor to push the crate outwards onto the unloading area.

"Come on. Time for us to get on the ground. Grab your cases," Josha said.

Marissa made her way back through the crew area, down the passenger stairs and to the door, the others hot on her heels.

About five minutes later, they were all gathered on the tarmac.

"Dad," Josha said, stepping forward to the transportation truck and giving him a hug.

"Good trip?" Wayne asked, slapping his son's back.

"Easy as anything, this jumbo. You wouldn't even say there was an elephant in the hold. Not like that moody rhino you carted to Peta a few years back," Josha said.

Obviously, they were a close-knit family, Marissa mused. The multigenerational aspect of the business appealed to her sense of loyalty. Like her and her own dad. She blinked away tears. "Dad, you would have loved this," she whispered.

Movement brought her back to the present.

"Good to see you all again," Peta said, shaking hands with Josha's dad, Wayne. "This is Marissa, Dawn, and you know Mitch. Excuse me for a minute, I need to call Joss and let him know we've landed."

Marissa nodded and shook hands with Wayne. "Are you going to cover the crate?"

"No," Josha said. "We won't do that because of the heat. She'll be better with a little breeze while we're driving."

"Love you. See you soon," Peta said ending call. She put her hand on her stomach and turned to the group. "We're on the home stretch. Joss, Amos, and most of the anti-poaching teams are outside waiting to escort us."

"Why the AP teams?" Marissa asked. "Mitch is with us." Despite both Declan and Mitch thinking it less likely Chad would come for her in

Zimbabwe, they had decided to keep up her 24/7 armed guard, but a whole AP unit was overkill for her.

Peta shook her head. "Mitch's here for you. The others are here to hold back the press and the rest of the mob," Peta said. "With the baby's death going viral, Joss said a lot of international press has started to arrive. You've read the stories the papers have run about the captures taking place. Seen the leaked pictures. You know about the huge outcry over the export of baby elephant. We should have expected that when we publicized the date we were bringing back an elephant that was taken." Peta spread her hand towards the fence of the airport where a large crowd was gathered, chanting.

Marissa frowned. "The publicity is good, as it's highlighting the plight of the babies."

Peta nodded. "The downside is that the press is camped outside. Not a sight we see often here. You thought your American population was passionate about Amalee leaving; well, ours are too, because she's coming home. The difference is when our people get together in a protest, riots occur. We can't afford to have people get hurt because of this."

"I expected the crowds, but not that," Marissa said. She knew Africa was different to America, but this was another level.

Above the noise of the drone of jet engines and the vehicles, Marissa could hear the shouting of the reporters and the people at the fence.

"Well, the press is your department. You know what you're doing. While we appreciate the publicity for the captured babies, I've got no desire to engage with those vultures," Peta said.

"This is madness," Dawn said. The cheering increased as Wayne and Josha's abnormal-load vehicle started flashing its lights and took its position in front of the flatbed truck.

"Welcome to Africa, at her finest," Peta said and knocked on the back of the truck twice. "Come on," Peta said. "We can go through the freight building and catch the trucks on the other side of that. Our team has a safe passage cleared for us."

YINGWE RIVER LODGE, BINGA, ZIMBABWE

Travelling on the back of the slower moving transportation truck, once inside Bongani's borders, had been a good decision. Marissa turned her head to watch Dawn's reactions when she saw the gates of Yingwe River Lodge come into focus.

"There are wild elephants!" Dawn said. "Look, Marissa. Elephants."

"I'm surprised we didn't see any on the way here. It'll probably be Ndhlovy and her herd come to welcome our new arrival," Peta said calmly. "They'll be an integral part of Amalee's rewilding. Let's hope they all make a good impression on each other."

Amalee and Dawn had waited so long to come to Africa and see elephant in the wild, and finally they were here together, right near the sanctuary. There were trumpets and rumblings sounds even above the truck's sound as they slowed to go through the gate. Marissa took pleasure in seeing Dawn's face, and each of her expressions of joy, fascination and wonderment, and smiled.

Marissa took a deep breath. She couldn't feel any vibrations coming from Amalee, but her trunk was sniffing the air. But Amalee might have been communicating beyond the frequency humans could detect.

"It's okay, girl," Marissa reassured. "They're your new friends. You'll get to know them soon and not be alone anymore."

"It's a way yet till we can let her out with the other elephant," Peta said. "She needs quarantine time."

As they drove past, the elephant herd they made no move to come closer to the truck, although Marissa had thought that might happen. Instead, they kept their distance, but they clearly knew there was something special in the box.

Once through the gate, the guardsman shut it with huge poles that would keep the local elephants outside of the sanctuary.

Marissa let out a sigh of relief. As much as she loved Ndhlovy, she didn't fancy the idea of wild elephant being around while they unloaded and settled Amalee.

Finally, the truck came to a stop beside the elephant stables.

"Hang in there, girl. Then you'll feel African soil once more," Marissa said.

"African soil," Dawn repeated. "I never seriously imagined her and I would get to stand on it together."

Marissa smiled and touched Dawn's shoulder as they stood close beside the crate that had travelled thousands of miles.

The staff came out of the building, and Marissa couldn't believe the efficiency with which they got ready to bring the elephant down from the trailer, all the while listening to Josha and Wayne, who had climbed up onto the truck and started to undo the side of the crate Marissa had had specially manufactured. They were helped down off the truck and stood next to it.

"Marissa, you ready?" Josha called.

She shook her head. "Dawn, do you want to walk her out? This was your dream longer than it was mine. Her first steps on the African continent."

Tears filled Dawn's eyes as she walked up the ramp.

Marissa took a deep breath. She knew that from the moment Dawn and Amalee had left the circus, this had been what Dawn had wished for. Never in Dawn's wildest dreams could she have imagined she would be here in Africa to actually achieve it. Marissa wished her father had been here to share the moment with them.

Wayne opened the crate, and Amalee turned toward the exit where Dawn was holding out a treat. Amalee didn't hesitate and started to walk down the ramp next to her, as if she'd done this a hundred times before.

"This way to her quarantine area," Joss said.

Marissa waited at the bottom of the ramp. "Ready, my friend? First steps home in Mother Africa."

Dawn nodded.

She stepped off the ramp onto the dirt of the sanctuary yard.

Marissa couldn't stop smiling as she walked next to Amalee on the other side.

"We're here, Amalee," Dawn said. "We're finally back in Africa." She gave her another treat, and Amalee took it in her trunk, popped it into her mouth, and looked for more in Dawn's hand.

Tears shone in Dawn's eyes and ran freely down her cheeks. Amalee reached up and touched them.

"Good tears, Amalee. Happy ones," Dawn said.

Amalee dropped her trunk back to Dawn's hand and then her clothing, clearly looking for treats.

"She doesn't seem to be concerned, does she?" Marissa said.

When Amalee couldn't find another treat in Dawn's pockets, she then turned her attention to see if Marissa had any.

Together, they escorted the elephant into the building and down the long corridor to the first of the holding cells, which Joss indicated. He stepped aside to let them in.

Amalee looked around.

"It's okay, girl. We're here; this is home now," Marissa said. "We'll be close; don't you stress."

Amalee put her trunk in the air and trumpeted.

Goosebumps ran up and down Marissa's body.

Mitch looked at the group around Amalee.

Marissa and Dawn belonged there. It was as if they anticipated each move the elephant made. He could only imagine what they were giving up to let Amalee have this life. Even if they were not successful in fully rewilding her, it was better than Amalee being on the wrong continent. Organizing the relocation would have been a huge emotional strain on Marissa, especially so soon after her father's murder.

Mitch had only been with her for the last two weeks and he was still in awe at her tenacity. He couldn't help but be proud of Marissa and the way she was holding up.

Peta closed the gate with Joss's help and rested her arms on the wood. "She transported well. It was as if she had complete trust in both Marissa and Dawn and didn't question what they were asking her to do or subject her to."

Marissa had come away from America, away from the threat from Chad. It was hard to imagine that, while she was so public about her elephant and the rewilding process, she was being so secretive that her own life was in danger.

That psychopathic cousin of hers could come after her, and if he did, Mitch's job was going to be a real challenge.

A sniper in Africa. There were so many places for him to nest and hide around the lodge, wait for the right time, and then take out Marissa. If that was Chad's endgame as Walter has said. It was a small mercy that he'd been given the information the US security team had put together on Chad. His

MO had clearly changed since he'd left prison. Apparently, he liked to make murder personal now. Get up close to his victim. And Mitch knew he would have a better chance of protecting her if Chad came in for the kill.

Mitch looked at the three females huddled together: the elephant, Dawn and Marissa.

All of them were potentially on Chad's hit list, and Mitch could only hope that between him and his team, they would be able to protect them.

Marissa had woven her way under his skin from the first moment he'd seen her walking through the doors at the airport just a few months earlier. She was everything he hadn't expected and hadn't known that he was waiting for. He knew that he might literally have to take a bullet to save her.

Instinctively he looked around, assessing the many places that Chad could use as cover if he came into the area. He saw a community working hard to settle an elephant who had flown thousands of miles, and yet, there was still excitement oozing out from Marissa. An infectious happiness. Here at Yingwe River Lodge, he was probably facing one of his most challenging adversaries he had to deal with.

An unhinged, trained ex-soldier with a vendetta.

He would need every one of his guards to keep alert, and ensure that nothing happened to Marissa, because he wasn't sure he wanted to live in a world without her.

"You did good, dear. It's not easy to let someone else take responsibility for something you're quite capable of. Especially someone so young," Joss said as he came to stand next to Peta and Mitch.

"It's quite novel to stand back and let others do the work," Peta said. "Young Josha is a credit to Wild Transportations. We need more young vets like this in Africa. Just look at him with Amalee. So confident."

Joss wrapped her in his arms, and Peta leaned back into him and said, "Besides, I get her for the rest of her life. I can't be jealous of his part now. Step one done and dusted."

Mitch smiled as they stood together, watching the small party settling the elephant in.

"He would have hated this amount of attention being on just one elephant," Tsessebe said, as he came to stand beside Mitch.

"Peta's late father?" Mitch asked.

"*Yebo,*" Tsessebe said.

Mitch smiled. "You'd know. You were his right-hand-man. What about you? What do you think?"

"Me?" Tsessebe asked. "It is amazing. Bringing a grown elephant on a plane all this way from America."

"I think so too. You doing okay?" Mitch asked. "You've seemed a bit lost lately."

Tsessebe nodded.

"You know you're always welcome in my camp," Mitch said. "Come spend some time there. Away from the lodge."

"Peta said I'm retired and should sit on the farm and drink Chibuku. But getting fat like an old man isn't what I want to do," Tsessebe said.

Mitch laughed. "I could do with someone to teach tracking; someone who knows the bush and is good with prickly people. We get some real porcupines with their quills up sent to us to learn more," Mitch said. "Marines are good for the fighting, but people with bush skills like yours are harder to come by. You have a gift that you can pass on to others."

"I will think about it," Tsessebe said as he looked around the stable.

Mitch eyes landed on Joss, who held onto the bump on Peta's stomach. "She's about to get really busy soon enough. You'll have a baby crying in their house one of these days."

Tsessebe grinned. "Perhaps a change for a while is good. Babies cry a lot."

"The door is always open," Mitch said.

"Mamma. Dada. Can I come in yet?" Sophia called from the outside of the quarantine area.

Joss nodded and Sophia walked through the gate to them.

Peta beamed at her daughter, then bent down and picked her up, hugging her tight. "Oh lordy, you're getting too big for me to do this. Growing too fast."

"It's good to see Amalee again," Sophia said.

"All three tons of her," Peta said, cuddling Sophia close.

Joss ruffled his daughter's hair.

Sophia looked across the stable. "Can I go sit with Amos?"

"Of course you can," Peta said putting her down, as Sophia was already wriggling to get moving.

"Have you made any plans for a potential attack from the psycho?" Joss asked in a quiet voice, once she had gone.

"A waiting game at the moment," Mitch said. "I got to see some of Marissa's skills while we were in the States. She's not someone who folds under pressure. I watched her on the shooting range over there; she's more than competent with rifles and handguns. She's got some impressive Taekwondo moves too."

"The question is if she'll freeze or use them against him. We won't get to test that, as the attack won't happen, because you will do your job and keep him well away from here, for all our sakes," Peta said, clearly listening in on their quiet conversation.

"There's got to be some benefit to having an anti-poaching unit made up of ex-marines. They're ready for this kind of detail. I've also called in some extra mates to help out. Her cousin isn't getting through us on African soil."

Peta reached out and touched Mitch on his arm. "I don't even think I need to threaten to hold you to that promise. Not with the way you look at her, and the way she looks at you. I didn't think I would see the day this happened, but I'm so happy for you both."

"Thanks," Mitch said, though their relationship was far from a done deal. She lived in America; he lived over here. There was a lot to still sort out. "But I'd still expect you to do that. I can't lose her. I can't lose any of them on my watch."

"You won't," Joss said. "You and your guys are top-notch. You'll stop him. Besides, from what you told me about the last attack on her, that elephant of hers has it in for him too, so you have a watchdog on your side. And talking elephant, Amalee doesn't look any worse for the long flight," Joss said, nodding toward Amalee, who was snuffling down game cubes. "She looks as happy as when I last saw her in Nevada."

"She was fantastic the whole time," Peta said. "She has a lovely temperament and is clearly bonded with Marissa and Dawn. All I can say is thank goodness Marissa has the means to stay here for a long while, so she can settle in and befriend other handlers. It's going to take time, I think. Lots of it."

"Mamma, can Amalee dance with me again, like we did at Marissa's stable?" Sophia asked as she returned to her mother's side.

"Oh, sweetie. You and this elephant are friends already, but I'd rather you don't go into her stable alone. Not for a little while," Peta said.

Joss smiled and turned away, his shoulders shaking.

Peta shook her head. "Just let me make sure she's settled before you–"

Amalee's trunk reached through the elephant fencing, and she wrapped it around Sophia. Regardless of what Peta thought, Amalee had her own ideas on how long they should wait.

Now Joss laughed aloud.

Josha was standing in the middle of the stable. He shrugged. "She wanted to come over to say hi, and Marissa and Dawn said she knows Sophia already."

Sophia reached out her little hand and stroked Amalee's trunk. "Hello, beautiful. Everyone here's going to look after you."

Mitch looked at Marissa who had walked along next to her elephant; he couldn't help the smile.

Marissa had tears in her eyes, but she was smiling too. "I think Amalee is happy to have a friend in her new home, and it will make her settling in so much easier for her, Sophia."

But her gaze was on Mitch.

He caught her staring at him, and a wide grin formed on his face as he winked.

He could see the blush start from her neck and go all the way to the top of her forehead.

Busted.

CHAPTER 29
NOTHING IS SECRET

LOS CABOS, MEXICO

24 November 2014

At ten o'clock in the morning, the yacht club café at Los Cabos, Mexico, was packed. Chad ordered another cup of coffee and a breakfast burrito to accompany it.

Sitting and watching the ocean had always calmed him. Its rhythmic waves crashing onto sandy shores. A smell of salt and freshness.

Freedom.

He needed that calm right now. Having bought a sizable secondhand yacht and sailed down into Mexican waters, he knew that they had bigger criminals to catch here than one little ex-U.S. Services felon. Besides, staying in the USA, with all the street cameras and the nice bounty on his head, was becoming difficult. His options were to go to ground and hide or to Mexico, while he waited for the heat to die down and the small army of private security she'd employed, to grow bored and leave.

Marissa was out of control without her father watching her spending. She didn't appreciate what she'd inherited. She'd spent millions on moving that stupid elephant back to Africa.

Time hadn't changed her, but it had changed him. He had learned patience.

Money first. Revenge second.

He picked the newspaper up again.

A few pages in, a headline caught his attention: 'Is history repeating itself between the USA and Zimbabwe?'

He read on about how the once rescued elephant brought to the USA was now being relocated back to Africa, at the same time that a new group of young elephants were being exported; couldn't they keep them in Africa?

The waitress put his order on the table. "These millionaires in the USA have too much money; they spend it to bring an elephant from Africa, then send it back thirty years later. They should come walk a day in our shoes and spend money here on people who will appreciate it so much more than an elephant."

"I agree," he said. "*Gracias.*"

She didn't linger near him but went about her duties. He liked that about her and always tipped her well. Another thing he'd learned in prison was not to underestimate the little people. Not only did they spit in your coffee when you were a dick to them, but they knew things. They paid attention to details. And if you paid for the information, they were always willing to give a little more in the hope of getting some extra cash.

He could not believe how quickly Marissa's up-front approach to the relocation had opened everyone's hearts, and more importantly, their wallets, to help other elephants in the same position who didn't have the means to go home to Africa. Her foundation would help with resettlement transportation and regular payments to the elephant sanctuary where the elephant would retire.

"Yeah, they are screwed up," he said aloud. "Don't mess with the new China."

Then he sat up straight, because right there, in black and white, was exactly where he could find her in Africa: Yingwe River Lodge in Binga, Zimbabwe.

He didn't even need to look for her.

He downed the last of his coffee, left a large tip for the waitress, and folded his paper under his arm.

The security firm she had working for her, after he'd dealt with her father, was well-trained and from one of the best protection units in the USA. He knew better than to try to get to her when they were around.

It was a different playing field now that she was in Africa.

It was time for a family reunion.

BEIRA, MOZAMBIQUE, AFRICA

27 November 2014

Chad's feet splashed down into the cool water of the sea off Macuti Beach, Beira, Mozambique. The dhow had brought him right up to the sand at high tide, just as he'd paid them to do.

Admittedly, his flight into Maputo had been exactly what he was expecting from an African country, where the officials wanted expensive bribes, which he begrudgingly paid to get through as fast as he could, and with as little scrutiny as possible. His new passport said his name was Charles Jones. He wore his hair longer and shaggier than it had been in prison, a white T-shirt, and khaki shorts.

Nothing about his outward appearance said that he was ex-military.

Or suggested him as an ex-prisoner.

After speaking to a man in the bar about the best route to Gorongosa National Park, he stole a car and made his way towards Beira, carrying his own fuel in the trunk in jerry cans.

At the small town of Nhanguo, he turned east to Nova Sofala.

This once grand town was almost forgotten to history since the Portuguese had left and was now partly reclaimed by the silting of the Buzi Estuary.

Leaving the car unlocked so that it was easier for the next person to appropriate, Chad walked to the seafront. He caught a local dhow to complete the twenty miles to Beira. Driving a stolen car into a big city could bring its own problems.

Problems he could do without.

He made his way down Olivera Salaza Avenida until he came to the avenue address he'd burned into his memory during his days in Somalia. A bolt hole, if ever one was necessary.

To call it upmarket, in American terms, would be an exaggeration. While it was a large house and may once have been grand, red brick now showed through the faded, flaking paint. A garden bed was scratched out in the beach sand, and sad trees hedged the perimeter, cut clear at the base so you could easily tell if anyone was trying to hide behind them. Barbed wire topped the fence that ran the whole way around the property.

He smiled.

There was no security outside. They didn't need it. The locals knew not to come near.

He opened the corroded gate and walked in.

There was no dog to greet him. Only the low hum of a generator running somewhere around the back.

At least someone was home.

The door opened before he had a chance to knock. In front of him stood an enormous Black man, his broad shoulders and thick corded muscles formed from years of hard labor and survival. His hair was shaved short to his scalp, his face covered with tribal scarring.

When Chad had met him in Somalia, it was explained to Chad that those scars marked him as being from the Mundari tribe in Sudan.

"Now, here's someone I did not think I would ever see again. Welcome, my friend."

"Jamiel," Chad said. "Somehow I always knew I would see you down the line. A friendship like ours is not easily forgotten."

CHAPTER 30
PROWLING

MUTURE, ZIMBABWE

2 December 2014

Chad and Jamiel crossed into Zimbabwe at the Mutare border post in an almost brand-new Range Rover and made their way into the capital, Harare.

They downgraded to an older Isuzu truck to be less conspicuous. Chad put the money from the sold vehicle in a backpack before they picked up five more men, who sat on the back, on top of the weapons cache and supplies. He was blowing through his nest egg fast to finance his revenge. Unlike Marissa, his inheritance didn't have that many zeros behind it. But it was worth it to get his hands on her cash, and to be able to give her the death she deserved.

Killing her would make him feel like the richest man alive.

"They are expendable muscle we might need," Jamiel explained. "Once we get to my friend's house in Vic Falls, I want you to stay inside. You're a *qorrax-la'aan* and will stand out even more than you did in Harare."

"A what?" Chad asked. "Speak English."

"A sunless one, who doesn't belong in Africa," Jamiel said. "And here they don't cover their heads and faces."

"I thought this was a tourist town?" Chad said. "Who's more touristy than an American?"

"It's becoming more common for tours to be in the townships, but mostly they stay in the tourist areas. The labor force lives very much apart from their paycheck. A few hard-to-break traditions remain after being an English colony."

Chad nodded. "Seriously? My cousin is sitting in one of those luxury lodges. How hard can it be to get me in there?"

"We'll see once we know more about where she is. Surely, after what happened in Somalia, you have learned not to be impatient and act irrationally? That is what got you caught."

Chad shook his head. "I–"

"You were given a chance to do that protection with me, and you blew it," Jamiel said, no emotion in his voice.

"You know killing Farid was an accident. You were there. I don't regret doing it. He deserved to die. Thinking himself so superior. Favoring his own daughter over anyone else–"

Jamiel nodded. "But we were paid to protect him, and one of 'our own' killed him. Did not look good for us now, did it?"

"I was there as a US Marine. It was a sanctioned protection detail. I wasn't informed why he was also under militia protection. You know, I never asked many questions about your other business. I was happy just to know who you wanted killed."

"We both know the militia considered you one of us. Ignorance is not an excuse," Jamiel said.

Chad looked out the window. More trees and poverty-stricken huts passed outside, people eking out a subsistence living. "I have paid for that mistake. Twelve years in a military prison. Do you have any idea what they are like?"

Jamiel grinned. "I have seen my fair share of jails. I suspect your American jails are like a hotel by comparison. All you and your marines had to do was make sure that he remained in his house. He needed to live. He would have been the one who ended the oppression in South Sudan. We know there will be another war soon, and millions will die again, which would not have happened if Farid was alive."

"I can't change the past, but I can get my hands on millions when I get to my cousin. It'll help ease the past for you. It'll be a simple job for the likes of us."

"I hope you're right, my friend," Jamiel said. "I like doing nothing, far away from trouble, sitting on my beach. Unless we can get in and out, and away clean, it doesn't happen."

Chad nodded. "The money is worth going after. What do you know about that place I said she was at—Yingwe?"

"Nothing, but by this time tomorrow, we'll have enough information to make a plan," Jamiel said. "Just remember, nothing is free in this world, and you owe me a big debt—enough to make me forget about Somalia."

Chad scowled. He hadn't travelled halfway around the world to not collect from Marissa.

She would pay, and then she would die.

CHAPTER 31
HERITAGE OF A GIANT

YINGWE RIVER LODGE, ANIMAL RESCUE AND REHABILITATION CENTER, BINGA, ZIMBABWE

5 January 2015

I felt the rumbles of the approaching wild elephant.

The vibrations came through the floor of my stable. The sounds carried on the wind.

They were coming to visit again.

Marissa, Dawn, and Peta had been talking more and more about the quarantine being almost up.

Marissa and Dawn stood outside my stable, but they were close. Peta was farther away, still behind the thick elephant bars, but she was there. My new family stood with her—Zola, who talked a lot, and Danie. Excitement vibrated off them all.

Something was happening today.

Did this mean I was about to see the other elephant who speak with me?

I had smelt them when they had been near the stable.

I had certainly heard them; they had been nearby since the first day.

They had been calling me since I arrived, but I had not seen them yet.

I had been alone for so long without one of my kind.

Would they let me be part of their herd?

The door opened, and the golden early morning light flooded in. It splashed all around the stable. I loved the color; it reminded me of a time when I was with my family long ago.

With a rumble, in came the one called Ndhlovy.

She was large. Impressive. And fast.

She didn't slow down but came right at the iron gate that separated us. Ndhlovy put her trunk through the gate, pressed her forehead against it. Trying to push it.

If it were wood, it would have broken, but the metal held.

Ndhlovy's trunk was reaching for me. She was encouraging me to connect.

To meet with her.

Tentatively, I put my trunk forward.

And for the first time in a very long time, I touched one of my own kind.

This was not a dream of days long past; she was real.

And as we spoke to each other, the bond deepened.

I touched Ndhlovy, and we stroked each other's trunks. It was as if we were sisters greeting each other again after a long time apart.

There was so much about Ndhlovy that was familiar. And so much to still get to know.

I touched her forehead, as she did mine. I put my trunk out and smelled her chest and body.

Marissa was smiling at me.

"Aww, look at them. Oh, my goodness, their trunks. It's as if they know each other," Marissa said, her hand on her heart.

I wanted to go to Marissa and tell her, as part of my herd, how exciting this was, but then the one called Khwezi pushed alongside his mother. She seemed reluctant to let him say hello.

I greeted Khwezi carefully. Children bite.

He was a male child, tired of waiting to grow up and forge his own future. He simply wanted to greet me. He didn't want to stay and talk and get to know me—not like his mother.

There were others from Ndhlovy's herd. Each came in and said hello.

Ndhlovy stayed close while I greeted each of them. They wandered back out into the now bright sunshine.

Except Ndhlovy.

Peta brought Ndhlovy's food and water. She ate outside the bars. She sprayed water at me.

I did the same to her.

I had not played with water with another elephant for so many years.

I ate chunks of sweet watermelon, one of my favorite treats, as did she.

As always, Dawn made sure I had enough food. Both she and Marissa were now in my stable with me.

They had been feeding me trees that tasted different.

Different textures.

Different smells.

Ndhlovy smelled like those.

The herd moved off to graze, I could no longer see them from my stable. But I could feel their rumbles in my feet and trunk, as they let me know they were still in the area.

Ndhlovy stayed.

Every so often, she would reach for me with her trunk, and we would talk together. There were years of each other's lives to learn about.

As the inky night began to fall, Peta and her Joss, with the metal legs, coaxed Ndhlovy out and away from my stable.

I was sad to see her go.

They shut the door, and I was left alone with Marissa and Dawn once again.

I trumpeted.

Just outside the door, I heard a trumpet back.

Tonight, I would not sleep alone; the herd would check on me throughout the night, until the door opened in the early morning as the sun lightened the sky, and my new herd waited to greet me.

CHAPTER 32
BABY STEPS

YINGWE RIVER LODGE, ANIMAL RESCUE AND REHABILITATION CENTER, BINGA, ZIMBABWE

7 January 2015

Mitch sat on the deck at the lodge and nursed his Zambezi beer. It had gone warm long ago, as he stared out across the lake. Joss, Peta, and Bongani were with him, although they seemed more interested in him than he was in his beer.

"You okay, Mitch?" Joss asked.

"Too much pondering time. Kat has to go and fetch Christine in Vic Falls, and Marissa is with Jason Carpenter, while I've got some paperwork to catch up on. He's got personal protection experience, so I figured he knew what he was doing well enough, but I have missed having her with me all day."

"You've had almost two months of not leaving her side. Good to hear you are giving yourself a bit of a break from the pressure," Bongani said.

"Mate, I'm not about to stop watching her back. Honestly, it's been a bloody treat. I think there might be more to us. She's so different from what I expected."

"Could it be that the mighty Mitch is off the market?" Joss asked. "Loving seeing your fall, man. Damn, I owe you a foot rub, Peta. You were right; it's a happy ever after in the making." He laughed.

Peta snorted. "You doubted a woman's intuition?"

Mitch frowned. "Don't count those chickens just yet. First, I have to keep her alive for that to happen. And then there's this whole living on different continents thing."

"Do not stress about it," Bongani said. "Things like that have a way of working themselves out. So, what is up. You called a meeting?"

"I had a rendezvous with Esulu Duzi on the side of the road again," Mitch said. "Not only did he say four went down on the last flight, but he hit me with another bombshell. ZimParks are already snatching another lot for China. This quota is fifteen. Those papers didn't lie. They're doing more trips with fewer elephants and filling the rest of the space with other wild animals. Despite the world's reaction to the last shipment, they are carrying on with the exports."

"What the fuck?" Peta said.

Mitch's head hurt. "That bloody Environment Minister still gave it the go-ahead, even though the ZimParks guys were reporting that the facilities over there were a joke."

Christine entered the deck and sat down on a chair that Bongani motioned to. Mitch nodded to acknowledge her arrival, but his mind was elsewhere.

Greed was clearly at play when the government overrode the experts. And a government that obeyed the law was a luxury they didn't have in Zimbabwe

He looked at his watch. 1:15 p.m.

He had been away from Marissa's side for half a day. A knot of fear burned in his stomach. An unfamiliar sensation.

Since the USA, and then her landing in Zimbabwe, they had spent almost every moment together; they had grown even closer.

Maybe too close. He feared he could no longer protect her objectively. Feelings were beginning to get in the way, just as Declan had warned him.

"Mitch? You with us?" Joss asked from across the table, bringing his thoughts to the present.

"Affirmative," he said, sitting up straighter to listen and get his head back in the game. Christine was thanking everyone for bringing her and her grand-mother home so quickly as there was something going on in the township.

"What do you mean by 'unusual activity' in the township?" Mitch asked.

Joss threw him a look of disbelief as if to say, *Really? Keep up!*

Christine took another sip of her water. "There's a white man who travels with a dark man, with heavy scars." She pointed to her face. "Lots of scars. Like tribal markings."

"Not Zimbabwean then?" Bongani said.

She shook her head. "Farther north, like Kenya, Sudan, maybe Nigeria, he was darker. Not like me."

"What was it about them that frightened you? I know you; you don't scare easily," Joss said. "You bringing your grandmother back here from her old-age home in her state means you're seriously worried."

Christine nodded. "Do you remember at Ephrem's funeral—the buses of supporters who were brought in? I saw the face of one of them, even though they knew they were defeated and their plan for attacking here had failed. He stood in the door of the bus, watching the lodge until he couldn't see us anymore. He's one of the men who travel with them, although his face has a burn mark on it now."

"Might be from when some of those buses met with accidents," Mitch said. "I remember thinking how cold Tichawana was for giving that order to kill those kids before he lost his life."

"My brother's hired troubled youths have become grown hired muscle," Bongani said.

Christine nodded. "He was the one who was at the markets, asking for a tracker. He said they didn't want to drive into the area and needed to go in on foot into the Chete Safari Area."

Joss drummed his fingers on the table.

Mitch swore. "Where were you when you saw him?"

"I was visiting with Julian Seziba. He sells *knobkerries*, walking sticks, and carved goods to the tourists."

Bongani said, "Did this man see you?"

"I don't think so. I hid by the clothes of the lady next door until he walked away," Christine said.

"If they were legitimate hunters, they would have been using a registered hunting outfit and using hunting quotas and permits for what they were going after," Joss said.

Mitch nodded. "Add to that, it's strange seeing a white bloke hanging around the township. What's he doing outside the tourist areas?"

"You think it's Marissa's cousin?" Bongani asked.

Mitch nodded. "Could be."

"She's such an incredible woman, and then this two-bit loser of a cousin wants to kill her? So unfair," Peta said. "How did he get on a plane from the States when they are looking for him for her father's murder?"

"People like us know how to disappear," Mitch said. "However, I suspect he's not going to have access to military information after a murder conviction, but he'd have prison contacts he could use. He'll probably still need hired help."

Christine stood as if to leave.

"Thank you. You have been most helpful. Let me or Lwazi know if you need any help with your grandmother. He is home from university at the moment," Bongani said as he got up and shook Christine's hand with both of his and she walked away.

"It's not too early to bring Gideon Mthemba in on this. He's still the member in charge at Binga. He helped us last time," Bongani said as he sat back down.

Mitch nodded. "Good idea, especially if it's nothing to do with poaching. He'll enjoy a change of drama from us."

Peta smiled. "That poor man was caught up in red tape for ages after the Tichawana assault. I suggest, if you're dragging Gideon into this, that you give him an expensive bottle of brandy before you even open your mouth. A KWV brand at least."

Joss laughed. "True. Mitch, will you organize that? You're always in and out of the police station. No one will think anything of it if you head in again. Gideon needs to know. I'm sure he would appreciate a heads-up if there's another fight coming to his jurisdiction."

Mitch nodded. His mind was working overtime on ways to keep Marissa safe. "I have another idea. Tsessebe has been at my camp for a few weeks now. Why don't we ask him to find them in the township, and then Gideon and his men can go and arrest Chad."

Peta exploded, slamming her fist onto the table. "Have you completely lost your mind, Mitch? Tsessebe's old. He's been with my family since—always! And you want to send him in to track a group of thugs and killers?"

"Hang on, Peta. Mitch might be onto something," Joss said.

"No. We're not asking Tsessebe to do that."

"Sorry to say this, but Tsessebe's a proud man. He still wants to work," Mitch said.

Peta shook her head. "But–"

"You realize that he's closer to Bongani's age than your father's," Mitch said.

"But he's always been here. What if something happens to him?" She frowned and hiccupped as she swallowed a sob.

Joss reached over his chair arm and hugged her. "This is unlike you, to be so emotional. Usually you just give us what for…"

"It's these baby hormones," Peta said, rubbing her tummy. "They are doing strange things to me and my body. You're probably right. I'm being overprotective of him, and I know my dad would have gotten a kick out of it if Tsessebe could help bring them to their knees."

"Now that is the truth," Bongani said.

So they had the beginnings of a plan–if Tsessebe agreed.

Mitch hoped he was wrong.

Hoped it wasn't Chad, somehow in Zimbabwe, and tracking Marissa down, but the chances of it being another white guy with some hired muscle, looking to cause chaos was slim.

In his gut, a sick feeling churned.

He had to protect Marissa. Her life could depend on it.

CHAPTER 33
ALL THAT GLITTERS

VICTORIA FALLS, ZIMBABWE

7 January 2015

Anger radiated in waves from Chad. Despite the beautiful environment he stood in, the gently falling mist from the Victoria Falls themself, he could not stop it bubbling to the surface.

He stood toe to toe with Jamiel, neither one backing down. "I didn't come all this way to turn around and go home," Chad said.

"I understand that," Jamiel said. "But with the information we have about this place, information I wasn't aware of when I said I would help you grab your cousin, this has become an impossible mission. We're walking into a rampaging buffalo herd. It's suicidal."

"I don't see that many buffalo," Chad spread his arms wide. "And if they are there, we just go around."

"Even if we could, the intel says that this lodge she's at is crawling with ex-military vets. They come to catch poachers, and the chief who owns the whole area where that lodge is, he and the resident ex-British marine, they took down Tichawana Ndou, the one who the underworld knew as King Gogo wa de Patswa."

"So?" Chad asked.

Jamiel took a deep breath. "He was a kingpin crime lord in Zimbabwe—had a thriving business before he lost control and went after his brother's lands. From the information gathered, he had many good contacts, and not everything was found by the police raids. Some other powerful people benefited greatly from having him removed. One of them is a lawyer for the government in Harare, Shumba Chitepo. It's rumored he reports directly to the president. Anything he wants, he takes. He took a chunk of what once was King Gogo wa de Patswa's and protects it fiercely."

"What are you saying?" Chad asked.

"In a way, these people who removed him, Bongani and Brennan, did not go after the King's men. They just took him out of the picture when he attacked them. They gained nothing but peace from his death. Shumba filled a vacuum, and he's worse than the King. He has the police's and the army's backing. He is set up well enough to stage a coup if he wanted to, and win. He might view them with rose-tinted glasses, as the people who gifted him much. He could become involved. Our militia does not want this fight. This is not a place where you can pick a fight with your cousin and win."

"You won't help me?" Chad asked, his voice threatening.

"The militia, no. But me personally, I'll help, on the condition you think carefully. One marine with artificial legs and a local chief, along with a few friends, took down the previous King. We know that the King had firepower and men. Now they have a whole anti-poaching training facility, so more bodies to throw at the protection. And the rumor is that the Chief apparently has a coven of *sahar*—uuummm– *sangomas* on their side."

"*Sangomas*?"

"Traditional healers, but more like witch doctors," Jamiel said. "The BaTonga people call them *n'Goma*s. We don't have enough trained people, and we do not know what bad medicine they have used. Until we know more about these protections on the land, the only ones walking into that lodge area are you and me. The others we picked up in Harare are local street fighters. They will run from a *n'Goma's* curse if they find out about it. We need to retreat for now, take her when she's in a different location. Not on this chief's land."

"Where? From here, she goes back to the USA. I can't get to her there. This is the weakest link in the chain. Right here," Chad insisted.

"No, this link is strong. Probably stronger than her home in the USA. I can't see how to do this—not yet," Jamiel said as he scratched his chin.

"How many million do you think she dropped bringing her elephant here? And she didn't hesitate to spend it. If I can get to her, I'll force her to transfer her money into my account. She's still scared of me; she'll pay. If not, then we take the kidnap route and demand a huge payout; we just fail to exchange her. With the size of her foundation, there is no way she came to Africa without insurance. She's going to die, either way. We just need to snatch her, then get the money—"

"I still do not like it," Jamiel said.

"I already know of an abandoned farm barn that will hold her securely for a few weeks; she'll have biometric scanners and complex passwords to get to her money. I need her alive to do all that," Chad admitted.

Jamiel turned away from him and walked to the edge of the trail overlooking the falls. He took out a Lion Lager from the pack on his back, opened it, and downed it. After a loud burp, he sat on the side of the path. "My friend, you're mad to keep someone hostage long-term. Do you know the size of the team you need to do that? Do you know how much it costs to pull something like that off?"

"I do," Chad said. "And not as much as you think. The hardest part is getting my hands on her. That's why I came to you for help. The rest will fall into place easily; besides, she's a prima donna, so she's unlikely to try to fight. Easy pickings."

Chad began pacing to the edge of the cliff into the falls, and back to the path.

Jamiel shook his head. "An abandoned shed, in the Zimbabwean bush, with no internet connection for her banking? No biometric scanner in that barn either. I do not believe that we should pursue this. Look at the intel. She's protected where she is. There is some baby elephant scheme happening as we speak that involves Shumba, and she's related to the elephant. She's already on his radar. Move against him in any way, and you will have your throat cut during the night. Don't you get it? Back away. Do not play here in Africa; don't poke the sleeping lion."

"Fuck, haven't you been listening?" Chad said. "It's millions of dollars. And she is *against* Shumba, not with him. She's the face behind the campaign to stop the baby elephant from being relocated to China. She's the one who is causing him trouble now. Not the people she is with."

"I have been. And it's not worth us dying for," Jamiel said. "We need a better plan than just going in guns blazing and snatching her. We're sitting ducks on land or on water. We have no escape route. Think this through properly; don't let that temper of yours rule you again."

"I'm not giving up," Chad warned. "You can bail if you want. I'm going to get her, one way or another, even if I have to live here for a year to find their weak point."

"I hear that. Are you sure you can achieve this without the militia?" Jamiel asked.

"I came to you as a friend, not the bloody militia," Chad said.

Jamiel nodded. "How do you plan to find out more about these borders that the *n'Gomas* protect, to get in and snatch her?"

"Patience. We'll find someone who knows that area. I have learned patience. According to her newspaper interviews, she said, 'Rewilding an elephant takes a long time.' She's not rushing back home to the USA."

Chad grinned at the thought of her transferring all her money to his account. And of her dressed in that racy underwear of hers, with the diamante sparkles, as he put a bullet in the space between her perfectly sculpted eyebrows.

"We don't need to rush this either."

CHAPTER 34
A THREATENING CLOUD

NEAR SINAMATELLA CAMP, HWANGE NATIONAL PARK, ZIMBABWE

8 January 2015 – 06:00

Shumba stood beside the baby elephant bomas in Hwange National Park. Milo was with him, and Frank flanked his other side.

"The next shipment is for fifteen and is due out in three weeks. The plane will land in the late afternoon, so there will still be sunlight to load. It will leave at seven o'clock. The heat issue on the tarmac will be avoided this time," Shumba said.

Milo moved his feet uncomfortably, shaking his head. "Frank, you will find himself loading at midday and transporting in the heat. A better solution might be for the plane to remain on the runway till nine-thirty-ish. If ZimParks brings in more trucks to make the delivery go faster, it will help. If we load here later in the afternoon, begin at say six o'clock, we leave the elephant till last. We'll need three hours to load everything, and delivery will bring us closer to nine o'clock. They should be able to load the predators first, then the sable and impala. Lastly, they get the babies on board and be away by nine-thirty. It'll mean floodlights at the airport."

"Go on," Shumba said as he glared at Frank. "What about the delivery?"

"We might be under for the quota this time," Frank said. "There are three babies that will not pass inspection to get on the plane. Two were extras we were going to send as goodwill for what happened last time, but there have been complications. They got sick just after they were given the rabies vaccinations. My men have tried everything, but they are still losing condition. We called Milo for help."

Shumba looked at Milo. "And?"

"I have done what I can, I cannot do more—not here. But there is a place that can. She'll help the elephant willingly, but there will be problems getting them back. The elephant orphanage in Binga. Where the stolen elephant just returned to."

Shumba nodded. "I know the place. I remember the paperwork for the license to bring that elephant home. The application was rushed through as the USA contact needed to move the elephant before their winter. Some foundation, give me a moment, and I will remember the name…"

Milo continued, "Usually, they only have one vet at the Animal Rescue And Rehabilitation Center. They call her maNdhlovu, the best vet with elephants, but she's pregnant. There are two others helping her at the moment. If we take these babies to her facility to heal, I think together they could get at least one of the three better enough to fly to make quota."

"You trust this woman?" Shumba asked.

Milo shook his head. "She can't be bought, that is for sure. She'll try to keep the elephant and do anything she can to stop the plane, but she's the best hope for these babies' survival. For us to make quota. We can't have any more die. The newspapers always get to know, and there's always trouble. I'm at a loss."

Shumba balled his fists.

"Three sick," Frank said. "We need fifteen for quota—"

"Milo, it is important to Zimbabwe that these elephants are well enough to get on the plane," Shumba said. "That is when their Chinese veterinarian examines them. I'm sure he can tell a healthy elephant from a sick one. It will be different to before. They have their own vet attending this time because of what happened. Call this woman. Tell her that ZimParks will pay her to heal the three babies. But they are to be returned for this next flight. She has three weeks. That is all."

Milo went to speak, but Shumba lifted his hand to silence him.

"Better yet, make sure she knows that if she doesn't comply and return them, I will make it my personal duty to have her license for her orphanage cancelled, and all elephant in her possession confiscated."

CHAPTER 35
WHEN WORLDS COLLIDE

YINGWE RIVER LODGE, ANIMAL RESCUE AND REHABILITATION CENTER, BINGA, ZIMBABWE

8 January 2015 – 07:00

Marissa and Mitch were in the stable; Marissa brushed Amalee, and Mitch sat near her on the night bed. As they talked, Marissa couldn't fight her smile.

At the time of the heartbreak over losing her father, something unexpected and good had found its way into her life.

She'd never shared moments like this with a man like him. Their relationship had progressed so much, and so fast that they were basically cohabiting. While Mitch occasionally left her under Jason's protection so he could do some of his anti-poaching work, it was the stolen moments of quiet like this morning that she appreciated as special. Neither wanted to leave the company of the other.

Amalee turned towards the door. Even before Peta walked in, she was sending out rumbles of greeting.

Marissa smiled. "She recognizes your scent."

"They're so intelligent," Peta said, handing an apple to Amalee and picking up a brush to help as her phone rang. She answered it and put it on speaker.

"Hey, Peta, it's Milo, state vet—"

"I know who you are," she said, smiling. "I'm pregnant, not senile. What's up?"

"I'm so sorry, but I need your help."

Peta frowned and picked up her phone. Mitch, instantly alert, shook his head, warning her to leave it on speaker. He moved closer. Marissa froze, and Amalee, sensing the change in the atmosphere, let out a low, comforting rumble.

Peta put her hand on Amalee and patted her trunk, as she held out her phone so everyone could hear. "Okay, what's happened?"

"Please don't hold this against me. I did not know it was going to–"

"Just tell me, Milo," Peta said.

"There are three babies in Hwange, meant to be on a transporter in three weeks. They started deteriorating after their rabies shots. I can't seem to stop the decline. I was asked if anyone else could, and I said you. But I never expected it to come at such a price."

"What price? What are you talking about?" Peta asked.

"Shumba Chitepo, the man behind the elephant deal. He said to get you to help the babies, but if you don't let them come back to me for the export, he'll cancel your orphanage license and take away your animals."

Marissa's hand covered her heart. How could a man threaten something like that? How could one man hold the power to do that? To strip away all hope and manipulate Peta like he was doing?

"Milo!" Peta shouted. "What have you done? What deal did you make with him? He's the devil. Why would you ever think otherwise? What if they die?"

"I'm sorry. I was only thinking of the babies. Giving them their best chance of survival," Milo said.

The three of them were silent.

Peta gripped the brush so hard she snapped the handle in half.

Mitch rubbed Marissa's arm in support, then laced his fingers through hers.

"Peta, you there?" Milo asked.

"I'm here. I'm just in shock." Peta said, tossing the broken brush through the fence bars and getting another from the bucket. "Am I allowed to collect the babies and bring them to Yingwe? Or do I have to wait for you to deliver them?"

"The fastest way into your care is if you can come and fetch—"

Marissa focused on the voice in the background, shouting something to Milo.

"Definitely, you come get them as soon as you can. I'll be here to meet you. Just come in the Mbala gate, towards Sinamatella Camp, and I'll be waiting to show you the way. Bring the anti-poaching teams; you might need them." Milo hung up the phone.

Peta stared at it for a moment. "I guess we're going to save three elephants for the government and China to keep our license and the babies we already have."

"I'm coming with," Marissa said. "They might behave a bit better with an international witness. Especially one who just brought her elephant back to her homeland and gained so much press coverage."

Peta nodded. "I think we'll need two rescue teams. Bring a full complement of anti-poaching guards with you, Mitch. It's going to take us four to five hours to reach Mbala gate and then another to Sinamatella Camp in the trucks. If we leave inside half an hour we can load and have them back here by say eight tonight. A thirteen-hour workday, plus care once we're home. Sorry, girl." She patted Amalee on her foreleg. "I'll spend more time with you tomorrow. Duty calls now."

Peta walked away, speaking on her phone. "Darling, you're never going to believe what Milo did…"

"I guess we're heading on another rescue, but this one's going to be a bit more hostile," Mitch said to Marissa once they were alone. "Bring your camera, even though you probably won't be allowed to take any photos. We're going where they keep the animals before they send them to China. The place is a dump. You'll wish you could scrub the images from your eyes after we've been there."

Dawn walked in just as Mitch finished talking.

"Good, you're here," Marissa said, but she couldn't summon her usual smile for her longtime friend. "We're heading off to fetch three more babies and bring them in for treatment. Would you mind staying with Amalee? She could feel how upset Peta was, and probably how mad I am, and she's giving us all this love, and we have to leave her to go get ready."

"Go," Dawn said. "Bongani was stopping by, and an elephant handler will be coming in for more time with her today. We'll be fine. You just take care, be safe."

Marissa hugged Dawn and then walked out with Mitch. She'd become so accustomed to having him with her that it was as if her shadow had drifted away when he wasn't there. She could tell his mind was already on the road as he lifted his cell phone from his pocket and dialed his unit, organizing the quick pulling of extra guards for the day.

Was this how her life would be if she lived in Africa?

All she could see in her mind was a vision of her and Mitch, together on a porch swing, both with grey hair and wrinkles, and holding hands, and she shook her head, trying hard to erase the image. It was too soon for happy-ever-afters and looking that far into the future.

But the picture lingered on.

NEAR SINAMATELLA CAMP, HWANGE NATIONAL PARK, ZIMBABWE

13:30

The smell hit Marissa's nose first: old dung lying around.

The sound of thousands of flies hit second.

She could see the babies who had become the center of attention in the China and Zimbabwe case in the elephant pens. Her heart broke. Elephants around three years old stood huddled together, their trunks down. They didn't even lift their heads to smell the air when all the vehicles arrived. It was as if they were disinterested in life.

Two workers in green overalls, with ZimParks proudly displayed, stood by the boma, looking as disheartened by the exercise as the elephant babies were. Both held sticks she had come to know as *knobkerries*, but she wondered how much poking or bashing they had done on the docile babies to break their spirits.

One of the men stared at Mitch, but didn't lift his hand or acknowledge him.

Milo exited from the vehicle that they had followed in from the gate, drawing her attention to him as he waited while Peta and Joss got out of theirs, then for Marissa and Mitch to reach him.

"Thank you for coming," Milo said. "I know I can never repay you for this, and I'm sorry to have put the orphanage in any trouble, but please don't underestimate the lengths that Shumba will go to in order to keep his word." Milo rolled his neck, and put his hand on his shoulder, trying hard to dislodge the stress he carried there. "The deal with the Chinese is his project. I'm just caught in the middle, between trying to ensure the elephant are humanely managed and alive. The one to hopefully say that the damage left behind after they've gone, is not as devastating as I fear it's going to be."

"I know, Milo. I've been in this situation," Peta said, softly placing her hand on his arm. She stroked her bulging belly with her other hand. "When I worked up at Matusadona. A rock and a hard place. I'll do my best for these babies, but what is he going to do if they die? Is he going to hold me personally responsible?"

"I don't know. But I do know that if anyone around here can save them, it's you."

"I can't promise that," Peta said. "Let's go and get them loaded. The sooner we transport them home, the better." She wiped sweat off her face with her hat, then put it back on her head, shaded from the harsh afternoon sun.

Milo walked towards the pens when his eyes focused on Marissa's camera around her neck. "No photographs."

"I know, but my camera goes everywhere with me," Marissa said.

"I'm trusting you," Milo said. "Heads will roll if he finds you take a single picture, and not just mine. There's a lot at stake here. Do not mess with Shumba."

She nodded.

They soon reached the pen with three little elephants, and the two men in green overalls greeted them. Marissa noticed that while the same man watched Mitch intently, he didn't acknowledge him any differently to the group—just nodded.

Marissa wondered what the story was between them.

"At least they're still separated from the other babies," Milo said.

"Might be a good thing," Peta said. "Where's the loading ramp?"

Milo pointed to a ramp not far from where they were. "The boys will bring them down the chute now that you're here. They still walk, although they're slow. I don't think they will give you any trouble on the way home."

Marissa couldn't get used to grown men always being called boys instead of hands or workers. She'd learned it wasn't an offensive term—it was just how things were—but she didn't like it.

Marissa climbed onto the pole fencing beside Peta. The gate was opened and the elephant were corralled out by the two men. The little babies moved as if they were cattle, used to being herded and listening whenever the stick was pointed left or right. Soon, they were down the chute and waiting.

Once the vehicles were backed up, the elephant were easily corralled onto the trucks, as if they knew they were heading to a safer location.

"Please keep me updated," Milo said, "so I can try and keep Shumba away from you. The last thing you want is him arriving at Yingwe."

Peta nodded as she climbed in the back of the truck with the two babies. Zola was already next to one doing observations, before administering tranquillizer. Peta signaled for Danie to go in the second truck. Each elephant had its own vet.

Mitch's team divided themselves up between the two vehicles and got ready to protect their cargo when they left the National Park. Their weapons pointed outwards, but dipped slightly to avoid any accidental discharges from hitting anyone.

"Are you coming to the orphanage with us?" Peta asked Milo when he remained standing at the side where she was starting her own observations on the baby she would be monitoring after delivering the sedative.

"If you'll let me. I would love to help. I could not do anything for them here. As you can see, they do not have the facility for me to treat them past inoculations, and my help was not wanted." Disappointment in himself showed on his face. But there was more. Fear for the three elephant, and the lives of each person who was now involved with them.

"Are you sure you and the baby will be okay up there?" Joss said, looking up at Peta from next to the truck. "Milo could do that, and it would settle my mind better to have you in the front with me."

"Of course, I'm fine. Just get us home as fast and safely as we can," Peta said, blowing Joss a kiss.

"Right everyone, load up. We're ready to move," Mitch said.

The two trucks began slowly inching forward, as AP guards climbed into the open back with the elephant, and others ran for Mitch's *bakkie*.

Marissa climbed into the third vehicle with Mitch and two of the AP guards in the double cab; the rest of their group were in the back. She didn't want to get in the way, and resisted the desire to run and open the gates to the boma, and let the other elephant out before they drove off.

"Don't even think about it," Mitch said, as if he was reading her mind. "There's nothing we can do for those ones."

Before they even had a chance to start forward, a smart new white Range Rover drove at breakneck speed towards them.

"Here we go—brace yourselves. Just what I was trying to avoid. Unfortunately, you're going to meet Shumba in person," Milo said loudly.

"If shooting starts, get down and stay down," Mitch said as he jumped out. The AP units now poured out of the vehicles, forming a protective barrier across the front of the two vehicles holding the elephant. Mitch remained close to theirs, protecting Marissa.

The Rover skidded to a halt, almost connecting with Milo's vehicle at the front of the convoy.

The driver ran around and opened the door, and a huge man lumbered out the back. Marissa couldn't tell whether he carried a firearm or not.

The man looked around and frowned. "I am Shumba Chitepo, legal consultant to the President. Which one of you is Peta?"

Mitch and Marissa looked to where Joss stood in front of Peta's vehicle, his handgun visible.

Milo walked towards Shumba. "Afternoon. As you can see, the elephant sanctuary is ready to help the babies. They are on their way for treatment."

Shumba glared at Milo. "Good. Now, where is the woman who runs the place?"

Marissa's hackles rose at the man's attitude.

"I'm Doctor Peta Brennan," Peta called from inside the back of the truck, beyond Marissa's line of sight. "If you want to talk, you'll need to come to the vehicle. I'm setting up an IV line, and I can't come out. Come on over; the elephant can't hurt you down there."

Marissa wanted to laugh at Peta's obvious condescending tone. A power play by Peta—she had the higher position and was forcing the suited man to look up to her. Clever.

He lumbered closer to Peta's vehicle but stopped more than six feet away —out of the splash zone if the elephant baby excreted anything.

Peta popped her head over the edge. "I'm listening, but busy. You know what they say about working with animals and children."

Marissa saw the roll that Shumba did with one shoulder.

"Milo has told you that these are destined to be exported in three weeks. We will need all back as soon as they are well enough for transportation," Shumba said, adjusting his suit, attempting to bring the buttons into line to close over his stomach.

"He mentioned it," Peta said, and turned her back on Shumba as she moved farther into the vehicle, with the elephant between him and her.

Shumba straightened his shoulders and clenched both fists.

Now forced to raise his voice to make sure she heard, Shumba said, "Milo will check in with me daily on their progress, and I will know if you are delaying their recovery in any way."

He waited for a reply, but nothing came.

Shumba said, "I expect them back here. Do not try to keep them any longer than necessary."

Peta returned to the side, looking down at him. "I got your threat about my license loud and clear. Know that the only reason I'm here and helping at all, is to save the lives of these babies. You do realize there's a chance that your mishandling of these calves has made them too sick to travel? Now and later?"

"That is not an option you want to explore," Shumba said, turning away, and then stopping in his tracks as Marissa walked up behind him. Mitch was standing to the side but still shielding her.

"It is, actually, now that you are here in person. Might as well ensure we both understand the predicament these baby elephant are in. Their health is uncertain. It's the way with animals—I can't guarantee they will live," Peta carried on. "You, of all people, know from the 2012 disaster, that baby elephant die when mistreated."

He turned back towards Peta. "Then I will see the bodies and attend the autopsies. In person. You will not swindle Zimbabwe by pretending they are dead."

He swung back around. "I assume you are Marissa Whitney, the American with the Zimbabwean elephant you stole?"

"I am, but it depends on whose side of the argument you're on as to whether it was me who stole it. I'd like to believe we're one the same side, as it was me who brought her back," Marissa said, "to Doctor Peta Brennan's sanctuary. Her outstanding reputation in the international community was one of the biggest drawcards for me to choose Zimbabwe as the refuge. So it is a huge privilege to be able to accompany her now and see first-hand how her work continues, and with these babies especially." Marissa did a wide sweep of the whole camp. "Since you were not at the airport on our arrival, would you like a photograph of us together now? The legal consult for the President and the person who returned hope for their wildlife to the people of Zimbabwe?"

Shumba was quiet for a moment, glaring at her with an expression of pure venom. He nodded. "Of course." He stuck his hand out to shake hers. "And every Zimbabwean appreciates the return of our elephant, but perhaps another time when I am dressed better."

Marissa stepped forward and shook his hand.

"No problem. Another time," Marissa said and as she walked away, she wiped the reptilian feel of him on her pants.

YINGWE RIVER LODGE, ANIMAL RESCUE AND REHABILITATION CENTER, BINGA, ZIMBABWE

19:00

Marissa realized that she had rescued more elephant in the few months she'd been in Africa than she had thought possible. Unloading the babies once they were back at the orphanage was as easy as loading them had been. But putting them inside a closed stable with a roof and walls did not go according to plan.

Marissa watched as if the elephant realized that here, there were different rules. Not only did the one chase Amos until he dived through a fence, but it also tried to plow through the fence to escape.

"Come on," Peta said. "I don't want to have to tranquilize you. You need to come inside the stable. I have to keep you isolated—all three of you. You can go together if you want."

Peta opened a partition between them, and the baby elephant seemed much happier, as if being apart had stressed them. Marissa could hear Amalee calling out to the babies. She'd wondered how her elephant was going to react to having others added to those already in the stable with her, and now she knew.

Amalee was going to be just like Ndhlovy, a nurse to all. A matron mother.

"Make sure you shower down before you go to see Amalee, Marissa," Peta said. "I don't know what's wrong with them yet, so take precautions. If they have something other than a bad reaction to the injection, they may pass it on if we're not careful."

Marissa nodded and she crossed her arms over the top beam of the stable as the team settled the baby elephant in. Although they had gotten very adventurous on arrival, they had quickly used up their energy and were now standing together quietly once again.

Zola and Danie were bouncing on the balls of their feet.

"*Ag* man, they're so sweet. A little bit bigger than the last one we brought in, but look at them. How can you not love that?" Zola said.

"Everybody loves babies," Amos said as he hung one blanket on the fence and, taking two in his hands, he slowly approached the three. None of them tried to run him down this time.

"*Sjoe*. It's like they're out of energy," Danie said, frowning.

"Too true," Amos said, quickly covering the first two elephant with a blanket each. Danie entered the actual facility through the bars and handed Amos the third for the remaining baby.

"This is not normal behavior," Milo said. "These little elephant are too placid."

"Definitely sick," Peta said. "Milo, did you do stool samples?"

Milo shook his head. "I was not able to do much. I couldn't even get into the boma with them—nor could any of the guys who were there. They see those green overalls, and they try and run them down every time."

"Ah, explains why they tried to hurt Amos. I'll make sure our guys don't wear their greens around these kids," Peta said. "I think blood samples from all of them and stool samples. Amos, Zola, and Danie—pick an animal, mark it with chalk on its forehead so you know which is which, and we'll start from the bottom. They got sick when they had their rabies injections. Is it contamination? Did you do that?"

Milo shook his head. "It was another state vet who did the vaccinations. I was on holiday in South Africa, but when I came back, he went on leave. I didn't even get to speak to him. When I realized the condition they were in, that was when I suggested that I bring them to you."

"Are all three in the next shipment?" Peta asked.

"Yes, while only one is left in the quota. They are going to send the others to make up for those that died last year."

"We heard four didn't make it off the flight alive," Peta said.

"I do not know for sure, but it might be true," Milo said. "We're loading at night this time, to make it less stressful for the animals in the heat. It's better than standing on the tarmac at midday."

"*Sjoe*, that's something. At least one good thing has come after the last disaster," Zola said.

"We also have a mixed delivery this shipment. Fewer elephant, but then they have sable, impala, and lion in the same cargo."

"That's gonna be interesting," Peta said. "Having the predators along for the ride."

"Same as last time. However, I have suggested that we keep the lions sedated. I'm just waiting for the all-clear from higher up. So far, they have listened to what I've had to say, including having a Zimbabwe vet on the trip back to China."

"So who got that job?" Marissa asked.

"Me," Milo admitted. "I have a contract to look after them for a year after delivery. Each time they come and go, I'll fly with them. It was the only way I could think of to make sure that they were transported more humanely, and their post travel care attended to properly, after what happened."

"Milo, what about your family?" Peta asked, frowning.

"My wife understands it's needed. I have no children; I can make a difference if I do this by seeing that they're looked after properly."

"She's a very understanding woman," Peta said.

"I think so too," Milo said. "But then, perhaps we're fortunate in

Zimbabwe to have such strong women, like her and like you. I didn't think you would want to help me after I got you on Shumba's radar."

"We've been on his radar before," Peta said. "It took us a while to get this license, but it was all done right, and I don't think, despite his position, that he'd be able to pull it so fast. Not with the international exposure we've had since Amalee came in. To take it away now would be stupid. Shumba may be a lot of things, but he's not an idiot. At least I don't think he's one..."

"Are the Chinese going to pay your salary?" Mitch asked.

"Yes; and a big bonus. It'll be worth it for me to be doing this, but I'll obviously not have a job to come back to, because people will believe that I wanted these babies taken away when in fact, all I'm doing is trying to look after them once they arrive in China. I might have to look to move overseas."

"Milo, you'll have a job here if you need. You have to do what's right for you in your heart. If you believe you can make a difference going with them, then do it," Peta said. "Bugger what everyone thinks, as long as you know the truth."

"That's so sad—you and your wife having to be apart for such a long time," Marissa said, "but I can understand the reasoning behind you taking the job. And I think you're wrong: getting these three saved now, that is making a difference. This is what people will remember you for. Being the one who stood up to Shumba and helped save these babies."

"Thank you," Milo said. "But right now, getting them here is just the first step. Shumba will keep his word. If they die, he'll want a body and a necropsy, and he won't flinch while you're forced to perform one, pregnant or not, Peta. These babies need to be in this quota, as much as it'll hurt every person here to see them go. In three weeks, I'll load them onto that plane. I can't be responsible for you losing your license and not saving so many more."

Marissa frowned. There would be no happy ending for the elephant babies.

It seemed like the fate of the three elephant was sealed, and there was nothing that they could do to prevent it from happening.

CHAPTER 36
TOPOGRAPHY

YINGWE RIVER LODGE, ANIMAL RESCUE AND REHABILITATION CENTER, BINGA, ZIMBABWE

10 January 2015 – 12:00

Chad lay on his stomach on the ground next to Jamiel, his body relaxed; his shoulders, which should have been tight with tension, were at ease. His legs, despite the long hike, hummed instead of cramping. Being on the hunt again brought him peace and calm.

He brought his scope up to his eyes and measured the distance the three men they still had left working for them had to cover before they crossed into Chief Bongani's lands. The two other men had absconded. The first had disappeared the night they arrived in Victoria Falls, having just gotten a free ride across the country. The man with a scar on his face had tried to run as soon as he became aware of where they were expected to go.

Things hadn't turned out quite as that guy had wished. He was now croc food downriver. Chad and Jamiel had made sure of that; they couldn't afford to have a loose end speaking to any authorities.

The remaining three were still testing the borders of the chief's land, trying to find out what bad medicine the *n'Goma's* used.

Jamiel had done the recon on the borders and what the locals had to say about the tribal trust land. It was filled with superstitions claiming to prevent people with bad intentions from entering, but then they'd heard others say the medicines only affected those who believed in the *sangoma*. The three expendables from Harare left were not worried about a Ndebele curse; they were from the Shona tribe, and poo-pooed the idea that traditional medicines would work on them.

The men crossed over the border.

None of them showed any signs of distress.

"Looks like the black bullshit doesn't work if you don't believe," Chad said.

"Give it time," Jamiel said. "Sometimes superstitions and traditional medicines works in different ways."

The first of the three men moved his weapon from hanging on his shoulder to in front of him; obviously, he'd heard something in the thick trees.

"What's he reacting to?" Chad said.

"It will show itself, whatever is there," Jamiel said.

Chad shrugged. "I don't believe in that hyped up police crap or the sangria-mojo stuff—"

"*Sangoma* or n'*Goma*. It's OMA at the end," Jamiel corrected him.

"Do you think any of the stories are true?" Chad asked.

"Which ones? That traditional medicine keeps people off this land, or that police in this area shoot first, ask questions later?"

"Both. It seems weird to me that a nation with such a corrupt police force would bother with the shooting of a criminal," Chad said.

"You're making a big assumption. They don't tolerate anyone bringing violence into their country," Jamiel said. "They have worked for many years to try to be a police force that was looked up to, because they have been so manipulated by the politicians. Many of them believe that it's their duty to make sure there's no violence."

"Interesting," Chad said.

"It's a hard place to live. They tread a fine line between criminal behavior and what people need to do to survive. With this inflation, the cost of living. How much they pay for a simple loaf of bread is crazy." Jamiel said.

"I cannot see how people would want to live here," Chad said. "There are better places."

Jamiel shook his head. "You do understand that many don't have the choice? This is where they were born, and this is their home country until they die. Same in so many African countries. They make the most of it and try to live in harmony, despite all the political rubbish going on."

The men Chad watched continued through the forest, skirting around the open areas. There was movement to their left. Now he saw what the men had reacted to earlier. A lion kept parallel to them, loping along at the same speed. It was larger than any lion Chad had seen. About a mile in the distance, Chad saw a truck gunning down the bush track in their direction.

"The lion is there again. You gonna pull them back, or are we going to test how efficient the anti-poaching guys actually are when they confront them?" Jamiel asked.

Chad picked up his radio. "Second unit, come in."

"This is second unit," the leader said.

"Anti-poaching coming in hot. Turn back," Chad said, taking his thumb off the button on the radio.

Jamiel shook his head. "That's five out of five times the anti-poaching unit came to investigate, every time we get inside those borders, no matter the direction we approach from in the daytime. Always, a lion appears and runs near them. How can that be? It's as if the trees themselves have eyes."

Chad looked through his scope. The men had turned and were zigzagging back towards them. The truck was closing the distance between them.

"They are not gonna make it to the border before that truck gets them," Jamiel said.

"Goddammit," Chad swore. "They know the deal. If they get caught, they're on their own."

"You know they won't keep quiet even though we've said we'd pay them to?" Jamiel asked.

Chad took his sniper rifle from its cover and started setting it up. "We're on the same page. I didn't think for a moment we'd get any loyalty from them."

Jamiel nodded.

Chad looked through his telescopic sight. The three men were making progress and were almost at the border of the chief's lands, but the anti-poaching unit was on their heels, five guards running them down; one in the vehicle, continuing to navigate where they were now off-road, and the other four on foot. The men seemed to have a way of moving through the bush as if they were part of it. They were so well trained and extremely fit; they were gaining on the city brawlers.

"I was hoping to get a better idea of access using them," Chad said, looking through his site.

"Then don't waste them all. If they catch them, take one out," Jamiel suggested. "The others won't open their mouths knowing you can get to them from even this distance. It'll make the AP unit stop, and the other two can get back to safety."

The city brawler at the back was rugby-tackled by one of the anti-poaching guards; as they rolled over, Chad could see it was actually a woman. There was a lot of shouting, and they could hear just enough of it. The two other men kept running, determined not to be caught.

With their one insurgent down, Chad checked his distance.

It was a long shot, but he could get it if he needed to. It would also be the ideal opportunity to check the response of the poaching unit when they came under sniper fire.

The man who was down was fighting with the AP guard, and another guard was there within moments. They had the man unarmed, tied up, and sitting on the ground in no time at all.

Three guards continued their pursuit, but the city men were keeping in front. The guards seemed to know exactly where their border was and stopped, their legal limit for maneuvering exhausted.

The remaining men kept running, putting as much distance between them and the AP guards as they could.

Chad looked at the one who had been caught. He knew he was defeated; his head was down, but he wasn't talking. Yet. He didn't even look to the place where they hid in the hills. His body language gave nothing away.

"Make your choice," Jamiel said. "If you shoot him now, they'll know you're here. If the man keeps quiet and his family collects his pay, you will still be a surprise for your cousin. Not many African snipers can take out someone at that range. They'll know it's a professional hit."

Chad hesitated. "If he talks, she'll know I'm here anyway. And even knowing her life is in danger, she won't leave that fucking elephant. I'd rather she starts sweating than get too comfortable in her tourist castle."

He took the shot and then watched for the aftermath.

As expected, the impact of the sniper's bullet smashed into the man's skull and out the other side. The women standing behind him buckled over as if he might have got a two-for-one bonus, then the shouting started. Even though he couldn't hear her, her mouth instructed the others. "Down. Shooter."

He could see her clothes smattered with red and grey as she rolled to the side and behind a large tree. He couldn't tell if his bullet had gotten her too, but he sure hoped it had.

The others had all gone to ground. Where once they had all been in the open, now they were behind trees and in thicker bush, where they blended in. He would need time to evaluate the scene below and flush them out.

"Time to go," Jamiel said, beginning to crawl backwards from their vantage point. "Now that they're aware we're here, the vehicle might not stop at the border and come looking."

"Collect our two survivors on the way," Chad said, and began packing away his rifle.

He hoped Marissa got the message. *I'm on your doorstep, Princess. Pay day is here.*

CHAPTER 37
IN THE SHADOWS

BINGA AREA, ZIMBABWE

10 January 2015 – 13:30

Mitch stood in what had been a sniper's nest just outside of Bongani's lands. Right at the top of the *koppie*, two people had watched their men test the border before they shot one of them.

He shook his head.

The cruelty of people sometimes still got to him, despite everything he'd seen.

"He lay right here," Mitch said. "He looked through his scope and shot the man in the head. Clean and calm as if it was an everyday exercise."

Joss nodded. "The second man lay next to him where I'm standing, a sniper and his spotter, or a sniper and his tracker. Either way, they are comfortable in each other's space, close together, even in this hot weather."

"As a bloke with a military background, I've got to hand it to whoever took that shot. He's got serious skill," Mitch said. "But mate, I'm just bloody relieved that when the anti-poaching unit came under fire, he didn't take them out too. There was nowhere for them to hide other than where they were; if he'd wanted to stay and kill them, he could have."

"There's no way your average thug would be able to take this type of shot," Joss said.

"Which means it might be Chad," Mitch said, nodding in acknowledgment. "We haven't considered that he may try take Marissa before he kills her. We know Chad is after her money, and he can't get to that if she's dead."

"Fair point," Joss said.

"The challenge is, if he's such a good sniper, how do we keep Marissa safe? If he chooses to shoot her, he can. He can take out anyone we assign as protection just as easily and then snatch her."

"True, but we have the advantage; he can't get above the lodge to have a look inside. We have the high ground," Joss said. "He can get to the tree line, but it's all flat land around us. Steep down to the lake and escarpment once you drive away from the fenceline."

"You know that if he's got a proper sniper weapon he won't care about a bit of distance. He'll be able to get her from a kilometer away easily," Mitch said.

"I think Gideon's confidence that the police can stop him is off. I doubt they will," Joss said. "Even though Tsessebe tracked them to their place in the township, basically packaged wrapped them for Gideon to follow their every move."

Mitch gazed across the valley. Vultures soared on thermal winds far in the distance. "Marisa said he served in Somalia. The violence in that war was something else. We both know that if he's bringing that type of warfare here we're in trouble; it's African militia carnage."

"It's not like we haven't faced a sniper before," Joss said.

"And most of the AP guards are ex-service at the moment," Mitch said. "But we'll need to keep Marissa inside the lodge and the stables—somewhere he can't line her up with a long-range rifle, at least till we work out how to flush him out. Good thing she's not in any rush to head back to the States."

"Unless he wants to get in near," Joss said. "Declan's file said that he got up close and personal for the fire and Marissa's father. It's not good enough for him to watch from a distance. He's been testing us, and we know it. So now we set part B of the plan. We get Tsessebe to bring them to us," Joss said.

"If Tsessebe approaches them about the tracker job, he can lure them to us. If we can capture Chad here rather than try to fight him, it would make things easier," Mitch said.

Joss nodded. "And there's probably a politician or two that could do with some bargaining power over the USA for something, handing over a wanted criminal from the US could give them more power. It could end up with diplomatic negotiations for extradition back to the USA, or he can rot in his Zimbabwe jail. At least we know he won't come out on an amnesty; not many white men get out of there once they're in."

Mitch had run through so many scenarios in his head.

Marissa's cousin was coming for her, but what Mitch couldn't prepare for was the fact that he was a sniper. They did their best fighting from a distance.

His hands shook as his skin prickled. Blood rushed through his veins and a dull throb began in his temples.

What if someone got to Marissa without him being able to protect her?

CHAPTER 38
THE N'GOMAS

BONGANI'S LANDS, BINGA, ZIMBABWE

11 January 2015

Mitch, Joss, Bongani, and Tsessebe stood in the middle of the bush. There were no huts around and no fences—just wild trees and grasses, with two *koppies* to the north and south funneling a natural valley between them.

"This is a good place," Bongani said. "From here, we can have our guys trap Chad and his team. What do you think?"

Mitch frowned. Other than a few scraggly trees dotted along the flatland, there was no cover for his team.

Bongani smiled. "There are always secrets in my land that will reveal themselves to you when you need them. Come, let me show you one." He walked about sixty-five feet north and stood on an iron grid. He took a bunch of keys from his pocket and used them to remove the padlock. "This is the beginning of a shaft where once my ancestors dug for gold. From here, the tunnel runs north. There is an exit about fifty meters away. There are channels at ground level that stretch about twenty meters east. If Tsessebe can bring them in here, we can hide underground until they pass, then climb out and attack. They will never see it coming, and what's worse for them is that there will be no retreat."

Mitch nodded.

Tsessebe looked around and smiled.

Bongani continued. "The river will mask your movements. You can run the whole way from the border until you see that *koppie*. Once you cut across and come around the side, you need to channel toward the middle. There are other mining dongas on that side–"

"But they are only about knee-deep, so they look like natural runoffs," Tsessebe said.

"That they are, but if you and the hunters use those, the AP teams will be better concealed on this side, where the dongas run chest-deep on a man," Joss said.

Tsessebe nodded. "A stranger could walk this valley many times and never know these are here."

"Sometimes, unless you are specifically looking for something, you will not find it. Come," Bongani said as they opened the grid and climbed down an old wooden ladder.

About fifteen feet down, Mitch could feel the temperature change. Then the shaft opened out. Bongani passed them all battery-operated torches, and they switched them on as they continued to walk where the earth had been dug by hands of yesteryear. Every half meter or so, wooden bracing supported the walls to ensure they didn't collapse.

"None of these additional tunnels go anywhere. They aren't very deep into the *koppie*, but that one?" Joss pointed. "It has a large area opened out at the other end. You will find old furniture in there, to make waiting in the tunnels more comfortable."

"Any gold left in here?" Mitch asked.

Bongani laughed. "The main vein was dug out many years ago. It was only a little; we are already almost at the other end."

Mitch could feel the incline increase under his feet and soon didn't need his flashlight anymore as sunlight came in through another grid, this time with no ladder. It was on the side of the *koppie*. Again, Bongani unlocked the iron grid covering the entrance.

Waiting on the other side were five *n'Gomas*.

The tallest was clearly the group's leader. Except for the tortoise-shell hat, she wore plain clothes, but at her waist was an impala-skin apron, decorated with a belt of trailing monkey tails. She had a sash running over her shoulder and down to the apron.

Mitch could have sworn it was genuine leopard skin.

The others wore normal clothing too, with various animal and ethnic prints; each wore a leopard sash and matching fur headbands. All the women wore bands of fur around their calves, and at their ankles and wrists were layers of what looked like bottle tops from Coke bottles, squashed and threaded together to chime as they moved. Each carried a flyswatter swatch, made from the tail of a wildebeest, and while the leader carried an elaborately beaded *sjambok,* the smallest one had a decorated *knobkerrie.*

"Chief Bongani," the tallest woman said, "we were on our way to your home, but we found you here."

Bongani nodded to them in greeting. Joss and Mitch did the same, while Tsessebe gave a small nod, but didn't make eye contact and quickly looked down, not daring to face them.

Mitch smiled openly.

"We are honored by your visit. What is the occasion that you are coming to see me?" Bongani asked.

"Our medicine is not strong enough to keep out the non-believers who come from far away and across the ocean. They do not run, even from a lion. This is a different threat against your lands that we cannot keep out. There is one who wants to harm the *Ndhlovu'udadewethu*. The matriarch of old, they call for her to be saved. The one who comes, he could be a leopard if he chose a different path, but he is the hyena. The one who sneaks around."

"The elephant sister—do you mean Marissa?" Joss asked. "Or the one they call Dawn?"

The smallest of the women shook her wrists, making her shakers rattle, as if annoyed that Joss was interrupting.

"There is blood in the clouds. We cannot stop it, but we can help when the time is right to change together once more, to keep evil from this place," the tall one said.

Bongani nodded. "Thank you, my sisters, for your sight and your help. We do know of these men, and there is already blood that has been spilled by them on their own. I hope this is the blood you speak of?"

The tall one shook her head. "No, Chief. There is still blood to wash into the water. Much blood to clean from the land."

"Did you see anyone else we must protect?" Bongani asked.

"maNdhlovu," the one on the right said. "maNdhlovu."

"Peta?" Joss asked.

The smallest of the women shook her wrists again. This time she stamped her feet too.

Bongani put his hand on Joss's arm, keeping him in his place. The tall one continued, "There is one who comes to harm. He is from Zimbabwe. He is of power, but he wears the skin of an old honey badger. It is baggy and does not fit. She is the matriarch. She is strong. The ndhlovu call for her protection. Without her, the ancient paths of the elephant become quiet. The matriarch and the sister must not fall."

The two women who had been still the whole time began shaking their wrists, as if beating drums in rhythm.

"We will come to the lodge when the baby is born," the smallest of the *n'Gomas* said. "It is one of us. It is of Africa."

Joss nodded.

"Tsessebe," the smallest *n'Goma* said, "we are happy to see you here. Part of this world. Keep this with you so we will know it is you who enters these lands with the evil ones." She held out her *knobkerrie*. "We will not harm you."

Tsessebe looked up at them, then walked to the *n'Goma,* and she put the *knobkerrie* across his palms before placing both of her hands on top of his.

He nodded to her, and when he attempted to back away, she held onto him.

"You need to let him go now, sister," the tall one said.

Slowly, the small *n'Goma*'s hands slid from Tsessebe's, and he retreated until he stood slightly behind Mitch, as if trying to hide.

"Take care, Chief. It is a time where the old ways and the new need to work together," the tall one said, lifting her hand. They all did the same, then crossed their arms, interlocking their fingers, straight and true, showing strong bonding.

"Thank you," Bongani said, bowing his head.

Joss and Mitch copied him.

Tsessebe stayed silent, not moving.

The tall *n'Goma* nodded, then let her arms fall to her sides before turning and leading the others away on the game path. Her tortoise shell bobbed as she walked.

Once they were all out of sight, Bongani turned and relocked the grid. "Well, that was interesting, as always."

Joss slapped Tsessebe on the back. "Hey, man, seems like that small one likes you. You might find a wife before long."

Tsessebe shook his head. "Never. Not a witch. No. No. I will carry this with me if it means protection from them, but I cannot marry a *n'Goma*."

Bongani laughed.

Mitch shook his shoulders out. "Why must they always be like that? Creepy–"

Bongani smiled. "The *n'Gomas*' role is to serve. There have always been five, in this territory, who work together. For many years, the medicines of *n'Gomas* and the ancestors have protected us. They serve the land. They serve the people."

"They scare the shit out of me," Tsessebe said.

Everyone laughed.

"Come on," Bongani said. "We were looking for the dongas on this side."

Mitch laughed. "A donga in Australia is a temporary home, like a shipping container, made into accommodation. I still want to laugh every time you say that here for a drainage gulley."

Bongani, Joss, and Tsessebe laughed, the tension leaving the group.

Mitch looked over the area and could not see the 'dongas' that Bongani had spoken of, but he kept looking. When the ground beside him began rising, he realized he was walking on one.

"Ideal place for a leopard attack," Mitch said.

"That it is," Joss said. "Many moons ago, there was a leopard family who lived here—a mother and her cubs. She was the reason I stopped coming to the mine; she needed space away from humans."

"Was there was really gold in the mine?" Mitch asked.

Bongani nodded. "During the Bush War in the seventies, these tunnels were used to hide when there were terrorists active in the area, to protect the women and children. Many of them are still on my lands, but it is not somewhere I would recommend children play. When the herds of buffalo come through, this is where they pass. They are ancient pathways the elephant also use to get to the lodge. That is one of the reasons there are no houses in this area. I have tried to keep corridors open for the game to pass through without too much human conflict."

"It's a good place for a trap. I'll bring them here," Tsessebe said.

"That is the idea," Bongani said.

Now on the other side of the valley, the small group continued walking until they reached the area where the dongas were not as deep.

"This is where you need to bring them," Bongani said. "They will still think there is cover, but it is not as good as what we will have if we can get them before they come out the other side of the *koppie*. There are a few houses there, but lots of trees to walk through, and you come up the escarpment near the lodge."

"Are we sure we want the shootout inside your land, Bongani?" Mitch asked.

"We already know the police are watching him, so we can always say we suspected poachers," Bongani replied.

"It's a good plan," Mitch said. "Now all we need is for Chad and his posse to take the bait."

And then finally, he would know Marissa was safe.

CHAPTER 39
A REVIVED JACKAL

VICTORIA FALLS TOWNSHIP, VICTORIA FALLS, ZIMBABWE

12 January 2015

Chad, Jamiel, and the two Harare crew sat down to eat dinner. The maid who was servicing their house had cooked a stew with sudza, but a few bites in, there was a knock at the door.

Jamiel stood up, drew his weapon, and walked to the side of the front door. "Who is it?"

"My name is Tsessebe. I came about a job for a tracker," a deep voice replied.

Jamiel opened the door, and from the table Chad could see an old man, probably in his sixties. His clothes were well worn but clean, and his boots were polished. He had taken time to wipe the dust off before knocking—a proud man. He carried a walking stick in his right hand.

"I am unarmed, except for my *knobkerrie* that I use for walking," Tsessebe said.

"Who told you we are looking for a tracker?" Chad asked.

"At the market. There are people who said you look for a tracker and couldn't find one," Tsessebe said.

"How did you know where to find us?" Jamiel asked. "We never told anyone where we were staying."

"This is Victoria Falls. A white man staying in a township, is an easy person to find. I followed his desert boot prints. But a little bird told me you have lost one man in the bush because you went into lands where you were not welcome."

"If you already know that we lost a man, why would you offer to be our tracker?" Jamiel asked, still standing by the door. He swept his gaze up and down the street.

"Because I know that place. I need money, and I heard you pay in US dollars," Tsessebe said. "I have tracked for many of the hunters in the area. People know me; when we walk into the bush, and they see me, they think I am once again working for a hunting company. They will not ask questions."

Chad nodded. The old man had a point. He glanced at Jamiel to see his reaction.

Jamiel's face was blank, not giving anything away.

"Like all trackers," Tsessebe explained, "I get paid half before I go into the bush and the rest once the hunt is finished. If there is a blood show of any type, I get paid as if you hunted the animal, even if you decide not to pursue one you have injured. Although that is a bad-bad practice—you should always find the animal and show mercy in its death."

Jamiel turned to Chad.

"Can you start tomorrow?" Chad asked as he got ready to shovel another spoonful of dinner into his mouth.

INSIDE BONGANI'S LANDS, BINGA

13 January 2015

Chad's heartbeat was at a regular rate, but his smile was wide. Once again, he lay on his stomach from an advantageous height, but this time they were inside Chief Bongani's lands.

"The old man is good. He knew there were gullies in the bush and took the men through those," Jamiel said. "I still can't believe he did not flinch when we told him we were not interested in the Chete Safari Area, but rather the Sijarira Forest Area just south of that. And his eyes lit up when we said we were looking for tuskers. And the fact he knew the lodge–"

"Yes. But we must not trust him. Too coincidental, his arriving and knowing this elephant path and that they walked through here to the lodge," Chad said.

"He knew about the bad medicine, and if he's been around as long as he says, then knowing the tuskers coming through this path and the lodge to feed seems reasonable," Jamiel said.

Chad shook his head. "Not convinced yet. Did you notice? No lion this time. Not a sight of it, after it dogged our every attempt previously. Strange."

"Perhaps. We'll see," Jamiel said. "Still time for it to show itself, but we took a very different entry towards this place. Perhaps the lion wasn't witchcraft after all, or it knows him?"

"A wild animal knows a man? Unlikely. Look where he's heading now, towards that escarpment, at the same height as this one. We'll need to break cover, follow, or catch up. Get our surveillance route in and out clear, then we can come back without him," Chad replied.

Jamiel nodded. "Somehow I don't think the old man would be up for what we are really hunting."

Chad laughed.

They both rose up, dusted off, and went to join Tsessebe and the two men. Moving quickly through the bush, Chad and Jamiel made their way down the hill and around the base, following the same gullies that the old man had. Moving faster than the scouting party, they were quickly behind the tracker.

They stood at the bottom of the escarpment. Up close, it was rocky and looked impassable.

"You sure there's a way up?" Chad asked.

Tsessebe nodded. "It's a well-worn elephant path that zigzags up the rocky cliff."

Chad followed him. It took effort to get to the top, and he was sweating from the heat. The old man kept walking, his stick tapping on rocks the only sound he made.

At last, they were at the top. From here Chad could see the lake in the distance, where it appeared to touch the sky.

Tsessebe carried on walking. "The moringa trees are this way. You cannot hunt near them as they have *askari*. Guards. We can stop to have a look. I would not recommend going closer. There are always many people around this place, but they will think we have come for their elephant if they see us. They don't take walk-in visitors. Everyone comes from Victoria Falls in a vehicle or by boat."

Chad nodded. At last, he was making progress. He had the way into the lodge mapped in his head. Now he could come and watch for Marissa.

The grove they walked into was terrible cover.

Tsessebe was concealed, but both Chad and Jamiel had to stoop to keep from being seen.

Chad turned all the way around to assess the surroundings, aware that anyone would be able to see him due to the stunted height of the trees. His head would be clearly visible above them. The trees were neatly arranged like a plantation; one could look both ways down straight lines, but unlike the pines at home, these were no more than bushes.

"Is it the wind that keeps these trees short?" Chad asked.

"No," Tsessebe said. "The elephant eat these trees. This is the moringa grove the tuskers come to feast on. It helps them to stay healthy." He stopped. "We cannot go closer; we will be spotted. The people, they are there, with the baby elephant grazing. And the other orphans, they are around. See the giraffe?"

Chad nodded, mapping it all in his head.

He couldn't see into either the stable area or the lodge itself from where they were, which was frustrating, but he didn't want to go any closer and alert the tracker to their own real plans.

Tsessebe stood up. "It is time to leave. Now. I see the lion, it is close. We must go back into the Sijarira Forest Area, for it will call the antipoaching guards."

Chad shook his head at the superstitious nonsense these people believed in but followed the old man. The lion had come even with the tracker being with them, it had just been delayed a little. Perhaps they could trust the old man after all.

Chad smiled.

He was another step closer to kidnapping Marissa and getting his hands on all the wealth that would come with it, before he killed her and left her body to rot in the African bush.

CHAPTER 40
A TRANSGRESSION

YINGWE RIVER LODGE, ANIMAL RESCUE AND REHABILITATION CENTER, BINGA, ZIMBABWE

13 January 2015

Chad and Jamiel lay low in the moringa grove. The lights in the lodge twinkled in the otherwise dark escarpment. In the distance, solar panels kept many of the huts alight. Floodlights and fences protected irrigated crops from elephant and antelope raiders.

Chad felt that Tsessebe was well worth what he'd been paid for the day, and he'd been told to report back at the house the next day at four o'clock. Not only had he shown them the path through the Sijarira Forest Area, but he'd shown them a route in to avoid the anti-poaching patrols. He'd suggested they move to hunt tuskers in the north of the Chete Safari area, nearer the Sinamwenda Crater. He'd even given them a hunter's name, to use for quota numbers if they were successful, so that they kept it looking legal.

Clearly the old man had worked with poachers' before.

Jamiel and Chad had snuck back to the lodge that same night without seeing the phantom lion.

Now they waited for the tourists to go to sleep. Many didn't stay awake long on safari, as they had to be up early for game drives and fishing trips. To avoid the heat, they retired to their rondavels and air-conditioned luxury pretty soon after dinner.

But not Marissa.

It had been her custom to go visit her elephant at night in the USA, and Chad couldn't believe the dumb bitch was doing the same here. The stables were easier to raid than the rondavels. The escape was faster along the path out, without tourists or staff getting in the way.

Chad and Jamiel crept closer, keeping in the shadows.

They could see the stables housed the elephant orphans. There seemed to be a lot of people wandering around the area.

"Let's get closer and see if we can hear," Jamiel said.

When they got to the area just behind the stable, they stopped. Still in the shadows of the trees, the elephant fence right in front of them. If they went any closer, they would have to cross open ground.

People were coming and going between the stables and the outside area.

Soon, three baby elephant were herded into the outside bomas. Marissa was followed by a tall, solidly built man who was clearly military-trained; he controlled every movement of his body, and was fluid, yet precise as a tightly coiled spring. He checked his surroundings and yet displayed ease in the environment he was in, despite carrying an unconcealed weapon on his hip.

Clearly used to being in Africa, not a USA import. The way the man moved and stayed close to Marissa made Chad think he was more than a bodyguard. There was a connection between them—subtle, but Chad could see it even from this distance. He was on the phone when he stopped, grabbed her arm, looked around, then guided her back into the stable area.

He didn't look back, but Marissa did.

"What? He can't know we're here. Something else must've spooked him," Chad said.

Jamiel nodded. "We watch for a while. If she comes out, we grab her, but I suspect going in there would not be a good idea."

Chad nodded.

Despite the mosquitoes buzzing hungrily around them, they remained and watched for another two hours.

Marissa did not come out.

By midnight, at last, the stables seemed to quieten down. The two babies in the outside bomas had settled in and gone to sleep. One elephant handler stayed with them, but it was obvious he was sleeping just outside the fence line, his stretcher within touching distance of the elephants' trunks if they needed him.

The lights inside dimmed as a quiet came over the stables.

"She must be sleeping with Amalee," Chad said. "She always does that. Good thing we brought along the right rifle to shoot that elephant."

Jamiel shook his head. "That is for protection in the wild—not for now. You can come back for the elephant anytime. You let off a shot with that, and every single anti-poaching guard will be on our tail. Keep to the plan. We snatch Marissa. That's it."

Chad nodded as he rose from hiding and slunk into the shadows.

He crept farther towards the back of the stable, where the lights didn't reach. Then he crouched over and ran to the wall, out of the light, keeping in the dark.

Jamiel followed. But when he caught up with him, Jamiel smacked the back of his head, as if trying to remind Chad that tonight was supposed to just be for reconnaissance.

Together they crept around the back of the stables, they looked for a doorway.

An elephant trumpeted.

Chad frowned and froze.

No way would Amalee be signaling to Marissa that he was there. They were on a different continent. Why would the elephant suspect him?

The elephant trumpeted again. A sound full of warning. Danger was in the area.

He could hear the other elephant joining in, even the babies, as they all started to trumpet together.

Jamiel put his hand on Chad's arm. "Tonight is not the night. We lay low and come again tomorrow."

"Fuck," Chad said.

"Come on," Jamiel urged, grabbing his arm and pulling him back down the wall towards the fence line. They ran together through the clearing and into the cover of the trees.

Floodlights clicked on. The whole area was as bright as daylight.

Chad shrank into the shadows of a tree and kept dead still. With light so bright, even a small movement would show up to any eye looking for it.

"That bloody elephant remembers my scent. I'm not going to get anywhere near Marissa as long as that fucking animal is around," Chad complained. "Jamiel, you're going to have to get her."

Jamiel spat in the dirt. "You remember, I told you this was a bad idea," he muttered, his voice low and edged with fatigue. I can't believe I'm letting you have your way."

"We won't get another chance after tonight," Chad said. "We barely made it out of the house before those police burst in."

"Too bad we have no way to contact Tsessebe because he's going to walk into that in the morning," Jamiel said. "He was useful."

"True, but there is no going back. No more waiting time. We need to get in here, do this or everything we have done is down the toilet," Chad said.

"If I'm going in alone, then I guess now's the time. When they settle again, I'll move. You get to cover. I'll wait till it quietens down, then I'll bring her out. Be ready to make the run to the vehicle."

Inching slowly backward bit by bit, Chad retreated deeper into the moringa forest. He could still hear the commotion of men shouting, elephants trumpeting and rumbling, but as Tsessebe had said, no one came through the moringa grove. He lay on his back and looked up at the stars.

When he had first got to the Lucky 7 Ranch, he'd been eager to learn the stars' names, as there had seemed to be so many more in the night sky than he had ever seen before. But the stars there had not sprinkled luck his way.

Here, nearly overhead, the brightest star in the sky, Sirius, burned like a beacon. The three stars of Orion's belt were easy to spot too. A satellite caught his attention as it tracked across the blackness, moving fast and disappearing out of view. He wondered which country it belonged to and what or who it spied on.

He looked back towards the stables.

He was so close to having Marissa, he could taste it.

CHAPTER 41
SENSES

YINGWE RIVER LODGE, ANIMAL RESCUE AND REHABILITATION CENTER, BINGA, ZIMBABWE

14 January 2015 – 01:00

Amalee refused to settle again.

Something had disturbed her, and she had spurned sleep.

Dawn hurried in. "What's going on? Why is she so upset? I could hear her from my chalet."

"I don't know," Marissa said. "I don't think I've heard her sound like that since … since the night of the fire. It's almost like she's warning me that Chad is here."

"The same trumpet," they said together.

Mitch said. "Tsessebe rang me earlier; Chad and his mate Jamiel crossed into Bongani's lands earlier tonight. We know he's here. The units are moving into position as we speak to take him down. The *n'Gomas* are ready."

"We knew he would come," Dawn said. "Let's get Amalee settled the best we can."

"I've been trying. She keeps going back towards the rear door of the stable," Marissa said.

"Then we leave her there. We know better than to question her when she thinks there's danger," Dawn said.

"True," Marissa said.

"I take it she's warning us that Chad's actually here, at the sables?" Mitch asked.

"We think so, or she had wind of him somewhere close," Marissa said, taking a deep breath. "She's a bit calmer now, so he must have backed off."

"The AP team is scouting outside. They'll find him if he's around. You need to stay in here, where he can't get to you. Even if he has infrared, this stable is made of concrete blocks—two layers to get through. It's like a bunker. Stay away from the windows and any doors, and you'll be fine."

Marissa nodded. She might be safe inside the stable, but she was torn. On one hand, she wanted Mitch out there, getting rid of Chad. On the other hand, she didn't want Mitch in danger.

Amalee sent her healing vibrations, and Marissa smiled. Her elephant was so in tune with her emotions, despite crossing the ocean and having so many more people around her, and being exposed to her own kind.

Amalee had seemed happy until tonight. She'd shown nothing but excitement when the babies had arrived.

Now she was clearly agitated.

"Mitch, any news I should know about?" Peta asked as she walked in from the corridor outside the stable and rested her arms on the thick bar of the fence.

Marissa turned to him, wondering why he would tell Peta something and not her, when it was her life in danger.

"Just the same stuff I've told Marissa. The intruders are here, but we don't know yet if it's just surveillance or a planned attack. The AP units are out there, tracking. Either way, they're inside the net and will go down tonight."

"Given that the elephant haven't reacted badly in a while, I would guess it's just surveillance, and they have scattered. It will take a while, but the elephant will settle," Peta said.

"I hope they do. It's kind of loud in here when they all get started," Mitch said. "But even if they have given up tonight on approaching Marissa, they will not get out. They will be taken in for trespassing at the very least."

"I'd rather loud, than have him sneak up on me," Marissa said.

Peta smiled and rubbed her stomach. "Fair enough. It's not the first midnight trumpeting session we've had, and I'm sure it's not going to be the last. They will calm down, eventually. I'm going to try to get some sleep. Do the same if you can."

Peta left the stable and Marissa could hear her talking to the animals as she went, reassuring each of them to go back to sleep.

"She has a point," Marissa said. "But I doubt I can sleep knowing that Amalee sensed Chad's near." She grabbed her pillow and flipped herself into the bunk. "But I can rest and be ready."

"That's my girl," Mitch said as he sat in the straw next to her, his back to the internal wall.

Dawn chuckled. "I know when I'm beaten. I'll borrow a bed in the next stable, but I agree—probably better to stay alert. We have to trust Amalee."

Marissa turned on her side and watched her elephant.

Amalee hadn't settled; she kept smelling the air as if there were something there she just couldn't identify. She was still agitated.

02:00

An hour later Amalee's rumbling changed.

Marissa felt it in her whole body—a menacing roll of danger.

Marissa was on her feet and by Amalee's side in a heartbeat. Mitch was with her just as fast.

"What is it?" he asked.

"Not sure, but something is not right," she said, patting Amalee's leg.

"Is your elephant ever wrong?" Mitch asked.

"Never," Marissa said confidently. "She always hated Chad, but she's really perceptive to any danger towards me, be it a snake or a drunk cowboy. She's never given me a false warning."

"Then we take it seriously. Be vigilant," Mitch said.

It looked as if the wall had come alive as a huge Black man in camouflage clothing climbed through the horizontal bars of the stable and charged.

Amalee trumpeted. A loud scream to warn of danger.

Marissa saw Mitch move before the man reached them.

The world slowed as they collided halfway across the stable. Mitch dodged the attacker's fists, and his own connected with the man's stomach. The man barely flinched.

The attacker was fast.

They traded heavy blows. Hard. Brutal.

Mitch got in several punches to the man's stomach before the attacker grabbed Mitch in a headlock.

The assailant couldn't hold him for long. Mitch broke away and stepped back, ready to go again. Even as he ran at the attacker, the man drew out a knife.

Mitch did too, and they circled each other.

The intruder was the bigger person. Heavier, with the tribal markings on his face, making him appear even more menacing.

Marissa drew herself into a defensive posture, knowing that Mitch would need help. As the attacker turned his back on her, she ran and jump-kicked, slamming her heel between his shoulders.

The attacker fell forward and rolled up, as fast as a cobra, and in one movement lunged at Mitch, then slashed.

Mitch put his arm up to shield his face, and the knife slid deep.

"I'll take you piece by piece," the attacker said. "And I'll still get the women."

Marissa kicked the man square in the jaw and he fell backward.

Mitch jumped on the attacker and held the man's arm under his thigh. Marissa stood on the intruder's hand, grinding until he loosened his grip, and she could kick the knife away.

Just as Mitch pulled a thick cable tie out of his pocket, the man jackknifed, and Mitch was thrown forward.

The man grabbed Mitch and a sick noise was heard as he smacked Mitch's head into the metal railings of the elephant fence.

Mitch slid to the ground. The man kicked his side twice in quick succession.

"No," Marissa screamed, running towards Mitch.

The man reached for Marissa, but she dodged and ducked.

Amalee trumpeted again and charged the man, but Mitch's body was in the way. Amalee backed up. She wouldn't stand on Mitch.

Marissa couldn't watch both Amalee and the man.

The choice was taken from her as all she could do was defend, arms up, hands protecting her face, arms tucked in so no punch could get through her block. When he came at her, it was faster than a warthog bolting for its burrow.

Marissa blocked his attack, redirecting his arms away from her, then delivered a roundhouse kick and immediately disengaged. He came again. She kicked his chest, and while it stopped his progress forward, it didn't knock him down. Drawing on all her training, she fought him. Blow for blow.

There are no rules; you do whatever it takes to stay alive, Mitch's voice echoed in her head.

She bent and gathered straw in her hand, and then as the man came at her, she threw it, blinding him with the dust for a moment. She thumped him with punches to his nose and the side of his head while he was vulnerable. Blood spurted from his nose, but he kept coming.

Amalee trumpet again, mingling with Dawn's scream of fury as she joined in the fight.

With the two skilled women fighting him at the same time, the man wiped blood from his eye and hesitated a moment too long, deciding who he would target.

Marissa did an off-balance sweep with her leg, and the man came tumbling to his knees. He struck upward with one hand, connecting with her windpipe, even as he went down. As she jumped and stepped back, Amalee ran and rammed him. She held him with her forehead on the floor of the stable, dropping to her knees as she tossed her head side to side, crushing him.

Marissa was trying to breathe.

"No Amalee, don't kill him," Dawn said.

Marissa staggered towards Amalee, still holding her throat, trying to force air down.

The man wasn't moving.

Amalee held him still. He was pinned down and unable to reach Marissa.

Peta climbed through the bars, a cattle prod in her hand. "Amalee, back up."

"No, Peta, be careful, Amalee doesn't know those," Marissa croaked.

Amalee remained where she was. A loud rumble came from her in a tone that Marissa had never heard before. Her body heaved.

"It's for this piece of shit, not for her," Peta said.

Marissa reached her elephant. "Come on, girl; I'm okay. Look, I'm fine," she whispered as she touched Amalee's side and patted her.

Amalee slowly got to her feet and released the pressure off the man.

Marissa stroked her trunk, calming her. Dawn was on the other side, also stroking Amalee's leg and speaking quietly to her.

"Dawn, stay with Amalee. Peta, you need to see if Mitch is okay," Marissa rasped. Her chest ached, and not just from the beating she'd taken.

Mitch.

He had to be okay—he had to.

She was almost afraid to look at him just in case he wasn't. "Mitch took a really bad knock to the head. I'll take the intruder. Can't have him hurting you and the baby."

Marissa moved to kneel beside her attacker. His chest looked caved in, and his left arm was in an unnatural position. She felt for a pulse in his neck. Nothing. She'd lived on a ranch all her life, seen more beaten-up men than she cared for. But this was the first time, she'd reached for a pulse and there hadn't been one. This man was never getting back up to hurt her again, nor Mitch, Dawn or Amalee. "He's dead."

"Mitch's alive. He's starting to come around," Peta said.

"Oh, thank God," Marissa said, and rushed to where he lay.

CHAPTER 42
THE MISTAKE

YINGWE RIVER LODGE, ANIMAL RESCUE AND REHABILITATION CENTER, BINGA, ZIMBABWE

14 January 2015 – 02:45

Chad waited in the moringa grove. Jamiel had been gone too long.

He heard the elephant trumpet and squeal, and the other elephants joining in. The floodlights around the stables had been turned on again, dulling the stars. This time they stayed on.

Something was wrong.

He grappled with possible scenarios.

Perhaps Marissa and her elephant have some of the weird voodoo magic protection? After all, he's tried to kill her three times before and failed.

"It was a simple hostage snatch, Jamiel. Go in, disable the guard, and grab the target. Like we performed hundreds of times together in Somalia. How have you fucked that up?" Chad said quietly.

Jamiel should have been out ages ago.

Chad needed to get closer if he was going to see what was going on. He owed Jamiel that much.

Creeping from tree to tree, he got close enough to see that while all the lights were on, the activity seemed to be inside the building. There were AP guards heading into the stable, and a squad of them was stationed outside, already looking outwards, behind barriers where even Chad couldn't get to them with his sniper's rifle.

Not a good sign for Jamiel.

He got his sniper rifle out, removed the night-vision scope, as it would be useless with the washout from the floodlights, and put on his standard scope for a better view. He felt safer in the bushes now that he was properly armed.

Shadows moving inside and indistinguishable voices shouted above the elephant's trumpeting. He couldn't hear their deep rumbles, but their trumpets were as if someone was ringing a big old church bell right next to his head.

Nothing of Jamiel. Obviously, he'd been captured or killed. It did not look very promising for him to be coming out of the building.

He looked at his watch

02H45. Soon it would start to get light, and his escape route would be inadequate.

Chad shouldered his rifle and began a shadowy retreat back through the moringas.

A bullet hit the dirt just to his left.

Chad dropped to the ground, attempting to hide behind a tree. Another bullet slammed into a tree trunk close by.

He had a choice: to lay down a base of fire now or run.

Either way, they were coming for him.

He let off rounds in the direction from where the shots had come, not aiming for anything in particular, just giving himself cover to get the hell out.

There was a squeal of something in pain. He hadn't heard a sound like it since a horse had broken its leg at the Lucky 7.

There was more shouting and trumpeting from the stables. He ignored it. Lifting his weapon to his shoulder, he let off two more random shots. Shouldering his weapon again, he fled.

He jogged down the escarpment. At the darkest hour of the night, when the moon waned, and the sun had not yet touched the horizon, he kept a steady pace along the well-worn path. At the bottom, he would cross between the two hills, the most open part of his retreat, before he reached the trees.

Cover. He chose not to run to avoid falling over an unseen rock, but still pushed himself to walk faster.

He stopped and listened. There was no sound of pursuit.

He took off at a brisk walk along the path, not sure how long it would be before the AP units came from the stables and picked up his tracks.

He heard a shot and felt something hit his knee.

He kept trying to walk, but his knee gave out beneath him. His rifle jerked off his shoulder in the fall.

He put his hand on his blood soaked his camos.

"Fuck," he cursed. Tsessebe had warned them about trip wires with bushpig guns, but he'd passed this way once already. And he was pretty sure he had retraced his steps perfectly.

Someone was out there. In front of him. His escape blocked off.

Still horizontal, he reached to retrieve his rifle from where it had fallen. There was no use laying down fire until he was mobile again, but that didn't mean he would be unarmed or unready to fight when the danger came closer. He took his 9mm from its holster and placed it in his lap. He sat up, but hunched over, still lower than the grass. Breathing deeply, he used his combat knife to cut open his pants to assess the damage to his knee.

He knew he should be feeling the most excruciating pain, with the amount of blood he was losing. Still, the adrenaline working through his system held the burning he knew was coming at bay for now. He had to get it sorted before the debilitating suffering began.

Chad cut his pants leg into ribbons with his knife. He ripped open the small blowout kit on his vest, grabbed the combat application tourniquet, and wrapped it just above his useless knee. He packed the injury with the Quik-Clot combat gauze, and finished by wrapping it firmly with a combat bandage.

Pain began to radiate out from the knee. Burning. Rolling upwards and down to his toes.

Damn it, nerve damage. Possibly tendons too.

The night grew darker, his vision narrowed.

He grabbed at his 9mm.

At least he'd tried to save his leg before the pain took over. He would live to fight another day.

He passed out.

CHAPTER 43
BATTLE READY

YINGWE RIVER LODGE, ANIMAL RESCUE AND REHABILITATION CENTER, BINGA, ZIMBABWE

14 January 2015 – 03:00

Mitch's whole body hurt, from the knock on his head that was now bandaged tightly, to the tips of his toes. His bruised and battered abdomen called for rest, but he couldn't—not yet. He'd been beaten, sliced, stomped on, and was strung tight. That he battled to breath against the bandages binding his ribs, which were severely bruised, if not broken, was an added discomfort.

From the moment he'd got the call from Tsessebe saying Chad and Jamiel had gone it alone, he'd known tonight was the night.

The easiest decision he'd ever made was to stay close to Marissa.

The hardest thing ever was trusting his team out there without him.

Marissa had become more important to him than anything in the world.

It was her skills that had saved him. She'd taken down Jamiel, with a little help from Dawn and her elephant. Marissa was safe, for now, but the threat was still on their doorstep.

Jamiel was dead but Chad was still out there.

A sniper who didn't need to get close to cause harm. Just as he'd proven when shooting the baby elephant newly arrived from Hwange. The sound of the baby's pain would haunt him for years to come.

Peta had been quick to give it an anesthetic and get it sleeping so she could assess the damage, and she had worked on its little leg along with Zola and Danie. They quickly had it patched up. Luckily, it had been straight clean shot. No bone damaged or lodged bullet to deal with.

Mitch was a strategist, and his AP teams had moved into their night ambush positions before the stable attack, but not soon enough to stop the attack. He'd already deployed Jason, Kat, and her team, and Joss had insisted on joining them.

Chad must have also been an expert in camouflage to get past his team.

Chade was ex-Marine, and Mitch would have done well to remember that.

The team had been stationed along the path and on the top of the escarpment where the lodge was.

Night-vision goggles were a godsend for all of them, and he was sure they would need them in the coming hours.

He was certain they would get Chad as he retreated.

It was like old times—he and his friends were in on the action, only this time, he wasn't right there with them.

CHAPTER 44
THE WARRIOR RETURNS TO THE FRAY

14 January 2015 – 03:00

Joss looked through his tactical headgear at a black-and-white-and-gray-toned vision of the land he loved. Once again it was under attack, and there was no way he would have stayed at home and not been in the field. He was a trained soldier, after all, and fighting for justice was his calling. Especially when it was for his home.

Kat was at his elbow.

Knowing the path helped narrow down where to look for Chad. Sure enough, he saw movement coming down the escarpment. He estimated it was just inside the six-hundred-meter mark.

A soft red light shone behind the movement, then snuffed out. A sign from the team that they had confirmation of incoming. A man.

Mitch's teams were well trained, and the man they suspected was Chad had gone right past the AP guard concealed in the bush.

About two minutes later, the next red light flashed and was off.

Five hundred meters.

The goggles allowed Joss to see the animals who shared the night with him and the AP team. If they knew what was coming, would they scamper away quickly?

A jackal jogged down the path in front of Chad, who seemed oblivious to its existence. Its shape was clearly identifiable to those who knew the bush. The interesting animal was the big lion padding silently behind.

Joss frowned. He hadn't noticed its arrival, but it was gaining on the intruder.

The jackal bolted off into the bushes, concealing itself, uncertain what danger came behind it.

Joss knew. A disgraced ex-soldier. A killer.

A man who had shot one of the Hwange baby elephant they had transferred to the outside boma. He didn't have all the information, but he knew the little elephant's leg had been hit. Peta would want this man's blood.

The lion got closer, picking up speed. Joss frowned. There was something about it that gnawed on his subconscious.

It reminded him of the time he had seen huge lion tracks in the sand beside the lake.

Joss debated whether he should simply leave nature to do its worst.

He waited.

"Three hundred meters," Kat counted off.

The man came into full focus. Joss had clarity through the night-vision goggles.

"Two hundred meters," Kat whispered.

Joss could see his face. He knew it was Chad; he'd seen the photographs and read Mitch's file on the reprobate.

If he confronted him, there would be a gun battle.

There was only one way to bring Chad down.

Thankful that Mitch had also provided him with a thermal clip on his weapon, Joss lifted his .303 hunting rifle, put Chad perfectly in the crosshairs of his scope, and then ran them down his body.

He wanted to put one through Chad's heart and never have the trouble of him endangering Marissa, Peta, or anyone in Bongani's lands again, but that would be murder.

Instead, he went an *eye for an eye*: a man's knee for a baby elephant's leg.

"One hundred meters," Kat confirmed.

Slowly, he squeezed the trigger.

Absorbing the recoil easily into his shoulder, he looked back up the path to see if the lion would rush in and deliver African justice.

Instead of a lion, five *n'Gomas* surrounded the man. Their arms and feet beat out a steady rhythm.

"Chad, throw your weapons down. We know you are badly injured. Let us take you in," Joss called.

"*Ulala, ulala,*" the *n'Gomas* chanted, their voices clear in the bushveld.

He blinked. The lion was back. Joss was almost certain he was hallucinating. It sat next to Chad, as if waiting for them, but in its mouth was Chad's handpiece.

Slowly Joss crept forward.

"Joss, he could shoot us," Kat whispered.

"No, trust the *n'Gomas,*" he said. "They chanted *him to sleep*. So, he's out by now."

"Eish, you're a white man. How can you believe that?" Kat asked.

"I'm a child of Africa. Even if I'm white. If they say he sleeps, he's no threat. We need to get in there fast."

Joss ran ahead toward the place he'd last seen the *n'Gomas.*

The place where Chad had fallen.

The lion sat there watching him. Joss nodded to the animal and gave it a small bow of respect. "Thanks, for your help, for your protection."

The lion lifted its body and stood before him. Joss looked at its huge face, and where it should have had amber eyes, there were dark black holes. He froze.

It came closer.

"J–o–s–s?" Kat said, a nervous tone in her voice.

The lion dropped Chad's 9mm sidearm at his feet and then loped off into the bush. A loud roar could be heard. The sound vibrated through Joss's body and into his bones. He shivered.

Surreal.

He checked Chad's handpiece had its safety on, popped it into the back of his pants and kicked the sniper rifle towards Kat. Joss leaned in and took Chad's pulse.

The pulse was there, but erratic. *Typical for someone in shock.*

Joss said, "Best not let him die out here and have to explain to Gideon why bodies pile up at Yingwe. Let's put double straps on him and real cuffs. Once he's secure, you can grab your first-aid kit. Looks like he attempted to attend to his own knee, and his tourniquet is controlling the blood for now. We should probably stabilize him."

Joss breathed out and looked upwards at the heavens.

The threat had been neutralized. Relief rolled through his body.

Thanks to a little *n'Goma* medicine, and their transfiguration into one awe-inspiring lion.

03:30

Joss radioed base.

"Mitch, come in."

"Mitch here."

"We have Chad. Jason and Kat are on their way back to pick up the 4x4s to fetch us at the old mine. Are you able to meet us at Binga Police Station? Four hours, max. We need to go via the clinic for a gunshot wound."

"Who got shot?" Mitch asked.

"Just Chad. We're going to need sedation. Despite having both hands and legs in restraints, now that the pain meds are helping, he's begun fighting."

"Idiot. Get Jason to administer. His first-aid certification tops Kat's. Less paperwork," Mitch said, but he smiled.

"Will do. So 07:00?" Joss asked.

"Affirmative," Mitch said. "07:00."

"Roger. See you shortly at the station, with the prisoner."

CHAPTER 45
WHEN TITANS COLLIDE

BINGA POLICE STATION, ZIMBABWE

14 January 2015 – 08:00

Mitch and Joss sat at Gideon's desk as he took Joss's statement. Chad was in a cell; he was now a police problem, not theirs.

"Are you sure this man was poaching?" Gideon asked again.

"He shot a baby elephant at the orphanage," Joss said, looking Gideon in the eyes.

Mitch hoped this would be enough to keep Peta's license enacted. God knows that Shumba would not be happy about the baby elephant being shot, even if it wasn't her fault.

Gideon looked tired. Harassed. A man who once again had bodies and people piling up on his watch and was not happy about it.

"We can collect the bullets; you'll see that they match his sniper rifle that Joss handed in," Mitch said, moving really carefully in his chair, his head still throbbing once again.

Gideon smiled. "This is Zimbabwe, not *NCIS* on the TV, Mitch. You know this."

Mitch shrugged and smiled. Joss chuckled.

There was a commotion going on at the front desk, and Mitch turned his head to see none other than Shumba demanding to see the prisoner. The policeman on the front desk was a younger man, a new recruit; his name badge said Constable Ketiwe.

"I am the president's lawyer," Shumba said. "This man you have here has shot one of the presidential elephant."

Mitch raised his eyebrows. If it was a presidential elephant, it would never have been in their care because none of the babies from the President's herd were being rounded up and shipped to China. He had to give Shumba credit; he was good at spinning his bullshit.

"Excuse me, Joss, Mitch," Gideon said as he stood and went to the front desk.

"Ah, the man in charge. At last. I demand to see this man in your custody. I want to see him face-to-face, and he must explain why he shot this baby elephant. And I will tell him how many years he's going to sit in a Zimbabwe jail. How his life is going to be from now on. You cannot mess with Zimbabwe," Shumba said.

Gideon sighed. "Normally, we would not let you do that—"

"I will see him," Shumba cut him off, slamming his fist on the counter. "Or the President himself will hear about you not catching this man before he shot the baby." Spittle flew from his mouth. His finger almost went up poor Gideon's nose as he pointed at him.

"As I was saying, before you interrupted, we don't normally allow this, but because you're the President's lawyer, we'll make an exception. Constable Ketiwe, bring Prisoner Whitney to the interrogation room." Gideon turned his attention back to Shumba. "You need to know there are cameras in that room, and our cameras work because we catch and prosecute criminals as well as poachers here in our police station."

"I suggest that you switch them off," Shumba said, looking down and straightening his jacket.

"I would if I could, but they are remotely controlled. There is no off switch in the station," Gideon explained.

Shumba looked at him and nodded.

Mitch wasn't sure whether Gideon's claim was true or whether Zimbabwe's internet was advanced enough to support such a setup. Still, the power transfer back to Gideon controlling his police station had been clear.

Gideon and Shumba walked to the back, out of Mitch's sight.

Mitch had a feeling in his stomach like he should get the hell out of Binga and be wherever Shumba was not. He looked at Joss.

"I feel it too. Keep an eye out," Joss said.

Mitch moved in his chair to get a better view.

The young Constable Ketiwe went to the holding cell at the back of the same room they were in, to get the prisoner.

He passed handcuffs through the bars to Chad. "Put these on."

Chad did as he was told, making a show of snapping them closed.

"Come. This way," Ketiwe said, opening the door, but not checking the tightness of the cuffs.

Chad sat where he was on the cot. "I can't," he said. "My knee is shot, and I cannot put any pressure on my foot. If you want me to walk, you have to help me."

The young policeman tisked, *"Eish."* He shook his head in disbelief but walked in and stood beside Chad to help him. They hobbled along slowly, Chad putting his full weight on Ketiwe.

"That is not good. He's a slippery eel," Joss said.

"Which one are you referring to?" Mitch asked. "Chad or Shumba?"

"Both," Joss said. "Can you see them?"

Mitch tipped his chair backward. He could see the interrogation room. Shumba sat on the far side of a table, facing the door. Gideon stood to the side of him, leaning with his back against the wall.

Ketiwe helped Chad to the table, heading directly opposite Shumba, but before Chad could even sit, Shumba was leaning over the table, shouting. "You idiot American. Do you think you can come here and just shoot the shit out of everything? That there would be no consequences? I am the legal consultant to the President of Zimbabwe himself. Do you understand what that means?"

Chad sat in the chair, his back to the door. He didn't move. He just stared directly at Shumba.

Shumba put his fists on the table.

"Chad's being given room to calculate. This isn't good," Mitch said, putting his chair on all fours and standing. Joss did the same.

"No? You are even more thick than I'd thought then," Shumba continued loudly. "It means that I have all the power here. I am the one who can simply make you disappear. For good." He snapped his finger and thumb together loudly.

Chad continued to say nothing.

Mitch and Joss stood in the passage, with an unobstructed view. Slowly, they tracked towards the interrogation room. Mitch drew his 9mm but kept it at his side, silently getting closer.

Gideon looked across the table at them, but nothing showed in his face that he was surprised at them being so close to them. He put his right hand down and unclipped his sidearm.

"Those people"—Shumba waved his arm about—"they said that you attacked an elephant orphanage and shot one of the President's elephant! I rationalize that as an attempt on the President himself. What did you think you were doing, coming to our country and attacking the President?" He crossed his arms over in front of his chest.

Mitch saw everything as if in slow motion.

Chad had his cuffs off and had disarmed Constable Ketiwe, who was standing next to him, of his service weapon. Still sitting, he put the Makarov pistol to Shumba's forehead, and before Shumba could even lift a hand to swat it away, Chad had put a round into his brain.

Shumba dropped backwards, smashing his legs into the table and making the chair scatter as his weight took him down to the floor.

Chad turned his stolen semi-automatic weapon towards Gideon.

"Gideon!" Mitch warned as he lifted and pulled his own trigger in one motion. His trained reaction was to double-tap his finger and hit Chad hard. *Always follow up with a second bullet to make sure.*

Gideon was quick on the draw; his weapon ready, he shot too.

Chad crumpled forward onto the table. His weapon discharged, but the bullet went wide, above Gideon's head, and lodged in the wall, dry plaster raining down over Gideon's already blood-covered face and uniform.

Mitch made his way towards Gideon to help. Joss ran, overtaking him in a few steps.

Ketiwe threw up.

Gideon's weapon was still in his hand, his finger on the trigger, his eyes wide. Blood and plaster covered his face and down his body.

"You okay?" Mitch asked, as he looked the room over. The wall just next to Gideon had two puncture marks from where Mitch's bullets had passed through Chad and continued their trajectory, and one slightly messier one where Chad's bullet had exited Shumba's head. There was a void pattern where Gideon's body had stopped the blood spray from hitting the wall, which was clearly visible now that he had taken a small step to his right. And the one from Chad that had gone wide and high.

"You look like shit, Gideon, but man, you're a lucky bastard. I thought Chad might have got you as a two-for-one," Mitch said. "Through Shumba and into you."

Gideon lowered his service weapon but held it tightly. "Thank God not."

Taking another step into the room, Mitch bent and smacked his weapon against Chad's hanging hand to dislodge the stolen pistol, making sure he was disarmed.

Gideon was staring at the wall. "That was too close. I think I could use a shot or two of that brandy you gave me last time you visited." He walked to where Chad's body lay against the table and checked for a pulse. He shook his head.

Mitch could see where his two rounds had entered Chad's back and where Gideon's had exited. Both his shots were kills through the heart. Gideon's would have done the trick too, taking out a lung. He looked to the wall behind Chad and sure enough, both him and Joss had been lucky too.

Lodged in the metal doorframe, at chair height, was Gideon's bullet. A few millimeters to the side and it might have got Mitch or Joss.

Gideon moved to Shumba. "I don't think I need to check his; he's clearly dead."

Joss bent down and felt anyway. "Always better to be sure, but yeah, he's dead. In combat, we have seen too many presumed corpses come back to kill again."

Mitch looked at Constable Ketiwe, who stood hunched over. He was no longer vomiting—just a retching noise came from him, the involuntary contractions after his stomach had been emptied. Now instead of having his hands on his knees, they were tapping his ears.

"Your hearing will come back soon. Don't stress," Mitch said, loudly. "The first time you see a dead body is always the worst. You'll get used to it. They were both pieces of shit. Just glad you and Gideon were not harmed."

CHAPTER 46
SUNSETS AND DREAMS

YINGWE RIVER LODGE, ANIMAL RESCUE AND REHABILITATION CENTER, BINGA, ZIMBABWE

15 February 2015 – 18:15

Marissa walked through to the deck and stood next to Mitch on a lounger. The sun was sharing its last crimson and orange light as it slipped lower to the Kariba Lake water, creating a golden backdrop on which to bid the earth goodnight. The distinctive sound of a Burchell's Coucal's bubbling call closely followed by guineafowls calling other flock members, to roost together high in the trees for the night.

Marissa smiled.

"Nice of you to join us," Mitch said, standing up and kissing her. Their bodies pressed close, fitting together as partners in a dance.

"Enough of that kissy-kissy stuff," Bongani said, interrupting Marissa's euphoria. "Some of us don't need to see that!"

Marissa sighed in resignation but continued to hold onto Mitch.

Mitch laughed. "No worries, mate. Just wait, I'm sure your turn is coming." He pulled a lounger next to him for her to sit on. And when she sat, he reached for her hand and entwined his fingers through hers, squeezed gently.

Peta and Joss sat opposite, Joss's hand resting on Peta's growing belly. Dawn sat next to Bongani.

"I never thought I'd find a place to not only rewild Amalee, but to want to call home. Are you sure it's not going to cause any problems if I apply for a visa to remain here a while longer, Bongani?" Marissa said.

"Apply for a forever one," Mitch said.

Peta laughed.

Marissa shook her head. "Slow down, champ. One step at a time."

Mitch squeezed her fingers a little tighter. They'd spoken about her helping Mitch in training some of the AP unit recruits and tending to the elephant while she continued her work for the foundation remotely. Thomas could continue to manage the Lucky 7. And of course, they could always fly to America should the need arise. Life was looking pretty-picture-perfect.

Bongani smiled and lifted his beer. "No trouble at all. I think you are more than contributing to the community and have earned a place here."

Marissa smiled. "So much changed so fast—my Dad, Chad and finally, Amalee being so close to leaving us. The first part of her rewilding was worse than seeing your child go off to school. Well in my opinion anyway."

"It's a lot to take in," Dawn said. "I remember Chad arriving at the ranch, and your father having so much hope for his lost nephew. Chad turned out to be such a nightmare. It's sad really. If he'd just tried, he would have found such a wonderful life."

"The danger has passed now, it's not something we need to think about again. Amalee's safe, and we are too. He can never hurt us. Thanks again to Joss, Bongani, and of course Mitch and everyone, for keeping us Americans safe," Marissa said as she raised her energy drink up high.

Mitch squeezed her to him and kissed the back of her neck.

Marissa giggled like a schoolgirl. She was finding she couldn't stop.

"I had an interesting conversation with Milo," Peta said. "As we know, the last shipment was one elephant short, but ZimParks were adamant they would make it up to the Chinese on the next quota. No one is looking for the 'spare' two that have gone into the bush with Ndhlovy, or the one the one we're still nursing. Amelee seems to be taking him on as her own so those three are in the clear."

"Yes!" Mitch said, punching the air.

Marissa shook her head. "Wait, there will still be another shipment? But–"

Peta interrupted. "But this is Africa, things take time, and stopping these exports, the fight is just starting. We can do so much more now that you are involved, and the world knows what is happening. However, a total ban, as much as we fight, it's still a while away."

"But Shumba is dead," Marissa said. "Wasn't he the one behind the shipments?"

"And his shoes were filled quickly by another power-hungry son-of-a-bitch." Joss said. "Milo's new Zimbabwean contact in office is Misheck Chitiyo. We don't know much about him yet, but I'm sure he'll make his mark on history soon enough."

"And the Animal Rescue And Rehabilitation Center? Is it safe now?" Marissa asked.

Peta was nodding. "An aid in the office, who's sympathetic to the plight of the elephant babies, said there is no paperwork at all around withdrawing the license. We're clear and free to continue to rescue animals of all breeds and sizes. No one outside of the immediate circle, Zola and Dani, Shumba and Milo, was aware of his threat."

Joss and Bongani were clapping. Mitch, Marissa and Dawn all joined in.

"Looks like a good day to celebrate all around," Bongani said.

Nyala, walked up to the group with a tray filled with drinks, and placed it on the table in the middle of the group.

"You timing couldn't have been more perfect," Marissa said laughing.

Two monkeys leapt from the trees up onto the deck.

Nyala took her apron off and, waving it around, shooed them away. They bounded back into the branches, where they sat shouting at her for having the audacity to chase them.

"That troop better move on soon; those trees are finished fruiting," Joss said.

"They always do," Peta said, "although that one male seems really taken with sleeping on the moon chair we put in the corner."

"Relocate the chair somewhere else," Bongani warned. "You do not want to encourage them to stay here." As he handed out the drinks.

Peta smiled. "Already done."

"I felt action," Joss said loudly, and put his other hand on Peta's tummy. "He kicked me."

"The baby kicks all the time," Peta said, but she ran her hand down Joss's face. "Maybe he wanted his dada's attention."

Sophia walked out of the dining room and towards them. "I heard you from inside. The baby's kicking? Can I feel too? Pleeease?"

"Of course," both Peta and Joss said at the same time.

Joss put his daughter's hands next to his. "Feel your brother?"

"It's not a brother," Sophia said, moving his hands away from Peta's stomach so she could fit herself in and snuggle into his lap, then ceremoniously plopping it back to carry on feeling the kick. "It's a sister. And maybe, when she's a bit older, Ndhlovy or Amalee can bring her a baby elephant of her own."

For the first time in a long time, Marissa was lost for words.

CHAPTER 47
AN ELEPHANT'S FREEDOM

YINGWE RIVER LODGE, ANIMAL RESCUE AND REHABILITATION CENTER, BINGA, ZIMBABWE

30 March 2015

Marissa and Dawn showed me a collar that was to go around my neck. I had noticed that Ndhlovy had one. She assured me that they did not hurt, but it made it possible for the humans to find her no matter where she was. I would get used to it.

Marissa opened the door for me to go outside where Peta, Joss, and Sophia stood.

Ndhlovy trumpeted.

Finally, I walked out into the sunshine to greet her.

There was no barrier between us—not now and hopefully not ever again.

We touched trunks, and she checked my new collar.

Dawn cried; it was not often I saw tears in her eyes. I walked to her and touched her tears.

"Go on, girl; this is what we came here for. You'll be fine out there." Dawn opened the big gate at the bottom of the stables.

Ndhlovy walked out of the area into the wilderness. The herd followed her.

I knew each one of them; I had spent time with them, and they were now as familiar with me as I was with them.

I looked back at Marissa, who stood with her mate, Mitch. His arm was around her. He was a good one; I could let him look after her while I was not around. But still, I turned back and went to touch her with my trunk, giving her comfort. I was not sure if it was for me or for her.

I remembered the awful day she was there at the circus to save me.

I remembered her in a pink dress, dancing with me.

I remembered her laughing and writing in her books with my trunk on her head.

I remembered when Chad came for her that first time, and all the other times afterwards. I hated that not all humans were inherently good. That I had to learn whom to trust.

I remembered the man I killed to protect her life too. And I knew I would do it again if she were in trouble. She was my child, and I would do everything for her.

But it was time for me to let her go. For her to live independently of me.

I had a new family.

She had a mate. I wondered who would have a baby first, or if I was already too old for such things. I was sure she was not.

I gave her one last kiss.

Finally, I touched Sophia—the second little girl who would always live in my heart, twirling.

Ndhlovy trumpeted again, calling me to the herd so that we could leave.

I followed slowly at first. I was not sure about going into the real wild. To leave the lands where Marissa and Dawn were. To go farther away than I had before.

But the herd waited on the other side of the gate, encouraging me to join them.

Calling me to adventure. A new life. A free life.

Their songs send sensations rippling through my feet and into my body.

I went to join them in the wild.

I looked back to see Marissa and Dawn holding each other, and I wondered if I should turn and comfort them more, but Ndhlovy trumpeted, bringing my attention back to the herd.

My own kind.

I walked out to greet them.

I knew the sweet taste of the trees here. I remembered them from before I'd returned to Africa, and I had tasted them in the stables. A memory of once having freedom and wildness. I was not scared.

I was free to come and go. I was part of the herd.

There was a time when I had only the humans as family, and those same humans brought me back to my elephant family.

I knew it was not goodbye forever. I would return to check on Marissa, and her whole human family. I could live in both worlds now. Just as Ndhlovy did. I would be by her side.

The sun set on a day the same here as it always had, and the sun would rise the next.

My homeland endured all.

And I along with it, with my own choices as a wild elephant.

GLOSSARY

aikona — (also spelled *aykona*) – *[eye-koh-na]* - no or can be an expression of strong disagreement, indignation or disbelief. A South African term used across various South African languages (including South African English and Afrikaans)
Ambulance chaser — derogatory term for an unethical lawyer who profits from accidents or disasters.
askari — [pronounced *ass-car-ee*] — protector, guard or soldier. Originally Swahili but adapted across Southern Africa.
bakkie — A South African word for a pick-up truck, a ute in Australian English
Banele — it is enough (Zulu, Xhosa, Ndebele, Swazi)
BaTonga (or Tonga) — An Indigenous Bantu group in the Kariba area. Historically they lived in harmony with the Zambezi River. A peaceful people, they were displaced for the constructions of Kariba Dam. They were resettled to new lands around Binga and Lake Kariba.
biltong – Spiced, air-dried meat strips. Common snack / meal in Southern Africa.
boetie — or shortened to *boet*. Also *boeta* – diminutive / affectionate of brother / bro friend – *groot boetie* and *klein boetie* can be used as distinction between big

brother and little brother. (Afrikaans and generally adapted South African slang)
boma — A fenced area used to keep animals enclosed. Also can be an area used for outdoor meals and parties. (Swahili but adapted across Sothern Africa)
Chete Safari Area — Situated on the shores of Lake Kariba between the Senkwe and Muenda Rivers. It is a controlled hunting area, and one of Zimbabwe's most rugged concessions.
Chibuku — a sorghum-based slightly sour beer, though it may also contain maize or millet. It is brown, opaque and thick. A commercial brew based on a traditional African beer.
Chizarira National Park — A large national park found in Northern Zimbabwe.
dagga boy — [often spelt dugga boy] – A male buffalo (Southern African slang)
dankie — thank you (Afrikaans)
dongas – rough pits, gulleys or holes in the ground, usually caused by environmental deterioration like over crazing soil stabilising plants, cutting down trees and leaving hill sides bare of vegetation, heavy rains. A word adopted by most southern African cultures, including Zulu, Ndebele, English and Afrikaans.
Duracell Bunny – an advertising mascot for Duracell batteries that continue to last a long-long time.
eish — (pronounced *aysh)* Wow, phew, oh boy, what? Expression of surprise (Xhosa / Zulu or Tsotsitaal)
Esulu — clouds (Ndebele)
gijima — run (Ndebele)
go-away bird – common nickname of the Grey Loerie, or by its Afrikaans name, *Kwêvoël,* due to its distinctive alarm call which sounds exactly like "go-away" or "*kweh*"
Gukurahundi — A 5th Brigade operation carried out between 1983 and 1987. Suspected anti-government elements among the Ndebele community were identified and eliminated, and the people involved were given indemnity by the ruling government. (Shona)
helivaced — a shortened term for helicopter evacuation, used in military, rescue, and by emergency services.

inja — dogs (Ndebele)
ja — yes (Afrikaans)
Jalabiya — (or *galabeya*) comfortable loose fitting traditional long sleeve robe worn widely across North Africa and Middle east
kapenta — (also known as *matemba*) — A Tanganika sardine – type of small fish that packs a protein punch – commonly eaten across southern Africa.
knobkerrie (or *knopkierie*) — An African club. Typically made from wood with a large knob (wood knot) at one end with a long stick protruding from it. They can be used for fighting or throwing at animals during hunting. Ideal size to also be used as a walking stick. Can conceal knives. (Afrikaans (*knop* + *kierie*) and Zulu, a weapon for Zulu warriors (*iwisa*).)
koppie — Also *kopjie* or *kopje*. A small hill rising up from the African veld (alt. spelling *veldt*). (Afrikaans)
kraal — An area where animals are kept, usually found inside an African village / settlement, and usually circular, with barricades to keep the stock inside. Can also refer to an African cluster of huts – like a family compound. (Afrikaans but commonly used in Southern Africa)
laaitie [pronounced light-e] — someone young, can refer to young male. (South African slang) ALT. English would be light-weight, as in young and doesn't have the weight behind the mouth to really fight / succeed.
leguaan – [proper Afrikaans *likkewaan* – k pronounced as g in goose – sound] — rock monitor (South Africa English)
Lowo olwa — He who fights; shortened to Lowla for this book (Ndebele)
Matusadona National Park — A large game park in Northern Zimbabwe
Mbala gate — Entrance into Hwange National Park
Mbuso — Kingdom (Ndebele)
Moloi — A wizard, witch, magician (Sotho and Tswana)
mukwa tree — Pterocarpus angolensis / bloodwood tree, a teak tree that appears to bleed when you cut it.
n'Goma — Traditional healers within the Nguni, Sotho, Tswana and Tsonga societies. The same as a sangoma. (Tswana and Tsonga)
Ndebele — An African language belonging to the Nguni group of Bantu languages. Spoken by the Ndebele or Matabele people of Zimbabwe. Also referred to as Northern Ndebele, isiNdebele, Sindebele, or Ndebele.
Ndhlovu'udadewethu — Elephant sister (Ndebele)

Nkazimulo — Glory. Radiance. Spender. Girls name shortened to *Nkazi* (Ndebele; isiZulu)
Nomalanga — sunny (Zulu name)
nyama — Meat (Ndebele) Also *nyamazane* – is another name for a buck – (Zulu.)
putzi fly – (*Cordylobia anthropophaga*), also known as mango or tumbu flies, are parasitic insects at the larval stage, particularly active during the rainy season. They lay eggs on damp clothing or soil, which can burrow into skin, causing itchy, boil-like lesions. Prevention involves ironing clothes and avoiding drying laundry on the ground.
qalcad — an ancient castle / fortress (Somalia)
qorrax-la'aan — a sunless one (Sudanese)
rondavel — A Westernised version of the African-style round hut with a pitched thatch roof. (Afrikaans)
sadza — A thick maize meal porridge, the staple food in Zimbabwe - of the African people. (Ndebele) – Also known as *stywer pap* – stiff porridge. (Afrikaans)
sahar (or *Sahir*): A magician or sorcerer, associated with fortune-telling, curses and black magic. (Sudanese traditional healers)
Salibonani — Hello or we see each other.(Ndebele)
sangoma — Traditional spiritual advisor and healer. (Zulu term)
Senzeni — what did we do? (Ndebele)
sharp-sharp — All good, looking great (South Africanism) ALT. *Shap-shap* – said quickly so r is no longer sounded out.
shebeen – informal tavern / pub serving alcohol and sometimes basic food and cigarettes, usually a tin shack / traditional hut or even part of a home / business. Usually without a liquor license.
shesha — Hurry up / faster (isiZulu)
Shumba — Lion (Shona)
Sifiso — Wish, what we had wished for, also S'fiso (Zulu)
Sinamatella Camp — Inside Hwange National Park
sis (English) also *sies* (Afrikaans) – expression of disgust / gross (commonly used across southern Africa.)
sjambok — A leather whip. It used to be made from rhino or hippopotamus hide, but is now made from plastic. Used as a fighting weapon in Southern Africa (Afrikaans)

sjoe — (pronounced "shoo") – 'phew' or 'wow', used to express admiration, surprise, relief, or exhaustion. Often used to describe intense heat, shock, or a difficult situation. (Afrikaans derivative)
taqiyah — a short skull cap or cultural head covering
totsiens — goodbye (Afrikaans)
Tribal Trust Land (TTL) — Now referred to as Communal Lands. Small scale and subsistence farming are the principal economic activities in Communal Lands. The farms of Communal Lands are traditionally unfenced and Communal Lands have resident traditional African chiefs who are supposed to see that the community as a whole is looked after
udakiwe – he was drunk (Ndebele)
ulala — you sleep (Ndebele; isiZulu)
ungaas — (also spelt *angazi*) — I don't know (isiZulu)
yebo — Yes (Zulu)
Yingwe — Leopard (Xitsonga) also *ingwe* – (Zulu)
ZESA — Zimbabwe Electricity Supply Authority
Zonke — All (Xhosa)

FACT VS FICTION

Fact: I have written a different ending for real-life British Marine Michael 'Mick' Laski of Signals Detachment, Yankee Company, 45 Commando Royal Marines, who died on 23 February 2009, from wounds sustained in the north of Sangin, Helmand province, Afghanistan. I called him Mitchell and 'Mitch' in respect… may Michael rest in peace.

Fact: Between 2012 and 2019, Zimbabwe sold 140 baby elephants to China, in five separate exports. 2012: eight elephants; 2015: twenty-seven elephants; 2016: thirty-five elephants; 2017: thirty-eight elephants; 2019: thirty-two elephants. All were taken from the Hwange National Park. During the period of exports, at least twenty elephant babies are known to have died. Figures from: *The Journal of African Elephants.*

Fiction: My characters are fictional and had nothing to do with these exports.

Fact: USA was involved in both Bosnian, Kosova war and the Somali wars.

Fiction: USA troops did not go AWOL and shoot indiscriminately. USA troops had nothing to do with joining militia groups in Somalia.

Fact: McDermitt is a real place in Nevada.

Fiction: The Lucky 7 Ranch and the McDermitt money for the McDermitt New Frontier Foundation are fictional. Marissa is also not based on any McDermitt relative, living or dead.

Fact: It is legal for an individual to own an elephant in Nevada, USA.

Fact: The Arthur Jones Jumbolair Elephants are real. Sixty-three elephant babies were 'saved from culling' in 1984 and taken from Zimbabwe. Ten died while still in Jumbolair's care before 1986, while about forty were transferred to zoos and circuses; the remainder have been lost track of. In 2023, only eighteen were still surviving.

Figures from: savenoseynow.org

Fiction: Amalee was not one of these real babies, but I wanted to rewrite at least one happy ending for them all.

Fact: Charlie, another Zimbabwean-born capture, became the last elephant at the National Zoological Gardens in Pretoria, South Africa. He was successfully relocated to the Shambala Private Game Reserve in Limpopo on August 19, 2024, and was renamed Duma (meaning thunder). His rewilding has been a success.

Three elephant remain as captives in Johannesburg Zoo: Lammie, Mopane, and Ramadiba. There is a legal and ethical battle in Gauteng High Court regarding their captivity, continuing today.

ACKNOWLEDGMENTS

Writing a book has never been a solitary act for me—from the first words to publication. It truly takes a village, and I am, as always, truly grateful for the unwavering support of my community.

Thank you to my editor, Lauren Clarke at Creating Ink.

Personal Thanks

My readers, for sticking with me over the last few extremely turbulent years.

Disney Animal Kingdom: For being so amazing and answering all my questions about having an African elephant in the USA.

The lovely ladies at Writing Tuesday Caboolture and Bribie Island. I love you all and hope we can spend many more hours quietly (sometimes not so quietly) creating stories together. Kaylene, Kerry, Elizabeth, Lisa, Diane, Angela (not Heather), Anne, Rita, Victoria and Jillian. And of course, our token male for RSL lunch – Tony.

Long-time readers and friends: Dot Rosebery and Lin Mogg – because you were always on at me to come back to Joss and Peta's world. This is for you two.

Robyn Grady and Gayle Ash, for cheering this book on, and who are always with me every step of the way. Sam Eeles for constantly reminding me to experience life too.

Joss Wood and Katherine Gebara for nightly sprints. R.L. Merrill (Ro) and Lorelei Buzzetta for the morning sprints. You are all amazing and I'm so lucky to have been able to join you.

Thank you to my sister, Dale Hardman, for stepping back in as a beta reader after so many years. Working across time zones was surprisingly seamless, and I still felt connected.

Last and most importantly: my darling husband, Shaun. Because even when my brain was poisoned, you still believed that I could write stories!

Shadows Over Africa

CHILD OF AFRICA

A thrilling novel of a courageous fight to save the children of Africa

DREAMERS

Kajaki Hydroelectric Scheme, Afghanistan, 2008

The four kilometre-long convoy snaked into the Kajaki Hydroelectric Plant. Joss Brennan watched the turbines arriving at the dam wall through his binoculars and wanted to dance around, even though he was just one of five thousand troops who had played their part in protecting Turbine T2. But celebrations would have to wait.

Seven sections of turbine, each weighing between twenty and thirty tons, had been transported the final one hundred and eighty kilometres from Kandahar air base, through the Helmand Valley and the desert and finally up to Kajaki Lake. Some optimist had painted holy slogans and an Afghan flag on the containers to try to dig deep into the patriotism the locals had for their country – T2 belonged to the people. It seemed to have worked, because the heavy convoy had arrived at its destination. The people of Afghanistan would soon have two working turbines, creating power and bringing them electricity.

Chinook helicopters flew overhead, loud as they passed low, sweeping the area.

Ten days of hell were almost over.

The eighty-ton crane was the next piece of equipment to come to a halt. As important as the segments themselves, it would help the engineers lift the parts off the trucks. Each minute the sections sat around was a minute longer that the troops had to protect them from the Taliban.

Joss adjusted his binoculars and looked further up the hill, following the line carefully, looking for anything out of place in the rugged terrain. The word in the barracks was that almost two hundred insurgents had been cleared on the route through and around the dam. He hoped that was true and they were unable to return, but there were always those who, like snakes, slipped through the cracks to come back to bite their butts another day.

He scanned the compound in a grid pattern, making sure no one would threaten this precious cargo, not after the epic mission they had just accomplished. This was his job, the sniper, the tracker, the spotter in his company. Who knew that watching the animals in Africa all those years ago would be such good practice for hunting the enemy when he became a British Marine Commando? Who would have known that the hours spent with his father and Bongani in the bush, learning the skills of a hunter, would help him be the ultimate marine?

Joss went over the grid a second time. 'Check two o'clock on the ridge. Shadow protruding beyond the wall,' he said into his mic. 'Definitely something moving in the compound.' But in the next moment, the shadow had gone, and all that remained was the edge of the wall.

'Affirmative. Suspect unfriendlies,' Mitch's Australian twang answered.

'Don't jump to conclusions, might be the locals. Eleventh troop mobilise. Sweep compound,' Lieutenant Colonel Johnathan Tait-Markham – Tank to his friends – ordered over the coms.

After a quick glance at the convoy still rolling in, Joss packed his binoculars. Mitch put his hand out to help him up.

'Crack on, we have a compound to clear,' came Tank's voice.

Joss bent and ran with Mitch just a few steps behind. The stones at their feet slid loosely until their boots gripped the baked surface beneath.

They reached the compound and were soon hot-footing it along the mud wall. Joss remembered this village well – they had previously cleared an IED from exactly where he walked now. They'd returned a few times since the initial clearing, but that didn't mean that there were no more IEDs. Insurgents could creep in at any time and rearm a place.

'Affix bayonets. Two break left, two break right,' Tank instructed.

Joss saw Mitch and Tank break left. He rounded the corner of the same hole they had blasted in the mud wall a few weeks back, Cricket, one of his fellow marines, with him. He heard the wasp sounds as bullets flew close to his head. He hit the dirt and rolled for cover.

'Contact. Contact,' Tank shouted into the mic.

Crawling after Cricket, Joss slipped into a room. They swept it quickly.

'Clear,' Cricket said.

'Wait,' Joss said as he saw a carpet hanging on the wall move. He indicated with his head towards it. Outside he could hear the shallow *pop-pop* sound of the insurgents' AKs and the deeper sounds of their own rifles.

'Joss, where are you?' Tank called. 'We need a sniper.'

'Clearing this—'

He got no further as the carpet came to life. Someone was screaming, and the whole thing came down, exposing an insurgent with his gun raised.

Cricket and Joss shot him down in a hail of bullets.

Joss approached the body. He kicked the AK-47 away, and looked at the man.

Correction.

Boy.

Joss knelt down and checked for a pulse, but there was none. He was relieved and sad.

No more than fourteen, the boy had only the wispy beginning of a moustache. His black turban still clung tightly to his head. He looked too young to be carrying a weapon and trying to kill them. He should still be in school.

This was someone's son. Someone's child who might not have wanted to be a soldier.

Or worse, this could have been a child who chose this path, thinking it was his shortcut to glory in the afterlife.

Joss swallowed. It was survival – if they hadn't shot him, they would be the ones lying on the floor. 'Dead,' he told Cricket, and together they moved out of the room, to help the rest of the troop.

The stone chips pitted Joss's face, flicked up by bullets that were unnervingly accurate and close. One whistled past his ear. Joss adjusted his scope. 'Bogie at three o'clock.'

He squeezed the trigger.

The man's head jerked back. Joss slid the bolt of his rifle, ejecting the shell and loading another.

'Three o'clock,' he said as he shot the next man who was keeping his troop pinned down.

Again he reloaded.

Taking a breath, he looked for the third insurgent he'd seen. He had gone to ground.

'Lost visual,' he informed Mitch.

Mitch looked through his binoculars, scanning the small hill on the other side of the village. 'Four o'clock, blue/black turban. Behind a wall – must be a ledge beneath it that he's using.'

Joss adjusted his weapon and took aim at the designated place, even though he could see nothing there. The turban rose as the man wearing it peered over the ledge to check where his enemy had got to. Calmly, Joss fired, and the man dropped out of sight.

'Hit?' Mitch asked.

'Affirmative,' Joss said as he reloaded.

Mitch nodded. 'Bad angle, I couldn't be sure from here.'

The firing had stopped. The silence that followed any fight was always deafening. The wait for the next shot terrifying in case it came right for you.

'Any more?' Mitch asked.

Joss took a deep breath and swept his scope over the side of the hill. A single goat nibbled at non-existent grass. 'Wait ... look left of the goat.'

Mitch focused on the goat, then left. 'Bogie,' he affirmed. 'He has a rocket launcher.'

They saw the tip of the man's head, his arms outstretched to launch the deadly missile at them or at the precious convoy of trucks.

Joss took him down. The sound of the single shot was loud in the silence that had descended.

The goat bleated and tried to run away, but it seemed tethered to the insurgent. Panicked, it bleated some more.

'Continue to clear area,' Tank shouted over the coms and the men came out from where they had taken cover to sweep the village.

'If we let that goat go, it'll lead us to where they came from,' Joss said. 'Find their base.'

'Negative,' Tank replied. 'It's getting late; we pass that on to the American troops to follow up. I'm in contact with HQ, and they have a command passing us in ten minutes. Check fire. Friendlies approaching from behind.'

Joss watched as the American marines chatted to Tank on their way through. He pointed to the goat, and their leader nodded. Then they were off, along with the goat, over the small hill and out for their night patrol.

Joss's company gathered and headed towards their temporary barracks, spirits high, adrenaline levels beginning to lower. Joss grinned. This was what he had been born to do – to wear his green beret and serve the greater good, just like his grandfather. To help people who were unable to stand up to tyranny. Fight for freedom and justice when those around couldn't.

Tonight he would pen another letter to Courtney, like he always did when something significant took place, then he would watch it burn, as was regulation. He would rewrite it when he got back to England, after he was out of the desert, a more sanitised version. An emotionless version that would never depict the true horrors they experienced out here, or the simple joys of just waking up, knowing that you had achieved something amazing.

It didn't matter that Courtney didn't write back often; he just wanted her to know he was okay out here in the world beyond Africa. He kept the letters he'd received from her in England, and any that he received while on the front line he would read, commit to memory, then burn so that the enemy would not get their hands on them.

Letters to his best friend, and phone calls to Bongani, his lodge manager, were his only connection to his home in Zimbabwe now that his parents were gone.

ALSO BY T.M. CLARK

ADULT BOOKS

Shadows Over Africa series

- Child of Africa
- Cry of the Firebird
- My Brother-But-One
- Nature of the Lion
- Shooting Butterflies
- Song of the Starlings
- Tears of the Cheetah
- The Avoidable Orphan

PICTURE BOOKS

- Slowly! Slowly!
- Quickly! Quickly!

www.ingramcontent.com/pod-product-compliance
Lightning Source LLC
LaVergne TN
LVHW030909080826
845145LV00010B/2819

9781923129313